ALSO BY
DARCY COATES

FROM BELOW

DARCY COATES

Poisoned Pen
PRESS

Published by Poisoned Pen Press, an imprint of Sourcebooks
P.O. Box 4410, Naperville, Illinois 60567-4410
(630) 961-3900
sourcebooks.com

Library of Congress Cataloging-in-Publication Data

Names: Coates, Darcy, author.
Title: From below / Darcy Coates.
Description: Naperville, Illinois : Poisoned Pen Press, [2022]
Identifiers: LCCN 2022002248 | (trade paperback)
Subjects: LCGFT: Novels.
Classification: LCC PR9619.4.C628 F76 2022 | DDC 823/.92--dc23
LC record available at https://lccn.loc.gov/2022002248

Printed and bound in Canada.
MBP 10 9 8 7 6 5 4 3

1.

The camera's view blurred, then sharpened again to focus on a woman's profile. Cove Waimarie bent over a table, a wash of wavy black hair hanging like a curtain over one side of her face as she scratched in a notebook with a thick lead pencil. Behind her, the lounge's large plateglass windows filled the room with cool light. Foamy waves rose into view as the boat tilted.

"Hey there," Roy said from behind the camera. "Guess what? We're live."

She lifted her head, a mischievous smile forming as one eyebrow quirked. "Got it running, huh?"

"For the moment at least." He adjusted the camera, forcing the lens to refocus. Cove's form bled into the searing light behind her before shifting back to reality. "Did you want to do an intro, or—?"

"The day I say no to that is the day you need to put me out of my misery." Cove straightened and leaned one hip against the table, her feet crossing at the ankles. The ship rolled with every wave that passed underneath, but she showed no signs of losing her balance. Just like her outfit—white linen pants and a tan blouse that emphasized her warm complexion—the pose looked both comfortable and effortless.

"We're moored in the Gulf of Bothnia between Sweden and Finland, a day's travel from port. Somewhere in the water beneath us is a lost shipwreck that has both captivated and puzzled the world for decades. Why did it sail so far off course? What caused it to sink? Over the next few days, we intend to find our answers. How was that?"

The final question was directed at Roy, not the camera. He kept the bulky recorder propped on his shoulder but freed one hand to give her a thumbs-up. "Did you rehearse that, or does it just happen?"

"My father always told me to find a job that I love." Her smile widened, shining white against bronze skin, her green eyes filled with laughter. "And I love talking, so here I am."

"Well, there aren't many jobs that involve watching movies all day, but I got the next best thing." Roy flipped the camera and held it up to capture his face. The close quarters distorted his broad jaw and filled the lens with a view of thick, dark stubble. "*Making* movies."

A man's voice, dense with frustration, called from somewhere deeper in the lounge: "You're a camera technician, not a director."

"Ah, ah, ah." The camera rotated again, its view rocking wildly across the metal floor and cracked paint before fixing on one of the darker corners of the space. A man lounged in a swivel chair, a circuit board held in one hand, screwdrivers and solders scattered on the table behind him. "That's our ROV wrangler. He was supposed to drop his little robots into the water and guide them down with a joystick. But just like with my film equipment, his robots went on the fritz sometime between leaving port and mooring. However, unlike my film equipment, he's been unable to bring them back online. Say hi to the camera, Sean."

Sean, with his buzzed hair and gaunt, heavily creased face, only glared at Roy.

"Some people would say it's a bad omen." The camera turned to catch another, much younger man. He sat forward in his chair, legs flung out at uncoordinated angles, a mug clutched in thin hands. A batch of freckles—swelling thanks to the ocean's inescapable sun—covered his pale skin. He seemed faintly shocked that the camera was facing him, like a child caught trying to take a chocolate from a box meant for the adults.

"Say hi," Roy prompted.

"Hey." A cautious smile formed. Unlike Cove, he had trouble making eye contact with the camera. "Um. I'm Aidan? I guess?"

"You guess?" Roy broke into heavy laughter. "If we're talking bad omens, I'd say forgetting your name is high up on the list."

"Sorry. I'm just saying." Aidan became aggressively preoccupied with his feet, tilting them in and then out again, his knuckles flushing white against the steaming mug. "It's kind of weird, right? The ROVs go out. The main camera and backup camera go out. Our navigation system glitched and sent us twenty miles off course…"

Cove crossed to Aidan's side and pressed one hand onto his shoulder, her other tucked into her back pocket. "You know, I like to think of it as excellent luck."

"Oh?" Roy lowered his stance to give the camera a better angle of Cove's smiling eyes.

"Yeah. Before, our plan was to send the remotely operated vehicles down for the majority of the exploration. Now? We get to do it. We're going to walk the *Arcadia*'s halls ourselves. That's pretty lucky in my books."

Aidan couldn't quite meet her gaze, but he couldn't hide a grin either. "Yeah, okay, that's pretty neat."

"As for the equipment malfunctions, Devereaux thinks we likely experienced a solar flare that damaged the more delicate equipment. The diving suit gear all seems to still be in good shape, and it sounds like Roy here saved at least one of the main cameras, so as far as I'm concerned, we're barely impacted."

Something clattered behind them. The camera turned just in time to catch a circuit coming to a halt on the desk where Sean had thrown it. The room was silent for a second, then Cove's voice returned, strong and encouraging. "Our dive isn't scheduled for another hour, and I've gone over the equipment so many times that my eyes have started to cross. Now might be a good time to introduce the team. What do you think?"

Roy adjusted the camera on his shoulder as he swiveled back to her. "Let's go for it. Speed run?"

"Speed run it is." Cove clapped both of Aidan's shoulders as she leaned close to him, tangling her hair into his. "You met Aidan. He's basically holding this whole show together."

His grin was growing more flustered. "I'm...I'm the uh...the assistant."

"He's modest." Cove shrugged. "He does everything from prepping food to assisting the rest of us with our work. *And* he's heading down to the ocean floor with us. Give him a few more years, and he'll be managing his own chartered adventures. Now, we have Roy. Camera, audio, lights, all the important stuff."

Still behind the camera, Roy whooped.

"Hell yeah," Cove called back. "We have some really neat gadgets for this trip. Because of the depth, we'll have limited time inside the *Arcadia*, so we want to make the most of it. Roy's ensuring none of the cool stuff fails on us. Next up, Hestie, who is somehow able to read at a time like this."

The camera moved to catch the opposite side of the lounge, where a thin, wiry woman sat with a paperback clasped in her lap. Her pale hair was aggressively, furiously curly, to the point where she used multiple scrunchies to keep it contained in a ponytail. Frizzy strands still spilled free, framing her face and pale-blue eyes. She smiled at the camera, showing large buck teeth but, like Aidan, struggled to make eye contact with the lens. "I'm a bit queasy." Her voice was soft, and Roy moved close to capture it better. "Just trying to keep my mind off it."

Cove made a sympathetic noise. "The first time my father took me onto a boat, I spent the whole time returning the seafood I'd eaten for lunch back into the ocean. Keep the ginger close and let me know if I can hold your hair back, okay?"

"Oh, I'm not... It's just nerves." Hestie cleared her throat, gaze flitting across the floor as she tried to find something to settle on. "Yeah. Thanks."

"Hestie's our marine biologist. She is *the* expert on the ocean in general and especially this region. We'll be going to her to identify every fish and sea sponge we spot."

The large teeth flashed back into view as she smiled, pleased. "Degree in biochemistry and microbiology, PhD in marine biology, postdoc in coral-plasticine interactions. Honestly, I'm just happy to be paid for something that relates to my career."

Aidan piped up. "I'm just glad to be paid period."

Both Cove and Roy laughed, Roy slapping the nearby wall for emphasis.

"All thanks goes to Vivitech Productions for that," Cove added. "Their sponsorship means the world. Not only do we get to explore this magnificent location, but we get to share it with everyone else too, thanks to this documentary."

"Thank heaven we still have the cameras," Roy said.

"Speaking of technical equipment, we can't forget Sean—" Cove's voice cut off as the camera turned. Sean was out of his chair and shoving through the lounge's door to disappear into the hallways below. A woman, climbing the stairs to reach the lounge, pressed close to the wall to avoid being shoved.

Roy made a noise that was halfway between a scoff and a laugh. "He's just salty because he thought his ROVs would be the star of the show, and now they're bricked and he has nothing to do."

"He'll have plenty on his plate," Cove said, her voice still warm. "We all will. Our dive window is limited, so it's going to be a hectic few days. We haven't introduced Devereaux yet, but I think we'll save him for later and cut straight to Vanna, our diving specialist. How are we looking?"

Vanna, entering to take Sean's place, carried a dry suit draped over her forearm. Dark, heavy-lidded eyes scanned the occupants. She was a few years older than Cove, crease lines forming around her lips and between her eyebrows, and her short-cropped hair was swept back from large eyes and a broad jaw. She failed to return any of the smiles directed at her. "We should begin preparing."

"I love your timing. We were just about climbing the walls up here." Cove pushed away from the desk she'd been resting against. Hestie took a short, rasping breath as she put her book down and joined Aidan in trailing behind the camera as the crew followed Vanna into the deeper parts of the ship.

Outside, the ocean swelled, heavy with dark promises.

2.

Cove kept her feet light as she descended the narrow stairwell. The metal slat steps clattered under their shoes and the scratched, white-paint-covered walls seemed to squeeze inward, as though wanting to crush her.

She'd never gotten around to introducing herself to the camera, but that was fine; they'd need to record a separate segment later, maybe even back at the studio, that would serve as the film's introduction. Cove wasn't exactly a foreign face for documentary enthusiasts either, though she was still waiting on her chance to break into mainstream recognition and cement her place in the world as a conservationist and educator.

The company sponsoring them, Vivitech, had a reputation for short projects and cutthroat budgets, but they still had the capability to create an award-worthy documentary...as long as they were given the material to work with.

Who knew? Maybe this documentary would be the one. That all depended on what they found waiting for them on the gulf's floor. Something visually stunning, Cove hoped. Even better would be clues to what happened in the ship's final few days. Everyone, herself included, was desperately curious to know how an ocean liner could vanish so thoroughly on what was supposed to be a routine voyage. And Cove, more than the others, *needed* the expedition to be a success.

They turned a corner, passing the mess hall, and descended a second flight into the storage area where their dive suits were kept.

She'd spent much of her life diving, mostly at warm-water reefs, but this was her first venture into the deep ocean. She was qualified. Barely. Just like most of her team.

It was common practice in the genre of documentaries she hosted to overstate a situation's danger. *Pretty woman in peril* was a motif the studios liked, even when it was rarely true. Cove had stood within twenty feet of wild lions as she elaborated on the ferocious crushing power of their jaws—failing to mention that those lions were safari regulars that had grown up comfortable and lazy around humans. She'd hiked mountains in blizzards, speaking in a rushed whisper to her handheld camera about the early signs of hypothermia, even though a tour guide and her crew were off to one side and a helicopter was on standby to carry her back to her hotel for the night. She wasn't the only host to do it either. They were all competing to make their situations seem the most hazardous, the most adventurous, to remind those at home that there was still plenty of adrenaline to be found out in the wild, even though half the time "the wild" was twenty meters off a paved road.

Cove thought this might be the first time in her career that she wouldn't have to exaggerate the risk. Mountain climbing and wild animals and swamp waters were dangerous, yes, but deep-sea diving was an entirely different field. It wasn't even uncommon to hear of divers with a lifetime of experience perishing in familiar waters.

And she and her crew weren't just diving to the ocean floor. They were going inside a wreck. Cove knew what that meant, even if the bouncy lilt in her steps maintained that everything was fine. Going inside the wreck meant poor visibility. Narrow passageways. No one to help if they became trapped.

They had an experienced diving instructor—Vanna—but Cove still wasn't sure what to make of her. She usually found it easy to read other people and easy to make them like her. Vanna was a no-go on both. She'd barely said a word since they'd cast off from shore, and that was two days ago.

They reached the landing, and Cove swung around to face Roy's camera. Eyes bright, smile warm, keeping her face at its best angle. "Through here's our storage room. We keep our diving equipment locked up tight when it's not in use. Check it out."

She stepped back so Roy could move the camera through the narrow metal door. Where they were, on the ship's lowest floor, was already technically underwater. The metal hull groaned as the vessel tilted. There was a strange, echoey hollowness to that level, and Cove couldn't help but feel that the ocean was already trying to suck them under.

"We have our food and fuel and spare bedding here too," she said, running her hands along the shelves as she approached the racks at the rear wall, "but we keep the good stuff over here."

The ship was technically larger than seven people needed, but the storage area still felt cramped and full of clutter. Roy, tall and broad shouldered, was struggling to fit between the shelves without ruining the shot.

Vanna already waited by the diving suits. They had five in total. Two of their crew—Devereaux and Sean—didn't have deep-sea diving certification. Those courses, required for anyone who wanted to go below what was considered the safe limit for recreational diving, weren't common.

Cove loved the ocean, but a tight work schedule meant she could rarely make more than five or six dives a year. This would be her first unsupervised dive at those depths.

She was pretty sure she could say the same for Hestie Modise. The wild-haired marine biologist had spent substantial time in the ocean as part of her degree, but her dive log suggested she rarely dipped under the water when it wasn't professionally necessary. Cove supposed it was possible to love the ocean but not love being *in* the ocean.

Roy Murray picked up a range of work as a cameraman, and his experience around reef filming meant he spent plenty of time underwater, but generally only at shallow depths and in tropical regions. He'd rushed through his deep-sea certification to join the expedition, dragging Aidan along with him. Apparently they'd met during a vacation and become close. Cove had been seeking a cook-slash-assistant, and the timid, self-conscious boy tested well on camera, so she'd taken him. She was now starting to second-guess that decision.

If just one or two of them had been inexperienced, it wouldn't have been a problem. But collectively, they amounted to perhaps one and a half truly good divers. And most of that was down to Vanna.

"We're lucky to have Vanna Ford with us," Cove said, putting one arm around the older woman's shoulders. She felt Vanna tense and hoped it wouldn't show on camera. "She has over four thousand logged dives. A good part of that is open-water scuba, but her true passion is cave diving. Would you say that's right, Vanna?"

The woman's bony shoulders felt cold under Cove's arm. She let the silence hang for a painful second, then said, "Yes."

Okay. This part's going on the cutting room floor. Cove let go of her companion and leaned on the racks instead. "My crew's safety is always my top priority. What's waiting for us on the ocean floor is a veritable maze of tangled metal and tilting corridors. That's why we wanted Vanna: she's unparalleled in navigating tight spaces, having been recognized as one of the top cave divers in the southern hemisphere. Vanna, how do you think we're going to fare down there today?"

Vanna's heavy eyes narrowed a fraction, giving Cove the sense that it was a ridiculous question. She took a beat to respond. "Fine. If you follow my instructions."

"We intend to. Especially since we have these." Cove picked up one of the helmets. "We're using full-face masks. That means our breathing apparatus isn't connected to our mouths, leaving us free to talk through built-in radios. Not just that but these masks are fitted with some of the best underwater cameras. Two of them per person, in fact, with matching lights: a set facing forward and a set watching our backs. If a shark sneaks up on us, we'll catch it in wonderful HD."

"There won't be any sharks down there," Hestie piped up. She and Aidan had been so discreet that they'd blended into the background. Even Roy seemed to have forgotten they were at his back and had to do a strange hopping step to get them into frame.

Cove nodded encouragingly. Hestie darted her eyes to the camera and back, uncertain where to look, before clearing her throat. "Normally, currents are constantly cycling the ocean's water, carrying in fresh oxygen and keeping everything, well, alive. But this is a bit of a dead spot. The Gulf of Bothnia has very slow water movement and therefore very little oxygen.

There will probably be some old barnacles—we like to call them rustacles—but no coral and no fish."

"And no sharks," Cove confirmed. "I don't know whether to be relieved or disappointed."

"Suit up," Vanna interjected. "We're losing time and energy."

Cove chuckled, nudging Vanna's side with her elbow. "A woman on a mission. I like it."

Roy had them wait while he positioned the camera on a tripod to record the room, then all five began pushing and pulling into their equipment. They were using dry suits, which had the advantage of a waterproof outer layer. It was more than a luxury in this part of the world—the wreck's depth and location meant the water temperature hovered a chilling two degrees above freezing. The dry suit would at least stop them from turning into human icicles.

The dry suits went over their clothes; that morning they'd all chosen warm, breathable fabrics that wouldn't trap sweat. The extra layers of wool knits and shearling fleece would double their insulation. While the dry suits weren't skintight like a wetsuit, they covered the entire body—boots included—and were a pain to struggle into.

No one was surprised when Vanna finished the suiting process first. She sat on the edge of a low desk, her face mask cradled limply in her hands, unspeaking and unmoving except for her eyes. She watched the divers closely as Roy tried to shove his feet down into the boots and Hestie hopped in a half circle as she shimmied into the suit.

Even Cove, used to every kind of scrutiny, felt exposed under the cool, appraising stare. She finished suiting up shortly after Vanna though and flexed her gloved hands experimentally. The suit felt oppressive on land, but she knew she'd be grateful for it once they entered the water. "All right, Aidan?"

"Yeah." The boy was struggling to zip up the back of his suit, but Roy took a break in straightening his own to help.

"You'll be fine down there," Vanna said, startling Cove. She held Aidan's gaze as she gave him a slow, thoughtful nod. "You're small. You'll fit into narrow gaps. A lot of cave divers wish they had your body type."

His laugh was weak and quickly petered out. "Oh. Gee. I don't know if I'm cut out for...for *cave* diving or anything."

"What about me?" Roy, finished with his own suit, rotated to show the room his handiwork. "I might not be supermodel thin, but you'd be surprised at how flexible I can get."

"Hm." Vanna offered nothing else, leaving the impression that she anticipated the giant of a man would become jammed.

"I'm ready." Breathless, Hestie fought to secure her hair into a bun. "Sorry for holding everyone up."

"No need to worry! You're fine." Cove tucked her helmet under her arm and scooped up her bundled diving apparatus: the fins, weight belt, wrist computer, and strap of tools that would help them navigate the ocean's floor. "If everyone else is good to go, let's head up."

The ascent to the ship's deck was less coordinated than their descent had been. Aidan, already seeming overburdened with his own equipment, had taken on Roy's so that the taller man could follow with their camera and continue filming. It was hard to know what would and wouldn't make it into the final cut, but Cove knew the moment they first plunged off the side of the boat would inevitably make for a good shot.

Biting wind cut into her face as she exited the ship's heated interior and crossed the deck. She was grateful. The slowly build-ing stress was fogging her head, and the cold helped to give her some focus. The sea provided good atmosphere that day: hazy clouds dulled the light and the swell, while not dangerous, was riveting. Angry gray waves, crested with flecks of white as the wind snatched at the most vulnerable peaks, swelled and dipped beneath them.

Their ship, the *Skipjack*, had arrived at its destination the night before and moored less than twenty feet from their target. It would stay there for the next three days as they fulfilled their mission and gained enough footage to make the executives at Vivitech Productions happy. Their contract stated twelve hours of footage at the dive site. Cove had negotiated that down from thirty. This wasn't a reef film or a warm-water dive where the crew could bob in and out of the ocean multiple times per day; deep-sea diving meant dealing with decompression sickness. Every minute they spent at depth would worsen the symptoms, and even with the special mixes of gasses in their cylinders designed to minimize the effects, they would still have to return to the surface in stages. Twelve hours was asking a lot, especially in the limited time they had.

They collected their air tanks and fins and then fumbled to strap on their belts, their dive weights, and their computers. Vanna circled the crew like a vulture, tugging at dry suit's zippers and rattling their equipment. The creases around her mouth and between her brows took on a strikingly defined edge in the muted light. She squinted at a fleck of salt water as she backed toward the ship's edge.

"I'm the safety officer on this journey. That means, as long as you're in the water, you listen to my instructions above all others. Understand?"

Her voice was stronger and harsher than Cove had ever heard it. The crew mumbled their assent, clustered close together against the gusting wind.

"The wreck will be filled with silt. The more you move, the more you kick up, the worse visibility becomes for all of us. Go slow and careful. If you can't keep your movements graceful"—a pointed glance at Roy, who, even behind the camera, managed to display a twist to his lips—"try swimming frog style: move your arms and legs to the sides, instead of up and down."

"Silt can take days to settle," Cove added. "And we don't have that kind of time to wait around for a clear shot. We need to get this right the first time, okay?"

More muffled assents. Aidan's skin had taken on a gray shade, and Cove knew that the sheer magnitude of what they were about to do was hitting him.

Vanna continued as though Cove hadn't spoken. "If you feel unwell, call an end to the dive and begin your ascent immediately. If you feel drowsy, call an end to the dive and begin your assent immediately. Follow the decompression routine as established. This is *not* the place to push your luck."

This was all information they were well familiar with. Cove glanced toward the door leading to the bridge. Through the smudged window, she saw Devereaux, their historian. He stayed in the warmth, a mug held close to his face so that the steam condensed against his white beard. He gave a small smile and a nod.

A dark shape merged into the shadows behind Devereaux. Sean. He shifted, and Cove caught a glint of one eye: harsh and unnatural in the gloom. She looked away, disguising her discomfort by moving to stand at Vanna's side as the woman continued with their instructions.

"We're operating on the rule of thirds with our air. One-third to get down and explore the wreck. One-third to decompress on the way back to the surface. One-third in reserve, in case of emergencies. We're bringing down three supplementary tanks as backup. They'll be left at the wreck's entrance, near the dive line, but we *won't* be using them because we're not taking risks. Agreed?"

Muffled yeses came back.

Cove braced against the ship's railing as she gave a final glance across the team. Roy stood several paces back, still carrying the camera. He'd pass it off to Devereaux once he'd gotten a shot of the rest of them entering the water. From then on, they would be relying entirely on the cameras in their masks.

Aidan's gray shade had worsened, and Cove was genuinely concerned that he might be sick. If you were going to lose your food, you wanted it to be on the surface, not at depth.

It's not too late. Tell him he won't be going on this dive.

Vanna's eyes were on her. Dark, heavy lidded, no trace of emotion inside but waiting nonetheless. Cove knew what for. Vanna was in charge of their safety underwater, but ultimately, Cove was in charge of the mission. Vanna wanted her to dismiss Aidan.

But the camera was still running, and Aidan was pulling his mask over his face and connecting it to the tanks with unsteady hands.

And she couldn't afford to dismiss anyone. Not when she'd gambled so much on this expedition.

Cove, breathing faster than she would have liked, pulled her own hood into place. It scraped her ears and snagged her hair as it settled over her head, creating a smooth surface for the diving mask and leaving only an oval of her face exposed. She hadn't realized how loud the ocean had been until the sound of the slapping waves and rushing wind faded beneath the hood. She pulled the mask on, flexible straps snapping around the back of her head to hold it in place, then turned on her air. Just like that, she was cut off from the larger world. For the next three hours, she would have nothing but this closed system to rely on. Every breath of air would come from the cylinders attached to her back. Her hands and feet could move but she would touch nothing but the neoprene inside her suit. She was an astronaut on her own planet.

Vanna made no sound as she fit her own mask in quick motions. Their tanks, the heaviest part of the gear, were strapped into place: two on their back, plus an extra, smaller canister on their sides to keep their dry suits inflated.

Cove was supposed to be in command, but she'd never felt so frantically out of control. Not when she'd been in the blizzard, not with the bonobos tugging at her clothes, not when her canoe sprung a leak during filming. She could do nothing as the rest of her team lined up against the railing, backs to the ocean, ready to tilt over and drop into the depths below.

Vanna was still at her side. Cove glanced down. For a second, she thought her mask had water inside and was distorting her vision, then she realized what she was really seeing. Vanna's gloved hand, gripping the railing, shook. She tilted her head and Cove had a split-second glimpse of the whites of her eyes, then Vanna fell backward and entered the ocean in a plume of frothy water.

I can still put a stop to this, she thought irrationally, but she couldn't. Hestie had already dropped in and Aidan followed immediately behind. It was done. The camera was on her, and if she hesitated even a second longer, it would show just how terrified she was, so she tilted backward and let gravity do the rest.

She felt the impact across her back, reverberations running through her lungs. Her face was pointed skyward, and bubbling water rushed across her mask, distorting her view of the boat and the sky. The glare-filled light began to dull as the ocean thickened over her and she faded into the abyss.

Her final image was of the camera lens aimed at her over the railing, watching her like a giant, black eye.

3.

18 April 1928
RMS *Margaret*, 135 miles off Ireland
Two days before the sinking of the *Arcadia*

"Pan-pan."

Phillip startled back to awareness. The clock on the dash ahead of him said it was shortly before four in the morning. He'd dozed off in the dimness of his corner, near the back of the RMS *Margaret*'s bridge.

He was alone on the bridge with First Officer Forster. Forster sat by the windows, his cap low over his eyes to dull the overhead lights, his skin seeming to sink into his skull as he stared through the windows at the empty night sky.

Phillip was certain he'd heard a voice, but Forster showed no reaction. Moving gingerly, twitching at a pulled nerve in his neck, Phillip straightened in his chair. He still wore the wireless signal headset, he realized. The cushioned earpieces were so familiar to him that he barely noticed their weight any longer. He'd been waiting on a confirmation from a different ship when he'd dozed off. Now, he touched the headset, waiting and listening. The voice came through again.

"Pan-pan."

It was a universal distress signal. Not as severe as mayday— that required lives to be at risk—but a sign that something had gone wrong. A failed engine, or noncritical damage to the hull, or a ship that had become stranded.

Phillip flicked a switch to put himself online as he leaned over his desk. "This is the RMS *Margaret*, Communications Officer Bowden. What's your situation?"

It was only after he spoke that Phillip realized there had been something...*off* about the voice. Communications personnel were known for being forthright to the point of bluntness. They spoke clearly and quickly, relaying messages with minimal excess words. They had to. Every ship shared the same handful of frequencies; to spend excess time hemming and hawing over your message meant you were potentially blocking other more important communications from getting through.

But that voice—the pan-pan voice—had been slow. Breathy. As though it had been starved of oxygen. As though the speaker was fighting to stay awake.

Phillip had an awful squeezing moment of terror. How long had he been asleep? How long had the unknown caller been breathing into his ear, waiting for an answer? Hours?

It came again, and this time, there was a real undercurrent of terror to the words. "Pan-pan."

"I hear you. This is the RMS *Margaret*. Please state your name and position."

There was a very long pause. Second Officer Forster had

turned from his post at the bow to watch with dark eyes. Phillip didn't like the tilt to the officer's jaw. It was as though Forster felt the same sticky, heavy dread that had infected Phillip. As though they had both been sucked into a nightmare they didn't yet fully comprehend.

The voice swallowed. A smacking noise came as lips were wet. Then, "I'm aboard the SS *Arcadia*. Things are going bad, old boy."

Phillip had his pencil poised at the ready. "What are your coordinates?"

"51.43 N, -19.26 W. Or 45.42 N, -14.17 W. Or…hell. I don't know any longer. I don't know where we are. How long has it been? There are too many. Too, too many…too many…"

Phillip's stomach churned. He knew the *Arcadia*. It was a regular on the transatlantic crossing. He'd taken calls from it before—not distress calls, just messages to be passed along, warnings of unfavorable weather ahead, the usual—and had passed back just as many. At no point had he received anything of this nature. He knew the *Arcadia*'s main communications officer too: Drummer. A good man. Steady, reliable. This voice was not Drummer's.

"It's 56.43 N, 2.87 W, I think," the awful voice continued. "Osman is dead, and Baines and Boswell and Rudd are dead, and I think Wilton may be gone as well. There are just too many—"

Phillip had written down all coordinates but underlined the last set. He hated the voice's gasping quality. The way every breath seemed to pain it. The phlegmy gurgle at the back of its throat. "What's your situation? What happened?"

"They're in the walls." The voice gasped, a choked laugh that curdled and quickly died. It seemed to say something else, but a hissing burst of static cut through the channel.

Phillip frowned, straining to hear. "Repeat, please."

"In the walls…" The voice from the radio groaned, and the sound seemed to travel not only through Phillip's headset but into his bones as well, causing them to ache. "*The walls.*"

"Please repeat—" The bridge's lights shimmered, flickering. Phillip pressed himself back against the desk as he stared up at the bulbs that sparked and threatened to blow.

Then the voice rose, flooding his ears, filling his head, raw and battered with terror: "There are bodies *in the walls.*"

FOOTAGE RECORDED ON THE NIGHT BEFORE THE FIRST DIVE

A shaky camera flickered to life. It captured dull gray metal walls, rivets in the ceiling, and then, as it straightened, Aidan. A triumphant smile bloomed. Harsh light flooded his face, washing his freckles into almost nothing, and created a crisp circle on the wall behind him.

"Hey." He spoke softly, glancing toward the ceiling as he did. "I've got to be quiet. The others are still at dinner. And I wanted to do this alone. If he knew, Roy would"—breaking into awkward laughter—"Roy's brilliant, and I'm so grateful he found me this job, but if he knew what I was on about, I'd never hear the end of it, y'know? And I don't want him accidentally spilling this to you, Pen, before I'm ready. So—"

Some part of the ship creaked, causing Aidan's head to snap to the side, toward the stairs. He was still laughing, but it held nerves.

"I'm in the storage room. The other cameras are all broken, including the ROVs. Roy says he can fix them, and I bet he can, but right now all we have are the mask-mounted cameras we'll be wearing underwater. So, y'know, fingers crossed they work just as well on land."

He shuffled back against the wall, holding the camera in both hands. The angle was crooked, cutting off the top of his head and one eye, and focusing the light on his grin.

"I'm pretty sure no one will be going through this footage until it's time to cut the documentary. I don't know if the studio will want to include this bit, but I hope they do. It's—ah, well, it's—"

He was laughing again, sparkling eyes and anxious, flickering smile betraying his nerves. The camera's view adjusted as he switched to holding the mask with one hand, the other reaching inside his shirt. When he pulled his hand out, it was clasped around a silver chain. A delicate diamond ring hung from the end.

"Pen, when I get back, I'm going to propose. And I hope the studio includes this bit in their documentary because then we can watch it together and you'll see just how long I've been thinking about this and how much I want it and how madly in love with you I am."

Again, the ship creaked, and Aidan snapped around before dropping his head with muffled laughter. "You can see why I'm doing this away from Roy. He's a good guy, a really good guy, but he'd give me hell."

Aidan let the ring drop back against his chest, on the outside of his shirt. "I've been carrying this for the last four months. Just in case I found the right moment. And then Roy mentioned this trip to me and I thought… I don't know. It's something big, right? It's important. People will remember it. Not many people, maybe, but some. Enough."

A heavy wave hit the ship's side, but the sound was dulled to almost nothing. Inside the hull, the storage room's walls were crowded with supplies and old equipment, the air unnaturally still and quiet. Only the gentle groan of metal walls reached the camera's audio equipment.

"I'm twenty-two but everyone treats me like a kid still. Like I need looking after. But not you. When you look at me, it's like you see a hero. Like I'm the biggest guy you've ever known."

He laughed. There was moisture in his eyes. "And I'm not. I know what I am. Puberty didn't do me many favors, and I'm past hoping for a late-stage growth spurt. But it's like you don't see that. You just see...I don't know...someone worthy. And I want to be that for you. And that's why..." He shook his head, biting his lip. "I know it's dumb. Even I can see that. But, like, if I go through with this, maybe I'll feel good enough for you. Probably still not your equal, because let's be real, you're in a whole other league. But doing something big, something with a bit of danger, maybe I'll stop doubting myself so much. Because I want to be your man. And I want to spend every day adoring you. And I want to start soon. So when I get back home..." He picked up the ring and tucked it back underneath his shirt. "We'll start then. And hell, you'd better say yes, because if the editors actually include this in the final cut and you turn me down, it's going to make for a very awkward premiere night. Okay. I love you, Pen. See you soon."

4.

The first dive

The water folded over Cove like a blanket. Jittering bubbles raced past her as they sought out the surface. She hung, suspended, limbs stretched out as she tried to find her new balance. Patchy beams of light, filtered through clouds, cut past her, illuminating a dark shape to her side—one of the other divers. She couldn't tell who.

Cove's primal instincts wanted her to hold her breath, but she pushed past it to take a long, deep lungful of air.

She'd been diving since she was a teen, but that knee-jerk, you're-underwater-keep-your-mouth-shut reaction still hit her as soon as the waves closed over her head. It would get easier as the minutes passed, she knew.

"Audio check." Her voice, at least, was calm and in control. "Run through your names, alphabetical, so that I know you can hear me."

"Aidan." Hearing the voice piped into her helmet was a disorienting experience. It came in both ears at once, robbing her of any sense of direction and making it impossible to tell which of the masked figures had spoken.

"Hestie."

"Vanna."

"That's great, you're all coming through beautifully." She raised her wrist to take a reading on the dive computer strapped there. Six feet down; air 99 percent; buoyancy neutral. "We'll just wait for Roy and then—"

As though on cue, the water to her back exploded in a froth of bubbles and dark limbs. Unlike the others, who had taken the classic back-first route to enter the water, Roy had opted for a cannonball. Hestie made a small shocked noise, which almost drowned out Vanna's sigh.

"He-e-ey," Roy called, uncomfortably loud through the speakers. "Let's get this party started, yeah?"

Cove couldn't repress a chuckle. There was a reason she'd hired Roy for her documentaries for close on four years. He never sacrificed a chance to add levity to a serious situation, and very often that was exactly what Cove needed. "That sounds like a plan to me. Oxygen's burning, so to speak. Everyone check your cameras are recording, then get ready for descent. As the most experienced diver among us, Vanna will be guiding us down. Follow her lead."

A buoy hung in the water close to the ship. Vanna had already attached their dive line to it and now began dropping downward, the crisp white cord trailing behind her. Once they bottomed out, the dive line would be secured near the wreck, then later the crew would follow it back up, ensuring they surfaced not too far from their boat.

Cove hung back to ensure she was the last of the group and could keep an eye on her team. The murky water disguised their forms, but she thought she could pick them out. Vanna led, her muscled legs guiding her down with graceful, effortless sweeps. Close behind was Hestie, less confident, her body taking on an odd shimmy as she flowed in Vanna's wake. Then Roy, enormous and unmistakable, and finally, Aidan. His fins moved furiously as he tried to keep pace with the other divers, but he was losing ground.

"Aidan, check your buoyancy," Cove said.

"O-oh, right, yeah." He paused to adjust the dive bladder—an inflatable pouch of air that counteracted the dive weights—and his descent sped up.

He shouldn't be here. Barely scraped through certification a week before we left shore, and only then because Roy was probably at his side and hiding his mistakes. Should send him back up. Should... should...

She recalled herself, age fourteen, scrawny and with bulging, too-eager eyes, standing stiffly as a Balinese tour guide explained in gentle, soothing words that she was too small and wouldn't be able to go white water rafting—not just yet, but maybe in another few years, okay? And Cove replying, hating the squeak in her voice, saying she was a great swimmer and knew what she was doing. And she remembered how the guide's reluctance had finally melted away as Cove's father appeared at her back, all muscles and sparkling eyes and, unlike Cove, unmistakably Maori, saying, "You'll let my girl join us, yeah?"

People had been trying to strip her dreams away for her whole life. It wasn't her place to do that to someone else.

She checked the computer strapped to her wrist. It was shaped like a chunky watch, multiple metrics flashing over the screen, with buttons along its sides to switch modes and record data. Depth: fifteen feet. Oxygen: 98 percent.

Cove was familiar with the way the water—and the divers— changed during their descent.

At surface level, nitrogen was a neutral, harmless gas. They breathed it in and breathed it out without registering its existence. But when nitrogen was put under pressure, it became soluble. That was the principle behind fizzy soft drinks. Inject pressurized nitrogen into the liquid, then when the bottle is unsealed and the pressure releases, it condenses back into tiny, sparkling bubbles.

But it wasn't just soft drinks that could absorb pressurized nitrogen. The human body could too, if the atmospheric weight was strong enough. And water could exert an enormous amount of pressure.

At just twenty feet, the nitrogen they drew from their tanks with every breath would soak through their lungs and absorb into their bloodstreams, their muscles, even their brains. It wouldn't be dangerous yet. Just like no bubbles could escape from a sealed bottle, the nitrogen would build up inside them, harmless until the pressure was released.

Returning to the surface opened that valve. Suddenly, the nitrogen inside them would reform. Bubbles would appear in their lungs, their muscles, and their joints. Small amounts would cause them pain. Larger amounts could result in permanent damage. Divers called it *the bends*, and it didn't end just careers but also lives.

That was why safety stops were a necessity. Anyone traveling deeper than twenty feet would need to take breaks on their way back to the surface to allow the reformed nitrogen to dissipate out again through their lungs. The deeper they went and the longer they stayed down there, the more decompression stops were required. It wasn't unheard of for a diver to spend fifteen minutes at a wreck and then need two hours to decompress on the way back up.

Cove checked her computer again. Forty feet. At sixty, they would transition from regular scuba diving to deep diving, a level most recreational explorers never entered. All of the advanced diving courses and certifications had been in service of that: the privilege of traversing deeper than the average person was supposed to go. And with good reason.

Turning the human body into a fizzy soda substitute wasn't the only thing pressurized nitrogen could do. At a hundred feet, nitrogen narcosis would begin to take effect. The greater the pressure and the more time spent down there, the more nitrogen would be drawn into—and stored inside—the body. And nitrogen, in large enough quantities, was a remarkably effective sedative.

Too many good divers had been lost to nitrogen narcosis. Their movements slowing, their reflexes dulling, a gentle, warming calmness washing through them and telling them everything was fine: *let your eyes close, let your mind wander, let the air in your tank dissipate as you drift deeper and deeper into the ocean.*

Cove and her team were going past the hundred-feet mark. They would be resisting the narcotic effects with trimix, the specialized blend inside their canisters. By substituting helium for part of the nitrogen, they could surpass their natural limits and dive beyond regular mortality barriers.

That didn't mean the depths wouldn't be hell for their bodies. The added pressure had become noticeable at only ten feet down. At a hundred feet, they would be breathing harder just to compensate against the squeeze. Anything over a hundred and fifty feet required even more specialized qualifications and prolonged training to withstand. By two hundred and twenty feet, even the oxygen in their canisters would begin to turn toxic.

Cove and her team were traveling down three hundred and twelve feet.

The dive line flicked ahead of Cove, guiding her. The pressure was increasing. Each breath grew tighter, and each foot down dimmed the ocean as natural light was filtered away. The lights atop her mask caught harsh flashes of Aidan's fins ahead.

The dark infinity surrounding them began to fizzle with vague movement as her eyes sought something—anything—to latch on to. Hestie had said there would be no sharks and no fish, but she imagined she saw vast shapes that rolled toward them before they bled back into the void.

The diving computer said they were passing two hundred feet. She could hear her companions' breathing through the communications system. They sounded ragged, even though the weight belts were doing the majority of the work to carry them down. She kept her ears alert for sounds of panicking.

Humans were never intended to reach the depths they were seeking. The only way they had was through a century of trial and error, of pushing the limits, of countless deaths in search of a way down. Cove had always found it fascinating that humans could have so much good, healthy land to live upon, but they still persisted in suffocating in search of a new summit or freezing as they struck out to find a pole or drowning as they sought the depths of the ocean. Now, the idea made her want to break out into frantic laughter.

She mentally checked herself. Giddiness was an early symptom of nitrogen narcosis. She searched for signs that her mind was growing vague or her limbs were turning heavy, but the trimix was doing its job and she remained alert. Almost too much so.

They were passing two hundred and fifty feet. Another minute and they would have eyes on the wreck.

There was still so much that could go wrong. They didn't even know if they were approaching the correct ship. The wreck had been found as part of an oil survey. Grainy, distorted imagery showed the distinctive bow of the *Arcadia*, but Cove's team would be the first humans to actually lay eyes on it. There could have been a mistake. It could be an entirely different ship, one with less mystery and less history. Or a rock formation that had unluckily created a close enough mimic to be convincing. The survey photos didn't offer many clues.

Two hundred and ninety feet. Their descent was almost deliriously fast. The waters were murky and impossibly heavy. Orbs of waterborne particles drifted past her lights. The white dive line twisted along her side, but it barely looked like anything Cove had ever seen before. This world was alien. Uninhabitable. Unimaginably hostile.

"Up ahead," Vanna said into the communication unit.

Cove leaned forward. Rocky formations rose around her. They'd reached it: the ocean's floor, three hundred and twelve feet from breathable air.

The angle of their descent altered. Instead of traveling straight down, Vanna led them forward at an angle. The mountainous rocks, softened by layers of snow-like sediment, rose on either side of them.

Then, ahead, she saw it. Cove drew a slow breath as the bow of an immense metal ship surged out of the darkness.

5.

The Adelaide Courier, 12 January 1929

WRECKAGE FROM SS *ARCADIA* WASHES ASHORE

Nearly nine months after the mysterious disappearance of the ocean liner SS *Arcadia*, some clues as to its final resting place may have arrived on the beaches of Poland.

The ship, which disappeared on a transatlantic voyage between the United States of America and Britain, has been the source of much speculation due to the unusual circumstances involving its loss.

Three ships reported receiving emergency messages from the *Arcadia* between 17 and 18 April 1928, though each of the messages provided different coordinates. Although an exact location couldn't be pinpointed, all agreed on one thing: the *Arcadia* required assistance.

Vessels in the vicinity searched the waters around the

reported coordinates, but no trace of the *Arcadia* could be located. After the final distress call, placed to the HMS *Margaret* at four in the morning on the 18th, all communication ceased and no further contact with the *Arcadia* could be established. When the ship failed to arrive at port, it was believed the ocean liner had most likely been lost at sea.

Theories regarding the vanishing of the *Arcadia* abound. Historian Richard Townsend published an article in this paper describing how the crew could have mutinied and broadcast their messages to confuse the trail before starting new lives at a remote port. Vincent Whelan, a naval captain with more than forty years of experience, suggests a simpler solution: the ship was overwhelmed during a storm. Other theories in popular circulation include the *Arcadia* being boarded by pirates, becoming beached on an uninhabited island, or hitting one of the many lost mines still active in those parts of the ocean.

To date, the true fate of the *Arcadia* remains unknown. However, new discoveries on the shores of Poland may have moved us one step closer to the truth and reveal that the search efforts for the *Arcadia* may have taken place hundreds of miles from where the ship sank.

Last Monday, a piece of oar bearing the *Arcadia*'s name was found on a beach five miles from the small town of Sopot, north of Gdansk.

It's reported that, although pieces of metal and wood occasionally wash up on their shores, it's rare that any items can be identified.

Officials from the Harland and Wolff shipyard believe the oar belonged to one of the *Arcadia*'s six lifeboats, which were stored on its deck. Its condition is consistent with having been adrift in the ocean for upward of six months.

Matthew Rostow from the Institute of Maritime Research, an expert in the ocean's currents, believes the location of the wreckage suggests the oar first entered the water inside the Baltic Sea. If this is true, it would place the *Arcadia* more than a hundred miles from any of the coordinates given during the emergency broadcasts and at least three hundred miles from its intended route.

When the ship left port on 6 April, twelve days before its last contact, it was under the command of Captain William Virgil and was manned by two hundred and sixty-five crew, along with four hundred and nine passengers. No bodies were ever recovered.

It's unknown yet whether this discovery signifies that the mythical ship was truly sunk at sea or whether the oar was jettisoned or simply lost during a storm. However, this is certain to add new fuel to the heated debate surrounding one of the British Navy's most infamous lost ships.

Sean paced the mess hall, a Styrofoam cup of coffee shaking in his right hand. It was only half-full and still needed to cool some. Only a fool would fill a cup any further on this kind of ocean. The swell was steady enough, and the boat was large enough to roll with the punches, but they were still rising and dropping upward of eight feet with every passing wave, and Sean was not in the mood to be mopping up spilled drinks.

He wasn't in the mood for much of anything, if he was being

honest. The crew had gone down for their first dive—something that shouldn't have happened for another three days. The plan had always been for his ROVs to handle the bulk of the exploration and for Cove and the others to get just enough footage to round out his work.

Instead, the ROVs had failed. All three of them. All at the same time.

Devereaux had posited some rambling, half-baked idea about solar flares damaging the equipment. The others thought that was a reasonable suggestion.

His ROVs were a thing of beauty: Alicia, the crawler; Hannah, the heavy-duty swimmer; and Judes, the tethered orb that could self-propel and responded to his joystick like a dream. Judes was his preferred vehicle, always. He could sit in the bridge, everyone gathered around him with bated breath as Judes relayed the first images of the *Arcadia* to his laptop. They would ask to look left or turn right with eager, hushed voices. They would gasp and jab fingers at his laptop screen—leaving prints on it, probably, but no one would care in the moment because the euphoria would be so great—as they found the ship's landmarks. They would clap him on the back and exhale in relief as the ROV finished its mission and returned to the surface.

It was a routine he'd done plenty of times before.

Instead, he was alone in the mess hall while the rest of them got to view the *Arcadia*.

The rub of it was that he could dive. He was damned good at it too. He'd been near the *Arcadia*'s depths before. Those dives hadn't exactly been aboveboard, to be fair, but if you paid admission to a popular diving site and brought your own equipment, no one much questioned how deep you went. He was just missing his final certification.

And that really showed how much of a sham the trip was. The kid—Aidan—who looked barely old enough to be away from his mother and who had scraped through a certificate by the skin of his teeth, was being allowed down. Because Cove was the boss, and Cove didn't much like Sean, and Cove was more than happy to take a shiny piece of paper over two decades of diving experience.

His ROVs were supposed to lead the charge. Instead, they lay scattered across the lounge, half-dismantled, as Sean tried to find out what had gone wrong. They were essentially useless. Just like he was. He'd been demoted from valued expert to little more than a tourist.

And thing was, he didn't think that was an accident.

He doubted Cove would have done anything to tamper with his equipment. She was reaching for celebrity status through these documentaries; she couldn't afford a possible scandal. But Cove wasn't the only one who didn't particularly fancy him. And she wasn't the only person to be excited that the three-day ROV exploration had been converted to three days of diving.

When Sean had discovered his ROVs were shut down in the permanent kind of way, Roy had been quick to add that his cameras were dead too. Not the dry suit cameras though; those were just fine. But the big, bulky, heavy cameras that were bound to give anyone a neck ache were nonfunctional. Though, hey, wouldn't you look at that, Roy managed to fix one of them right when it was needed.

Everyone else had just accepted it, but Sean had spent too long on the earth to believe in those kinds of coincidences.

The coffee cup was empty. He dunked it into the trash can, then turned toward the hallway that led to the lowest level's cabins.

If Roy had truly sabotaged the ROVs, he would have left some kind of trace. The machines looked fine from the outside, which meant it hadn't been as crude as hurling them against the ship's walls until they broke. He must have dismantled them somehow. And that would mean a screwdriver at the very least. Maybe loose chips or circuits. If he'd thrown them overboard, then Sean would have nothing to go on...but he didn't think Roy was that kind of man. It was more likely he'd hidden them.

He wasn't going to *do* anything about it, he swore to himself. No fistfights. No screaming. He wasn't even out to ruin the other man's reputation. But he needed to *know*.

They each had a bunk and a locker to store their bags in. The lockers technically had combination locks, but this wasn't a tourist charter where strangers might steal from you. They were a team of professionals, so no one bothered to lock their items away.

As he reached the stairs landing, Sean checked his watch. The dive crew would have finished their descent by this point. That meant they would have, at minimum, a couple of hours decompressing on the way back up. Devereaux had placed himself on the bridge, close to the comms in case any kind of emergency came through, and showed no signs of moving.

It was just Sean, the bunks, and whatever he could find inside.

6.

Aidan hung suspended, less than fifteen feet from the ocean floor. His hands moved in sweeps as he adjusted his balance. Ahead, rock formations, at least twenty feet tall, dwarfed him. Something dark and massive was wedged between them.

A burst of bubbles escaped his rebreather. They poured past his eyes as they shot toward the surface, vanishing into the vague layers of light and dark above.

"Wow," Roy said.

The massive hull appeared in the faint, diffused glare of their flashlights. It was unfathomably large. The diving instructors had said something about that: their face masks, paired with refracted light through the water, made objects appear a third larger and 40 percent closer than they actually were. It didn't make a difference. Even telling himself it was magnified, even telling himself it was smaller than other megaliners of its day, it was still so much bigger than he'd ever dreamed.

A body—Cove, he thought—moved past him. Her fins created

ripples through the water as she approached the ship with the grace of someone who had been swimming for as long as she could walk.

"Incredible," she whispered.

The others had shown Aidan photos of the *Arcadia*. It had been a beautiful ship, built not long after the *Titanic's* fatal maiden voyage. Even though the *Arcadia* had been repainted multiple times, it had still held the hallmark of ocean liners from the day: at least eight levels, porthole windows staring out of its sides, and two smokestacks rising from its back.

As he awkwardly fumbled closer, Aidan tried to make sense of what he was seeing. They were still far enough away that he couldn't make out much except a monumental shape that seemed to dwarf the landscape around it. It merged into a point, and he realized they were facing the bow.

Roy's voice piped through the helmet. "Remind me, how far are we taking this dive?"

"Full penetration," Cove replied, and Roy broke into his signature clenched-teeth laughter. Cove, a smile in her voice, added, "For the viewers at home, no penetration is where you look at the vessel from the outside but don't try to interact with it. Partial penetration is where you explore the ship, but only as far as the natural light will take you. Full penetration means going into the parts where the only things standing between us and blindness will be our headlights."

"*Ful-l-l-l* penetration," Roy crooned, and that time, even Aidan had to laugh.

"She's certainly a beautiful ship," Cove said. "But I didn't come here just to *look* at her."

The others were drawing ahead, but the largest body—Roy—hung back. When Aidan caught up, Roy tapped his forearm, a silent question: *You good?*

Aidan gave him a thumbs-up before remembering the international sign for *okay* in diver language was the finger-and-thumb circle. He corrected.

Roy gave him an okay in return. His mouth wasn't visible behind the breathing apparatus, but his eyes scrunched up in their familiar smile. He couldn't say it while the others were still online and listening, but his message was clear: *Just relax and breathe slow.*

That had been his mantra during the diving training. They'd spent the lessons virtually glued together. Half the entries in Aidan's logbook had been falsified just to make him eligible for the advanced course. Roy had done that, but then, Aidan hadn't objected, so he reasoned he might as well take responsibility for it.

Roy, for his part, was as comfortable underwater as he was on land. He'd stayed with Aidan through all of the flooded quarries, the underwater forests, the accidental silt-outs, and the questioning dive instructors.

Even then, Aidan suspected he'd only passed the last class because the instructor had been more interested in a frail older diver who kept trying to go beyond the recommended depths. Every time Aidan had begun to breathe too fast or fumble his equipment or show signs of panic, Roy had tapped his arm and nodded with such rigid calmness that Aidan found it easy to let go of the fear.

Just relax and breathe slow. That's all you need to do, man.

He did that then, letting his movements calm and become more fluid, allowing each breath to linger in his lungs a few seconds longer than his instincts wanted. That was the trick to diving, everyone said. Move slowly. Even if you're running out of air, don't fight your way to the surface, because you'll end up expending more oxygen than if you take it steady. He wasn't entirely sure he believed them on that last part.

Roy tilted his head, indicating that he was going to catch up to the rest of the group, and Aidan nodded as he leaned his body forward.

He had hoped that closing the distance would put the vessel's size into context, but it only grew. The water was clogged with tiny particles that flashed white in his light and muddied his vision. He still couldn't make out much of the ship except for the sheer, harsh curves of the formless bow. Its edges were rough. If the smokestacks were still standing, they were too far back to see.

They passed Vanna. She'd stopped to secure the dive line to a nearby rocky formation, and then clipped a second line—their safety line, the one they would be using to find their way back out of the maze of the wreck—to the same rock.

The bow kept growing. It was pure monstrous size, hiding everything behind it. The ship listed at an angle, one side propped against the rocky formations it had fallen between.

The ragged edges weren't a figment of his imagination or an effect of the water, Aidan realized. They were drawing close enough that their headlights could pick out details. The ship was crusted with something. *Rustacles*, Hestie had called them. A ragged coating where the ship's hull and the water merged. Many decades of sediment had settled on top, giving it an unsettlingly alien appearance.

Cove led, and she began swimming upward, one hand fiddling with her buoyancy compensator to help her rise. Aidan mimicked her, bringing more air into the pouches until they were lifting him up.

Above, the bow's edge was adorned with railings. They were perfectly intact: ragged, just like every other part of the ship, blurred by time and sediment, but otherwise exactly as they'd been above the surface.

He wanted to touch them. To know what the coating felt like. Soft, like the sediment appeared? Or would it be more like rust, delicate and flaky and painfully sharp all at once?

Cove had been focused on something else though, he realized. She floated, hands moving in gentle sweeps to hold herself upright, as she faced the lettering on the ship's side.

"*Arcadia*," she said, a ferocious smile filling her voice. "We found her."

Her light swept across the word. Each letter was the size of Aidan's torso, built that large to be visible from a distance. They were made out of flat plates of metal and fastened to the ship's side. Even covered in the unsettling crusting, they were still visible against the darker hull.

Giddy laughter broke out between Hestie and Cove. Hestie swam forward, gloved hands reached out. She was visibly shaking as she pressed both palms into the ship's hull.

Cove's helmeted head nodded approvingly. "Congratulations. You're the first human to touch the *Arcadia* in more than ninety years."

"O-oh." Hestie pushed away from the ship, swimming in a tight loop. "It's incredible. It's so intact—almost perfect—it's like the gulf put it into a time capsule."

"No signs of collapse," Cove replied, agreeing. "This part of the hull is still intact, at least. Minimal corrosion…"

"It's the water." Hestie returned to the ship's side, hands reverently touching the crusted metal. "The sea is saltwater, but the gulf is fed by melting ice. Cold. Minimal salt content. And no currents to beat at the ship or drag it across the ocean floor. And look at all this sediment—that's magic for preservation. If it's like this inside—"

"Who knows what we'll find."

Roy interjected, "Ful-*l-l-l-l* penetration."

Aidan couldn't hold back. Hestie had touched the ship, and she was the marine biologist, which meant it had to be allowed. He kicked closer to the railing and reached for one of the lower bars. He could feel the crunch of the crumbling material through his gloves.

It was accompanied by a flash of terror.

He let go, allowing himself to float back from the ship, his heart skittering too fast. The awe and anxiety were being replaced with something darker. Dread. In the brief moment he'd touched the metal, he'd felt the danger of the place. This ship wasn't a gem on the ocean floor, waiting to be found. It was a trap. A monstrous, hideous trap. Unfeeling, unyielding.

The image that came to mind was of deep-ocean fish. Their bodies bloated and gray, their eyes whited out in blindness. They lay among the rocks on the ocean's floor, their enormous frog-like mouths open and yawning as they waited for small, delicate morsels to swim inside.

"Look down," Cove said. "It's buried nearly to its waterline."

Something turned in Aidan's stomach. Cove was right. The ship's hull had been painted blue above the waterline, black beneath. It had settled so deeply into the sediment that only a thin stripe of black was still visible. He'd been in awe of the ship's size, and he hadn't even been able to see the full scope. It wasn't just *big*. A little voice in the back of his head whispered that it was *too* big, unfathomably so, *dangerously* so—

A tap on his arm. He'd been holding his breath, and somehow, Roy had realized even when he hadn't. He inhaled slowly, trying not to alert the others through the comms units. He was shaking. Sweat bled into the fleeces underneath his dry suit. His legs had become jelly, and if the buoyancy controls of his suit hadn't been holding him in place, he was afraid he would have crumpled and sunk down into the ocean's floor, where the layers of waterlogged sediment would fold over him and bury him so deep that the light would never find him again.

Hestie still touched the ship's side, leaning so close that she looked ready to kiss it if the helmet hadn't been in her way. Aidan couldn't understand why she didn't seem to feel the awful sinking, sickening dread of the place.

His ears had gone cloudy. A voice floated to him through what seemed like an immeasurable void, but the words were nothing more than murmurs. It was only when the other divers began examining their dive computers that Aidan realized Vanna had called for an oxygen check. Their answers came back in quick succession: ninety, ninety-one, eighty-seven.

Aidan fumbled to check his own. Oxygen: 75 percent. The lowest—and by a long stretch. He'd swum too hard, burned too much. Each ragged breath depleted more.

Just relax and breathe slow. That's all you need to do, man.

Vanna had said they were working on thirds. One-third to get to the seafloor and explore the ship, one-third to decompress on the way up, one-third spare. But they'd only just found the ship and he'd consumed most of his first allotment. If he told them his number, then Vanna—as cool and unyielding as the ocean itself—would call the dive off before the others were ready to leave.

They'd all turned to watch him: dark, sleek bodies floating in the void, legs moving in slow pendular motions, their masks unreadable under the glow from his light. They were waiting.

"Eighty-five," he said, hoping they wouldn't hear the shriveling anxiety in his voice. He hated lying. It was a skill that came easily to Roy—fudge the dive numbers, tell the instructor you've done this before, act like you belong in the restricted section and no one will pay you any notice.

But there was a key difference between his lies and Roy's: Roy's never felt malicious. They were the oil that greased the wheels of social interactions, smoothing everything over, making everyone happy. When Aidan lied, it felt like barbs, cutting the people closest to him no matter how good the intentions were.

This would be fine, he swore. The words ran on a loop in his head, circling just as rapidly as the air in and out of his lungs. *This will be fine. This will be fine.* Vanna was budgeting a third of their air for emergencies; he could dip into that surplus if it helped the team's first dive be a success. He could get his breathing back under control, make his movements smoother, be more efficient with his air. This would be fine.

Vanna was silent for a moment, and Aidan felt the press of terror that she'd guessed his deception, but then she said, "Okay. We have enough to go inside the ship. Keep an eye on your numbers and tell me when you fall under seventy-five."

Even as Aidan watched, his oxygen meter clicked down to 74 percent. He put his arm down, his throat tight and eyes burning, as he shifted forward to follow Cove's lead.

7.

Sean pressed the cabin door closed behind himself. They'd been given double-berth rooms: bunk beds stacked against one wall, lockers at their foot, a narrow folding desk and chair against the opposite wall. The desk would consume all of the walkway, so it had been stowed, fastened into the wall until it was called upon.

Space was always at a premium on ships, but this was one of the nicer ones he'd been on. Not exactly luxury-yacht stage—no hot tubs and no party dance halls—but with more consideration given to the occupants than research dive teams were often afforded. The last ship he'd been on had put him in a room with four bunks, eight occupants total, and it had been so cramped that they were tripping over each other trying to get dressed. Never mind the shower facilities. This time they had one shower for every two people. Absolute hedonistic luxury as far as Sean was concerned.

The reason for their current level of comfort was the ship's owner: Devereaux. Sean hadn't spoken to him enough to know the man well, but he'd gleaned plenty of insight simply from context clues. Devereaux had money, even though he was a historian—a career that, traditionally, did not result in an awful lot of money. Devereaux had been born into a life of comfort, had extended that same model to his ship, and was happy to loan the ship to the research crew on the condition that he came along for the journey and could be interviewed for the documentary. An arrangement that worked just fine for Cove apparently. Sean couldn't blame her. Ship charters were expensive, and now she had an extra talking head to fill up the camera reels. Win-win-win.

Sean had been bunked with Cove. He'd feared that their people-person leader would want to talk until all hours, but he'd lucked out. She didn't make much noise, she didn't disturb him more than was necessary, and she turned her light off at a reasonable hour. The holy grail as far as bunkmates were concerned, and Sean was happy to afford her the same courtesy.

Sean stood in the room Roy shared with his friend, the kid, Aidan. Sean had to admit, the berth was tidier than he'd expected. Both beds were made and the floor was clear of any personal possessions.

Give it time. It's only day two.

He didn't have to be Sherlock to know which bunk he wanted. Roy and Aidan had a benevolent-older-brother-figure-grateful-acolyte dynamic. Roy was served his food first. Roy had first shower. If there was ever a queue for anything, Roy was ahead of Aidan.

It was a no-brainer to know the older man would have the lower bunk. Sean crouched to reach the locker at the foot of his bed. As expected, it swung open without resistance. Inside was a large duffel bag and a spare set of boots. Nothing had been unpacked yet, and there were no suspicious screwdrivers or wires tucked behind the bag.

Sean didn't love the idea of pawing through someone else's possessions, no matter how valid his motivation, so instead, he searched around the bed first. The pillow hid nothing except clean white sheets. He found a used tissue stuffed between the mattress and the wall, but that had likely come from a previous voyage, so he threw it away with twisted lips.

Then, when he peeled the mattress up from the wooden holder, he found something. A small black book tucked underneath the mattress, easily accessible.

The book was too thin to be a novel and not labeled in the way dive logs were, which meant—*will surprises never cease?*—it was a journal. He never in a million years would have pegged Roy as having a rich enough internal life to necessitate or even allow for a diary, but he also wasn't about to look a gift horse in the mouth.

Reading a journal was arguably a step worse than opening the duffel bag, but it was also his most promising avenue for finding out what Roy had done to his ROVs. He slapped the book on top of the sheets and knelt before it as he flipped it open.

Small, neat script filled the pages. Each date was marked in the upper-right corner. Occasionally illustrations, scratched in the heavy black ink of a ballpoint pen, clustered in the margins. The writing was tidy. Too much so.

Sean squeezed his eyes closed. He'd seen Roy's writing before. It was wide and messy, full of the kind of energy that usually only inhabited golden retrievers. This wasn't Roy's journal. He'd picked the wrong bunk.

More than that, he realized, looking back at the neatly stowed duffel, he'd picked the wrong *room*. Those boots didn't belong to either Roy or Aidan. They had to be Vanna's. No one else on the dive team owned such austere clothing.

Give it up for Sean, legendary detective, so observant that he can't even remember which room his crewmates sleep in.

Vanna had the lower bunk, which meant Hestie's had to be the top. It was no wonder the room was as neat as the day it had been built; Roy couldn't have imagined a more rigidly law-abiding duo. The lack of boxer shorts and socks scattered over the floor should have been his first clue that he'd made a wrong turn.

He moved to close the journal and return it to its hiding place but stopped. The final line on the page had caught his eye, and once he'd read it, he couldn't turn away.

You watch as they drown.

He blinked, his mind going oddly empty as the words unfolded inside. It wasn't the sort of thing you expected to find in a dive instructor's book. Clearly, he was missing context. He glanced at the line before.

The bubbles vanish from their gaping mouth.

His skin had begun to itch as sweat flooded out. His mind was still empty, and he felt like he was trapped in a void, grasping for the answers he knew *had* to be there, except they clearly weren't.

Sean wound back to the top of the page. It was dated a week prior to the ship's departure. Eight lines ran down the sheet, every alternate line darting inward like some kind of poetry, except there was no rhyme and no meter.

The black holds them in its hands.
The void, beautiful, voracious.

They want more air but there's none to take,
just the deep thick water.

Skin turns white as they try to hold their
  breath inside.
They can't.

The bubbles vanish from their gaping mouth.
You watch as they drown.

A strange sound escaped Sean. He didn't even know what it was; he only knew he'd never heard anything like it before—whining, gasping, so unlike his usual self.

The emptiness in his mind had been replaced with *too much*. He thought he was pretty skilled at reading people and understanding their behavior. Apparently not.

Vanna had struck him as an odd person but no more odd than the usual fare on these kinds of highly specialized jobs. She wasn't social, but then, neither was Sean. He'd thought if there was anyone on the ship whom he could tolerate, it would be her.

Though that wasn't from any fondness forged by positive traits but simply a lack of irritants. Sean's measure for cohabitability began and ended with the ability to be quiet, something Vanna excelled at.

He knelt on the cabin's floor, wedged between the bunk beds and the stowed desk, elbows braced on the mattress as he stared at the writing and chewed the edge of his thumb ragged.

How much did he really know about Vanna? Her eyes moved often as she watched her companions, but her mouth stayed still. The previous night, as they ate dinner, he'd watched her physically stand up and walk around the table to pick up a saltshaker instead of asking someone to pass it to her.

She did a lot of cave diving. How many had Cove said she'd logged? Four thousand? A lot, anyway. More than Sean, and Sean spent more time in the ocean than almost anyone he knew.

So why was she writing about people drowning?

Maybe it was a form of therapy. A dream journal or a way to confront her own fears—if the stonelike Vanna had ever actually experienced an emotion as strong as fear in her life. He turned the page. The next entry was much shorter.

I would lie down with you, put my arms around you, feel how cold you are as you roll, rigid with death, on the ocean floor.

"Ah." He pushed the journal away as though it had burned his fingers. There was something deeply upsetting about how melodic and gentle the words were when paired with something as hideous as drowning.

Is this some kind of fetish for death? Some kind of…repressed…

Sean stood and began pacing. His palms were damp. The ROV situation, which had been his whole life just two minutes before, suddenly seemed blindingly insignificant.

At the same time, he was trying to bargain with himself. *Step off the ledge. This is weird, but plenty of things are weird if you don't understand them. This doesn't mean she…*

He turned back to the journal, this time fueled by a wild, desperate need to understand. Pages turned under his hands, moving faster and faster as he tore back through the entries. Words seemed to float off the page toward him, all penned in that same beautifully neat script.

Drown...

In the deep...

You'll drown...

Images had been scrawled in the margins. The black ballpoint pen had scored the pages so deeply in some places that it had torn through. Not all of the tight, urgent images were clear, but the ones that were made Sean sick to his stomach.

A breathing apparatus floating among seaweed, no human in sight.

Bubbles rushing up the page's margins.

A hand, so pallid compared to the darkness surrounding it, poised in a way that was just limp enough for Sean to believe the owner was no longer conscious.

The book fell open to the final entry, dated that morning. Vanna must have penned it while Hestie was in the shower. It was short and to the point, surrounded by scribbles that reminded Sean of rust and barnacles.

I'll watch you drown.

8.

Cove's heart sang. Until that moment, she hadn't been able to convince herself that they had truly found the *Arcadia*. It was lying on the ocean floor so far from its intended route that she'd half believed they were expending expensive supplies on a trip down to visit a very fancy rock.

But not only had they found a true ship, they'd also been able to confirm its identity. The footage their cameras captured as they arrived at the massive steel name would serve as a point of great emotional intensity for the documentary's eventual viewer, just as it had for Cove. It would probably be a key part of the trailer, maybe even the poster. The image of those seven letters floating out of the darkness and speckled sediment was more than iconic; it bordered on a religious experience.

The others had already drifted over to view the ship's other side in search of a way in, but Cove couldn't bring herself to move just yet. Her headlight's beam flowed across the name as she drank it in again. Covered by the effects of ninety-odd years in the Gulf of Bothnia, the clear-cut letters had blurred at the edges but still had enough contrast to be unmistakable.

Hestie's voice came through the speakers in her mask. It felt disturbingly close, considering that they were on opposite sides of the ship. "There's a hole in the port side."

"Coming." A flood of bubbles escaped her rebreather as Cove turned.

A jolt passed through her, startling her into stillness. She wasn't alone, like she'd thought. A dark body floated in the water behind her. It had half merged into the depths, its dry suit a perfect camouflage against the endless expanse of black water.

Cove, her heart racing slightly too fast for comfort, raised one hand in greeting. The floating figure didn't respond.

It was upright and seemed alert, hands drifting in nonexistent currents to make microadjustments to its position. Its face was the most unsettling part. At close quarters, Cove could see her crewmates' features beneath the plastic headpieces. At a distance, they vanished behind a sheen of pale reflection.

"Aidan?" she tried.

"Hi, I'm here." His voice came out tight, anxious. Like he thought he was about to be yelled at. It wasn't good to be that stressed at this depth. She could picture him twisting around, searching for Cove through the water, trying to find the source of her voice.

The floating form didn't react though. Its gloved hands were spread at its sides. Its legs swung in slow motions, the fins curving lightly against the water's resistance. Cove was struck by the disturbing impression that the figure wasn't staring at the *Arcadia* but was instead staring at *her*.

And for all she knew, beneath that blank white sheen, it was.

It's not Aidan. Not big enough to be Roy. Legs are too thick for Hestie—

"Vanna?"

The helmet twitched a fraction. The voice that answered was smooth and cool. "Yes?"

Cove grit her teeth into a smile, knowing her voice would sound warm even if the expression wasn't genuine. "Hestie thinks she's found a way inside the ship. Are you ready?"

Instead of answering, Vanna leaned forward and let her powerful legs propel her in a wide arc around the ship's bow. Cove felt the currents snag at her. She watched until Vanna was out of view, then tilted forward herself to follow in her wake.

The bow passed to Cove's left. She reached one hand out and lightly brushed the edge. Fragments of rust and dust spiraled away under her touch, leaving a comet's trail behind her hand.

On the ship's other side, she couldn't make out the divers' bodies, but she could find them by their lights. The beams zigzagged through the dark, crossing over one another and hitting the hull and rocks. Cove adjusted her buoyancy to go down and leaned into a dive.

The hole Hestie had found was low down on the bow, only a few meters above the smooth layers of waterlogged sediment. The ship leaned against the rocks on that side. It only left a narrow gap between the steep vertical walls and the bow. Cove twisted as she joined the others in the space.

"Look at this." Hestie indicated the edges of a ragged hole that tore through the plate hull and the interior walls, exposing rooms beyond. "We can fit through here without trying to open any of the hatches."

Roy, identifiable by his broad shoulders, repeatedly swam toward the ship and used an outstretched hand to press against the metal and bounce back when he got too close. The movements were languid in the heavy water, but Cove still had to bite her tongue to keep herself from telling him to stop. She didn't want their first visit into the ship cut short because he frittered his oxygen away or caused a silt-out.

"This has got to be it, right?" Roy said, once again hitting the ship's side and pushing back. This time, a plume of sediment flicked up, clouding around him, and he finally stopped. "We can at least put a tick mark against one part of our job: what caused the sinking. The *Arcadia* hit land, breached its hull, and dropped like a stone."

Hestie leaned away from the hole, her head tilted back. "I'm not sure. Look at the rocks up there. They're damaged. I'll wager this happened post-sinking."

Five sets of helmet-mounted lights turned toward the rocky protrusion behind them. The same heavy sediment had settled over the stone, but Cove could still see clear marks running down its length. She could picture the ship, sinking bow first, gushing a flood of air in its wake as it rocked toward the ocean floor, only to hit that stone and tear a fresh hole in its side. She would bet anything that, if they explored the outcrop, they would find well-aged pieces of metal wedged in the ragged surface.

"Hestie's right," Cove said. "It's not something to discount, but I don't think this caused the ship's sinking."

Aidan's voice joined in. "There was the, uh, the—" He cleared his throat and tried again. "The emergency messages. They came through over, like, a couple days. And they didn't, uh, didn't mention striking anything—"

"They didn't mention much of anything though, did they?" Roy, apparently unable to stop himself, kicked toward the ship again, arm outreached to propel himself back. "Except for the bit every single Creepypasta-style docu-video likes to focus on: *they're in the walls.*"

Cove said, "I get what Aidan's saying though. A hole this large should have sunk the *Arcadia* in maybe an hour or two. Even if they were pumping the water, I doubt they could have gone past five or six. Based on the time span of the messages, whatever happened to the *Arcadia* took at least two days."

Hestie lingered near the opening. The dark, ragged chasm in the ship's side was only a little wider than a person but twice as tall. A dark line cut across it horizontally: the floor dividing two levels. Even with it blocking the way, they could still squeeze above or below without too much stress. The lowest part of the narrow gash disappeared into the sediment below the waterline. A ship with that kind of damage wasn't likely to stay afloat for long.

Three hundred feet beneath the surface and wedged against a rock wall, the gap was almost pitch-black. When their lights swept across the opening, Cove could make out flashes of the insides: dark steel walls on the lower level, wood fittings on the upper. The *Arcadia* came from an era when that kind of opulence was not only tolerated but desired.

Modern cruise ships opted for minimalism. The more expensive a craft, the less clutter it aspired to hold. Equipment could be tucked away, storage areas kept out of sight, even chairs and beds sleeked down until they vanished into the room's walls. And the walls themselves were always bare. The more money that went into a ship, the less likely you were to see rivets or even seams.

The *Arcadia* had danced to a different tune, one from an era with significantly fewer safety regulations. Wood paneling— deadly if a fire took hold but considered worth it for the aesthetic. Carpet floor runners. Lamps fixed into the narrow hallway walls, each one posing a unique concussion opportunity. And Cove's favorite, a legitimate staircase leading between the living areas—not cramped and metal, but fitted with carpet and wood bannisters and wide enough to carry multiple passengers at a time.

She lifted her head, bringing her light from the lower level to the higher one. At the last second, just as the light vanished from the deeper floor, she thought she saw motion inside. Something large, shifting just outside of her view.

She brought her light back down, but the dark chasm was once again empty. If there had been something inside, it had moved deeper into the maze of hallways.

A fish.

They loved old shipwrecks for the shelter they provided. Diving communities were full of stories about turning a corner and coming face-to-face with a massive grouper or having a curious barracuda sneak up behind. Cove worked her jaw.

Hestie said there wouldn't be any sea life here.

That was true as far as she could see. The water was a biting three degrees above freezing, something she couldn't have survived for long without the layers of fleece and dry suit. And although the Gulf of Bothnia connected to the ocean, the water flowed *outward*, rarely in.

Still. It wasn't impossible that something had swum this distance, was it? The area didn't offer much food, not even the aquatic-plant variety, but a lost fish wouldn't know that.

Cove switched on her interview voice—the engaged, politely curious tone used to tease information out of the experts on her documentaries. "Hestie, in your opinion, what are our chances of encountering sea life inside the *Arcadia*?"

"Oh!" Hestie, seeming to guess that the question was intended as B-roll to provide reference for the everyman viewer, matched Cove by switching into her lecturer voice. "Almost zero. The Baltic Sea offers fantastic fishing opportunities to the south, but the farther north you go, the less life there is to find. This part of the gulf is almost entirely devoid of oxygen. Without oxygen, nothing lives—not fish, not plants, and not even bacteria. It's as close to a sterile environment as you can find underwater."

In a normal interview, Cove would have fired back with banter or another question. But she was struggling to turn her head away from the back corner of that lower floor, where she could have sworn she'd seen movement.

The ocean liked to mess with divers' eyes. The human mind couldn't cope with looking at *nothing* for very long and, in sufficient darkness, quickly began to create its own images of what it thought belonged there.

Still…

"Which floor are we taking?"

Roy's question, bright and full of life, snapped Cove away from the dark corner. She took a breath as she coaxed her mind back into order. The gash in the ship's side gave them equally viable access to the two floors. She wanted to say they were taking the higher level—the one with wood paneling, the one without the shape she may not have even seen—but instead, she said, "We'll vote."

"Upper," Roy instantly said, to Cove's relief. "It looks more interesting. The lower one's probably storage."

"I'll second," said Hestie.

Then, from Aidan, "Yes, the higher one."

"Good." For a split second, Cove wondered if any of the votes had come because the other divers had seen the thing she had—the cold, pallid thing that had been there for a fraction of a second and was then gone again, retreating into the dark it lived in—but she didn't want to speak the question into being. They were starting on the higher floor. She was more than okay with that. And it was time to do her job. "I'll lead."

9.

Fitz stared at the opposite wall.

Harland didn't know how long the ship's stock master had been standing there, but his eyes, normally unnaturally bright, had a glaze across their surface.

The *Arcadia's* metal frame rattled as the steam-powered engines shifted her through the water. She sounded as though she ached deep in her bones. Harland couldn't blame her. Some nights as he lay awake in bed, plagued by the insomnia that had haunted him since he was a child, he listened for signs that she was finally collapsing under the unreasonable burdens they put on her.

It was a bitingly cold day, but that wasn't unexpected for the area and the time of year. Memories of ice still hung in the air. Even so, the ship's insides were cooler than Harland remembered from previous trips. They hadn't seen a day of sun since they left port. He was due to start his shift on deck and was dreading the eternal chill that surrounded them and the way it wormed through the two layers of wool gloves he wore in an effort to protect his fingers.

Harland was already on the verge of failing to report on time, but he still stopped when he saw Fitz. The older, whiskered man had been kind to him when they'd been roommates the previous year. Fitz, wiry and weathered and with a head that seemed too small for his body, even with the beard helping to fluff it out, was known to be a hard taskmaster to his underlings but unendingly kind to his friends...especially when he'd had a bit to drink.

That was Harland's first thought now: that Fitz had foregone waiting for the evening and had dipped into his rations—or, more likely, into the private store he'd brought on with his luggage— and was now showing the effects.

Except the ever-reliable stock master was never inebriated on the job. And he wasn't rosy in the face. The opposite, in fact. His skin seemed to have been drained of blood. The glazed eyes didn't blink but stared, as though possessed, at the plain paneled wall of the midship walkway.

"Fitz?" Harland, already knowing he was going to get a dressing down for missing the start of his shift, stomped his feet to get some blood moving through them.

The man's tongue darted out to taste chapped lips and wet the whiskers that were maybe a couple of days past needing cutting, but he didn't respond.

"Fitzgerald." Harland moved closer to his companion. He folded his arms across his chest, hunched against the way winter seemed to have invaded their hallway, and stared at the wall that had obsessed his friend. The view was, as far as he could tell, no different from any other on the ship. The wood paneling had chipped in some places. Scuffs and scrapes and dents marred its form.

Then Fitz moved. He tilted toward Harland, his head twisting on its stiff neck even though his eyes remained fixated. "Do you hear it?"

The man's voice had always been cracked and raspy, but Harland had never heard it sound so hollow before. His friend's eyes were glazed but not from sluggishness or alcohol, he realized. They were glazed with fear.

Harland stamped his feet again, teeth clenched against the way his scalp suddenly prickled. "I hear the way my ears are going to ring if I don't get to my shift."

"Ahh." The wiry man straightened in gradual, twitchy movements but still didn't shift his eyes. "Only me, then. I heard them from the hold. I followed them up. Lost them here though."

"Fitz, you're supposed to be on shift, aren't you?"

The stock master's job wasn't complicated. It was his duty to answer any passenger queries about their stored goods and to watch the cargo and ensure it arrived at dock fully accounted for and with no water damage. It wasn't uncommon for Fitz to wander the ship to burn time, and the officers rarely bothered him for it. Still, some irrational part of Harland wanted to send Fitz back down into the holds. He felt that, if only the stock master returned to his domain, he might reset back to the sharp, funny man Harland had befriended, instead of this terror-eyed stranger.

Otherwise, what else was there to do? They were days from shore. But Fitz remained unmoving. His eyelids seemed to be withdrawing deeper and deeper into the sockets, leaving the eyes to bulge like giant glassy marbles.

"Back to your duties," Harland said, interjecting sharp authority into the words.

It shouldn't have worked. Fitz was his superior in both age and position. But the stock master swayed, then finally turned from the wall and shambled toward the stairs.

Harland watched him until his bony shoulders disappeared from sight. He was monstrously late but still bargained for another moment before surfacing. Fitz had left him uncomfortable in a slow, creeping kind of way.

Do you hear it?

Alone in the hallway, Harland could hear the ship's aching groans as she rolled across a wave. The reverberations started in the distance, then grew closer and closer until they had washed over him and faded near the ship's stern.

Men called to each other on one of the upper floors. The furnaces had established a constant, distant rumble beneath his feet.

And then, almost inaudible beneath the other sounds, he caught it.

Tiny scratching, tapping noises.

Despite the aching cold, sweat beaded across Harland's forehead as he slowly, warily turned to face the age-cracked wall.

THE FIRST DIVE

Sean stopped in the bridge's open doorway. The stairs at his back plunged downward, leading to the lounge and dining areas, and it wasn't wise to stand on that edge with the way the ship rolled with each wave, but Sean had never felt comfortable on the bridge.

Devereaux had truly opted for the best his money could afford. Sleek dashboards looked like something from an '80s sci-fi film set. Sean had spent half his life on boats and was certain he could pilot the *Skipjack* back to shore if necessary, but he still had no idea what half the buttons and dials were for.

Two seats had been left free to the port and starboard sides, each with their own set of screens and controls, but the ship was small enough that Devereaux himself was the only one needed at the helm at any given time.

The captain's seat, where Devereaux currently resided, was plush and swiveled on the pole attaching it to the floor. The chair reclined slightly as he, wrapped in fleece blankets to ward off the chill, read a paperback novel.

"Hey." Sean took half a step forward, putting some space between himself and the treacherous stairwell.

"Oh, hello, Sean." Devereaux didn't lift his eyes from the pages, but one foot leveraged against the dashboard to rotate his chair enough so Sean didn't have to speak to his back. Devereaux was a small man, and plump, but radiated comfort in himself and his situation. His white beard covered the lower half of his face. Sean had yet to see the man wear anything other than cardigans and slacks. "Why don't you get a cup of something warm and sit with me as we wait for our intrepid explorers in relative comfort?"

Sean tried for a smile but dropped it when it didn't work. "No. I think you should call them back up."

Devereaux finally lowered his book, his pale-blue eyes squinting behind gold-framed glasses. "End the dive early, you mean? What for? Has something happened?"

The question hung between them. Sean held the small black journal at his side, index finger tapping its cover with increasing agitation. He suddenly wasn't certain that he wanted to show the writings to the older man.

Devereaux wasn't accustomed to unpleasant situations. When everything in a person's life went *right* on a consistent basis, it was hard to imagine anything turning seriously, truly *wrong*. He'd want to downplay the journal. Laugh it away or say it really wasn't a big deal, and why was Sean snooping in his crewmate's personal possessions anyway; that wasn't very nice, was it?

Sean sucked on his teeth a second, then said, "I need you to trust me on this. We should get them up."

"Aah." Devereaux placed his paperback on the console, then braced his hands on his knees as his beard puffed up in a smile. "Did the young fellow's talk of bad omens spook you? I'll admit, it gave me a quick chill as well, but I've found sailor's superstitions are usually not something to fret over."

"It's—" Sean hesitated, the finger drumming faster and faster on the black-bound journal. It would be easy to turn away, tuck the book back under Vanna's bed, and simply wait to see if the crew came back up. It was very likely that they would. He was aware that, even at this stage, he was probably overreacting. Vanna had participated in thousands of dives with no reports of misconduct.

But the words continued to play like a twisted record in the back of his head. *Watch them drown...*

"Look, just call the crew up, okay?"

Devereaux lowered his head so his eyes could watch Sean over his glasses. The scrutiny was unexpectedly intense, but Sean met it without flinching. He'd said his piece, and the silent tactic wasn't going to drag anything further out of him, no matter how long Devereaux let them hang in that uncomfortable empty space between words.

Finally, Devereaux sighed. The fingers flexed on top of his knees as he gave a small shrug. "I would, except I can't."

"What?"

"I'm supposed to have contact with the dive team. Our setup was going to allow me to listen to their chatter and send them tips as they explored the wreck. But whatever took out the cameras has also put my communications system on the blink. I'm assuming they can hear each other, or they wouldn't have gone down, but there's nothing I can do from here except wait."

Sean wasn't sure what he hated more: not being able to speak to the dive team or the realization that Devereaux may have actually been right about the solar flare. Roy would have had reason to tamper with the ROVs to steal the limelight and extend his dive time, but there was no reason for him to bother with the communications equipment.

Except...

Maybe Sean had been placing blame at the wrong feet. He'd assumed that Roy, most eager to get into the water and most eager for his footage to be used, had the only motive. But if there was any weight to what he'd read in Vanna's diary, he might have pegged the team wrong.

If Vanna planned to do something to the team during the dive, she'd want to avoid having too many cameras watching. The helmet cameras were only worth anything if they came back to the surface. The ROVs, remotely operated, would have to go though.

The same for Devereaux's communications system: the only avenue for those aboard the ship to know what was happening under the surface.

The journal could only amount to a hundred grams, if that, but it felt like an enormous weight in Sean's hand.

Devereaux still held him under that beam of scrutiny, but Sean wouldn't—couldn't—return the proffered smile.

"Sorry, my lad," Devereaux said. "They'll be up in a couple of hours. Get a cup of something. It will be nice to have company while we wait."

10.

Cove entered the *Arcadia*. Her gloved hands fixed over the ragged metal where the ship's hull had been breached and used it to help guide herself inside.

The horizontal line marking the divide between the two floors grazed her stomach. Cove inhaled to rise as she slipped inside the ship, then gave her fins the smallest push to move her clear of the opening so the others could follow.

Her headlight flashed over a room's paneled walls. It was a cabin and probably second or third class, based on its size. Two simple bunks were still in place. The wood frames were bolted to the walls, but the mattresses had come free. One lay flat on the floor, buried under the snow-like sediment. The other had come to rest halfway out of the bed, its closest side still propped up on the frame, the other side slouched against the floor. It formed a small cave underneath and Cove tried not to feel bothered that her headlight was at the wrong angle to see below.

"This is incredible." Hestie's voice alerted Cove that the

marine biologist had, surprisingly, been the first to follow. Cove languidly turned to see her companion. "Even the mattresses are still here."

"I'd be more worried if they'd wandered off," Roy said, but they all knew what Hestie was referring to. As a rule, ships were not designed to be filled with water. Most wrecks faded quickly, their contents the first to perish, either decayed or consumed by the microscopic denizens of the deep, until even the shell was eroded by time. Mattresses were not just a bonus. They were a holy grail. Even ones like these—tattered and disguised under inches of silt.

Hestie made a soft groaning sound. "These are the sheets—"

Another dark shape—Aidan—pushed through the narrow gap, and Cove moved deeper into the room to make way. The door was open. She could glimpse the hallway through it: more paneling, dark wood, with shreds of wallpaper still clinging to sections like cobwebs. She leaned through the opening and tilted her head to spill the lights in each direction. The hallway continued on for as far as her light could pierce in both directions.

She hung there for a minute, letting her flashlight fight to cut into the dark water, but the black swallowed her view within fifteen feet. She could make out the lines of the paneled walls growing fainter, then…nothing.

A gust of bubbles escaped her mask. They were using rebreathers for the specific purpose of not introducing too much oxygen and bacteria into the fragile shipwreck, but the rebreather, although filtering most of the air back into the tanks, still occasionally released some. Cove found herself disoriented by the direction the bubbles chose. Not up past the top of her head, but shooting out at an angle toward the opposite wall's upper corner.

The ship lists. It was easy to forget. Weightless in the water's embrace, and with the pale glow of surface light so completely erased, Cove had very little reference for which way was up. Her mind wanted to trust the rooms' angles and believe that the floor was down and the ceiling was up, but in reality, the *Arcadia* lay at a sixteen-degree angle. No matter how familiar the halls felt, she had to remember that everything was just slightly tilted.

"Don't touch it!" A note of panic entered Hestie's voice. Cove turned too fast and a gust of sediment washed up in front of her. She grit her teeth, silently cursing herself for disturbing the delicate material, until she realized it hadn't entirely been her fault. Through the smoky haze, she could make out Aidan swimming backward. He'd tried to get a closer look at the blankets, but in doing so disturbed the inches of featherlight sediment that had gathered across the material.

"I'm sorry, I'm sorry!" His voice was impossibly tight. "I wasn't thinking. I'm sorry—"

"We're okay." Cove was gifted with a smooth voice. No matter what intensity of emotion she experienced, she had the ability to always sound calm. It didn't fail her then either; those two simple words silenced both Aidan's frantic apologies and Hestie's too-quick breath. "It's not too thick. Vanna, do you still have the dive line?"

"Yes."

Cove couldn't see the woman through the haze, but the comms system made her sound incredibly close, and the coolness in that single word sent a strange lurch through her stomach. "Okay, Vanna, move up front with me. The dive line will be coming inside the ship with us, so worst-case scenario, we can use it to make our way back out as well. In the meantime, let's get out of this room. Move carefully. We don't want to drag up any more of this stuff than we need to."

As she finished speaking, she heard Roy mumble, almost as though he thought he could whisper to Aidan through the comms, "Stay calm, man."

Cove moved gently as she pulled herself into the hallway. Silt-outs were a diver's nightmare. Even the lightest kind impeded vision. When they became thick enough, a diver was as good as blind.

She tried to imagine herself swimming through the *Arcadia's* maze of hallways when she couldn't see more than an inch ahead of her mask. Her outstretched arms would disappear into the hazy, sandy, gray blur that flooded the world like static. Blinded that badly, even just this short distance into the ship, would she be able to find her way out again?

It was a key reason for why dive lines were so vital. The silt was extraordinarily fine and would hang in the water indefinitely. A bad silt-out could take days to settle. The limited air in Cove's tanks meant she had, at most, an hour to find her way out. Even with zero visibility, she could use the dive line instead of her eyes, running one gloved hand along the cord as it brought her back into the outside world.

Cove stopped in the hallway, watching the haze spread through the cabin and spill from the open doorway. She couldn't see the opposite wall, but she could make out two of the closest figures as they hung, suspended, waiting.

Vanna emerged through the fog, the dive line unspooling from her belt as she joined Cove in the hall. Cove sent her a smile, though she knew it would be unreadable in the low light.

"Follow us through," she said. "Move carefully. Let's keep most of it contained in that room, yeah?"

Faint noises of assent reached her as, one by one, the remaining three divers carefully floated through the narrow doorway.

Each body brought a wash of the dust with them, but no currents flowed inside the ship, and the sediment barely spread.

It wasn't as though the deeper parts of the ship hadn't been corrupted by the sediment though. Over years, dust and debris had filtered down from the gulf's surface and gradually flowed into the ship, coating the floor and clinging to the fixtures.

This was definitely the third-class level, Cove decided. The hall was narrow enough that she couldn't spread her arms as she swam. The wallpaper, once covering the walls with intricate red and gold overlays, had lost most of its color. Now, submerged, most of the glue had given way and the paper hung in tatters. It twisted and danced with every small eddy and gave the illusion that the hallway was alive with writhing life-forms.

Cove led her team right, toward where the halls became swallowed by the endless dark. They passed many other doors, most to the right, facing the ship's external side. Those would be more cabins. Some doors hung open still, and Cove paused to send her light and camera's view into each space.

Most were replicas of the room they'd entered through. The sediment was less all-consuming but instead looked like a pale coat of dust across the surfaces. It collected in the corners where the ship listed, giving the impression of an off-color snowbank.

Many of the porthole windows were still intact, but Cove found two that had been broken by water pressure as the ship sank. One still had part of a pane, leaving an age-dulled sliver of glass.

"Kind of weird."

Cove's world had been reduced to the sounds of breathing for so long that Roy's voice came as a shock. Cove glanced over her shoulder. Hestie's slim form hung suspended immediately behind her, and beyond, she could barely make out Roy's broad shoulders. "How do you mean?"

"So many of the doors are open. Which would make sense if the *Arcadia* hit something in the middle of the night and the crew had to rush out of bed to reach their lifeboats, except none of these rooms have any, like, suitcases or anything."

He was right. She'd seen mattresses and old, discolored sheets, but no personal possessions.

"They weren't sleeping here," Cove realized. "The *Arcadia* was less than half-full when it set sail. No passengers were assigned to this hall."

"Yeah. And ships liked to keep stuff locked up when it wasn't in use. So why are all the doors open?"

The question hung in silence for a second. Ahead of Cove, Vanna had halted her progress and turned to look back at them. Her face was invisible behind the head-mounted light. The safety line floated from her belt, a white cord that ran along the left-hand side of the group, vanishing into the dark behind Roy.

Hestie disturbed the silence. "It could be the water pressure as the ship sank. These doors were getting old even before the ship went down; their latches could have given out."

"Could have," Roy conceded. "But I still think it's weird."

Cove didn't want her opinion captured in the audio, but she had to agree. Hestie's theory was a good one, depending on how quickly the ship sank. But she couldn't shake the idea of the *Arcadia*'s crew racing through the lower decks and throwing open doors as they...searched for something? Or tried to hide from something?

She pulled her thoughts back before they could travel too far. The darkness and claustrophobia were making her too tense and too quick to imagine monsters on her periphery.

They'd traveled at least forty feet into the ship. Mentally, Cove knew that wasn't much. But realistically, in the cramped hallway and surrounded by heavy water that wanted to smother their lights and turn the very air they breathed toxic, it seemed an insurmountable distance.

The *Arcadia* had two main hallways running the ship's length like dual spines, with rooms and smokestack channels filling the space between them. Crosswise passages would connect the two main paths at regular intervals, and usually contained stairs to get to higher and lower floors as well.

While the doors to their right were mostly open, the doors to their left were still closed. Cove brought herself to a halt beside one of them. The dull metal handle was barely visible against the wood. "Hold up a second, Vanna. I want to see what's inside."

She reached for the handle. Hestie's voice sounded like it was being whispered directly into her ear. "Careful. The water salinity is low, but it might still be rusted closed."

The handle ground as she tried to turn it, then wanted to seize up. Cove put the tip of her tongue between her teeth. They needed to be careful of the ship's remains; the ocean floor was doing its fair share of damage, but they didn't want to inflict much extra on top.

But she wanted to *know*. The interior doors were spaced less frequently than those leading to the cabins. They could be simple storage or passageways to staff-only areas or anything, but the closed door felt almost more ominous than the open ones.

Cove gave a hard wrench to the door, trying to knock the jam free. She had to kick her feet to counterbalance and immediately regretted it as flecks of silt rose from the floor. There was less to disturb than there had been in the entry room, but in an environment this tenuous, any amount of silt was a problem.

The latch scraped and opened though. Cove pushed the door inward. The hinges didn't want to respond, but she wasn't about to be beaten and pushed harder. Even through the full mask, she could hear the groan of swollen wood scraping its frame as it moved.

Immediately ahead was a square window. Something large and dark was suspended just beyond. It was shaped like a human, its long body seemingly hung in the water, facing her.

Cove's light hit the glass at just the wrong angle to obscure its face, but she had the impression of something flat and blank and emotionless. No eyes. No mouth.

It's an illusion. Something shaped vaguely like a human but not.

The thing's hands moved, reaching toward her, and Cove's body turned to ice.

"What is it?" Roy had closed the distance behind her and strained to see around her as she blocked the doorway. "What's in there?"

"A mirror." Cove closed her eyes for a second, her heart pounding out of control, even as she laughed. "I'll be damned, but I spooked myself with a mirror."

The window wasn't actually a window but the frame of a rectangular mirror hung above a sink. She'd seen her own blank, helmeted face, and her own hands sweeping in slow arcs to keep her stable. For a brief second, she really had thought she'd come in contact with something horrendously inhuman living inside the sunken ship, and her pulse was pumping like she'd just run a marathon. *That* wasn't going to be great for her oxygen situation. She took a long, slow breath as she tried to coax her heart back to a steady beat.

Her light flashed across tiles and porcelain. They'd found a bathroom. Many tiles were cracked or had even come out of the wall wholesale, and the grouting was crumbling. The destruction was so bad that not all of it could be attributed to the sinking either. Someone must have damaged the room before the *Arcadia* went down.

Cove tried to ignore the way her dark, shadowed reflection mirrored every movement as she leaned farther into the room to ensure the camera caught as much as possible.

There was no sign of habitation in that room. A scrap of foil floated near her feet—probably a wrapper that had become stuck behind the toilet or under the sink and come free—but there were no towels or soap containers, confirming her suspicion that this level had been left empty.

"Try the taps, there might still be water," Roy suggested, then laughed at his own joke.

"I wouldn't want to make the sink overflow." Cove used the doorframe to gently push back into the hallway. It was easy to keep her grin in place, not so easy to slow her heart rate or reduce the sweat seeping into her wool layers. "Lead us on, Vanna."

Their formation resumed. They passed more doorways: cabins to their right, closed doors to their left. Cove knew she could spend a week just exploring that one slice of the ship, but if they could reach one of the inhabited areas, the payoff would be so much greater.

Cove glanced over her shoulder again. She could see Hestie and make out just the edges of Roy. She knew Aidan had to be following, but the beams of light—one facing ahead, one to the rear, to keep things visible for the dual cameras—overlapped and made counting the sources of light difficult. She couldn't see Aidan. And she realized, she hadn't heard from him for a while either.

"Aidan, you still with us?"

"Yeah." His voice sounded distant. That shouldn't happen with the comms units. He was speaking quietly, almost as though there was something nearby he didn't want hearing. As though he was trying to creep past a monster.

The thought, created by the paranoia of three hundred feet of water pressing on them, unnerved her. But as always, her voice remained calm. "Oxygen check. I'm at 81 percent."

"Seventy-nine." That was Roy.

"Eighty." Hestie.

Then Vanna: "Eighty-four."

Silence hung for another beat before Aidan's voice returned, even fainter than before. "Seventy...seventy-eight."

"Okay. We're good for a bit more." Cove couldn't see much ahead except for the canisters attached to Vanna's back. They flashed in her circle of light, shining unnaturally in this world of dullness and cloudy water and tattered, grasping fingers of paper. "If we keep straight, we'll be surrounded by more cabins. But we could try to find the stairs to reach one of the higher floors and explore the living areas—or move downward, to the cargo hold. Knowing whether the crew jettisoned any of their supplies might give us some clues as to what happened."

Then Vanna spoke, her voice utterly devoid of inflection. "There's writing on the wall."

11.

"Writing?" Cove kept the sweep of her fins slow to avoid disturbing the water more than necessary as she caught up to Vanna. The woman had come to a halt near an intersection. The main hallway continued forward, likely leading to more rooms. The branch to their left was wider though. That meant it had to connect with the stairs, though the visibility was too poor to see them from that distance.

Vanna faced the patch of hallway right before the corner. Like the rest of that level, it had paneling on its lower half—the wood swollen and dulled by the sediment, like everything else—and the awful patchy wallpaper on the upper half. Shreds of the paper had come free, but what remained bore some kind of dark paint.

The hallways were narrow, and their head-mounted lights had tight beams. At close quarters, the illuminated circles were uncomfortably small. Cove put her back against the opposite wall to widen the light as much as she could. She knew it wasn't possible to sense the undulating shreds of paper through her dry suit and air canisters, but she swore she could feel them running across her back regardless.

Her light slid across the wall, trying to pick out the lines of paint between the broken surface. There wasn't enough light. She felt in her belt, where she always stored a backup light in case the main one failed, and flicked it on. The second beam helped a little but not enough.

"I can make out a *here*," Roy said. He'd come up to Cove's side, his shoulder bumping hers. One hand swept in a motion to trace what appeared to be the final word. It had been drawn half over the wallpaper and half over the paneling, making it the best preserved. Cove squinted, nodding slowly. The *h* was fairly clear. After it came something like an *e*, then an *r*, and the beginning of several straight strokes that had to be another *e*.

There were at least two words preceding it though, and possibly a third.

"I can try lifting the paper back into place," Hestie said. "I don't want to tear it, but…"

"Yes, try that." Cove's back bumped against the wall. She, Vanna, Roy, and Aidan were now lined up, all of them bringing both their headlights and secondary lights onto the message. The beams fought for dominance, passing over each other like searchlights, often leaving blocks of darkness between them as they struggled to cover all of the painted section.

Hestie gingerly slid her glove underneath a strip of paper that had come almost entirely free. She lifted it slowly, and as it slid into place, part of the first word reappeared.

The letters were painted in large strokes. The lines were ragged, as though made with a thick-bristled brush, and they became streaky at their ends as the drawing implement was abruptly pulled away from the wall. They had a manic kind of energy to them. As best as she could tell, the words covered a length of wall wider than Cove could reach with both arms outstretched.

"*The*," Roy read. "*The* what? Try the next bit, Hestie."

She gently lowered the paper back into its original position, then moved forward, alternating her attention between the wall and the watching audience. Cove was struck by how much her movements were like the hostess on an old episode of *Wheel of Fortune*: pick a letter, and if it's on the board, Hestie will turn it over. Even her motions were graceful and gentle. Only instead of letters lighting up, they were trying to read wild scribbles, and instead of a luxury gown, Hestie's form was distorted by her dive gear and her face was only partially visible behind the mask.

"That's a *y*," Cove said. "And...an *o*?"

"*You*?" Roy suggested.

"I can't see the *u* though. The next letter looks more like an *a*." Cove blinked furiously. The lights were playing tricks on her eyes, catching on every flake of grime their disturbance sent up, making the message harder to read than it already was. "No, wait. It's not an *o*; it's a *c*. And it's the beginning of the next word. The first word isn't *the*, it's *they*."

"Keep going," Aidan urged.

Hestie's rebreather let out a gush of bubbles as she slid along the wall. The next scrap of paper was gone entirely, but she lifted the one after that. It bore an unmistakable *e*.

Cove let her lips twitch, spelling out words, her eyes darting back down to the second set of letters beneath. Then she drew a sharp breath. "*They came through here.* That's what it says."

The others were silent for a moment as they traced the words themselves, then Aidan said, "Yeah, I see it."

Hestie released the paper she was holding up and leaned away from the message as though she no longer felt safe that close to it. She moved to her companions, placing herself between Cove and Vanna, and in the glancing light, Cove saw the whites of her eyes.

"What's that supposed to mean though?" Roy's voice had lost some of its joviality. Out of nowhere, he sounded irritable.

"There's another line," Aidan said. He cleared his throat. "There. Going around the corner."

Cove saw it too: a horizontal line marred the lower paneling. At first glance it looked like an underscore, except it continued past where the words ended, to the edge of that wall.

She swam forward, taking the corner, and saw it kept going. It ran on for another five feet before tilting downward and stopping near the floor. At its tip was a wedge. It wasn't an underscore; it was an arrow. A path to trace.

"*They came through here,*" Roy repeated. "And...went into the floor?"

The arrow's tip did seem to indicate toward the lower level. Whether the unknown *they* had taken the still-unseen stairs or whether the line-drawer had made a mistake, Cove couldn't guess.

A deep, sonorous groan passed through the ship. Cove jerked back, her tanks hitting the wall, her heart in her throat. The sound moved around them, running through the floors above and below, as the massive metal structure flexed. Spots of paint dropped free from the ceiling, spiraling past them like snow and further dampening visibility.

All of them held their breaths. The *Arcadia* shouldn't be making sounds like that. It had been stationary, wedged between two rocks, for the last ninety years. Their intrusion had been delicate. The presence of five divers couldn't have caused it to shift after all this time, surely.

The reverberations died out slowly, their final echoes lingering in the water long after the metal had fallen still. The dust, shifted from the walls, hung like fog in the water, small tendrils of it spiraling lazily.

"Cove," Vanna said. "End the dive? Your call."

She licked her lips. "Our air's still above the threshold. We can go a bit farther."

The dark helmet turned toward her, and Cove could imagine Vanna's frown, the black eyebrows pushing deep creases between them. "We need to allow enough time to exit the ship."

Cove closed her eyes. One of the rules of diving was that if a party tapped out, the rest had to surface with them. She couldn't refuse Vanna's right to call an end to the exploration. Vanna hadn't explicitly asked for it yet, but the implication hung in the air: she wanted to go.

Then Roy said, "Come on. My air's still more than 70 percent. That's plenty. At least let us find the stairs."

The dark helmet turned away, a voiceless sign that Vanna wouldn't argue.

The decision to continue the dive was borderline at best. They'd only have a few more minutes left inside the ship, one way or another, and the writing and the sounds of shifting had put them on edge. Cove knew that she should call them out. But... those few extra minutes of footage would be valuable. Their sponsor had demanded a quota inside the ship, and failing to meet that would put the contract into contention. A few minutes extra wasn't much, but with their schedule as tight as it was, it might make all the difference.

"Aidan, Hestie, are you both okay to continue?" Cove asked.

They were both silent for a second, long enough for Cove to read reluctance into it, and she was on the verge of calling the end herself when Hestie said, "Yes."

Following after her was Aidan's voice, softer, almost whistling. "Sure."

"Okay." Cove nodded, breathing slowly, trying to ignore the itching uncertainty creeping over her skin like insects. "Let's find those stairs."

12.

Harland could still taste the mist on his tongue.

It was a bad mist. Stinking, full of rotting sea life. So thick that it seemed to drip into his lungs with every breath. So dense that the watch was as good as useless. Still, he was sent onto deck for hours at a time, hunched and squinting into the bleak, endless white as the unnaturally dense fog choked him. It beaded on his face and on his clothes. It found every crevice it could to squirm up sleeves and down collars and wet his skin.

Now, even after changing clothes and hurriedly washing himself with a cloth and water that was as cold as the Arctic itself, the smell refused to leave. He sat in the mess hall, nursing a bowl of dubious-looking slop that had been labeled breakfast. And he could still smell the fog.

If anything, it had grown stronger in the lower levels of the ship, as though it had absorbed into the wood walls and tacky runners and had become a part of the vessel herself.

He'd smelled far worse things in his short career on the ocean. Things that made him retch or turned him off food for the remainder of the day or left him dizzy. The fog did none of that, but somehow, it was even more unbearable. Because there was no escape. Nowhere inside the ship or on deck could he get a single mouthful of fresh air. And he wasn't adjusting. This heavy, wet odor seemed to grow stronger hour by hour with so sign of reprieve.

A pewter mug tapped down, then a body slid into a seat on the table's opposite side. Fitz leaned over the wood, bony hands laced as he bent forward, resting his upper body's weight on his elbows.

Harland tried not to let his discomfort appear on his face. His shift meant he had a late breakfast and the mess hall was near empty. Four of the passengers clustered around a table in the back corner, speaking in quiet voices as they nursed drinks, and an odd assortment of off-shift hands scattered themselves around different tables, all of them seeming to prefer solitude.

There were enough empty seats that Harland knew his friend had sought him out in particular. He'd normally welcome the company, but the previous day's encounter had left him sour, and the fog's smell was winding his nerves painfully tight.

"Bad weather," Fitz said, as though this were any other morning. As though the situation were so mundane that they needed to resort to small talk.

Both men knew better. Harland couldn't bring himself to touch the supposed food, even though he knew he should be hungry. And Fitz looked as though he hadn't slept the previous night. His whiskers needed cutting. They were starting to creep down over his upper lip.

More than that, his face looked hollowed out. As though the

hours of wakefulness had been spent fixated on something deeply consuming and deeply harrowing.

Harland put his head down. He didn't want to endure the sick air any longer. He didn't want to listen to the scrape of spoons coming from nearby tables or the whispered voices of the passengers. Or to Fitz's slow, gasping breathing, slightly too wet, slightly too raspy. He sounded like he needed a doctor. Knowing Fitz, he would simply pour himself harder into his work until the labor killed him.

Fitz swallowed phlegm, then asked, breathless, "How'd you sleep?"

More small talk. Except, it wasn't. Harland met Fitz's gaze for the first time. His eyes were bloodshot and shining. Thinning eyelashes and withdrawn lids left them looking pale and strangely desperate. Harland couldn't look away. "Not so good, I suppose."

"No." Fitz crept a fraction closer, and suddenly his breath was mixing with the stinking air and Harland's stomach turned. "Look about. No one did."

The mess hall was quiet. That wasn't too unusual. But Fitz was right. None of the bodies there were moving quite right. Or *looking* quite right.

The passengers in the corner were huddled close together, not wanting their conversations overheard. They weren't supposed to be in that mess hall. They had their own, closer to the ship's bow, one with nicer amenities and better food. But for whatever reason, they hadn't wanted to be there, and no one had tried to stop them from sitting in the crew's space.

"They hear it. They're just too scared to say so." Fitz's pupils shimmered in the dim lights. "Are you?"

He wanted to say, *Hear what?* The words made it as far as his tongue before he closed his teeth on them. The words were tempting because they would let him stay coiled in the safety of ignorance.

But he wasn't ignorant. Not any longer. Not after lying awake the previous night, staring blindly at the bunk above while distant sounds teased at the edges of his hearing.

"The tapping," he said, and the fog tasted like sickness on his tongue. "I hear it."

"Yes. *Yes.*" Fitz nodded, his shimmering eyes too large for his head, his sweaty face painted in the off-yellow glow of their lights. "The tapping. Yes."

His admission didn't bring the relief Harland had hoped for. If anything, it made the weight heavier. "What's causing it?"

"I don't know, lad. Spent last night trying to find out." Fitz kept his voice to a rough whisper. "But I can tell you this: the captain knows something is wrong."

"What makes you say that?"

"I've been watching the bridge. The captain stays in there and paces all night. Officers go in. Officers go out. More than should during that hour. Lots of anxious voices. Can't make out what they're saying, but something's got them rattled."

Harland closed his eyes. Even then, even in the mess hall and surrounded by other people, he thought he could hear a distant scratching sound. Just faint enough that he couldn't be sure whether he truly was hearing it or whether the rhythm had infected his brain during the night and he now carried it inside like some parasitic presence.

"The engines," he said abruptly. "If the sound's coming from—"

"But it's not." Harland jabbed his fingertip into the table. The nail was slightly too long. It bent the finger back at the first knuckle when he pressed hard enough. "I've been checking in on the leading stoker down in the boiler room. He knows something's wrong too. Not sleeping much. Watching the furnaces like a demon. But it's not coming from them. I heard it yesterday. Coming from one of the hallways. I followed it. Couldn't catch up to it though. Every time I thought I got close, it was off again."

Harland didn't know how to reply. He should have been grateful it wasn't the engines. If something went wrong enough with the massive boilers, the whole crew and every passenger could be dead before they had time to say a final prayer.

But at least a fault with the engines would *make sense*. It would give them something to watch, something to fix.

"This ship's cursed," Fitz said at last. He raised his mug, examined the contents, then returned it to the table. "I've known it since the very first time I boarded her. There's something not right with the *Arcadia*."

The officers and captains tried to dissuade rumors of cursed ships among the crew, but they could rarely ever succeed in the face of so much evidence. Ships would run aground, would lose power inexplicably, would collide in clear weather—as though possessed with a need to disappear beneath the foaming waves.

"People died building her," Fitz continued.

"Not unheard of," Harland muttered. Ship construction was a dangerous sport. A liner that hadn't tasted blood of some kind was a rarity.

Fitz looked at his drink for a second time and then, for the second time, put it aside. "Maybe not. But this beast chewed through them like they were candy. And I think that's got to do something to a ship, yeah? It's got to leave a mark of some kind."

"What are you saying?"

"I'm saying maybe those lost souls are wanting retribution."

Fitz rose, jaw working as he shambled toward the exit. He had to raise his voice for his final words to reach Harland, and every other head in the room turned in response. "I'm saying maybe the ship isn't done eating."

Then Fitz was gone—perhaps down to the hold, perhaps to watch the bridge some more, perhaps to rove the hallways like a man who had lost his mind—and Harland was left alone with an untouched bowl of slop and the memory of the stinking fog plastered on his tongue.

13.

THE FIRST DIVE

The lights darted across the narrow hallway, revealing snippets in brief flickers but never enough to make Hestie feel like she knew what her surroundings truly looked like.

An impulse had risen inside of her: reach out and turn the light on. She knew that wasn't rational. There *were* no lights beyond what they carried on their heads. But she felt, if she could just see the space in its entirety, the disorientation would fade.

Beneath that was another darker fear. That maybe she *didn't* want to see clearly. That maybe there was something about the hallway that was hiding just outside of their lights, and she was better off not knowing it was there.

Cove's voice broke through her thoughts so suddenly that she twitched. "Ahead and to the right."

Hestie turned her light where directed. When they'd entered the ship, they'd followed one of the two long passages that ran the length of the vessel. The turn had carried them into one of the paths cutting across the ship's width. The hallway was slightly wider than the first one they'd traveled down but still only allowed them to move two abreast. She was near the back of the cluster, behind Cove, Vanna, and Roy, and inhaled deeply to raise herself enough to see over their backs.

The edge of a wide stairwell flickered into view. The lowest steps were curved outward—scallop shaped—and they narrowed as they disappeared inside the walls, leading upward.

Hestie's head pounded in a way that made her feel almost delirious. It wasn't from the air; the blend in her tanks ensured that she would be...well, not safe—a person could never truly be safe when diving, even at shallow levels, and their current depth was closer to protracted suicide than swimming. But it at least made life *viable* at this level, even if that was only for short lengths. And it wasn't causing the throbs through her brain or the shivers in her limbs, she was fairly certain.

Those could be attributed to the ship. Or at least, what the ship represented—the adrenaline of discovery. The all-encompassing threat of death that loomed over them and gradually worsened with every moment they spent underwater. The subtle nagging at the back of her head that this very moment was possibly the most significant one of her life and she couldn't do much except grin maniacally behind her mask and wish it were over already.

It wasn't that she didn't want to be there. She did—and very much so. But she wasn't great at moments of pressure.

She could get through them, just like she'd gotten through her thesis defense—and then promptly staggered outside and vomited in the bushes. But she didn't *thrive* in moments of tension, not like other people did. Not like Cove, classy and bright and always knowing the best thing to say. And not like Roy, who was never short of a one-liner. Even Vanna, resolutely quiet, seemed utterly at peace in this underwater maze. But the pressure was slowly unraveling Hestie. She was pretty sure she could keep her lunch from plastering itself across the full-face mask, but she also knew she wouldn't truly feel in control of herself until they surfaced again.

And the water…

Hestie wasn't convinced she was the kind of expert who could contribute to this dive in a significant way. She was a marine biologist. The word biology was literally in her title. She studied life. Specifically, *ocean* life.

There was none of that here. The water was as close to dead as it was possible to get.

That was a blessing; the ship was incredibly well preserved. The water was too cold for shipworms to devour the organic elements. No coral to crust over and aid the decay. No microorganisms even.

An absolute perfect environment for the ship. Literally useless for Hestie. The best she had was a crusting of long-dead barnacles from before the ship had sunk, and while she had nothing personal against barnacles, they weren't exactly riveting material.

When she'd heard the dive's location, Hestie had done some gentle probing around that very issue: *You know the water is pretty close to sterile there, right? I'm not an expert on ships. My experience is mostly around tropical locations…*

If she'd been a little less anxious and a little more ruthless, she never would have asked those questions. She would have kept her mouth shut and put on a good show and picked up her paycheck. That was the smart thing to do.

But Hestie had never been capable of that, even when she was picking up shifts in a call center to afford rent. Lots of people wanted to work in marine biology. Not so many people wanted to pay them for it. The job market could be described as ruthless on a good day.

It had been a terrible choice financially to question whether they actually wanted or *needed* a marine biologist to go to a location with no marine biology. But Hestie had book smarts, not street smarts, so she'd asked anyway.

That hadn't deterred them.

It had taken Hestie a few minutes of talking in circles to understand: she wasn't being hired because they needed her insight for the expedition's success. She was being hired because it would look good for the viewers at home to have an expert on the team.

She'd almost laughed. Nine years of studying and thesis writing and she *still* couldn't get a job that used her skills. Even this offer was hiring her more as an actress than as a biologist.

But she'd taken it, and she'd taken it gratefully. If they wanted her to sling around science-y words to give the documentary some extra authority, she'd give them as much as they wanted.

And who knew? Maybe this documentary would be something truly exceptional. Jobs had been gained through notoriety before. She might even have a chance at one of the coveted education positions in her city's marine institution.

She just needed to hold herself together for the next three days.

Cove led the group, turning lightly at the stairs and rising along them. It was a strangely unnerving sight: the steps were right there, such a familiar shape, something they all used on a daily basis, and yet she floated over them. One light kick from her fins lifted her up and into the darkness of the higher floor.

The next body up was Vanna's, white dive line trailing behind. Roy hung back, pressing against the opposite wall, head tilted in a strange way. It took Hestie a second to understand what he was doing. Even though he had exactly the same equipment as the rest of the team, he was still thinking from the perspective of a cameraman. Watching the sleek bodies rise along the stairs would be captivating, so he was framing the shot the best he could in their narrow environment.

That put Hestie next. She wasn't sure if Roy's camera could see through her face mask, but she tried to return her features to a more neutral state just in case. It wouldn't be a good look for the documentary if their marine biologist was constantly gawking or, worse, terrified.

She was at the steps. Wooden railing curved outward at the entrance. Sediment had fallen in through the upper level, which meant there was likely another opening to the ocean close by.

In that moment, Hestie felt transported to another world. The stairs belonged in some long-forgotten mansion. The sediment was like dust, accumulated over a hundred years. And she floated over the carpet runner nailed into the steps, her hands held toward the railings but not touching. She was disembodied, drifting through the ceiling and into another realm.

The barrier between levels passed around her as she surfaced into the upper floor. She breathed deeply to rise, then adjusted her buoyancy compensator to keep her at that new depth. Vanna and Cove were to her left, their headlights competing to light the dim hall. Hestie drifted right, clearing the landing for Aidan.

Different wall decorations had been used on this floor. It was hard to be certain at their current abysmal visibility, but Hestie believed they might have found one of the first-class quarters. There was less wallpaper, and the paneling was more intricate. Lamps were fastened into the walls at regular intervals. They were in one of the crosswise passages, and Hestie moved to its end to look down one of the halls that ran along the ship's length.

Her headlight struggled to get through the dense water, but

she could imagine it with the lamps lit. An endless passageway, just barely wide enough for two passengers to slip around each other as they passed. Pools of artificial yellow light competing with the endless dimness of this windowless world. Dark red wood, carved to remind the viewer of twisting leaves and berries, a haven for dust even during life.

And farther down the hall, something interrupted the dark, scuffed wood.

Hestie glanced behind her. Aidan had exited the stairwell, and Roy's light filled the dark tunnel as he followed. Vanna and Cove were approaching the hallway on the ship's opposite side.

They were still close. And she couldn't lose them as long as the audio communication stayed up. She turned down the hallway.

One of the berth doors was open. Hestie slowed as she neared it. The room had absolutely been first class, she realized. The floor was fully carpeted. A double bed was pressed to the closest wall, its canopy curtains pulled back to reveal the blankets still folded down after all this time. It had once also had goose feather pillows, but they had been disturbed in the sinking, and now existed as confused, lumpy shapes on the floor.

A shock traveled through Hestie. This room had been occupied. The rooms on the lower floor—the third-class bunks—had been left in a state waiting passengers: beds stripped, pillows missing. This room had been in use. Someone had turned these blankets back just hours before they died.

The porthole window had broken and allowed sediment to cover every surface generously. But as she moved farther into the room, she began identifying shapes. A chair, overturned. There was the sink attached to the wall, a collapsible writing desk built in beside it.

The passengers' luggage lay open. Three dark cases in total, left discarded on the floor. Their contents had been rummaged through. They looked nearly empty.

This happened in a rush and on the day of the sinking. Maybe they were trying to get warm clothes. Maybe they were trying to salvage possessions before running for the lifeboats. But if they were that short of time, why not just bring the cases with them?

Hestie swam as close as she dared. She held her breath as the light rippled over the crumpled, coated fabrics left behind. One small, rectangular shape appeared on top of the others, the size of a finger.

Lipstick.

The sheer everyday banality of that stung. This must have been the lady's favorite shade. She'd kept it close to wear through the voyage and so she could look good when they docked. And while digging through the luggage on her last day on earth, she'd picked it up and then discarded it again. The cap was off. Maybe even in the stress and helplessness of those last hours, she'd applied a final coat, clinging to the routines that felt familiar enough to be safe.

Hestie let herself drift back from the luggage. She was starting to feel rising nerves from being separated from the team. Technically she was only a hallway away, but they weren't supposed to drift out of sight during this dive.

It felt as though it would be disrespectful to call the others into this room. This was a sanctuary. She could capture it on the camera to show them back on the ship, but now wasn't the time to be bringing more bodies through.

As she made to move back to the door, her light glanced across the external wall bearing the broken porthole.

A dark, twisted shape floated beside it.

Hestie fell still, her lip burning from where she'd bitten it too hard. Her pulse thumped hard enough to hurt. She held still for a breath, then moving cautiously, she swam toward the shape.

At a glance and filtered by the water, the figure had looked as real as any human. But it was only a drawing. Not even a drawing but an outline, like some chalk victim in a crime movie. Thin, scratchy lines had been used to represent a body partway up the wall. Its arms were folded around its chest, its head thrown to one side. The feet were off the ground, giving the impression that it floated.

Hestie squinted as her headlight oversaturated the woodwork when she got too close. The image had been drawn with a different material than the cryptic words in the lower hall. Those had been painted on with a brush. These marks were thinner and midtone gray. As Hestie leaned even closer, she thought she saw some texture to the material. She reached out one gloved hand and drew her index finger across a line. Even after all that time, it smeared. She had no doubt that it would feel waxy on her skin.

Lipstick.

She glanced back to the open suitcases on the floor.

Maybe the lady wasn't trying to hold on to familiar routines in her last few minutes. Maybe she was trying to leave a message.

A message...saying what?

"Here's another one."

Hestie flinched. The voice seemed to come from just behind her ear. She turned, fins kicking, but the room was as empty as it had been when she entered.

It took a second to recognize the voice: Cove's. The dive leader had to be on the other side of the ship, but she'd sounded like she was right behind Hestie.

Her pulse was still too fast, beating a frantic rhythm in her throat. She'd already been separated from the other divers for too long.

14.

Hestie left the room and its crude facsimile quickly. It was a short trip to the hallway intersection. The water seemed to be growing denser from their movements disturbing the sediment, and her headlight became less and less effective every minute. She forced herself to keep her movements slow and smooth to avoid creating currents as she passed the stairwell and turned the corner into the opposite hallway.

Sharp wedges of light marked her companions' positions. They were all facing the left-hand wall at a clear patch of paneling between doors. The largest form—Roy—had his hand on the smallest's shoulder. That would be Aidan. Hestie couldn't tell whether Roy was doing it to keep his friend calm or to keep himself steady.

"At least it's legible this time," Cove said. Her voice was still upbeat, but Hestie thought she could hear traces of the stress that she herself was trying so hard to hide.

Hestie stopped at Vanna's shoulder and tilted to see the wall.

The letters were smaller and tighter than the message on the lower hall, but it seemed to have been painted with a similar brush.

"Someone must have run through the halls and written weird messages while the rest of the crew were distracted or asleep," Roy said.

"I think this one might be by a different writer," Hestie managed. "It's a lot narrower—"

Roy made a faint snorting noise. "The other one was written in a panic. That'll change a person's style a fair bit."

Aidan tilted his head toward his friend. "The, uh, the Ts are different, I think?"

"We'll compare the footage back on the ship." Cove's voice was like a balm on the rising tension. "We might even be able to call in a handwriting expert if it's in doubt. One artist or two is a question that could hold some significant insight into the ship's fate."

For a beat, they were all silent, hanging in a clump as they faced the tight, rigid words.

DO NOT LET HIM OUT

Roy had turned to stare farther down the hallway. The hallway should have continued on beyond the limits of their vision, but his headlight teased the edges of an indistinguishable shape.

Hestie suddenly found it hard to breathe. She fumbled for her dive watch. Oxygen: 71 percent. The pressure was still acceptable too. The tightness was coming entirely from her own chest.

Struggling to breathe was frightening enough on land. Submerged, it was like a living nightmare. She closed her eyes. The knowledge that water enveloped every inch of her, that the only way she could get oxygen was through a narrow tube and a small metal container strapped to her back made her abruptly nauseated.

Just breathe. You have air. A small amount. A finite amount. But you have it.

She loved the ocean. It was her passion, her calling, her life's purpose. But sometimes she found it easier to love the ocean when she was sitting at her desk.

Something touched her forearm. Hestie's eyes shot open. A dark form floated ahead of her. Its headlight hit her eyes, blinding her, before the head tilted up slightly to give her relief. She recognized the face underneath: Aidan. His wide eyes searched hers, questioning. He was trying to check on her.

She couldn't breathe well enough to speak, but she could manage a smile and to lift a hand in the okay symbol.

He hesitantly gave an okay in return but still didn't leave her side. She didn't want to think he could guess how stressed she was. She was nearly twice his age; she was supposed to be the one leading *him*. So Hestie gave his forearm a firm press in return, then began swimming after the other divers. They were moving closer to the dark shape blocking the hallway. It was only after Aidan had fallen in line behind her that the idea occurred to Hestie that maybe he hadn't *wanted* an okay, that maybe he was hoping she'd stop the dive.

She looked over her shoulder. Aidan leaned forward, using his arms to propel himself without creating too many currents. He didn't look up.

The other three divers had come to a halt. Their bodies blocked the hall almost completely. Hestie rose until her head came close to bumping the ceiling to see past them.

"I guess this is where we're not supposed to let 'him' out from," Roy said. His tone suggested he was trying to make a joke, but there was no laughter in his voice.

The hallway ahead of them had been entirely blocked with

furniture. A bed had been unbolted from the walls and forced in at an angle. Multiple chairs, just like the one Hestie had seen in the first-class room, were jammed together, their legs tangling. Rope and cables had been used to lash them all together. Their loose ends drifted limply in the water.

The blockade was so tight that Hestie couldn't see through it...or over its top. It filled the hallway so completely that she suspected it would take half a day to clear it.

They were trying to keep something—or someone—contained.

The idea was like a punch to her stomach. She let a slow, measured breath out as she dropped lower and tried to untangle the problem of what they were seeing. "Disease was—and still is—a major concern in maritime travel. They might have had an outbreak of something they were desperately trying to quarantine."

Roy was backing away from the blockade, shaking his head furiously. "If you get *the plague*, you lock them in a faraway room. You don't just—just—"

"The emergency messages didn't talk about anyone being sick," Aidan added.

Cove made a quiet noise in the back of her throat. "They *did* mention deceased crew members though."

Hestie was finding it harder to breathe naturally. It should have been an autonomous action, but somehow the idea that she was *underwater* had become lodged in her mind and she had to deliberately draw and release each breath or else her subconscious would attempt to hold it instead.

"Either way, we're not getting through here." Cove checked her dive watch. "And our time's just about up. Let's head back, yeah?"

Hestie should have felt relief at those words, but somehow, they only screwed the dread in deeper. *Time's almost up.*

Then Roy said, "I want to look in one last room."

Time's almost up.

Cove was already squeezing around them, her hands lightly brushing their sides as she passed them in the narrow passageway. "Slow down, cowboy. We'll have plenty of time to do that tomorrow."

"It's on our path back. I just want to glance inside. It will literally take a second."

Time's almost up.

Cove clicked her tongue as she considered. It made a strange noise as it was transferred through the communications system. "Which one were you thinking of?"

"I'll show you."

They returned along the hall, moving single file. Every few feet, Hestie thought she saw something out of the corner of her eyes. She would twitch her head toward it, only to find out it was a speck of dust catching in their lamps or a strangely shaped scuff on the wall or a shadow cast by layers of lights and bodies.

The ocean could make a person paranoid. The lack of light, the exhausting pressure, and the sensory deprivation led to the brain grasping at anything it could to make sense of its environment...with very mixed results.

Hestie stayed close behind Roy, with Aidan in her wake. Vanna brought up the back of the pack, using the handle on her cable spool to reel the spare cord back in.

They reached the hall that cut across the ship. To their right, bannisters showed the entrances to both the stairwell down and the stairwell up.

The opposite wall held ornate double doors, and Roy moved toward them. Hestie tried to scramble through her memory of the ship's layout to remember where the path likely led. They'd come in near the bow, which meant this was...one of the lounges?

Hestie moved back to give Roy more room as he struggled with the stiff handles. Something shifted behind her, and she corrected just in time to avoid bumping into Vanna. The woman hovered with her back to the stairwell, the slack in the safety line held in one hand. Her fingers twitched around the cable as though she were burning to follow it back down and out.

The handles turned with some coaxing. Roy's breath whistled as it was drawn through clenched teeth, the sound magnified thanks to the communications system. He pressed on the doors, but they were frozen in place.

"Oh," Cove said, signaling that she'd figured out where they were going and why Roy wanted to get in there. She joined him at the door and put her shoulder against one.

Small gusts of sediment rose around their feet as they kicked for momentum. Vanna's gloves flexed around the safety line, and Hestie was hit by the abrupt, terrible idea that their guide could leave at any moment, disappearing into the lower floor and taking her line with her, leaving them disoriented and lost inside the *Arcadia*'s mazelike insides.

She's not going to do that. Hestie tried to see through the glare on Vanna's mask to read her expression, but she was a blank canvas. *Four thousand cave dives, and she's never left anyone behind before.*

Roy swore under his breath. "We can get it," Cove said, breathless but fierce. Aidan, who had hung back near Hestie, abruptly swam forward and planted his hands on the door next to Roy.

A low, deep noise rose around them. Hestie flinched, thinking the rattling sound of the ship settling had returned, before realizing it was the sound of fused hinges beginning to turn.

"Yes, good," Cove said, seemingly oblivious to the way the water's cloudiness thickened until they nearly vanished inside it. Hestie bit her tongue until she tasted blood. The left-hand side of the door was moving inward. The grinding, whining sound became louder as it followed a path it hadn't used for nearly a hundred years.

And then Cove, Roy, and Aidan dropped back. The door wasn't fully open, but it was wide enough for a person to swim through. Roy, breathless but laughing, raised a hand. "Would our intrepid captain like to go first?"

"Thirty seconds," Cove said. "Just enough to glance inside. Then we're calling the dive and heading out. Okay?"

"You got it."

She tilted her body to slip through the narrow opening. As her fins disappeared around the carved wood, Roy followed. He was less graceful, and his mounted tanks sent up a heavy metallic noise as they bumped the door's edge. It didn't slow him down though. Aidan glanced at Hestie, then he too moved inside. She swallowed, the tightness in her chest almost painful, the urge to hold her breath a constant enemy that needed battling.

Then she leaned forward and let her momentum carry her into the gap.

15.

The captain had increased the watches. The order had come through at dinner, and Harland, barely finished washing the stinking, sticking fog off his skin, had been sent back outside again.

They hadn't been told what they were watching *for* or how they were supposed to see it when the fog made anything beyond two rail posts away invisible, but it had been made a priority.

Traditionally, watches consisted of one man in the crow's nest with a direct line to the bridge, but now an additional four paced the decks. As Harland had surfaced to take his watch, he'd been passed a lantern, a whistle, and a spyglass—all tools he normally made do without. He took his position on the first-class portside promenade with the whistle hung from a sling around his throat and the lantern held at shoulder height.

He could see two distant lamps from other watchmen. Their glows were smothered until they were barely more than a touch of yellow at the periphery of his vision, but they were some of the only relief in the endless expanse of white. They seemed too far away. Parts of Harland doubted if anyone would even hear his whistle should he need to use it.

The lookout's job was rarely necessary when they were this far out to sea. It was normally composed of hours upon hours scanning the horizon in search of other ships or, rarely, land if they had drifted off course.

None of that was possible with the mist. Harland couldn't even see the water below his station. And yet the ship surged forward at an almost reckless speed. It wasn't being piloted by a man who feared potential rocks in their path. It was being driven as though hell itself were on their heels.

And Harland still didn't know what he was supposed to look *for*.

His lantern swung uneasily as he turned. Scraps of mist clung to his limbs and spiraled in his wake. It had wet through his cap and soaked his hair. It soaked into every pore.

He breathed through his nose and felt as though he were suffocating in it. He breathed through his mouth and the sickly taste plastered itself across his tongue and teeth. No amount of alcohol could remove it. He'd wake up the following morning and it would still be there, setting his stomach on edge before he'd even risen from bed.

A distant, soft tapping noise started. Harland turned, the lamp rocking, and pressed one hand to his brows to shield his eyes... as though that could do anything to help. He saw one of the distant lamps flicker. To his side, the railings ran in an unyielding line along the promenade's edge. The metal balustrades came to waist height, heavy cables strung between them. They dripped endlessly, soft plinking noises that reminded Harland uncomfortably of the tapping he'd heard, but this new noise was something else entirely.

It drifted through the endless white, first to his right, then sliding somewhere to his left, always just out of sight. The spyglass hung from his belt, but he didn't reach for it. It had been a laughable thought, really. No amount of magnification could help a blind man.

Harland took a step toward the sound, then backed up again. He had the strange, panicky idea that if he moved too deeply into the mist, he'd become lost and never find his way out again.

That wasn't possible, he knew. The promenades were finite. If he walked far enough and stretched out a hand, he would find the ship's walls again, maybe even see the blue paint underneath the dripping, sticking fog.

He stayed by the rails regardless. The rails, at least, were safe. As long as he could see them, he couldn't become lost.

The sound grew closer. It was different from the drips from the railing and different from the scratching, tapping sounds he'd heard as he tried to fall asleep. This was a steady, recurring thud. Like hands slapping the wooden flooring. Or like Harland's own heart caught in the irregular, skip-beat rhythm of death.

It was so close, he should have been able to see what caused it. His breaths were fast, whirring in and out of his throat, leaving their residue over his tongue again. He stretched the lantern out to his arm's limit, felt the icy air bite at where his sleeve pulled away from his wrist, and imagined it was like a top layer of skin being peeled off his body.

The sound was nearly on top of him. Not quite a perfect beat, each thumping note was divided by a silence of two or three seconds each. Harland's ears strained for each new noise, trying to pinpoint its location, trying to guess how close it was.

Then fog swirled ahead of him, and something dark emerged through it.

The figure was still at least ten paces away, Harland thought, though it was impossible to be sure in this senseless landscape. It was shaped like a person but distorted and blurred by the fog. The head turned in Harland's direction. He imagined he saw the eyes as dark pits inside the gray blur, but that was impossible.

He was frozen, his mouth open, the tacky water dripping over his lips as he watched. The shadowed figure stared at him for a beat, then leaned forward and continued moving, its feet creating the irregular sound as it staggered.

Passengers weren't allowed on the decks. The captain had given the order the previous morning, though no one quite knew why. Still, even without the captain's decree, no civilian in their sane mind would want to step into the fog, no matter how claustrophobic the floors below were.

The figure skirted around Harland, teasing at the edge of his lantern's light. Its edges were smudged by the fog, giving it an ethereal, unreal kind of tinge. Like one of the malicious spirits from Fitz's stories. The damned, chewed up by the ship during construction and now come alive again to take revenge.

"Ho there!" Harland took a step toward the figure but could go no farther. It didn't respond to his call. It had set its gaze on something and now moved toward it with unerring certainty. Harland blinked liquid out of his eyes as he watched the form reach the railing.

It planted its hands on top of a balustrade. If the day had been different—if the sun were out and the deck were busy—it could have been a traveler pausing to admire the way the ocean frothed along the ship's port side below them. Now, however, Harland felt his queasy stomach turn afresh at the way the stranger leaned over the rails, staring into the void below.

The ocean's sounds were blurry and distant, as though transported to them from another world. Harland himself had already looked over the railing's edge at the start of his shift. There was nothing to see. Nothing but more of the endless, poisonous white.

But the stranger seemed to find what it was searching for. Its face lifted to the sky. One foot rose to stand on top of the second metal cord connecting the balustrades. Using it like a ladder, the figure rose up, its other foot perching on the highest cable.

Harland watched in the same way he would watch a stage play: with curiosity but unconnected to the events unfolding. His heart could swell and fall in rhythm with the actor's motions, but he was powerless to do anything as the body rose on top of the railings and hung there for an agonizing second, arms loose at its sides, head toward the bleak, blind heavens above.

And Harland watched as the figure pitched forward, dropping over the edge, and was swallowed into the endless white below.

He wasn't certain if he heard it hit the water. Part of his mind insisted that he had, but he couldn't be sure if it was interpreting messages from his ears or if he simply believed he had heard a splash because he knew he *should*.

Harland gripped the railing in one hand and raised his lantern over the edge as he peered into the void below. Fog, thick as soup, claiming everything as far as the eye could see. There were no visible waves. Not even the ship's blue hull or portholes were visible beyond ten feet.

Harland leaned back, dizzy. The idea that he'd just watched some pantomime play out onstage lingered. Was he supposed to do something? *Should* he? No one else had seen the unearthly figure walking across the ship or climbing over the rails.

Then his head cleared, and true panic bit into his heart. A man had gone overboard. At this very moment, he was likely drowning. Harland grasped for his whistle, his breath too shallow and his pulse too fast.

The metal tasted of the fog. Harland's tongue tried to crawl away from it as he blew a piercing call. It was deafening in his ears, but once it faded, there were no echoes. In the distance, the two points of light stayed motionless, and Harland had the dark idea that perhaps the other watchers had left their lanterns behind and disappeared downstairs, and he was the only body left on deck.

No one is coming. No one can hear me...wouldn't hear me even if I screamed...no way out...no one coming...just this white, forever, no way out—

He blew the whistle again and again, as hard as possible, his lungs burning and his ears ringing, and finally the distant lights began to move. He dropped the metal as he sucked in the thick air, dizziness flowing through his limbs as he tried to stay upright, to not stagger backward and tumble over the same railings as the distant figure.

Then footsteps began to pound toward him. Men appeared through the white. Their faces were blurred in the mist, but he recognized two officers by their hats. A taller, broad-shouldered man pushed to the group's front. Captain William Virgil. He must have been close by to respond to the call so quickly; if he'd been in the bridge, he never would have heard the whistle, no matter how hard Harland blew it.

The captain's jaw held a brush of whiskers. He'd always carried sagging skin beneath his eyes, but it seemed exceptionally pronounced that day. Harland could only remember what Fitz had told him: *pacing the bridge all night...*

If Captain Virgil was missing sleep, his voice didn't betray it. Crisp, hard notes seemed to break through the disorienting effects of the white. "What is it?"

"Man overboard," Harland said simply, pointing to the railings.

No one seemed surprised. One of the officers crossed to the railing and leaned over, just like Harland had, to stare into the nothingness below. It was almost as though they'd been expecting something like this.

Captain Virgil asked, "Did you see who it was?"

"No, sir. The fog was too thick, sir."

The captain stared at Harland, hard eyes taking his measure, then said, with very little inflection, "Pulley, take a census of the ship. Find out who's missing. Start with the passengers."

"Aye, Captain." The smaller figure at the captain's side touched his cap, then vanished into the fog.

Captain Virgil tilted his head back as he stared into the distance. There was nothing to see—there never was in the abhorrent mist—but something sharp and glinting in the captain's eyes suggested he could see something in the layers of nothing that the rest of them could not. He was silent for so long that Harland was forced to shift the lantern to his other hand to save his aching muscles. Then the captain said, "As you were, all of you."

He turned back the way he'd come. The officers followed behind, while the other men disappeared in their own directions. Their footsteps persisted far longer than Harland's ability to see their dark backs.

It wasn't until Harland turned back to face the railing that the true significance fell over him. There had been no orders to turn the ship back to look for their fallen man. The chances of rescuing someone who went over the railings was fleetingly small on any day, but in the fog, it would have been nearly impossible. Still, there was something about the bluntness of *as you were* that left Harland cold in his bones.

He had the horrible idea that, whatever they were trying to get away from, one man's life was an acceptable loss to not lose speed.

Harland found himself hunching under the weight of his wet uniform as the shift dragged on. His gloved fingers turned numb. Sometimes he swiped a sleeve across his face, but it couldn't do much to clear the water.

Sometimes, when his focus began to lapse, he imagined he could hear a churning, splashing sound in the water far below, interspersed with faint cries for help: a drowning man calling to be saved.

Every time he snapped to attention, the sounds faded again, leaving him alone at his post, perfectly isolated except for the two distant lights, disconcertingly still, belonging to the other watchmen.

As real as the sounds seemed in the moment, Harland knew they had to be a product of his mind. The fallen man would be a long way beyond saving at that point. He'd likely succumbed within minutes, either to the biting cold of the ocean or from being dragged under by the churning motors that created their wake.

Still, in the remaining long hours of his watch, Harland couldn't stop himself from imagining the stranger, lost several knots behind them, managing to stay afloat on the ocean. The *Arcadia* long out of earshot. No other ships. No land, no rescue. Just the white wherever he looked and the endless depths of the ocean below, waiting for him.

The census was only partially completed when the lost man's identity was uncovered by coincidence. A Mrs. Carraway was found wandering the halls, grasping at the sleeves of every passing sailor as she asked if they had seen her husband. He'd said he was going on deck to get some fresh air, but he'd been gone for hours and she was worried for him.

The story was in furious circulation at the next morning's breakfast. Harland later heard that the now-widowed Mrs. Carraway sat alone at a dining table, staring with a blank, dry face at her breakfast. She was young. She had married her husband just six months previously, and they had reportedly been excited to begin a new life together in America. Mr. Carraway had no debts, no recent griefs, and seemed delighted to be married. No one could say what had driven him into the dark that evening.

It wasn't an isolated incident though. The following night, the starboard guard watched Mrs. Carraway cross the deck in slow, measured steps, climb the railing, lift her head toward the heavens, and tip overboard, following in her husband's wake.

The ship did not turn around for her. It didn't even slow.

16.

THE FIRST DIVE

The gap in the doors was only just wide enough for Hestie to fit through without becoming jammed. Even so, she had to tilt her body to keep her canisters from trapping her. She was so focused on watching behind her and making sure her fins didn't become caught that she didn't look up until Cove's reverent, "Oh damn."

Her first impression was *cathedral*. In their narrow lights, the space seemed impossibly immense. Hestie tilted her head back and almost moaned. There was no ceiling. The space simply stretched up and up, until her lights only barely grazed the remnants of skylights above. It had to encompass at least three floors.

"Is this—" Aidan started.

"The dining room." Roy's voice was full of deep, rumbling laughter. "Isn't it incredible?"

They drifted inward, rising above the scattered, dust-covered tables. The first-class dining hall had accommodated nearly five hundred diners during the busiest crossings. It took up three floors, with a balcony circling the walls close to the ceiling.

Utter decadence, even at the time. The skylights were present only as hints of shine at the periphery of Hestie's view, but when the ship sailed, they would have poured sunlight into a vessel that could feel stiflingly gloomy elsewhere.

She turned her gaze down. The floor, coated in sediment, at first appeared to be made of one material but pocked with irregular gullies and ridges. Those she realized were actually tables, most round, designed to hold either four or six individuals, but some longer dining tables had been established to accommodate larger groups. Some of them still had chairs tucked neatly in. Hestie dipped down low enough to get a better look.

The tables had been set when the ship sank. Most of the settings had been washed to the floor as water flooded the room, and broken plates, shattered glasses, condiment pots, and napkins were visible in piles between chair legs.

Hestie squinted to pick out shapes in the debris. They were all drowning in the blanket of gray, but frequent wineglass stems appeared among the other shapes.

Several tables were overturned, though most had managed to stay upright, but the currents had swirled them around just as badly as the settings. They were often grouped together, especially against the walls. Occasionally they still held lopsided tablecloths.

"Want to know the really good news?" Roy asked. He appeared to be attempting a shimmery dance but couldn't move his limbs very fast *or* very far without stirring up the water, so instead the movements just came across as odd twitches. There was no mistaking the blatant delight in his voice though. "Those skylights imploded when the ship sank. We can start our ascent right here and pop out the top, instead of having to go all the way back down to the cabin. Pretty cool, huh?"

"Oh, nice!" Aidan said, before catching himself and twisting to look over his shoulder at the others. "Is that...okay?"

"Of course it is," Roy said. He leaned farther down and selected a sleek object from one of the tabletops. As he lifted it, the shape came up with a comet's tail of sediment. Their collective headlights flashed off it, and Hestie recognized it as a shard of glass the size of her head. "The skylights broke when the ship went down, and they're now our own personal portals out of here."

Cove tilted her head back to examine the ceiling, and Hestie did the same. They could barely see the place where the glass had once belonged. Most of Hestie's view was disturbed by the perpetually suspended dust that flashed like dull fireflies as it passed through their lights.

It was possible not *all* of the glass had fallen, and that the skylights would still bear jagged shards, much like the broken portholes they'd examined earlier. Still, there were twelve sky-facing windows in the ship's design. Surely one of them would have a wide enough gap.

And it would be a spectacular shot, rising through the three-level dining hall.

Vanna's voice cut through the audio system's white noise. "We should stay with our plan."

Roy said, "Chill. You want to get out pronto, right? I just found us a shortcut."

Hestie turned. She couldn't see Vanna. Was it possible the woman had never entered through the door behind them, but was waiting in the hallway outside?

"My safety line goes through the cabin. I need to rewind it."

"You can collect it next dive." An edge of irritation had

entered Roy's voice. "Come on, this way's faster *and* we get some spectacular views on the trip up."

"We only need to swim along the bow to find our dive line once we get out," Cove mused. "This is making sense to me, Vanna. But you're the expert, and I don't want to override you if this is throwing up red flags."

The silence only lasted for a few seconds, but to Hestie, it felt like an eternity. Then Vanna said, "Very well. We'll begin ascent here."

"She's such a pain," Roy muttered, and Hestie couldn't tell whether he'd forgotten the audio systems were constantly live or whether he'd actually intended for Vanna to hear him.

No one commented on the remark, and after a beat, Cove cut through the uncomfortable silence. "Everyone set your dive computers to track your ascent. We'll have plenty of stops ahead."

The five divers clustered together near the room's center, beneath the broken skylights, their heads down as they pressed buttons on their wrist-strapped computers. Cove waited until they were finished before tilting her head up. "Let's go."

Decompression stops were a necessary pain for every deep diver. While most of Hestie's prior diving experience happened around reefs, she'd still experienced her fair share. Dives over fifteen feet required a stop before the surface. That day, they were following a protocol that would require at least twelve stops on the ascent. The full process to reach the surface again would take a little more than two hours. That was the price they all had to pay to visit the deep realms of the ocean without their bodies literally tearing themselves apart on the way back up.

They rose in a loose cluster, Cove leading the way, Hestie a few feet behind. She couldn't stop herself from directing her lights at the floor below them, to soak in as much of the view as possible before the water cut the light's reach. From that height, the gray-coated tables and toppled chairs looked remarkably like the ocean floor itself: ridges and rocks poking above the sandy ground, all of it blending together in unexpected ways.

Their dive computers beeped. They were at their first decompression stop, and they hadn't even reached the skylights yet.

"Was this a plan or was this a plan?" Roy asked. "We get the view of a lifetime while we wait."

"There are definitely worse ways to spend the time," Cove replied. They'd come to a halt at the balcony. The scalloped seating areas jutted out of the walls like a ledge, but although they narrowed the open channel through the room, it was still vast enough that the five of them could hang there with no risk of touching each other or the balconies.

Hestie allowed herself an extra foot of height to see over the railing. More tables dotted these higher, more-private dining nooks. Many of them had curtains drawn over the entrances. The effect was of a box seat in a theater. The fabric's color had been turned into a deep, grim gray by the depths, but Hestie suspected their true shade was a rich red.

She turned slowly. Floating there, high above the tables, was a strange sensation. A small anxiety dug into the back of her mind that gravity might spontaneously kick in and drop her to the floor below. She imagined herself plunging, limbs shattering as she glanced off the tables, head cracking open as she impacted the floor.

Where did that come from?

Hestie tried to laugh, but it came out as a nervous gasp. It was the environment. She was surrounded by shapes that were all perfectly familiar: tables, chairs, napkins. But they'd been changed. These dust-clouded artifacts barely seemed to belong in the world any longer. They were some alien construction that could be examined but never touched. Never returned to the state they'd once been. This ship—this goliath—had been carried into a dimension it was incapable of returning from.

She checked her dive clock. Only two minutes and then they could ascend through the shattered skylights above. She could see them clearly now. Some still carried glass chunks, like she'd feared, but three were empty and wide enough for a body to fit through comfortably.

Roy seemed to have already grown tired of the view he'd praised. He floated toward one of the curtain-covered balcony boxes.

"Stay your depth," Cove said, faint amusement in her voice. "We're not delaying this ascent because you want to bounce up and down like a Ping-Pong ball."

"Chill, I'm fine." He'd reached the railings. His gloved hands braced on the edge, disturbing the soft coating, as he tried to peer through the narrow gap in the fabric. "I'm staying steady. Just thought I saw something in here, that's all."

Hestie, despite herself, found curiosity pulling her toward him. "There should be a table behind there. Maybe one of the six-seaters."

"Yeah, just thought I saw something above it. Right there! What is that?"

Everyone—save for Vanna—had been drawn toward the box. Aidan accidentally bumped Hestie's shoulder and mumbled an apology. Roy was blocking their view, craned as close to the curtains as he could manage, head bobbing as he tried to get a spear of light through the opening. It was only an inch wide, and Hestie knew it would be a nightmare trying to make out details without clearer light.

"What do you see?" Cove asked.

"It's like..." His neck craned, and through the refractions on his mask, Hestie glimpsed his expression. His jaw was set, his eyebrows low, a shimmer of something like fear glinting in his eyes. "No, it's not."

She couldn't stop herself. "Not what?"

"Screw this," he muttered. The gloves left the bannister and gripped the curtains instead.

Cove barked, "No," at the same moment Hestie drew a pained gasp. Just touching the curtains sent a cascade of sediment floating through the space. Roy didn't stop though. His arms wrenched outward. Even through their masks, they could hear the scrape of aged rings dragging along filthy runners.

The curtains billowed as they were thrown open. The heavy fabric hung as though enchanted in the water, the movement dragging in slow motion.

The sediment rolled out like some unnatural fog. It consumed the group. Hestie impulsively drew a sharp breath and clamped her mouth closed, her eyes squinted nearly shut as she tried to shield herself, only to remember how foolish that was. There was no need to hold her breath when she wore the mask.

Though it was hard not to feel itchy as the cloudy substance spread past them. Roy's impulsive tampering had disturbed not just the decades of dust on the curtains but what had accumulated in the space behind as well. Hestie could no longer see the walls. She could barely see her fellow dive crew members.

"Damn it, Roy," Cove muttered, somehow managing to balance exasperation with traces of fondness.

He didn't seem to be listening. Hestie thought she could still see him, ahead and slightly to her left, his large shoulders forming a dark outline in the muddy water. One arm raised to point ahead of himself, into the box. "Look."

Cove said, "Roy—"

"*Look!*"

The urgency in his voice silenced them. Hestie leaned forward, squinting, straining to see through the clouded water.

Something was emerging from the dining alcove.

Something human shaped.

It's not—it's an optical illusion—

Five sets of lights aimed straight at the silhouette. It drifted toward them, dragged out by the eddies created when Roy opened the curtains.

It's not...

It had arms. They floated at its sides, weightless in the water. Just like the hair, a blur of darkness on top of its head, swaying like algae in a current.

It wore clothes. Some kind of uniform, Hestie thought.

And it had a face. A strange, deformed, bloated face. The body was rotating as it moved closer and turned heavy-lidded eyes toward the group. One of the arms drifted upward at the same moment, and the limp, rising hand appeared to point at them. An accusation.

The hand was aiming at Roy. He jerked backward, a sharp cry dying in his throat. The light on his helmet flickered.

The dead face resolved in terrible increments as it moved toward them through the clouded water. Aidan screamed, and once he started, Hestie couldn't prevent her own hoarse voice joining the chorus of cries and garbled shouts.

17.

Five bodies hung on to the dive line. Like grapes on a vine, Cove thought, or like the clusters of tiny air sacs inside their own lungs.

They were approaching the surface after upward of two hours of decompression stops. Sunlight speared through the water above them. She could see the base of their dive marker bobbing not far above, casting a shadow across her team.

She'd kept them to the decompression schedule. It hadn't been an easy task, not when Roy repeatedly tried to break rank with thirty seconds left, but she'd somehow gotten them to hang together and hold their positions down to the second.

And she'd squashed any talk of what they'd seen in the dining hall.

They'd speak about it, she'd reassured the team, but not while they were still underwater, not while they were in a space where panicking could compromise their safety. They'd wait until they were aboard the *Skipjack*, until they could get some food and return their blood sugars to an acceptable level, and until they could revisit the footage on Devereaux's computers.

She'd encouraged them to think about anything *except* what they most wanted to think about. *Focus on family,* she'd said, *or your pets, or where you'd travel if you won the lottery, or try to guess which celebrity couples have broken up since we last watched the news. Anything from the dry world. Anything that makes you happy.*

Except, based on the expressions she kept glimpsing around her, no one was actually following her instructions. Aidan's face was white as a sheet, his head sagging, sweat dotting his features. Hestie kept shooting tense, questioning glances toward Cove.

And Roy refused to look at her but kept muttering sharp, unintelligible phrases under his breath.

She couldn't blame them. *She* was incapable of following her own advice. Every time she blinked, she saw the face in her mind's eye, drifting out of the haze of dust. She managed to keep her expression neutral, but she couldn't wipe her mind free.

If anyone had managed the task, it was Vanna. She actually seemed the most relaxed she'd been all day. She gazed into the empty ocean around them, occasionally nudging a fin through the water to keep her upright. Her body language was languid compared to the rigid muscles on the rest of them.

"It was a mannequin," Roy blurted. He turned back to the rest of the group and his features abruptly cleared as he repeated, "It was a bloody mannequin! Someone brought it onto the ship as a lark and—"

"Mannequins don't generally have beards," Hestie murmured.

"Save it for the ship," Cove said.

Roy ignored her. "It was one of those, one of those wax things, then. They make them realistic. They're almost identical to a real human. Obviously it couldn't have been—"

"Save it." Cove introduced some snap into her voice, and Hestie, who'd appeared to be on the verge of saying something else, bit her lip, looking ashamed.

Vanna, her back to them, continued admiring the sun-dappled water. Aidan had his eyes glued to his dive computer. Just like Cove, he'd been obsessively watching their times. As he dropped his wrist, he closed his eyes again, nostrils flaring.

"It was a wax figure," Roy said, but this time he seemed to be speaking only to himself.

Cove's dive computer beeped. *Thank mercy.* The team unclipped their cables from the line and began to rise once more, ever closer to the surface, ever closer to having to face the realities of what they'd seen on the *Arcadia*.

12 APRIL 1928
EIGHT DAYS BEFORE THE SINKING OF THE *ARCADIA*

The atmosphere on the ship was changing. It had been bad for days, but something shifted after the deaths of Mr. and Mrs. Carraway.

Passengers no longer walked the halls alone. When they moved between their rooms and the dining areas, they did so in huddled groups, shooting anxious glances at the walls surrounding them, as though the *Arcadia*'s wood and metal were poised to slide inward and open like a maw to consume them.

Harland was loath to call that paranoia though. The ship's crew felt it too. No one was outright showing cowardice, but they clustered together whenever practical. There was safety in numbers.

Safety from what?

Whispers passed from crew member to crew member, then to

the passengers, then back again. It seemed to be the kind of thing you weren't supposed to speak of in a loud voice or share to any group larger than three. As though something bad would happen if it was spoken of too boldly.

But people rarely spoke of anything else, and the whispers all circled around the same thing: the knocking sounds coming from inside the walls.

Some crew and passengers still claimed not to hear it, but they were in the minority. Crew members were arriving to their shifts disheveled and exhausted, having been unable to sleep because of the sounds.

That lapse in uniform protocol would have been treated harshly on any other voyage, but the officers were turning a blind eye. They understood the agony of a sleepless night plagued by the soft *scratch-scratch-scratch* coming from the other side of the metal just beside their heads. And they had no remedy.

It was no longer just Fitz who suspected something was amiss. It was now common knowledge that the captain barely left the bridge and held council with his officers in frantic, hushed voices.

And there was nowhere to escape it. Desperate passengers attempted to get relief on deck, only to be driven back down by the stinking fog. The boiler room stokers would abruptly leave their posts to dash to the near-empty hallways, only to creep back down again when the hallways provided no respite.

The brutal double watch duties continued. Harland still did not know what he was watching for. But at least being on deck gave him something to *do*. He couldn't eat and could barely sleep. Whatever free hours he had were a burden.

He hadn't seen Fitz since their breakfast together, but in among the whispers about the tapping sounds circled stories about the older man. He'd been caught in the cargo hold, staring at one wall and whispering incoherent words, they said. An officer had pushed him back up to the crew berths. Scarcely an hour later, he was back in the hold, returning to that one stretch of metal as though obsessed.

Harland was trapped in a two-hour gap between his shifts. He chose to spend it in the crew's mess hall. It was better there than being alone in his cabin, sitting like a mindless puppet on the edge of his bed or, worse, lying there with closed eyes as he attempted to ignore the scraping, scratching sound long enough to fall asleep.

It wasn't a constant noise. It was elusive, arriving when you least expected it and fading again whenever you tried to listen closer. Like some phantom teasing them, arising for just long enough to break any chance of sleep before falling back into maddening silence.

The best chance of escaping it was to be somewhere busy, like the mess hall. Silence left a gap for it to fill, and it would do so unfailingly.

And yet, although noise seemed to ward off the hellish tapping, by unspoken consensus, the crew avoided it at all costs. Even orders by the officers were passed along in hushed tones.

Even now, with the mess hall near capacity, there wasn't enough noise to break through Harland's stupor. Spoons scraped bowls. Pewter mugs tapped down onto tables. And people whispered. Hunched near each other, eyes downcast, they whispered and whispered as they tried to understand.

Groups of passengers had infiltrated the staff's mess hall, likely under some misapprehension that the sailors knew how to keep them safe. They remained huddled in their own small gatherings, shawls and jackets bundled over their shoulders to keep the intense chill out. No one tried to make them leave. *Safety in numbers.*

Fitz entered through the starboard door. His sharp, bony form was easily identifiable, even with the lanterns allowed to grow as dim as they had been.

Harland had been unconsciously waiting for him, as though the older man's arrival was inevitable. He put down the still-full mug he'd been nursing as he waited for Fitz to take the bench opposite him.

Fitz didn't. Nor did he carry food or drink, but only an old, grimy rag that he compulsively twisted into knots with equally grimy hands. He bent across the table to speak to Harland, and the sound of scrunching fabric was almost loud enough to drown out his whispers. "I found it."

"It?"

The cloth was untwisted and then retwisted. Fitz's knuckles bulged as he squeezed the fabric. "*It*. The source. Where all of this is coming from. I can't tell anyone else. Not sure if I can trust them with it, but you—you understand, don't you, boy?"

Harland didn't know how to reply, so he only nodded. Fitz's whiskers were no longer just a day or two past shaving but far gone. The gray hairs on his lower jaw were damp, and Harland had the horrible mental image of Fitz standing for hours, staring at a wall, lips slack and saliva running over.

"D'you want to see?" Fitz asked.

Do I?

The answers collided: *yes, desperately* and *never in a thousand years*.

Harland knew in his bones that he wanted to be nowhere near whatever was inside the walls. But he also knew there was no escaping it. Not until they made port, and that was still days away. Whatever happened, they were trapped together in the *Arcadia*—a ship somehow vast and yet also nowhere near large enough—and he was likely going to have to know this thing better, whether he was willing or whether he was dragged to it.

Fitz didn't stay for Harland's answer. He twisted the cloth around his right hand a final time and turned, shoulders hunched as he retreated through the door he'd arrived from.

Harland rose, his stomach sick and his head filled with a cloud of fear as thick and impenetrable as the fog, and followed.

The narrow passageways seemed impossibly dim. Lights were going out, and no one seemed to be trying to fix them. Fitz didn't glance back as he shuffled along the familiar paths. A pair of stewards passed them, heads down but sneaking brief, mistrustful glances. Harland tried not to meet their eyes. There was too much poison inside.

Fitz led him deeper down. The boiler rooms' furnaces rattled beneath their feet. Harland had heard that the stokers were hurling coal into them as fast as their arms would move. It was a dangerous game with the impossible fog smothering them so severely. Not even a lighthouse would be visible from any kind of distance. He just had to hope that the captain's sailing was keeping them on their plotted course.

Still deeper, then turning abruptly into a room Harland had only seen a few times before. The aft cargo hold.

Large parts of Fitz's time were spent in the cramped rooms. His job involved watching over the storage, preventing water damage, and ensuring that no unlawful tampering occurred. Whenever an item needed to be retrieved or inspected, it was Fitz's keys that went into the lock. The *Arcadia* was carrying a small fortune in goods to be delivered to merchants back in England, and their preservation was paramount.

He wove through the stacked, net-bound crates with deft ease. Room was at a premium in the storage quarters, and even on a voyage below capacity, the hold seemed close to bursting. Harland had to turn his body sideways at several points to squeeze through narrow gaps.

Finally, they entered a patch of ground that had been left clear. Ahead were the steel walls making up the *Arcadia*'s hull. The empty space was large enough not just for Harland and Fitz to stand but for a dozen other men, if they'd so chosen.

Was this space set aside for something? Was a shipment canceled at the last moment?

Harland looked behind himself and realized he'd been mistaken. The area had most likely been as full as every other quarter of the cargo hold; only, its crates had been shifted. They had been dragged and stacked and shoved into any available gap around them, blocking other walkways through the mazelike hold, to make room. Harland could only assume this was Fitz's doing. He'd wanted this space clear.

"Do you hear it?" Fitz continued to weave the rag across his hands, scrunching and knotting it compulsively. It was filthy, but so were his fingers. When he squeezed the cloth too tightly, cracks appeared around his nail beds and knuckles. Beads of blood formed there. The fabric's dark stains were not grease evidently.

"I don't hear anything." Harland's mouth was dry. His head pounded in time with his heart. The wall shouldn't have inspired anything in him; it was bare plated metal, just like many of the crew-assigned parts of the ship. But he didn't dare look straight at it.

Something about this area was *wrong*.

"Listen," Fitz urged. He leaned close to Harland, their shoulders bumping, the old man's whiskers brushing Harland's shoulder.

And it struck Harland that this was the wall the officers had found Fitz staring at, engrossed, for hours at a time. The wall he returned to no matter how many times he was pushed away.

Harland looked at it. Dark gray metal plates were punctuated by rivets. The wall, clear from storage, seemed too large. The cargo hold's ceiling should not be this high, surely?

"Listen," Fitz whispered.

Tap. Tap. Scrape.

Like fingernails digging at the metal.

Like something that desperately wanted to be let out.

18.

THE AFTERNOON OF THE FIRST DIVE

Aidan sat in the bridge surrounded by the other returned divers. Someone had draped blankets over their shoulders—Devereaux or maybe Cove. Mugs of strong coffee had been placed at their sides.

At first Aidan had thought the extra care was overkill. The ocean was achingly cold and the air biting, but the full-body dry suits were like a tiny sauna strapped to their bodies. It had kept him comfortable, if not warm, in the icy depths of the gulf. Once they actually tried to climb back onto the ship, bringing up their heavy equipment with them, Aidan had felt uncomfortably hot.

Sean had been waiting for them. He'd seemed anxious and had come up alongside Aidan while he was stripping his tanks and weights off, but Aidan had been too exhausted to fully focus on his questions. He'd asked something about Vanna. About whether she'd seemed strange.

But the line of questioning had been interrupted as the queasiness that had dogged Aidan all morning had led him to be sick over the boat's edge.

Sean had left, and his presence was replaced by Cove. She'd patted his back, telling him he could lie down, that he'd be excused from the meeting if he didn't feel up to it.

She thought he'd been sick because of what they'd seen in the dining room. The *thing*. The human-shaped lump of debris or the optical illusion or, if Roy was right, the inexplicable wax mannequin that had floated toward them through the curtains.

That hadn't been on his mind though. If anything, he wished he'd been able to see it properly.

Instead, Aidan had carefully placed his hand over the dive computer so that Cove wouldn't notice his oxygen reading—6 percent.

Aidan bent forward in the rolling chair they'd brought up from the lounge. Even now, his head pounded and his stomach churned at the thought. The blanket and warm drink had felt unnecessary when they were given to him, but now, as the adrenaline faded and his body temperature dropped, he was inexpressibly grateful for them.

He'd been checking his computer's numbers compulsively in the latter half of the dive. Every minute, the desire to surface had grown more urgent. But he'd been incapable of vocalizing it. Roy had become short-tempered. The others had wanted to spend time with the messages on the walls. Again and again, he swallowed the words, while the numbers ticked below fifty, then below forty, then to thirty.

He'd been trapped in an insane loop of trying to be calm when his frantic heart literally pumped his lifespan away before his eyes. The closer he came to death, the more he panicked. The more he panicked, the closer he came to death. He'd tried, again and again, to break that cycle, but it had proved impossible.

Roy had promised to stay at his side during the dive. Technically, he'd never been far away, but his attention had been wholly absorbed by the ship from the moment they entered it. Aidan couldn't blame him. It was exactly what Roy had promised: an unparalleled experience. The kind of thing that no amount of money could buy.

The first people to enter the *Arcadia* in close to a hundred years. Though, perhaps, the ship hadn't been completely empty.

They huddled around the large screens set up on one side of the bridge. They'd initially been intended for Sean's ROVs; the plan had been for a singular dive to end the week, with the raw footage being packaged and shipped to the documentary producers largely unseen. Now, though, Sean uploaded the footage from Roy's front-facing camera for them to review.

Devereaux sat at Sean's side, one hand resting on the back of the younger man's chair as he watched. Cove stood, her blanket discarded but the mug clasped in both hands. She'd leaned back against the desk's edge. Long legs were crossed at the ankle. She seemed to have no problems balancing, even though Aidan was fairly sure his legs would turn to putty if he tried to stand.

Hestie had taken a seat next to Aidan, swaddled in a thick blanket just like him. There was a third seat for Roy, but he paced, alternately folding his arms and forcing his hands into his hoodie pockets. He was more on edge than Aidan had ever seen him before. Roy had always been the mellow one. The confident one. Comfortable. Unfazed by anything.

Now, he seemed almost to be crawling out of his own skin.

Images flickered across the screen as Sean fast-forwarded through the footage. Aidan glimpsed fragments of the first and second hallway messages, then the blockade, then the dining hall.

"Just a few minutes from here," Cove said.

The footage slowed back to a standard replay. Roy finally stopped pacing, and Hestie leaned in as they watched a first-person view of Roy approaching the curtained box. His voice played through the computer's speakers: "Just thought I saw something in here, that's all."

With the camera's color correction, the dark gray curtains appeared red. Aidan knew the principle but not the actual mechanics. It had something to do with light refractions and whatnot in deep water; past a certain depth, red shades were filtered out and, if you went deeper, yellows. On a scuba trip he'd attended with Roy, one of their diving buddies had cut his hand on sharp rocks. They'd all gathered around and watched in awe as green blood seeped from his hand. Aidan's knee-jerk reaction was to think some kind of exotic fish had bitten him and he was seeping poison; it wasn't until they reached the surface again that they were able to confirm his blood was still as red as the rest of theirs.

The cameras had been designed to counteract this and show true colors. While the earlier glimpses had all seemed familiar, this view of the balcony was jarring with its unexpectedly vibrant crimson streak.

The camera craned close to the gap in the curtains. The lens struggled to focus as a narrow spear of light cut through the opening. There was a flash of something pallid. Then something that might have been an eye or might have been a clump of dust.

Roy's recorded voice played again: "It's like…" A pause, then, "No, it's not."

Aidan knew what was coming. He took a deep swallow of coffee. It was strong and bitter, missing the sugar he knew he shouldn't have but never managed to resist. The burn of hot liquid down his throat helped ground him.

The camera blurred again as the curtains got in the way. Even dulled by the computer's speakers, Roy's voice was full of an anxious kind of frustration: "Screw this."

The screen exploded into flickering grays and blacks as the curtains were thrown aside and thick layers of sediment billowed outward.

Cove's voice, sounding distant: "Damn it, Roy."

Aidan's eyes burned, but he couldn't bring himself to blink. *It* was coming. He couldn't see it yet; the water's all-consuming cloudiness hid the balcony and everything beyond. But it was there, whether they could see it yet or not.

Something blurred at the edges of the screen. Static, almost unrecognizable among the blinding, flashlight-lit specks twisting through the water. Hestie made a small sound beside him, and Aidan's skin crawled. The cameras were expensive, designed to be reliable above all else. There was no reason for the recordings to lose fidelity. And at that moment, of all...

A shape began to take form behind the clouds of dust. For a second it was too indistinct to even see, just a vague sense of something dark moving in the distance. But it drew closer and closer, and the outline of the hanging arms began to appear and then the head and then the swirling haze of hair—

Everybody on the bridge was motionless. No one breathed. No one spoke. They were all tense enough to snap as they leaned forward, scrutinizing the figure as it drew ever nearer, the body seeming to consume the camera's view.

One of the arms drifted upward. Reaching toward Roy, or perhaps pointing; as it rose into frame, the fingers became clear: strangely deformed, limp, nails still visible in their nail beds.

Then Roy's recorded voice cried out, and the camera jerked backward. The static intensified, and the light used to illuminate the camera's view flickered. Sean rushed to turn down the audio as voices began to scream. Aidan realized, with a pang of shame, that one of those voices was his.

Then the camera's view became unrecognizable as Roy fought to get away from the balcony. The screen was nothing but a blur of water and dark, dry-suit-clad figures, all submerged in that soup of sediment. Sparkling, fizzing static stabbed in from the edges, sometimes strong enough to blind.

Cove was barking orders for them to rise through the gaps in the ceiling. The image cleared and the static abated as Roy neared one of the holes. He'd blindly risen to one that hadn't fully cleared of glass, but he didn't back away; instead, his gloved hands grasped at the glass, breaking shards free and letting them swoop down in slow motion to join their companions on the dining room floor.

Then he was through, and the view was of deep, dark ocean in every direction.

Sean paused the film and began winding it back. Still, no one spoke. They watched the skylight repair itself. The camera sank back down, deeper into the clouds of dust. Then the lens turned back to the balcony seat and the figure drifting toward the screen.

Sean paused the film there. The view captured the body's torso and most of its head, as well as the raised, deformed hand.

The bridge was almost impossibly silent as they stared at the image. Aidan swallowed the last of his coffee to give himself something to do.

Then Roy—the real Roy, not the recording—spoke. "It's not *real.*" He broke into laughter on the last word, as though they were all realizing that they'd been the butt of some practical joke, and they were probably in the right to be annoyed, but no harm done really.

No one else joined in. Now that Aidan could see it more clearly through the camera, there was no mistaking that it was a human figure. It had a beard, like Hestie had noted: short, dark stubble poking through a malformed chin. It even had eyebrows, and though the sediment was still too thick to be sure, Aidan thought he could see part of the eyelashes too.

The skin was strange though. It had an uneven, lumpy texture that almost seemed to have a shine in the camera's harsh light. The effect was especially pronounced across its cheeks and nose, but it was also noticeable on the hands.

"It's not *real*," Roy said again. He was still trying to laugh, hands rising at his sides before flopping back down again in exasperation. "No one's been to the ship since it sank. *A hundred years ago.* Even if—even if crew had been trapped inside—they'd be skeletons by now. It *can't* be real."

His chuckles were dying as the rest of the dive team remained silent. He looked at Aidan, sheer desperation in his eyes, silently asking for agreement. Aidan tried to smile in return. He didn't know what to say.

"I should have known this would be possible," Hestie said. She sounded very small and stared intently into her coffee mug. "I'm not…uh, my work was always focused on warm-water locations. Marine reefs and the like. I've never been to a shipwreck like the *Arcadia* before. I should have known better. I just didn't think—"

"What are you saying?" Roy asked.

She glanced at him, then looked down again. "Do you remember me talking about how we wouldn't get any sharks around the *Arcadia*? How there wouldn't be much of anything, because the water was too cold and there weren't enough currents?"

Roy didn't answer, so Cove stepped up instead. "I remember." She still leaned on the desk near the screen, her hands braced on the wooden surface. She gave a reassuring nod for Hestie to continue.

"Well, the reason for that isn't just because of the cold. It's pretty near freezing down at the gulf's base, but the main reason you don't get plants or fish or even parasites down there is because there's no oxygen. Oxygen enters the water at the surface, and in most oceans, there are enough currents to circulate it to the ocean floor and sustain life. But the gulf has very little water movement. Especially in the deeper parts, like where we visited today."

Cove gave another gentle nod, encouraging more, and Hestie cleared her throat as she rubbed her thumb over the lip of her mug.

"Well, no oxygen means no life of any kind. Including no bacteria. It's as close to a naturally sterile environment as is possible to get."

"The mattresses didn't decay," Cove noted. "The tablecloths didn't decay…"

"The *bodies* won't decay," Hestie finished.

They all turned back to the image frozen on the computer's display. One limp arm seemed to want to reach through the screen to touch them.

"But…" Roy appeared to lose inches off his height. He fumbled for the chair reserved for him and collapsed into it before trying again. "It's been *a full hundred years.*"

Hestie was struggling to correct him. "The human body has naturally occurring bacteria in it. That's what kick-starts decay when someone dies. But just like every other living thing in the natural world, bacteria can only survive for as long as it has access to oxygen. The decomposition process would have started, but like a flame under a glass, it would have consumed all available oxygen and burned itself out quickly."

"The water is just shy of freezing too," Cove said. "And that's how modern mortuaries preserve the dead."

She was exceptionally calm. Aidan couldn't tell whether she was just very good at adapting to surprises or whether she might have already guessed these facts while they were waiting on their decompression stops.

"It's an actual body then." Roy looked at the screen with a heavy kind of resignation around his features. "You're certain."

"Well, I suppose you'd need to examine it more closely to be 100 percent certain." Hestie gave a nervous smile. "But...I don't think it's a wax figure."

They lapsed into silence. Sean stayed close to the screen, two fingers pressed to his lips in mingled fascination and repulsion as he examined the clouded details of the dead man. Hestie finally dipped her head to drink from her coffee, then grimaced, apparently as shocked by the bitterness as Aidan had been. Devereaux leaned back in his chair, his hands folded over his stomach as he stared through his gold-rimmed glasses at the ceiling.

The agitation had been drained from Roy, but it hadn't been replaced by anything that could be called *calm*. His eyes were disturbingly disconnected as he watched the figure that had seemed to reach toward him. After what felt like an hour but was likely closer to a minute, he asked, "What does this mean? For the dive?"

Cove pulled an elastic band out of her pocket and used it to snap her wavy black hair into a ponytail. "That's something we'll need to discuss. But I suggest we do it on a full stomach. Aidan, want some help with dinner?"

"Oh—oh, right!" He jumped from his seat too fast, startling Hestie, and mumbled something apologetic as he began gathering their cups. He'd been hired as a cook-slash-assistant, but the only thing he'd done since arriving back from the dive was let others look after him. Cove's reminder of his duties was as gentle as it was possible to be, but he still felt ashamed. "I'll get started on that right now."

"I'll give you a hand." Cove glanced over the remaining members in the room. "The rest of you, take a shower and put on some fresh clothes. We'll meet in forty minutes."

19.

When Cove had asked Aidan what kind of meals he was good at cooking, he'd enthusiastically responded with *spaghetti Bolognese*, so that was what they prepared. It was a solid choice—full of carbs and good comfort food—but the fact that only a single dish had been volunteered by their cook suggested they might be eating a lot of Bolognese through the remainder of their trip.

Cove stood at the head of the long mess hall table as the rest of the crew arrived in response to her bell. Aidan jogged between there and the kitchen, bringing out cutlery and bowls of frozen vegetables that had been thawed in the microwave.

Devereaux was the first to take his seat at her right-hand side and reached for the parmesan while his meat sauce was still hot. Cove could appreciate a person who prioritized properly melted cheese, even during a less-than-ideal situation. Most of the others sat without trying to touch their food. Sean settled into a seat at the opposite end of the table. He'd brought a small black book with him, which he placed neatly at his side.

Roy had been one of the first to arrive, and he'd brought his camera. Cove kept silent as he set up the tripod in the doorway to capture the room. She'd have preferred to go without film. It altered the atmosphere. People were less likely to be candid when their words could be replayed.

Still, Roy was rattled, and Cove knew letting him work would help. He settled the headphones in place, one cup over his left ear to monitor the audio quality, the other ear free, and dropped heavily into his seat.

Aidan was the last to sit and immediately bounced up again, muttering apologies for forgetting the salt and pepper. Cove waited for him to return.

They were still missing one other party: Vanna. She hadn't been present for the film replay either, and Cove wasn't sure what to make of that. Normally she would have said that a lack of morbid curiosity was a *good* thing, except in a situation like this, it seemed somehow unnatural.

Aidan finally returned, clutching three salt and three pepper shakers, which he spaced along the table. No one touched them. Aidan took his place at Roy's side, and Cove figured that if Vanna didn't want to be present for the conversation, she wouldn't force the woman.

"So," she said, folding her hands and resting her chin on the knuckles. "I think it would be an understatement to say that today's dive was a rough one."

Aidan and Devereaux nodded, but Roy was stony faced and silent. It was going to be difficult to warm him up.

"We all have a lot of questions, I'm sure. Things you'll want to know from me. And things I'll want to know from you. But I believe the key questions are whether we'll be continuing the dives, and if so, who will be a part of them."

Aidan had been cutting his spaghetti into bite-sized pieces but looked up at those words. "You're...thinking of continuing?"

Cove had to phrase herself carefully. The camera's red light blinked at her over Roy's shoulder. "That's what we want to answer. And we'll need to come to a consensus tonight because of how short our schedule is. But I have to be up front with you—our contract requires a certain number of hours of footage inside the ship. If we don't get that, I can't guarantee that any of us will be paid."

She tried to gauge the reactions without seeming like she was putting them under scrutiny. Sean and Roy both appeared indifferent. Devereaux wouldn't be impacted, she knew, though he continued to eat quietly and watch what unfolded with great interest.

Only Hestie seemed disturbed. She'd made a start on dinner but put her fork down and instead frowned at the tablecloth. Cove could almost see the calculations taking place in her head and felt a pang of empathy. Vivitech wasn't exactly paying them a fortune, but the company's fees had included airfares and accommodation in a nearby hotel, and having to cover those out of pocket would hurt almost everyone at the table.

"How much more footage do we need?" Roy asked.

"At least another two dives' worth."

He grimaced, then scratched at his stubble. "Well, the ship's big. We already have some decent footage of the dining room, so it's not like we'll need to go back there. We'll just stick to the parts of the boat that don't have hundred-year-old corpse soup."

The rest of the team grimaced and muttered pained words at his description, but Roy only shrugged, as though daring them to call it anything else.

"That raises a question." Sean still hadn't touched his food. He leaned back in his chair, head tilted to one side as he fixed them all with a languid, uncaring gaze. "What are the odds that it's not the only body down there?"

Cove had already considered that, but she didn't want to be the one to break *all* of the bad news that night. Instead, she turned to Hestie, knowing she would be knowledgeable enough to answer in Cove's place. "Thoughts?"

"Well, it depends on many factors, but most particularly what happened the day the ship sank." Hestie picked up her napkin, stared at it as though she hadn't realized what she was doing, and folded it beneath the edge of her plate. "We didn't get a chance to see how many—if any—of the lifeboats had been launched. If the crew had ample warning the *Arcadia* was going down and they attempted to escape, the ship could be empty. Perhaps the individual we found in the dining room was the one person who refused to leave."

"Or got trapped or lost and was left behind," Aidan suggested.

"Exactly. The *Arcadia* wouldn't have had enough lifeboats for *everyone* to escape—that's just the way they did it at the time; they were only required to have lifeboats for a certain percentage of the people on board—but since the *Arcadia* wasn't running at full capacity and assuming they had at least two or three hours' notice, it should have been possible to clear the entire crew and passenger list onto the lifeboats."

"They never made it to shore," Roy said.

"No. They rarely do. Lifeboats from that era weren't designed to power their occupants to the nearest port; they'd have oars, but they weren't much help when the sea was rough or a current wanted to move them in the wrong direction. Mostly lifeboats were just that—a way to preserve life until another ship passed close enough to notice and pick them up."

"And if the rescue boats were searching in the wrong ocean?"

Aidan looked like he'd immediately regretted the question as Hestie turned a grim smile to him.

"During that time in history, lifeboats were occasionally found with corpses in them. Or with just one or two out of twenty left alive. More often, though, if a ship went down in heavy weather, the lifeboats were likely to be tipped over with it, and all lives lost. That could have happened to the *Arcadia*. If that's the case, the bodies would have decayed on the surface, where there was plenty of oxygen to help the process, or scattered far and wide over the ocean floor. If we assume the lifeboats were filled and launched in time, that body could be the only one left in the *Arcadia*."

"An oar *did* wash up," Cove added. "Almost a year after the ship's sinking, it was discovered on a beach in Poland and identified."

Sean shook his head. "That means nothing. Sure, there might have been a lifeboat that capsized or something. But it's just as likely that the oar got knocked free from its stowage when the ship did its whole nosedive into the deep. Shipwrecks aren't gentle affairs."

"I'm inclined to agree with Sean." Everyone at the table turned to stare at Devereaux, who had finally broken his silence. He seemed unconcerned with the attention but kept his chin tilted up so he could examine a forkful of elegantly twisted spaghetti through his spectacles. "I'm in no way an expert on diving—I could barely survive in a swimming pool—but I *did* request to join this exploration for a reason: a lifelong fascination with shipwrecks."

Cove smiled. She'd hoped Devereaux would join in, and now that he had, he wasn't disappointing. "What are your thoughts on this all?"

"Well." He carefully placed the spaghetti into his mouth and paused to chew and swallow. At the other end of the table, Sean tilted his head toward the gray ceiling and ran a hand over his closed eyes, but Devereaux paid him no attention. Instead, he returned the fork to the remains of his meal as he cleared his throat. "The *Arcadia* had a manifest of those on board, including crew members, staff, and passengers. Not a seam-splitting number, as we said, but a significant one regardless. The chances of a shipwreck having a high survival rate balances on a calculation of proximity to shore, time taken to sink, and number of individuals needing to evacuate. The *Arcadia* may have taken some time to go down, but that would be the only element in its favor."

"It wasn't close to shore," Roy noted.

"Precisely. If someone in a dire situation can see a way out—that is, if there is land nearby—they may struggle to reach it. But if they can only see ocean in every direction, history has shown us that many people will prefer to cling to what they are familiar with, even if it's a ship that's in the process of sinking. It's irrational but, when panic sets in, all too common. It's why we have evacuation drills these days. A person who has visualized climbing into a lifeboat and being winched down the ship's side is more likely to follow through if the moment ever arrives."

"And the more people on board, the more likely you'll get herd mentality, where they plant their feet and refuse to move," Hestie said.

"That's the basic psychology of it, my dear."

"So you think there *are* more bodies in the *Arcadia*." Roy said it as a statement, rather than a question.

Devereaux lifted his hands into a gentle shrug. "I would not be surprised."

"Most of the ship was relatively watertight," Hestie said. "We didn't notice any enormous breeches in the hull where...*things*...

could have been washed out during the sinking. Most of the furniture was still in place. It's likely any additional bodies would be too."

Roy grimaced. "And you couldn't have thought of this *before* we went on the dive?"

"I'm a marine biologist." Hestie's voice dropped as she turned her focus back to her food. "Specializing in corals and plasticines. That's on par with asking an astrophysicist to explain the star signs. It's tangential at best."

"You don't have to be such a—"

"Back to our question," Cove cut in. She shot Roy a warning glare. He pretended he didn't see. "Are we diving again tomorrow? Knowing this might not be an isolated incident, but also knowing that our contract voids if we don't."

For a beat, no one spoke. Then Aidan took a stuttering breath. "Are there, uh, laws about…this kind of thing? Like, swimming with dead bodies and filming them and stuff?"

"In essence, no." Devereaux pushed his plate aside and reclined, hands laced over his waist. "In rare instances, a shipwreck will be declared a grave site and divers forbidden from exploring them. Military wrecks are often given special protections like that. But human remains are found infrequently enough that laws are created on a case-by-case basis. And since no one realized there was still a body on the *Arcadia*, no one has brought it up."

"This can't be that rare though," Roy said. "There are *thousands* of shipwrecks out there. Lots of them as big as the *Arcadia*. I've gone on dives to a bunch of them."

"Commercial wrecks," Hestie said. "Close to the surface. Warm currents. Fish. Bodies never last very long there. The *Arcadia*'s position is very, very unique: the anaerobic water, the temperature, and even the depth are all in perfect balance to make this possible."

"The *Titanic* took many bodies down with it," Devereaux continued. One hand shifted, and Cove had the distinct impression he was wishing he could reach for a glass of port. "The ROVs sent into it have captured photos of shoes on the floor. *Pairs* of shoes, you understand? You could almost draw an outline of where the bodies once were, with remarkable accuracy. But the *Titanic* rests at twelve thousand feet, not three hundred. The water's pressure quite literally dissolved even the bones a long time ago."

Hestie nodded. "Exactly. The oceans cover the vast majority of our world, but there are very few pockets where preserved bodies can exist. I've heard of them in the Great Lakes and in the Dead Sea. It's possible, but not common. We had the sheer bad luck of diving to a wreck that simply will not decay."

Sean flicked one hand up to get their attention. "You're still not answering the question."

"We have permission to dive to the wreck," Cove said. "Vivitech secured it on our behalf several weeks ago. The *Arcadia's* resting place hasn't been designated a grave site—yet. Legally, we won't be in trouble."

"Ethically?" Aidan asked. He caught Cove's inquiring glance and dipped his head. "Sorry. Never mind."

"Ethically," Devereaux murmured. "You could ask ten people and get ten answers. Is this any less ethical than walking through a graveyard? Or of viewing a mummy in a museum? Does swimming near the bodies count as disturbing their resting place?"

Aidan was growing increasingly flustered. He looked to Roy, who gently pressed his arm. "I think Aidan's less worried about a course in philosophy and more in, say, what the newspapers would print about this."

"Mm, yes, public opinion." Devereaux's eyes were half-closed as he considered the question. "People tend to care the most when the shipwreck is recent. In particular, if there are surviving relatives who remember their departed, you understand? There's an argument that the *Titanic* should count as a grave site. The bodies may no longer be present, but we know where they lay, which isn't too different from a traditional graveyard. However, so much time has passed since its sinking that many people view it as a location of historical significance, deserving of further research. I suspect the same will be true for the *Arcadia*. It borders on being an urban legend by this point, and curiosity will outweigh many shades of moral objection."

Cove took a slow breath. "I think ethics is something each of you will need to figure out in your own way. And ethics aside, whether you would actually be comfortable diving to the shipwreck twice more. We can avoid the body we know about— but we won't know whether there are others down there. Or for that matter, how many."

There was a pause in the conversation. Devereaux, apparently happy to be a bystander, picked lint from his cardigan. Roy scratched at his stubble before shooting a glance at Aidan, who gave a tiny shrug.

"Take the evening," Cove said. "Sleep on it. I'll need your decisions by breakfast tomorrow to prepare for the next dive—if it's happening. On that note, even if you're all prepared to return, we can't go down without Vanna. I'll need to check in with her and see if she's still on board."

"I am."

Cove managed to hide her flinch better than almost everyone else in the room. Sean, normally unmoving, half leapt from his chair. The voice came from the open doorway behind him.

Vanna's silhouette was next to invisible against the dark hall. Cove had no idea how long she'd been listening in, silent.

She stepped into the room, her heavy eyes scanning their faces as she approached her seat. Instead of taking it, she picked up her plate of spaghetti Bolognese and cutlery, then turned to leave again.

Cove felt as though she should say *something*, so she called out, "You're certain, Vanna? Tomorrow's dive will be on a voluntary basis, and that includes you."

She paused next to Sean. One of her muscled arms reached out and her fingertips lightly touched down on the black leather-bound book Sean had brought to the table. He stared up at her, a pulse jumping in his jaw. One hand twitched as though he wanted to grab for the book but didn't.

"I'm sure," Vanna said. She stepped away, taking the book with her.

Sean watched her go, then turned back to the table, nostrils flaring and eyes hard. He seemed on the verge of saying something, so Cove waited, but he simply shoved his plate aside, gaze fixed blankly on the tablecloth.

"Well." Cove looked down at her own half-finished meal. She doubted she had room in her churning stomach to complete it that night. "Think it over."

The ship tilted as an abnormally large wave dropped them into a trough. Cove put out a hand to stop a saltshaker from sliding over the table's edge. The lights above them flickered— just once—then stabilized again, returning their room to the pretense of normality.

She stood, a calm expression masking the anxiety gnawing through her insides. "I'll expect your answers by morning."

20.

Fitz had been removed from his post. The news reached Harland secondhand. He hadn't seen Fitz since the previous morning, when the man had taken him into the storage hold. If he was being fully honest with himself, he'd been trying to avoid Fitz. Not that it was a hard task, when half of his time was spent in isolation as a watchman on deck and the other half he kept to himself in his room. But guilt and relief had flooded Harland in equal measure when he'd found he would no longer be bumping into his friend in the mess hall.

The story was that Fitz had been locked in an empty passenger room. Someone brought him food twice per day. There was no mention of court-martialing or punishment or word that he'd broken any laws. But his whispers had been stirring up the men, and the implication was that he needed to be *contained*.

No one had replaced him in his role as stock master. The safety of their storage room felt like less of a priority when there was such a pervasive sense that their very lives hung by a thread.

One of the chief stokers had been found in a passenger bathroom. It was uncertain why he'd traveled so far from his quarters, but by the time he was discovered, the mirror and many tiles had been broken, and the sink and floor had been smeared with the blood he'd begun retching.

He'd been taken to the liner's hospital, where he lay catatonic. One of the men who had helped carry him there had scrubbed at his bloodstained arms until they were red and raw and now lay unresponsive in his own room.

Just hours later, one of the junior stokers had failed to turn up to his shift. There were murmurs of a figure seen staggering through the fog and slipping over the ship's side, though they were just that—rumors. The man on watch hadn't made any official report. Harland couldn't blame him. None of the prior reports had led to any action.

By captain's orders, the passengers were being restricted to their rooms save for meals. They had to be led between their quarters and the dining halls by crew members, and all other passenger areas—the lounges, exercise room, promenades—were off-limits.

It was perhaps for the best. They were having trouble with the lighting. Although the remaining stokers were keeping the engines running, the bulbs set into the walls and ceilings were failing at an alarming rate. In some parts of the ship, as many as half the bulbs were dead.

Supposedly, someone was working to fix them, though Harland had yet to see anyone on the task.

When passengers inquired, the crew were supposed to explain

that something had gone wrong with the wiring and it would be fixed shortly. It seemed like a simple enough explanation, though it didn't account for *what* had happened to the wiring or why it impacted virtually every part of the *Arcadia*.

Every time Harland had to explain that to the passengers, a single thought bounced through his head.

It's in the walls.

THE EVENING OF THE FIRST DIVE

Aidan lay on the top bunk, arms folded behind his head, one knee raised just inches from grazing the ceiling. The lights were out, but their cabin was never actually dark; the hallway's light still filtered in beneath the door, and surprisingly harsh LEDs shone from the alarm clock and portable music player Roy had set up on the windowsill.

He could feel the ship moving beneath them. That was supposed to be something he became more adjusted to with each passing day, until he no longer even noticed it, but it was only his third night on the *Arcadia* and Aidan was exhausted from the perpetual rocking.

Hestie said that part of the gulf was as dead as an ocean could get, but that night, with the glowing lights in his periphery and that evening's talk still ringing in his head, the water felt unpleasantly alive. As though something pulsed between them and the shipwreck three hundred feet below. As though it was calling to them.

Aidan rolled over to face the wall, knees tucked up to his chest. Their window had a blind that could be pulled down, but Roy left it open. The stars were shockingly bright. They created a haze of light across the room, letting Aidan pick out every tiny flaw in the wall's paint—the minuscule bumps, the scratches, the place where a flake of paint had chipped away entirely. He pressed his fingernail against the edges of that chip and pushed another flake of the paint off the wall.

Roy sighed in the bunk beneath. It wasn't the relaxed, contented sound he made when he was on a beach or prying the cap off a bottle of beer. It sounded frustrated.

"Hey," Aidan whispered. "Still awake?"

"Yup."

He felt like he should say something more. Roy had been short with him ever since the dive. To be fair, he'd been short with everyone else too, but Aidan still couldn't shake the feeling that he might somehow be to blame.

"What are you thinking about tomorrow? Will you go down again?"

"Course I am, bud. I got us into this mess, so I'm sticking with it until the end."

That's what a man does, huh? You stick with things. Even when they get unpleasant. Even when you don't want to.

Aidan was wearing thick layers of fleece to ward off the chill. He touched his hand against his chest and felt the firm pressure of the ring against his skin.

"What about you?" Roy asked. "You're joining me tomorrow, right?"

"Yeah. I think." His hand folded around the ring beneath the fleece. "I'll...I'll regret it if I don't, right?"

"Mm." Blankets rustled as Roy rolled over. "This is the kind of thing you'll be able to point to when you're eighty and say, *I did it. I was an explorer in an age when there was almost nothing left to explore. I left my mark on history, make no mistake about it.*"

"Yeah." A thin smile flitted over Aidan's face. "It's worth it, right? Even with...even if..."

"Nothing big was ever achieved without a little risk." Roy took another deep breath and let it out as a languid sigh. "That's basically my life motto, bud."

"I thought your motto was *eat five Hot Pockets or die trying*."

"Same thing, really."

They both laughed.

It took Aidan another hour to fall asleep, but when he did, he was still holding on to the ring.

Sean paced through the ship. He and Cove bunked in the same room, but he'd been sitting on the edge of his bed for more than an hour and he was sick of waiting for her. Only problem, he didn't know exactly where she was.

The wind whistled unpleasantly against the windows as he looked into the mess hall and kitchen with some vague idea that she'd stayed up to have a drink. Both empty. Both dark. The ship, all sleek, modern lines during the daytime, took on a distinctly cold, hostile aspect at night. A house could feel like a home. In Sean's opinion, the same was true for certain kinds of ships... but not this one. It knew it wasn't designed to be lived in for any longer than a few nights at a time. It remained professional. Clinical. Unwelcoming.

He jogged up the stairs to reach the bridge, but instead of opening the door, simply looked through the circular window. The overhead lights had been dimmed, but enough screens were still on to illuminate the slumped shoulders behind the dashboard.

Devereaux flexed his neck muscles, one hand tapping keys on the computer. He was reviewing their footage from the day. He'd have a lot to get through. They'd spent more than an hour in the *Arcadia*, times five individuals, times two cameras each. Though, Sean supposed, this was what he'd wanted when he'd volunteered his ship for the documentary: to live the adventure vicariously through them.

There was no sign of Cove in the bridge, and Sean backed away from the door without disturbing their sponsor.

The showers weren't running; he would have heard them otherwise. It was too cold to spend more than an hour on deck. And the ship didn't have very many other quarters to lurk.

Sean circled around to the only remaining room: the narrow lounge. He'd passed it earlier, but no light came from under the door, so he hadn't bothered with it. Now, he shoved the door open. Cove's face, illuminated only by the laptop she'd propped in her lap, turned toward him.

"Hey," she mumbled. "Thought you'd be asleep by now."

"I could say the same to you." Sean felt like he was intruding on a personal moment. He leaned on the doorframe and shoved his hands into his hoodie's pockets.

The laptop's blue light glanced off Cove's face in strange ways. She had a strong bone structure—one that played well with all kinds of cameras. Now, however, it served to make her seem half-alien. Her eyes shone a vivid, almost glowing shade of green. They blinked languidly as they watched him. "I'm trying to read up on…well, preserved shipwreck bodies. Figure we might need to know a bit about them if we're heading back down tomorrow."

Sean chuckled. Cove spoke differently when she wasn't in front of a camera and when she wasn't trying to impress too many people. She dropped the positive, upbeat energy. He liked her better this way. "Fair enough. I wanted to talk to you though. It's important. And I know the timing's horrendous, but…"

She reclined on the couch. "You don't live in the entertainment industry without getting used to surprises. Come on in."

Sean used an elbow to nudge the lounge door closed behind him and, hands still in his pockets, approached the chair Cove had indicated. "How well do you know Vanna?"

Devereaux's eyes ached: a symptom of spending too much time in front of the harsh computer screen. As a child, his parents had always harped that spending so many hours reading would ruin his eyesight. They had passed before computers became household items, but he imagined they would have a synchronized meltdown over the hours he spent in front of his laptop. Not that it would stop him.

On most days, he would accept that his eyes had reached their limit and go for a nap before a headache had a chance to set in. Not this day though. Not when the insides of the *Arcadia* were at his fingertips.

The computer's screen flickered as he tapped through the footage. He'd already viewed the front-facing cameras for Roy, Hestie, and Cove. He'd saved screen captures and noted time stamps of the most intriguing moments: the three messages on the walls, the stairwell, the broken bathroom, and, of course, the dining hall and its unexpected guest.

Roy's files had been his favorite. His training as a cameraman meant his footage was the clearest and the best framed: he knew what moments would make a cinematic banquet and had lingered on them appropriately.

Now, however, Devereaux had returned to Hestie's footage. She'd made the ill-advised but highly productive choice to diverge from the group, and hers was the only recording of the first-class bedroom with the silhouette drawn on the wall. Devereaux had already watched the front-facing camera, but now he switched to the rear, hoping for a clearer view of the furniture. Unlike Roy, Hestie moved around a little too quickly and often stood too close to things for the camera to get their full measure.

He played the footage inside the room at half speed to be sure he wouldn't miss anything. The front camera naturally faced whatever Hestie was looking at, which meant the rear view often only captured the walls or the ceiling. Still, Devereaux hoped he would get a complete shot of the wall and its scribbled outline when Hestie left the room.

He leaned close over the computer, rubbing one finger into the corner of his burning eye as the camera jittered over the bed's posts. The view, which was blurred from the movement, became still. This would be when Hestie stopped to look at the silhouette. The rear camera tilted down as she turned her head up, and its new view was of the floor and the bed's feet.

The screen hung there for half a minute, then Hestie turned to leave the room and rejoin her companions. Devereaux caught a glimpse of the silhouette and felt vague disappointment that the rear light wasn't strong enough to illuminate it properly. The shape probably would have appeared dark gray to Hestie at that depth, but with the camera's color correction, it was a vivid, vicious red.

Still, his disappointment was inconsequential compared to a small spark of intrigue. Devereaux wound the footage back. The camera's view returned to the lower half of the bed. The room had carpet, though that was now smothered by a snow-like covering of sediment. The bed's wooden legs were dull but still reflected enough light to tell Devereaux they had been highly polished once. The gap between the mattress and the floor was almost pitch-black, at the wrong angle to catch either the direct light or any refractions.

Devereaux let those thirty seconds of stillness play through again, then wound back. This time he set the speed to one-quarter as he played it again.

A pallid shape shifted beneath the bed.

He watched as long fingers drifted into view. The footage was too hazy with silt to be certain, but to Devereaux's eyes, the fingertips had been stained crimson in the same shade as what marred the wall.

Unbeknownst to the dive team, they had uncovered at least one other body inside the *Arcadia*.

The hand moved forward, giving the illusion that it was reaching out toward Hestie's foot. The movement would have been caused by tiny eddies in the water, pulling the figure out from where it had settled beneath the bed.

Though it did seem that the fingers extended a fraction in the second immediately before Hestie turned back to the door.

He would show this to the crew—but not just yet, he decided. They were already uncomfortable about the figure they'd discovered in the dining hall. Although they had aptly guessed that more bodies were contained inside the ship, he couldn't imagine this footage would be a welcome sight when they were already torn on the idea of a second dive. It could wait.

Devereaux noted down the time stamps and the camera number and took several screenshots of the pale, clawlike hand. Then he closed out of that footage track and returned to Roy's.

21.

THE SECOND DIVE

Cold spits of rain cut across Cove's face as she strapped her tanks into place.

No one had dropped out. Not even Aidan, the most shaken by the previous day's trip, had shown any hesitation when Cove had asked for their decisions over breakfast.

She glanced at Vanna. Fresh lines seemed to score deeply around her lips and eyebrows. The black-haired woman didn't return the look.

She and Vanna had talked for upward of an hour that morning while the sun rose. They had been the only two souls awake, huddled in the dim lounge area, far from prying ears.

Their conversation had been intimate to an uncomfortable degree. Unpleasant. It left Cove with the sensation that she'd cracked open a turtle's shell to see what was inside, and now the turtle was squirming and helpless on the cold ground. She didn't like it, and worse, there was no way to fix it now that it had been done.

And you can't even verify what she told you. Not fully.

On a better job with better circumstances, Cove would have dismissed Vanna from the crew. But Vanna was the only member of their party with significant deep-water diving experience, and losing her would have forced Cove to cancel the remainder of their visits to the *Arcadia*.

She couldn't afford that. She *needed* Vanna. And she quietly hated herself for it.

During interviews and behind-the-scenes footage of her other documentaries, Cove often spoke about crew safety. It was something she'd always prioritized and always been proud of. *No matter what, the crew comes first.*

Turns out she didn't have the luxury of that any longer. Their deadline was too close. They needed more footage. And she was becoming the thing she had always looked down on: the producer who pushed people just a little too far and a little too long, all the while hoping and praying that nothing snapped. *Two more days of footage. Please. That's all I need.*

After their talk, she'd half expected Vanna herself to refuse to return to the water. But Vanna had shown up to breakfast that morning, stony faced and pale, and then had returned to the hull to prepare her equipment with the steadfast focus of someone who had never considered otherwise.

So against Cove's expectations, and perhaps, even against sense, all five of them were returning to the ship.

They lined up at the railing, backs to the ocean. The sky was heavy with threatening rain clouds, but where they were going would be impervious to the fickle weather of the surface.

Roy said, "Let's get wet," and Cove knew he was still rattled because he didn't laugh at his own innuendo. One at a time, they tipped back.

The water crashed over Cove. She had one final glimpse of the undulating blanket of the sky before the bubbles and steely water flooded over her.

The impulse to hold her breath was stronger than it had been the day before. Her throat tried to close over. It stung to draw tank air into her lungs.

Shake it off. Do your job. Keep the team together.

"Audio check," she called, and the bright tone to her voice sounded horribly foreign, like she was listening to someone she didn't recognize. "Alphabetical order."

"Aidan."

"Roy—oh, shoot, Hestie was supposed to be next."

"Hestie."

"Okay, Roy again, official this time."

The silence hung about them for a moment, and Cove turned, counting the dark figures about her. There were four, as there were supposed to be. "Vanna?"

The shape to her right twitched. "Yes?"

"Okay, just checking your mic." *Keep it together. Keep them together.* "Let's go get ourselves some killer footage of this wreck, yeah?"

"Killer," Roy mumbled, as though he was trying to figure out if he could turn that into a pun. Cove was unfathomably grateful when he didn't.

Cove put herself into a dive. They were following the line Vanna had laid the previous day, which would take them right to the edge of the wreck.

The natural light faded rapidly, and with each foot descended, their headlights became harsher. Cove's rebreather seemed too

loud as it exhaled a burst of air. The white line of rope danced
ahead of them, a narrow point of focus in the endless void,
growing smaller and fainter as it twisted into the dark.

"Cove." Vanna's voice was void of any feeling, and Cove
couldn't tell which direction it came from. "You were hoping to
get your footage with three dives, yes?"

"That's the goal." She already dreaded the idea of having to
force her crew back down for a fourth sojourn.

"We should split into teams. We can cover more ground that
way."

At that moment, Cove was immeasurably glad that Sean had
kept his discovery between himself and Cove. She couldn't share any
part of that morning's conversation, and if Sean had revealed what
he'd suspected to the rest of the crew, they would never in a million
years have agreed to being isolated with Vanna inside the ship.

"That's a good idea." Vivitech's contract had specified *viable,
unique footage.* Blurred or indistinct footage wouldn't count as
viable, and five viewpoints of the same image wouldn't count as
unique. If they could split up, they would be that much closer to
fulfilling their contract.

It would have to be into two teams. One of the most prevalent
diving rules was to have a dive buddy, and while plenty of lone
wolves went down solo on their own time, Cove was not about to
stray into that territory when their risk margin was already so steep.

The dive line appeared to undulate, swirling in the still, dark
water. They were already closing in on the *Arcadia.*

"I want Aidan," Vanna said.

"O-oh?" He sounded shocked. Shocked and somewhat
pleased. Cove hoped he could enjoy the sense of being chosen
first without realizing Vanna was picking him because he was the
least experienced, and she wanted to keep an eye on him.

"Aidan and I dive together," Roy said. "He'll come with me. The rest of you can make up the second team."

Cove grimaced, grateful that the mask would hide her expression. Pairing Aidan, easily swayed, with the overconfident and risk-seeking Roy could only lead to disaster. And yet, the undertone to Roy's voice made it clear that he wouldn't agree to Vanna tagging along.

"Hey." The bright spark that inhabited her voice didn't come out quite right. "How about this? Roy and Aidan come with me. Hestie with Vanna."

It was the closest she could get to a compromise. Roy liked her well enough, and he also *listened* to her, something she couldn't count on if he was paired with Vanna. Cove might not have Vanna's experience, but she at least had a level head.

"That's fine," Vanna said. "I'm going to retrieve the dive line we placed yesterday. Hestie, we'll enter through the torn hull and make our way to the dining hall before retracing our path. There should be time to look into rooms along the way."

"Okay." Hestie seemed perfectly happy to let someone else set the plan.

"Which means…" Cove closed her eyes for a second to steel herself. "Roy, Aidan, how about we try to get into the lower level? While the others go *upward*, we'll go *down*."

"Hell yeah, fresh ground." Roy's enthusiasm was returning. "I want to know if they jettisoned any supplies. We should get an idea of that if we can find the hold. Maybe we can check the boiler room while we're down there."

"Time permitting," Cove replied, agreeing.

The dive line was curving slightly, signaling they were closing in on the end of their descent. Cove strained to see the *Arcadia* through the dense water. Her lungs ached, and she realized she'd been holding her breath.

The bow came into sight faster than she'd anticipated. One second, she was straining at a phantom shape that *might* have been the edge of something, and the next second the ship's silhouetted bow was cutting across her field of vision, sharp and dark against the ocean's depths. It gave the disarming impression that the ship was surging toward her, meeting her halfway.

A true ghost ship. A phantom of the deep, manned by the bodies of the dead.

Prickles spread across her skin as every hair on her body rose. The ship was utterly, overwhelmingly vast. They only had three dives to visit her. That wasn't enough time to cover even a quarter of the winding halls and narrow rooms.

"Same rules as last time." Vanna's voice, crisp and hard, startled through Cove's thoughts. "Dive ends when the first of us has reached 65 percent air. Signal me once you're at seventy so we have time to find our exits."

"Yeah, whatever you want," Roy muttered.

How he could be flippant at that moment, Cove could never understand. She'd climbed Everest. She'd stood at the base of trees that made her feel as small as an insect. She'd leapt from a plane, her life in the hands of a parachute strapped to her back.

Nothing compared to the awe-inducing dread the sight of the *Arcadia* inspired in her.

Nor had she ever felt so utterly cut off from the world.

If we die down here, our bodies may never be recovered.

The thought came out of nowhere, slamming into her and stealing her breath. It was the truth. Any single small mistake could leave her tangled in the wreck, sharing berth with the century-old bodies of the crew, and odds were that no one would be able to get her out.

You always pay, her father had told her once when she was a teenager. *When you go somewhere most people can't or try something dangerous, there is always a fee. You either pay with caution and a level head, or you pay with your life.*

They moved around the ship's bow like a school of large, sleek fish, following the safety line Vanna had laid the day before. Their path narrowed as they moved between the hull and the jutting rock wall. Ahead, Cove glimpsed the dark gash in the ship's side. They slowed as they neared it, straightening, hands lightly pushing the water to hold their balance.

Five sets of lights jittered over the dark chasm. The top half looked into the third-class berth they'd entered through the day before. Vanna's safety line vanished inside. It would continue through the open door and along the hallway, though Cove couldn't see that far.

The water was still muddied from the silt-out they'd caused the day before. It wasn't as bad—the thickest particles had started to settle—but the haze was still enough to block out anything more than two feet into the room. It wouldn't fully clear for another few days at least.

The floor cut through the middle of the gash: a hard, divisive line marking the difference between the decorated passenger quarters and the darker, steelier crew space below.

"Remember, speak when you reach 70 percent," Vanna said.

"Will do." Cove cut in before Roy could say anything. "See you both on the other side."

Vanna entered the room first. She moved with a grace born from years of navigating caves. Her movements created tiny swirls in the water-suspended sediment but didn't kick up anything fresh.

Hestie waited until Vanna's fins had begun to fade into the haze, then followed, slightly less coordinated and accompanied by slightly more agitation.

Cove let her gaze drift down. Her light didn't reach inside of the lower half of the gash so easily. All she could make out were dull metal walls.

A memory—the flash of motion, right on her periphery, gone when she looked at it—resurfaced. She drifted closer to the opening, her skin crawling, her throat tight, but as she dipped her head to see beneath the horizontal line, her headlight only managed to illuminate dark rivets in the walls and stacks of grim crates.

She raised one hand behind her and signaled to Roy and Aidan, then leaned forward and slipped inside.

22.

14 APRIL 1928

SIX DAYS BEFORE THE SINKING OF THE *ARCADIA*

The mist had entered the ship's lower decks.

It was thin enough that Harland couldn't see it unless he was facing down a long hallway, but he knew it was there.

The stench—wet wood, rotting sea life—always on his tongue, filling his lungs with every breath.

That alone would have been enough to send him mad.

But the sounds in the walls were growing bolder. Louder. Sometimes, if Harland pressed his ear against the cold steel, he could hear it far too clearly: broken fingernails digging at the metal, seeking a way out. He wondered if those clawing hands had left scars just out of sight, on the other side of the metal. The fingers must have been scored and worn, skin cracking, blood seeping—

Fitz, rubbing his hands on that cloth, smears of red across the fabric...

—and he questioned how far that trail of marks might extend.

He was scheduled to lead a quota of passengers to the dining hall, thirty of them from the port-side second-class passenger accommodation. That was their limit. Thirty passengers at a time. They would wait inside their rooms until he passed, knocking on each door, then follow him, silent as wraiths, for their meal.

At first, some of the louder passengers had complained. That had fallen off quickly. Everyone sensed just how precarious the ship was, and no one wanted to make the trip between the quarters and the dining room alone.

The first-class chef was missing, presumed dead. There was an increasing number of those: another eight men had failed to turn up for their shifts that morning. They couldn't be found in their bunks, and searches of the ship had largely been futile. Although Harland had been a part of the searches, he hadn't been there for the one recovery that *had* been made: a steward, found crammed into the narrow gap beside one of the boiler room furnaces. He'd been there for some hours and the heat had cooked the skin off his bones; identification came from a monogrammed handkerchief in the breast pocket of his uniform.

At first, the officers had believed it was murder. The boiler rooms were manned around the clock to keep the engines running; it seemed unfathomable that the steward could have accidentally fallen into the space beside the boiler without being heard. All stokers and coal trimmers who had been near the engine room that morning had been questioned. Other crew members had been asked to come forward if they had any knowledge of what had happened to the deceased.

The questioning had abruptly ended when the surgeon made his ruling: it was impossible for the steward to have been stuffed into the cramped space. The position of his arms indicated he had dragged himself inside.

The stokers testified that they would have most likely overlooked small amounts of noise and movement. The furnaces were loud, and the boiler rooms—like most other quarters on the ship—were home to rats; small disturbances were simply ignored as routine. However, they all insisted they would have heard screams. There had been none.

His fate had been by his own choice. Something had terrified him so fiercely that he had willingly crawled into a scorching death.

He had been the only one of the eight missing crew who could be recovered. Harland wondered how many of the others had gone overboard to be embraced by the chilled ocean and how many of them had found more creative hiding places, whose decomposing remains might be uncovered inside cupboards or under machinery weeks later.

The steward's death wasn't the only one that day. The surgeon reported that the stoker—the one who had torn apart the second-class bathroom—had stopped breathing during the early hours of the morning. It didn't come as a surprise to anyone, considering the blood he had lost.

Those two bodies had been wrapped in canvas and laid in a storage room designated as the temporary morgue. They were far enough away from the engines that the heat didn't reach them, but lay in the near-freezing temperatures of the outside world, it was as close as they could get to preserved until they reached port.

It was far from unheard of for deaths to occur on a liner. Not every passenger was in a fit state, and not every crew member stayed alert enough to remain aware of risks. But it was considered unlucky to have two deaths occur so close together, and for them to happen in such a grizzly way.

Harland was desperate to reach land, to escape the eternal fog and the ship that seemed bent on carrying them to their damnation.

He reached the end of his hallway and began retracing his steps, rapping on each of the doors as he passed. The passengers were ready. Doors creaked open and bleak, dull eyes pressed against the gaps to reassure themselves that he was one of the crew and not some imaginary phantom. Then, one by one, they stepped out and followed Harland as though he were some grim pied piper.

As Harland knocked on the hallway's final door, he glanced behind himself to take a head count. That stretch of hallway was supposed to contain exactly thirty passengers. His group was composed of less than that.

A faint idea occurred that he should return to some of the doors that hadn't opened and look inside.

To see what?

He imagined finding bodies in their beds. Couples huddled together perhaps. The lumpy figure of something that was once human hiding beneath blankets.

Or worse: he might open the doors to discover rooms that were perfectly empty. The passengers vanished, just like the eight missing crew members, leaving nothing but questions in their wake. Vanished to *where*? Might they eventually be found? Or were they just gone, their fates forever uncertain?

The first question resurfaced and danced inside his head. *Where could they go? Inside the walls?*

Harland twitched as he faced forward again. His group was less than thirty, but he wasn't going to stay to find out why. Instead, he moved forward with quick, hard steps. Men and women shuffled in his wake, their bodies pressed close enough to each other that their clothes rubbed together. It created a strange whirring noise, as if the hall was full of hissing insects bearing down on Harland.

The ship was a maze of hallways, but he knew them well enough to follow them in his sleep. That was a skill that was needed that day; more of the lights had gone out. Some parts of the hallway were still lit by sickly yellow bulbs, but they were separated by long stretches of grim shadows. Both Harland and his tow increased their speed as they moved through those darker areas. The whirring scratch of heavy jackets brushing against one another was nearly enough to mask the scrape of raw fingers from within the walls.

Ahead, where the passageway turned to the left, Harland glimpsed a band of crowded figures following the path Harland himself was taking. Another crew member was leading his own charges to the dining hall. Harland would have liked to catch up to them—they were only supposed to travel thirty at a time, but the quiet voice in the back of his head said it would be safer with more company—but they were moving almost as quickly as he was and were gone before he could get near.

Then, a lone figure turned the corner, this time moving in the opposite direction.

Harland squinted. That patch of the hall was dim; five out of the six lights were gone, and the only remaining light flickered plaintively. But he could have sworn he recognized the stooped figure. The too-long beard. The wild glint in shimmering eyes as Fitz glanced behind himself.

Already, the man's shuffling footsteps had faded. As far as Harland knew, Fitz should still be locked in his room. The officers had implied that he would be staying there until they made land.

Harland looked back at his trail of passengers. They had all come to a stop behind him. Pinched, pale faces and dark-ringed eyes stared into him. They showed no emotion, but Harland imagined a sentiment boiled underneath those blank canvases: resentment.

He moved forward again, only a step, then hesitated a second time. They were close to the dining room. And yet, he couldn't stop staring in the direction Fitz had vanished. That hall led toward the ship's bow. And he was fairly certain he could guess where the older stock master was headed.

Harland turned after him, stepping into the long stretch of hall that held no lights. The scratching, insect-like sound of scraping fabric followed him. None of the passengers had noticed that their route had diverted. Or perhaps they did not care; their eyes were glazed with the same exhaustion Harland himself felt. They would simply follow instructions until they dropped.

More lights appeared ahead, giving small patches of illumination along the wood-paneled halls, but Fitz had moved too far ahead to be visible. Harland could hear him though. Heavy shoes landed on metal stairs as the stock master climbed down.

Harland stopped at the top of the stairwell. He was breathing too hard, too fast.

How long has Fitz been out of his room?

He should tell someone. Except he was nowhere near any of the officers. They tended to cluster around the bridge those days, waiting on the captain's inevitable summons and the private meetings that sometimes resulted in hoarse, angry voices screaming at each other and the crash of breaking furniture.

In this part of the ship, Harland was alone. Below was the boiler room where the steward's baked body had been discovered. Fitz wouldn't be traveling there though. No. Harland already knew what the stock master's mind had fixed on.

The storage room. The blank metal wall. The scrape of finger-nails, clearer than anywhere else on the ship.

Harland hadn't returned there since Fitz had first shown it to him. The wall roused some deep, primal horror that overrode every logical part of his mind and filled his body with sickness.

But it also fascinated him. When he lay awake at night, waiting for his next shift to begin, his thoughts roved back to the strange, cold wall. And a dark private part of him longed to see it again. To touch the metal, perhaps, and see if he could feel the reverberations through it. To see what else he might hear at that point where the curtain between their world and the *other side* seemed thinnest.

He wanted to know that room as well as Fitz seemed to know it.

Harland stepped onto the narrow metal stairwell and began creeping down, a drum of footsteps in his wake.

23.

THE SECOND DIVE

"Oh," Cove murmured.

The passenger hallways had been narrow to the point of rousing claustrophobia, but these storage spaces beneath the waterline were a hundred times worse.

They'd entered into what had to be one of the holds. The *Arcadia* had four of them, all positioned to the front of the ship, while the boiler rooms took over from the midway point to the ship's rear.

While the *Arcadia* was known as an ocean liner, its human charges weren't the only valuables stored inside the ship. Passengers—merchants especially—would bring large quantities of almost everything on the voyage with them. The remainder of the ship's storage space was then sold to private individuals who would arrange for the goods to be picked up at the docks.

Cove had seen snippets of the manifest. It included everything from bulk cases of pencils and gum to artwork.

And while the pretense of luxury was maintained on the passenger decks, the cargo hold was treated like a game of Tetris. As long as the ship didn't compromise its seaworthiness with overloading—and it wouldn't have, with the passenger berths so comparatively bare—every unused foot of space in the holds was treated as lost money.

Cove's first impression was of a tangled forest made of crates and ropes. There were gaps between the stacks for the stewards and stock master to keep watch on the goods, but they were only just wide enough for a man to squeeze through. Everything had been lashed into place. When the stacks of boxes grew tall enough to be precarious, the space above them had been occupied by hanging nets full of more.

Roy whistled. "How much d'you think this all would've been worth?"

A lot. Cove didn't answer him, preferring instead to keep the comms unit open in case Hestie and Vanna needed to give instructions to each other while navigating the dust-clouded upper halls, but she knew any sinking like the *Arcadia*'s stole not only lives but fortunes. More than a few merchants and wealthy businessmen had filed for bankruptcy when a long-awaited shipment was lost to the ocean. It was a hazard they had all dreaded but was many times impossible to avoid.

Cove inhaled to rise to the nets' height, squinting as her headlight picked up layer upon layer of storage. She wasn't sure they could get through it. If they tried, there were reasonable odds that they would go blind from the dirt their efforts kicked up. But beyond this hold was a passageway that would lead them to the boiler rooms, and Cove had no guarantee that any of the other routes would get them to it any more easily…especially in the tight time frame they had.

She clipped her dive line to one of the nets next to the opening in the hull, then beckoned to Roy and Aidan. "Move carefully," she said. "Keep low; the nets will swing if they're bumped and give us an impromptu display of underwater snow. I'll try to pick a safe path, but tell me if you don't think you can fit. Yeah?"

"Yeah" came two replies.

Cove turned back to the storage room and pushed forward. In life, the walls would have held a solid line of storage, but the breach in the hull had torn enough free to allow Cove and her crew inside. She turned her body at an angle, legs straight out behind her and shoulders tilted to make her narrower, and eased herself between two blocks of crates. A logo was branded on their sides. Alcohol. She slowed just enough to capture some footage of it, then moved forward.

It was impossible to turn around far enough to check that her charges were following. She instead had to trust that they would call out if they became trapped. The mental image of collapsing crates invaded her mind. Boxes of heavy weights tumbling over the dark divers, pinning them in place, hiding them under tons of cargo.

She kept her fins still, letting her legs drift behind her, and instead used her hands to pull herself forward. The crates offered an abundance of handholds. Each time her gloves fixed into a crack or curled around an edge, a small plume of sediment broke free, but it was still better than the currents her kicking legs would create.

Occasionally, the gap between spaces narrowed until both sides of her shoulders and hips grazed the walls. Eventually, she had to rise to where the crates were replaced with suspended nets. She held her breath as she eased herself between them, trying her hardest not to bump any and set off a chain reaction.

From that higher vantage point, she glimpsed a watertight doorway in the distance and grinned as she dipped back down to move between the crates. They were more than halfway there.

Then Aidan's voice cut through the muffled quiet. "No—Roy—!"

Cove tried to turn. The gap was too narrow. Her shoulder hit one of the crates, sending a small cloud of dust into the air.

Roy began swearing. The suit's helmet and dampening effects of the water blocked out almost all of the outside world's noises, making it difficult to hear more than the rhythmic sounds of breathing coming through the communications systems and the low squeaks of synthetic materials and metals. Beneath that, though, she thought she heard a deeper noise. Something heavy, crashing as it fell through the water.

Cove turned, so she was upright, and pivoted. The stacked crates behind her were being swallowed in a silt-out. It merged through the room, swallowing everything in its path, and, as the dust washed over her, Cove had to repress the instinct to hold her breath. "Roy! Aidan! Speak to me."

"I'm okay, I'm okay." Aidan's voice was higher than normal, pained, and she could hear sounds of struggle. "A crate fell on me. But it's okay."

Fearful nausea came, quick and heavy. She fought the impulse to rush forward. Moving when visibility was this bad could only make things worse. Instead, she swallowed the metallic fear and called, "Aidan, are you pinned?"

"No." He was either trying to laugh or trying not to hyperventilate. "It just kind of…bumped me as it fell. Gave me a fright."

"Roy, what about you?"

"I'm fine, but damn. Sorry, Cove."

"Yeah." She tried to stay stationary by pressing one hand

into the box at her side, but the silt had robbed her of any sense of direction. No matter where she looked, all she saw was the disquieting blur of gray. "I think we're done with the hold for now. Roy, Aidan, do you both have ahold of the dive line? We'll follow it back out."

"Hang on." There was a moment of silence as Roy searched. The impenetrable dust felt like it was physically pressing on Cove, and she closed her eyes so she wouldn't have to feel it so acutely.

"I found it," Aidan said. "It's, uh, it's near the floor. Roy, can you find my hand?"

"Got it."

Okay. Getting out will be harder now that we can't see. But at least we have the line. At least we won't be trapped—

Then Roy said, "Uh," and Cove felt her heart drop.

"What is it?" She still held her position, but she couldn't tell if she was even facing up any longer. One of her legs bumped into a box, and she pushed away from it, only to feel her opposite shoulder nudge something hard.

"Hang on. Let me—Aidan, hold my shoulder. Don't let go. Let me just—"

A deep, grinding noise echoed through Cove's layers of protection. It sounded similar to the sounds that had reached her when the box first fell, only slower. She kept her eyes closed but could imagine fresh waves of sediment spreading around her. As though she weren't blind enough to begin with.

"Okay, we have a problem," Roy said. "It wasn't just one box that fell. It was, like…a lot of them. I can't find a way through."

Her tongue was dry and tacky as she ran it over the back of her teeth. "Do you still have the dive line?"

"Yeah." The heaviness in Roy's breathing told Cove he was still searching, clawing through the dust blindly as he hunted for a way through the fallen crates. "It's pinned to the floor. There might be a way around this. Maybe if I get to the ceiling I can—"

"Don't leave the line." Those words, harsh and fast, came from Vanna. Cove had forgotten that she would be listening in.

Roy didn't reply, but the sounds of struggling stilled.

Don't leave the line. Vanna, cave diver, would know that better than anyone. The ship's hold was dangerously disarming because it presented itself as *a room*. As long as they continued to think about it in that context, it could carry them into a false sense of security. Because who could become lost in a *room?*

Except, it wasn't a room. Not in the familiar sense. In a traditional room, Cove's feet would never leave the floor. If nothing else, she would have at least that one point of reference to orient herself to.

Here, free floating, she'd already lost context for which way she was facing. She could reach for a surface she thought was the floor and instead touch one of the walls or the ceiling. Gravity no longer weighed on her body in the traditional sense, and with every visual cue robbed from her, she wouldn't be able to correct that. Not even the tried-and-true diving method of following the direction of the bubbles to find the surface would help. Not when the bubbles vanished into the fog before she even got a second to look at them.

They were trapped. Surrounded by narrow passages of crates and hanging nets, their environment was closer to a cave than anything. Infinite new passageways led them in discordant directions, making their chances of finding their exit one in a hundred.

"I'm coming to find you," Vanna said. "Hold still until I get there."

Cove raised her wrist to get an oxygen reading from her dive watch, but even pressed against her mask, the water was too clogged to make out the numbers.

We have maybe an hour, hour and a half. That's enough time. Assuming Vanna can reach us. Assuming the collapsed crates haven't completely blocked us in.

"Aidan, Roy, follow the dive line to reach me." Cove was grateful that her voice sounded calm at least. "We need to keep hold of each other."

"Damn it," Roy muttered. Then, again, "Sorry."

"We're fine." *As long as we can get out. As long as Vanna can figure out a path to us. As long as...*

Cove blinked. A vague memory resurfaced. When she'd risen up to the nets to gauge their distance to the door, she'd noted that a line of them had been bunched together. Instead of containing crates, like most other storage containers in that hold, those nets had been packed with cloth packages. And they'd led almost perfectly to the rear wall.

"Vanna, I'm going to try to get us to a corner." Cove's fingers, still resting on the crate at her side, were shaking. "It should make it easier for you to find us."

"Good. It will help if I can follow a wall to reach you."

Cove kept her eyes closed as she tried to visualize their route. They'd been nearly three-quarters to the hold's rear wall.

The dive line attached to her belt shivered as Roy and Aidan picked their way along the cable to her. A large hand bumped her arm, and Cove managed to suppress a gasp. She felt through the void, and her own hand fastened on an elbow. "Roy?"

"Found you." Relief and barely concealed stress crackled through the words. "Aidan's in tow. He's got my shoulder."

"Good. Roy, hold on to my foot. We're heading up to the nets."

She tried to push in the direction she thought was *up*. Instead, she hit a crate. She was probably shaking all kinds of fresh particles into the water. That was one small mercy of being in such a severe silt-out: it was hard to make it worse.

Cove felt to her side and located one of the stacks. She traced along the boxes' edges, using them to guide her direction. Within seconds, her head bumped into one of the hanging nets. She pressed her fingers through the gaps in the netting. Soft material. Fabric, long waterlogged.

Vanna's voice crackled through the speakers. "Hestie, stop. I think the line's loose."

Cove reached for another net. It held smaller rectangular crates, and the difference in sensation was immediately noticeable. She pushed it away and felt for more.

Roy's hand was a steady pressure on her ankle. He was holding her slightly harder than he needed to, but Cove appreciated it. She needed to know they weren't about to lose contact. Even a brief slip of the hand could leave them grasping to find each other again. They weren't exactly deaf, but with the communications units unable to indicate which direction a noise was coming from, they may as well have been.

Vanna's voice came through again, tenser. "Cove, did any of your group touch my dive line before you entered the ship?"

She hung essentially upside down, one gloved hand clinging to the underside of the net as her other hand felt for a second. It took all of her focus, and Vanna's words reached her as though from far away. She needed a moment to focus on them. "Not that I saw. But I went in first."

Vanna clicked her tongue off her teeth. "Roy?"

"Hey, why are you singling me out? Aidan was behind me."

"I didn't do anything!" The boy was stressed and hiding it worse than any of them. "Wait, was I supposed to do something?"

"My dive line's untethered." Vanna didn't seem pleased about it. "Roy, if you tampered with it—"

"Jeez, I didn't, chill. Weren't you splitting away from us specifically to collect it, anyway?"

"Yes. But we needed to reach its end first—the end near the dining hall. That way we could rewind it without losing our guide out. But it's loose. It's either been pulled off the rock I tethered it to...or it was cut."

"Guess you couldn't have tied it off properly, then."

Cove was only keeping half an ear on the increasingly heated discussion. Her hand fixed around another net with soft contents. She used it to pull them forward as she hunted for a third. Every few seconds, she opened her eyes, as though that might do anything to help. All it managed was to flood her vision with a sheer wall of flashing gray specks. The constant motion bordered on making her nauseous, so she kept her eyes closed instead as she clawed them forward one foot at a time. "Vanna, are you still able to reach us?"

"Yes. I can remember our route. I should be back at the opening in the ship's side in about three minutes."

Another soft net. Cove dragged them forward, fighting to keep her breathing moderate even as the nausea swelled. The nets swung in response to her movement, bumping off each other, and Cove could only imagine what they must look like. Their bodies were probably dusted with heavy layers of silt shaken out of the nets, like some kind of sweet treat coated with powdered sugar.

One more net. They were getting easier to find. Whenever she pulled forward, Roy's large hand yanked on her ankle in the second it took him to match her speed. She knew she could trust him to call out if he'd lost his own charge, but her anxiety was too heady to stop her from double-checking. "Aidan, you still with us?"

"I think so."

That made her chuckle. In the maddening, blinding, sensory-depriving storage hold, it was hard to be sure of much of anything.

She stretched out a hand for one more net and instead touched something broad and solid. Cove brought their motion to a halt as she ran her hand across the surface. It wasn't another stack of crates; it was too large and smooth for that. A rivet under her hand confirmed that they had finally found the back wall.

Now, she just needed to keep them level with the nets and carry them left to reach the corner. It should be easy for Vanna to find them there. Then Vanna—or more importantly, Vanna's dive line, assuming it still worked even after being broken—could guide them out.

Aidan gasped, a sharp, shrill cry, before breaking out into choked laughter.

"What?" Cove asked. "What happened?"

"It's Vanna." He was still chuckling as his panic gave way to relief. "Give me some warning next time. You startled me."

Vanna's emotionless voice responded. "What do you mean?"

"That's you, right? Or is it Hestie? Someone's holding on to my foot."

The silence dragged out for what felt like an eternity. Then Vanna said, softly, "No. We're still on the higher floor."

24.

Moisture dripped down Harland's face. His first thought was sweat; his heart was pumping as though he'd run the length of the ship, instead of down a single flight of stairs, and every breath came rough and painful.

But it was too cold for this much sweat. He was in the lowest levels of the ship, with the boiler room too far behind him for its blazing furnaces to do much more than rattle the ship's walls. In among the storage holds, it was bitingly cold, and Harland's hands ached even through his gloves.

A trickle of liquid ran over his lip, and he licked it away. It tasted fetid. Like stagnant swamp water. Like rot and poison. *The mist.*

The halls were hazy with it. He'd thought it must have only made it into the passenger areas, where doorways and hatches gave it a chance to slink inside. But for it to penetrate this far down into the hull—

He'd lost sight of Fitz. But he knew where he would find the older man. The second hold on the port side. Sealed off like most compartments on this lower level with watertight doors. Something about making the ship safer in case of a collision. The shipyards had all but given up on the term *unsinkable* after one catastrophic failure a few months before Harland's eighteenth birthday.

He still led his compartment of guests. They hadn't questioned where they were going, but they had started to lag farther behind. When he twisted to look back at them, they were clustered at the other end of the hallway. The lights didn't have elegant sconces like on the passenger levels but were bare bulbs surrounded by metal brackets, and the four at that far side of the hall had all failed. Harland stared into the gloom, and the only trace of his guests was the dozens of glinting eyes staring, unblinking, back at him.

He pressed on. The second storage hold was close. He could hear noises coming from it. A scrape, a metallic whine. So similar to the sounds he heard through the walls when he was on the edge of sleep but magnified a thousand times.

The watertight door was closed. Harland pushed on the stiff handle. It shuddered and clattered as it turned. A faint hiss told him the seal around the door had been broken. He pushed on it, and the sounds became far, far louder.

It sounded like screaming metal. The pained whines were interspersed with a man's raspy, phlegmy gasps.

The lights in the storage hold were out, but a distant glow told Harland that Fitz had brought a lamp. He left the door open, so the hallway's lights could guide his steps, and moved in.

Something made of heavy metal groaned. The reverberations spread through the floor beneath Harland. His shoulders became wedged between two stacks of crates, and he had to shove them to create an inch more room. The lamp's glow was growing closer though. And the mist was growing thicker.

"Shh, my beauty. Wait a moment, dear one."

That was Fitz's voice but gentle and beseeching in a way Harland had never heard it before. He had the stark impression that the man was trying to coax something wild and panicked out of hiding.

And then came the groan of strained metal breaking apart.

Harland stepped around the last layer of crates. He was panting, suffocating in the air that was somehow achingly humid and ice-cold at once.

Fitz stood by the wall he'd shown Harland days before. He'd stripped off his outer layers, until he wore just an undershirt and linen pants. They were both filthy, yellowed from sweat and dotted with stains from his cracked fingers.

He'd crudely bandaged his hands, but the cloth was past due for changing. It had started to unwind from its knots, and straggly ends hung down to his elbows, exposing patches of yellowed skin. Stains had bled through and dried, and brighter spots from fresh bleeding marred the edges.

If the cuts hurt Fitz, he didn't show it. Instead, he held a metal bar that had been fashioned into a sharp point at one end and wedged it into the metal wall as he pried the plates off. The heavy metal screamed as he leveraged it out, and a rivet, pushed past its limit, popped free.

Harland was gasping, mouth open, on the edge of suffocating. "What…" Drips of moisture trickled over his cheek and entered at the corner of his mouth. He swallowed it. "Fitz…don't."

The older man glanced over his shoulder at Harland, and his lips pulled back into a wide, eager grin. "You made it. Good. You need to see. Everyone needs to. Just wait…just wait…"

He shoved against his homemade crowbar, thin, wiry muscles straining under the yellowed shirt, and the plate of metal bowed farther out.

Harland was watching his friend tear apart a wall. The *hull* wall. The only thing between them and an infinity of seawater. He needed to stop him. But his body wasn't working right. He felt numb, his head too heavy, his arms too light. He could only watch as the walls peeled outward like a tin being opened.

Footsteps ran toward them. Distantly, Harland registered the voices of two officers. He knew this could become bad. Fitz would be sentenced back to confinement—or worse. And Harland himself would be treated as an accessory to the crime, simply because he hadn't tried to stop it. But the mist was inside him, inside his *head,* and he was incapable of anything more than staring, wild-eyed, at how the lamplight flashed over the peeling metal.

"Belay that!" an officer called, shoving through the crates. Harland was jostled as the man pushed past him and nearly lost his balance. Fitz turned, his lips pulled back to expose narrow, yellowed teeth in a snarl as he raised the sharpened metal bar. The officer pulled back just out of reach, and the two of them wavered, both waiting for the other to make the first move.

Then a deeper, calmer voice spoke: "Stop. All of you."

It took Harland a second to recognize the speaker. Then he turned, slow and full of dread.

The passengers he'd inadvertently lead into the lower levels had followed him into the hold. They were positioned around the edges of the cleared section, their backs against the crates, their faces expressionless and cold. In the dim light, they seemed to blend into the storage as though they belonged there. The cargo and the passengers, together. None of them made any sound but simply waited.

Three officers and a half dozen sailors had joined the growing crowd, and more filtered in through the gaps in the stacked crates. Someone had seen Harland take the wrong passageway and had raised the alarm. Or perhaps his group had been noticed as missing at dinner and a search party established.

At the growing crowd's head stood Captain Virgil. He seemed neither shocked nor angry, but instead his cold eyes took stock of the state of the wall as though he'd been expecting something like this the whole time.

"You found something?" he asked Fitz.

Fitz only grinned. "Aye, Captain."

Captain Virgil nodded, an instruction for him to continue. The officers stepped back to take their places behind the captain. Fitz, still holding his sharpened bar raised, turned and stabbed it back into the gap in the wall.

They all watched, as though hypnotized, as the metal was peeled back an inch at a time. The bandages around Fitz's hands grew more ragged and more discolored, but he dug with the desperation of a starving man being offered food. A string of spittle flew from his clenched jaws as he pried the bar into the metal again and again, and the hull was filled with nothing but the dull hum of heavy breathing and the scream of tortured metal.

Then the metal panel fell away entirely. They had exposed the second layer of hull—the final barrier between them and the ocean. A gap had been created between the two walls, less than a foot wide, segmented with frequent crossbars of metal: a safeguard against leaks.

Fitz had exposed a span of exterior hull four feet by five feet. And, inside, he had revealed a shriveled, twisted corpse.

25.

THE SECOND DIVE

Hestie held her breath, her ears ringing with Aidan's voice, which grew increasingly frantic: "Who is it? Who's holding my foot? *Cove?*"

Cove's own voice remained unexpectedly smooth. "Stay calm, Aidan. It's most likely a rope that's become tangled—"

"They won't let go." His fear was turning to panic, his breathing becoming ragged, and Hestie imagined him thrashing as he tried to break free.

"Ow—hey, stop—" from Roy.

"Aidan, relax—"

"*Make them let go—*"

Hestie shot a look to her companion. Vanna hung in the hallway just ahead of her, as motionless as a statue, one end of the dive line clasped in her glove. Hestie couldn't read the woman's expression through her mask, but every muscle in her body seemed to have become tense as she listened to the exchange.

Roy's voice rose, almost painfully loud. "Aidan, hey! Stop clawing at me!"

Then Cove: "Relax, Aidan. Breathe. Nothing's going to hurt you."

He was no longer speaking, only breathing in urgent, panicked gasps.

Hestie swallowed. She didn't dare speak. This far away from the hold, there was nothing she could do to help except stay silent and pray the three trapped divers could work through it.

Then Roy's voice, louder yet again, making Hestie wince as he bellowed: "I said *cut it out.*"

The words were accompanied by a sharp hiss, then, abruptly, the communications unit went silent. Hestie waited, her own breath held, for an update. None came. As the seconds stretched out, she realized she couldn't hear *anything* through the unit, not even breathing.

Did the audio system break? Did Roy overload it? Surely not...

"Hello?" she tried. The word sounded hollow in her own ears. There was none of the subtle echo that the unit normally created, just herself, in her own bubble.

Ahead, Vanna raised a hand to gain her attention. She tapped the side of her head, where the unit was built in, and then swished her hand in a sideways motion: *no sound.*

Hestie nodded, then pointed down. *Are we going to find them?*

A single, firm nod from Vanna, then the dive instructor turned back to the hallway.

The team normally avoided speaking unless they had something important to communicate, and much of the dive had already been spent in silence, but this felt different. Her sense of connection to the others was gone.

Hestie's stomach churned. The hallway felt too calm, too

serene after the rising panic that had come through the audio. The old-fashioned wallpaper and wood paneling surrounded her in a surreal cocoon. She'd felt the sensation before: as though she'd been transported into a different dimension. A dimension that looked very similar to her own but was deeply, fundamentally *wrong*.

Vanna glanced over her shoulder to check that Hestie was keeping up. She swam with her body inclined fully forward, straight and smooth, only the swish of her fins propelling her forward. Hestie raised one hand in the universal *okay* sign.

She felt very far from okay though. The other half of their team was only separated from them by a single floor, but it might as well have been the other side of the world.

Shreds of loose wallpaper shivered in tiny eddies as they moved forward. With just her and Vanna to light the hall, the darkness seemed that much deeper, the layered shadows more intense. The water was still heavy with silt from the previous day's dive—not as much as they were dealing with in the hold, but particles had floated in through the open cabin door and now hung like flakes of dust in the air, reflecting Hestie's lights back at her and making anything in the distance feel vague and clouded.

The door can't be far. We'll be out soon—for better or worse.

Vanna had wound her dive cord back into her belt. Hestie had tried to get a look at the end to tell whether it had been severed or had simply come loose from its tethering point. If Vanna had been using a cheap cable or some kind of homemade rig, Hestie could have easily imagined it snapping as it rubbed against the ragged metal along the edge of the gash in the ship's hull. But Vanna was a cave diver, and her gear was some of the sturdiest money could buy. Hestie couldn't imagine her using anything less than professional dive line—and the cord was designed to hang over sharp coral or rocks for months without fraying.

Plus Vanna didn't strike her as the kind of person who would be flippant with the tethering. But unlike Vanna, Hestie couldn't imagine anyone else on their dive tampering with it. Roy was loud and could become abrasive, but he wasn't cruel. And Aidan was so fearful of upsetting the crew that he wouldn't in a million years touch anything he hadn't been instructed to.

They'd followed the dive line as far as the massive dining room entrance. The left door was still open a crack, the way they'd left it, and Hestie had willed herself not to look through, but her self-control had been weak. Was the body still floating where they'd left it, up near the balcony? Had it fallen to the floor? Was it hidden between the clustered tables and chairs, or had it come to rest on top of one of them?

She'd only managed a brief glance before turning away, and the narrow band of view had failed to provide her answers. The cathedral-like dining hall had been clouded from the disturbance and was too dark to make out any shapes beyond one of the nearer tables.

Vanna had clipped the discarded dive line onto her belt and began rewinding it as they retraced their path. That was when she'd noticed the cable was looser than it should have been. A quick tug brought it snaking to her without resistance. Her expressions were hidden under the mask, but it hadn't been hard to picture her lips tightening and eyebrows descending.

We'll be out in a moment. For better or worse.

At least Hestie, despite the way her heart thundered and her mouth had turned dry, wasn't in any danger. Even without the dive line, they had a very clear path back outside. She was fairly certain that, once they were out, Vanna would signal for Hestie to stay put as she entered the hold to search for the others.

From there, it would be a simple waiting game.

Simple. The word seemed fundamentally wrong. Nothing would be simple about drifting in the near-freezing ocean, entirely cut off from the others, unable to see or hear the humans she had been sent down with. Waiting to see if they came back out. Waiting to see *how many* came back out. Aidan had been frantic. That would sap his oxygen like nothing else.

They still had the backup canisters: Vanna had tied their two spares to the same outcrop where she'd tethered the dive line. And at least, unlike the dive line, the canisters couldn't just drift away. Maybe Hestie could retrieve one and hold it as she waited outside the ship, in case it was needed. It was as close to useful as she could be.

Vanna came to a halt, straightening with a gentle sweep of her arms, and Hestie snapped out of her reverie. There was no reason for Vanna to stop prior to reaching their exit. She craned to see ahead. The doors in that part of the hallway were all closed.

Some cold emotion entered Hestie's bloodstream, chilling her further than the layers of dry suit and wool should have allowed. She'd been so utterly focused on keeping pace with Vanna's fins that she hadn't paid much attention to where they were going or *how far* they were going.

They should have reached their door already.

A long time before, actually.

Vanna's blank mask faced her, unreadable, uncomfortably silent. Hestie tried speaking, even though she knew the audio was still out. "Vanna?"

No answer. Not that there could be one. The other woman just stared at her, silent, arms moving in languid arcs as she held balance.

Hestie turned. The hallway behind her was still clouded, making it impossible to see more than fifteen feet, but all of the doors within view were closed.

The tether was supposed to lead us out. The tether that was now wound tightly in Vanna's belt.

That shouldn't have meant they were lost though. They just needed to retrace their steps. Down one flight of stairs, turn left, turn right, and follow the hallway.

It should have been impossible to miss their exit. The door had been open and the room was rife with silt, clearly disturbed. They should have reached it before now. She was certain the hallway hadn't been that long when they'd first come through it.

And she would have noticed if they'd passed an open door, wouldn't she? *I was distracted. Wrapped up in my thoughts and my anxiety, not paying enough attention to my environment. A stupid thing to do this far underwater, even on a good day.*

She looked over her shoulder. Vanna had moved closer. Close enough to touch. Hestie licked parched lips, dearly wishing that they hadn't lost their communication units.

They were in the right hallway, she was certain. The path had been too straightforward for them to end up in the wrong section. Though, the decor wasn't helping. The halls were all filled with the same dark paneling, intricately carved but the details lost under the sediment, beneath strips of wallpaper that had faded and loosened and shredded into the free-floating strips that reminded her so deeply of cobwebs. She was sure there had to be unique features, but everything blurred together so perfectly that she could have been on any part of that level or the one above and not been able to tell.

This is fine. We'll backtrack. If we missed the door, we'll find it. If we somehow entered the wrong hall, we only need to return to the dining room to orient ourselves. We clearly made a mistake, but it shouldn't be hard to correct.

It wasn't as though the door could have been closed since they last passed through it a mere fifteen minutes before.

Something cut the rope though...

The thought startled her. Until then, she'd been close to convinced that the tether had been somehow pulled free from where it was tied. But now the idea burrowed itself inside of her, like some kind of insidious insect, and it wasn't coming out.

*Something cut the rope...something cut the rope...some*one *cut the rope...*

Hestie turned sharply, beckoning for Vanna to follow. They were going to retrace their steps. Hestie would lead, and she would count every single door they passed.

As her headlight washed over the seemingly endless walls and the shreds of gently billowing paper, she realized this was her first time at the head of the group. She'd always been more comfortable following, and the natural leaders—Cove and Vanna—had always gone first.

She wasn't sure she liked being at the front. She glanced behind herself once to check that Vanna was in her wake. She was: a sleek, faceless presence, arms loose at her side, body undulating in minute rhythms as she followed. Hestie faced forward again. Within seconds, the urge to look back once again began to itch at her. She repressed it. Glancing over her shoulder too often would only make her appear on edge. Diving teams were about trust. She had to trust that Vanna was keeping pace, that she wasn't turning down a different path.

Or edging closer.

A second intrusive thought, this one even harder to dismiss. She pictured Vanna in her mind's eye. Faceless, voiceless, those powerful legs moving just a little faster as she gained ground.

Reaching a hand toward Hestie's ankle. Careful, silent, eyes focused and unblinking like a shark's.

No, it wasn't just her imagination. She could *feel* it. A slight resistance to the water as her feet glided through it. Something was there, not yet touching her, but so close that it disturbed the water's perfect stillness.

Don't look back.

She was gasping, her lungs burning, her mind turning blind with the cutting fear. If she turned back, it would happen. The hand would fasten around her leg. Pull her back, deeper into the abyss. Into the dark. Where she would never be seen again.

"*El—no—*"

Hestie gasped as an involuntary twitch shook her. A distant voice crackled through her headgear. Masculine, she thought, but it was so badly distorted by static that she couldn't tell if it came from Roy or Aidan.

She hung still for a second, waiting, but only the deep emptiness answered her.

"Hello?"

The dull, echoless silence confirmed the connection had been lost. She closed her eyes, breathing slowly, willing her wild heart to calm. It wouldn't. It *couldn't*. She twisted to face the woman behind her.

Vanna had also come to a halt. The unreadable, blank sheen of glaring plastic marked where a face belonged. Hestie's stomach twisted into knots. It was worse than facing an empty hallway. She was facing something alive, something sentient, but it barely looked human.

Eyes flashed through the gloom. Not Vanna's though. *Behind* Vanna. Hestie opened her mouth, the useless words dying on her tongue before she even knew what they were.

Something hung in the hallway's gloom fifteen feet behind the dive instructor. Hestie's headlight only grazed the edges of the dark shape. In between them was water thick with particles, blinding Hestie to the point where she couldn't so much as guess what she was looking at.

But she'd seen eyes. Sheer white, like an animal's. Flashing.

Flecks in the water. That's all. Two large flecks catching your light and frightening you.

She wished she believed her own reassurance. Instead, she fumbled for the spare flashlight she kept in her belt.

Vanna, poised between her and the presence, tilted her head to one side. Her back was to the disturbance. She hadn't seen it.

Hestie pulled the light from her belt and switched it on. The beam flickered once, then settled. She raised it, holding it near her head so its light would pass over Vanna's shoulder.

It was less help than she'd wanted. The tens of thousands of tiny specks filling the hallway lit up brighter, but the two beams combined could barely reach much farther. But a sliver more hallway came into focus. Just enough for Hestie to see that it was empty.

See? It's nothing. Flecks in the water. Your own mind, painting phantoms.

Vanna glanced to where the light was pointed, staring down the endless length of closed doors and shredded wallpaper, then looked back at Hestie: a wordless question. Hestie tried to smile. Her lip, too dry, cracked. She licked across the stinging mark and tasted blood.

In the second she'd raised the flashlight, she'd thought she saw movement. Just a fraction. One of the hallway doors, the doors that had been shut for a century and would likely remain that way for a century more…closing.

That was as much a fantasy as the flashing eyes. Except for the tiny swirling blot of sediment where she thought she'd seen the motion.

A burst of air gushed from her rebreather, sending sparkling, dancing bubbles up and at a slight angle. Her rebreather's natural purge happened infrequently enough that it shocked her. She waited as the bubbles cleared from her vision and vanished into the dark corners of the hall. Then she lowered the flashlight, switching it off and preparing to return it to her belt.

A deep, aching, groaning sound rose from the vessel's metal. The water seemed to shake with it. The sound traveled the ship's length, rising first from the hallway behind Vanna and then rushing past Hestie and toward the bow. Even with the muffling dive suit and headgear, the sound was deafening.

Trails of dust shook free from the ceiling. Vanna's head tilted up, watching the walls, waiting. Hestie held her breath. The noise faded into the far distance, to be replaced by the slow ticking sound of metal settling back into place.

The communications units crackled. Roy's voice, sharp and terse, broke through the static: "What the *hell* was that?"

26.

"Roy?" Hestie reflexively reached out a hand. Her gloved fingers fell between the layers of peeled wallpaper and she pulled back. "Can you hear me?"

"He-ey!" His tone immediately brightened. "We're back! Hestie, what's good, girl?"

She wasn't entirely sure how to answer that but managed a weak laugh instead. "What, uh—is Aidan—"

"We're okay." This new voice was Cove's. It was still distorted, still crackling, but clear enough to be familiar. "Aidan was tangled in a rope. He panicked. But we're out of the storage hold now."

"Outside the ship?" Vanna asked.

Hestie found the audio to be unexpectedly uncomfortable. Vanna still floated ahead of her. The woman barely moved save for microcorrections to hold her position. She was so still that it created a disconnect with the voice; Hestie *knew* she had spoken, but with no face and no movement, it was comparable to trying to convince herself that a mannequin had said the words. Just very slightly unreal.

Cove answered: "No, we're still inside the *Arcadia*. I found the back wall and followed it to a door. We just got through. The water's clearer here, so we can actually see where we're going now. Are you out?"

"No," Vanna said.

There was a second of uncomfortable silence. Hestie cleared her throat and filled in the gap. "We're trying to find the cabin we came in through. But it's like it's not here anymore."

"It can't just walk away," Roy said. "Retrace your steps and—"

"That's the thing. We did. I'm pretty sure we're in the right hallway, but without the dive line, we can't find the door."

"It could have drifted shut," Roy said. "Like, with the currents or whatever."

No currents in the gulf. Hestie ground her teeth.

"It might have something to do with the audio loss," Cove suggested. "Or that movement we felt a moment ago. Our presence could be causing the ship to settle, and it's affecting the environment. Regardless, we're ending the dive for obvious reasons."

Aidan. Panicked because he felt a hand on his ankle. It was just a rope, most likely, but it's not safe for him to continue the dive.

Cove's voice was like a salve on Hestie's raw nerves as she took charge. "We're still on the lowest levels, somewhere between the holds and the boiler rooms. The gap in the hold is a no-go, so we'll be looking for a way up to the higher levels, where we'll attempt to meet up with you. While you wait for us, try to find a way out. Either the berth we came in through or an alternative. Worst-case scenario, we can always get out through the dining hall's ceiling."

"Nope." Roy made a small noise of disgust. "I'm not going near *that* thing again."

"Which is why Hestie and Vanna will look for another way

out." There wasn't a trace of stress or irritation in her voice, which Hestie thought was something akin to a superpower.

"I'll tie the dive line to the stairs outside the dining hall," Vanna said, cool and remote as ever. "If we lose contact again, follow the line to find us."

"Good. We'll do that."

As the communications fell silent, Hestie chewed her lip. The paranoia was rising again. Cove had said they were fine. But she hadn't heard Aidan's voice—at all. If something had happened to him, and if he'd been left in the storage hold, would Cove had told them? Or would she have deemed it safer to keep the news quiet until they surfaced?

Stop it. That's ridiculous.

Still, the fear began to dig at her and wouldn't stop digging. Against her better judgment, she blurted, "Hey, Aidan, are you feeling okay?"

"Yeah, I'm good." He sounded weak. As though he barely had enough breath to keep moving. But he was still there. Hestie closed her eyes, both unceasingly grateful and embarrassed that she would have even thought otherwise.

"C'mon, man," Roy said. "Don't cry."

"I'm *not*." It came out high and hiccuping, like a child trying to protest their innocence. Aidan must have heard what it sounded like too because he cleared his throat and attempted to correct it in a deeper, louder voice. "I'm not." The result was only half-successful. Roy sighed.

Hestie slowly turned to examine the hallway behind her. The waterborne silt and shredded wallpaper confused her eyes. Vanna still waited behind her, but if she hadn't been there, Hestie wasn't certain she could have remembered which direction they had come from.

Cove gave us a mission. Find the right cabin or find an alternative. The cabin would be the simplest, surely; we know for certain that we can get out through it if we can just find it.

She was struggling to think clearly and checked her dive watch to buy herself some time. Her oxygen was already down to 68 percent. Even if Cove hadn't called an end to the dive, her anxious consumption of air would have forced an end.

Okay. How do we find the berth? We could retrace our steps to the dining hall, then follow the path back down. If we missed it the first time, that would make it impossible to miss again, surely.

She opened her mouth to suggest that next step to Vanna, but the diving instructor was no longer looking at her.

While the cabin doors along that stretch of hall were all closed, one of the doors to the ship's internal areas was still open. Vanna stared into it. Without turning her head, she raised one hand and beckoned to Hestie.

Her tongue was tacky. She tried running it over her lips, but that only started the split in her lower lip stinging again. She moved closer to the dive instructor, until their shoulders were nearly bumping, and followed her gaze through the narrow doorway.

It was a bathroom. The mirror above the sink reflected their blank, unnervingly dark faces back at them.

Hestie's headlight flashed across a web of broken tiles along the walls and floor. She recognized this room. They'd gazed into it shortly after entering the ship on their first dive.

A small, choked chuckle escaped her as she nudged off the doorframe to look around Vanna's broad shoulders. They were in the right hall after all. Not only that, but the berth they needed had to be close. Just along the hallway, near…

The door I saw drifting closed. The eyes. Not real. But they seemed real.

"Let's look for another way out." The words came before she could judge their rationality. She committed to them though, grasping the small amount of relief the idea presented. "Higher levels will have larger windows. The water pressure would have broken them. It shouldn't be hard to, to, uh, find a different way—it might be easier, even—"

She didn't know why she was trying to explain herself. Vanna gave a single mute nod and gently nudged past Hestie so she could take the lead. Hestie, grateful to not have to be in front any longer, fell into place behind. Unlike Hestie, Vanna didn't seem to feel the constant urge to look back every few seconds. She supposed she had more practice at it. A caving instructor with four thousand dives must have done this so often that she could handle it in her sleep.

Then Vanna twisted just enough to glance over her shoulder, and Hestie suppressed a smile. Perhaps not. Perhaps the instinct to check on your charges was something a person never completely got over.

They followed the hall to reach the stairs. Again, Vanna led the path up them, gliding above the dark, clouded steps like some mythical being. The ceiling cut her headlights off from Hestie's view, and she was abruptly very grateful they were diving in teams. That second when Vanna's lights vanished gave Hestie a taste of what it might be like to be in the *Arcadia* alone. With only a single circle of illumination to guide her way, she was close to blind. One disk of view, immediately ahead. Darkness pressing in on both sides.

She'd had a recurring nightmare very similar to that when she was a teenager. Something enormous and monstrous was chasing her, but she couldn't get a good look at it because her vision had reduced it to a tiny circle. The more she searched for her hunter, the smaller the circle got, until it was just a pinprick of vision in an unceasing expanse of black.

The memories of the nightmare hit her harder than they might have on land. Hestie drew a sharp breath and rushed up the stairwell, nearly colliding with Vanna's legs as she exited at the top.

If she'd startled Vanna, the woman didn't show it. She simply unfastened the end of her dive line from her belt and began weaving it around one of the bannisters at the top of the stairs. Then she drew it across the stairwell, tying the end onto the second bannister. That effectively created a rope blocking the stairs. It would still be easy for a diver to pass over or under, but it made the cord unmissable.

As she tied the knot, Vanna's helmet tilted toward Hestie. It seemed like something of a challenge. *See? I know my knots. I'm not leaving it loose. My tethers don't come undone on their own.*

Hestie gave a small smile before remembering her face was all but invisible and made the okay symbol instead. Vanna fell still, almost as though she'd been surprised, then gave an okay in return. Hestie, grinning despite herself, let her body drift away from the stair's edge as she waited for Vanna to finish the knots.

She'd promised herself she wouldn't look into the dining hall again. The left-hand door was only open a crack—enough for a glimpse, nothing more—and besides, she hadn't seen anything on the first pass down.

But for the second time, she found it impossible to stop herself. It was the door itself, she thought; fully open, it wouldn't have been such a lure. But its gap was only just wide enough for a human to squeeze through. It teased at the corners of her eyes. Drew her toward it.

She turned just enough to let her light flash through. She only let her glance last for a second—any more and Vanna might guess her morbid curiosity. Hestie turned her back to the door again as Vanna finished tying the dive line and straightened.

She was grateful for the masks then. They hid her expression. Vanna wouldn't be able to see the wildness she was sure must be in her eyes or the way her skin had gone cold or the blood beading at the place she'd cracked her lip.

Vanna wouldn't guess what she'd seen through the door, and she wanted to keep it that way.

Their headlights flashed across the hall's age-dulled wood and the shards of peeling paint gradually separating from the ceiling. A gush of air left Vanna's rebreather, racing above and away until Hestie's light couldn't follow it any farther.

Vanna pointed to the stairs leading up and to the hallways leading away. It was a question: Which direction did Hestie want to try first? She didn't need to think about the answer and pointed to the hallway. The stairs would carry them up alongside the dining hall. Maybe even allow them access to the curtained balcony booths.

They had already ventured down the hallway to the right; it had brought them to the blockade of furniture and the strange scrawled message.

But the hallway to the left had only been partially explored by Hestie herself on the first dive. From what she'd seen, the remainder of it was clear. It should lead them to another stairwell eventually. And, hopefully, to windows large enough to swim through.

Vanna moved first, circling the stairwell's bannister, the dive line unwinding itself from the clip on her belt and floating in gentle arcs in her wake. Hestie followed, trying to keep her rough breathing quiet enough that it wouldn't disturb the others.

Through the narrow gap in the door, she'd glimpsed the drowned man. He'd been neither up near the balconies nor down on the floor, like she'd imagined. Instead, the form had hung just above the tables. His body was slightly curled, knees pulled up, feet pointing downward from loose ankles. His arms had drifted near his torso, the fingers slightly curled. The thin shimmer of hair hung about his head like a cloud. The pose wasn't wound as tight as a fetal position, but it was a memory of it.

He'd hung suspended above the tables, in the room's center. As Hestie's headlight flashed through the narrow gap, it had illuminated him in awful, grotesque clarity. His skin was marbled with unnatural, off-white lumps. His clothes drifted about him, weightless and dull. She could have sworn she'd seen his eyes beneath the heavy lids and that they'd flashed. Just like the eyes from down the hallway.

She hoped they would never have to go near the dining hall again.

27.

Harland had never tasted the stinking, sticking fog as acutely as he did at that moment, as the body was revealed in the wall.

It wasn't one of the missing crew members. Or one of the likely missing passengers. Unlike the unfortunate steward found beside the furnaces, this body hadn't died within the last few days.

A mummy. He'd seen photos of them in the history books he'd never been able to afford at the nicer stores. The body was shriveled and black. Its knees were drawn tightly to its chest, its chin resting on top, cramped hands coiled around. The mouth was open and the lips had receded, leaving rows of yellow teeth and black gums visible. The teeth looked almost too fragile to still be embedded. Harland thought, if he just gave one a tap, it would pop right out of its socket and clatter across the metal floor.

Unlike the mummies in the expensive picture books though,

this one had hair and clothes. At least, Harland thought they were clothes. They were the same dark color as the skin. The color of dried meat.

He turned aside so that he wouldn't be sick.

"There." Fitz was gasping. Bright color, forced by the exertion, turned his face blotchy. He threw the makeshift crowbar aside and staggered backward, forcing officers and two of the stray passengers to step aside so he wouldn't touch them. "There. That's it. That's the thing causing all this. The body in the walls."

Harland had a flash of realization. Fitz had said that shipyard workers died while constructing the *Arcadia*. That wasn't unheard of now and would have been even more likely back when the *Arcadia* was first constructed. Fitz believed the deaths had done more than simply cost a man his life though. Fitz thought the deaths had somehow painted the *Arcadia* in blood. That the ship was cursed from them—cursed and doomed to carry the crew and passengers down to a wet grave.

He wondered how it must have happened. The ship's interior walls had been laid first, and the outer wall—the second layer of skin—applied on top. A narrow gap had been left between the two, with the idea that damage to the outer wall wouldn't always compromise the inner layer.

As the walls were built higher and higher, it could have been very easy for a worker to lose his footing and fall between them. His fall might not have been noticed. Or—a worse thought—maybe it had, but he hadn't been very well liked, so they just left him.

The foreman would have noticed one fewer worker turning up the following morning. Not an exceptional circumstance in the shipbuilding business. It would have simply taken a few more days before he was removed from the payroll.

Did he die straightaway? Hit his head on the way down and bled

out? Or was he alive for a bit, stuck and with no way to get free? The
way he's sitting would have made it hard to get much air. No room
in his lungs to scream.

Fitz, apparently satisfied, turned away from his work and
shoved through the crowd. He passed close enough to Harland
that, for a second, the reek of sour sweat and bile cut through
the unceasing fog and stung his nose. Fitz slapped his hand onto
Harland's shirt to get his attention. The watery blue eyes danced
with fever. "You know now, boy. This is why it's happening."

Then he slipped past, disappearing into the crowd as he moved
back into the ship. Captain Virgil showed no sign that he wanted
to stop him, and the officers wouldn't move without an order.
Apparently, Fitz was no longer going to be contained in his berth.

Harland glanced down at his shirt. Fitz's hand had left an
imprint. A smear of dirt and grease, but more prominently, a
hundred tiny spots from where his saturated bandages had
pressed against the fabric. Harland knew, at that moment, he
would not try to salvage the cloth. He'd carry it with him when
he next went on watch and discard it over the ship's side.

There were very quiet whispers passing between the passengers. Harland tried to catch who was speaking or even some of
the words, but they eluded him. Everywhere he looked were
blank, sallow faces and cold eyes, all faced in the same direction:
the mummified corpse that had been living inside their ship.

The whispers were growing in intensity though. A quiet,
paranoid part of Harland's mind said he needed to know what
was being said. But the words were overlapping as a dozen voices
spoke at once, like a harsh wind cutting through trees, the leaves
all scratching together in a deathly rattle.

"Quiet."

At Captain Virgil's word, the whispers immediately ceased.

The silence that followed was somehow a hundred times worse. Now, the only things Harland could hear were their quiet breathing and the slow, aching groan of the ship's hull straining in the choppy water.

Harland bit his tongue to hold himself silent. The rasping breaths came from every direction: behind him, beside him, and worst of all, ahead, where the cleared floor led to the hole in the interior walls.

The corpse isn't breathing. It's not. It can't.

He hunted across its chest, looking for any sign that the shriveled remains were moving. The body's eyelids were almost entirely closed but not completely, he realized. There was a tiny crack in the lids, like a man who was feigning sleep so he could watch his companions. Beneath, Harland could only see darkness.

Captain Virgil had been standing as still as the others, simply regarding the pitiful creature in the walls with cold, unfeeling eyes. Abruptly, he drew a deep breath and let it out as a sigh, disturbing their tenuous quiet. "Remove it," he said. "Store it in one of the other holds. We will not speak of this again."

And then he turned and left. Crates and tethered boxes creaked as he pressed between the stacks.

It took a second for the officers to respond. One stepped forward first, gingerly edging nearer to the blackened remains. Another picked up Fitz's discarded crowbar, then looked at his hands in disgust, apparently having felt the moisture Fitz had left on the metal.

A third tipped bundles of expensive fabric out of a cloth bag, leaving them scattered over the hold's floor, and brought the bag nearer so that the body could be transferred into it.

Harland wanted to look away from the macabre sight but found it impossible to turn aside as the crowbar was wedged behind the body. It had been fused to the external walls, and the skin made an awful sticking, ripping noise as it came away in increments.

Someone should have directed the passengers back upstairs, he thought. That job should most likely have been his. But he made no move to leave or to shepherd the watching crowd. They, like him, were transfixed.

A tearing noise echoed through the room. The body dropped down, hitting one of the walls as it was hurriedly shoved into the bag.

But not the entire body. Part of it had been left behind: a layer of skin, still affixed to the wall, a black scar in the approximate shape of a coiled-up human.

The officer carrying the bag cinched the opening tight, sealing the corpse inside. He'd barely finished when the noises started again.

Fingertips: tapping, scraping, clawing at the insides of the ship's walls.

Iced dread flooded Harland's stomach. The sounds came from all around. Growing louder. Drawing nearer.

"There are others," a woman whispered.

The words hung for a moment. The wall to Harland's right was alive with scraping fingertips, prying at the overlapped metal panels.

"There are more," someone else echoed.

Then the words were caught up and repeated by others, baying over each other: *There are others. Other bodies. Other mummified remains.*

The officers seemed to want to control the crowd but didn't know how to. One yelled, "Quiet! Quiet!" repeatedly, as though he could invoke the captain's ponderous command just by parroting his words.

The officer with the sack hauled it up to his chest. The body couldn't have weighed much; the moisture had all evaporated while it was still in the shipyard. But sweat dripped from his face as though the task were herculean.

Or maybe it wasn't sweat. Harland's own skin was damp with the sticking fog.

The officer bearing the sack shoved through the crowed. They would follow orders and store the corpse in a different room. Harland wished they would throw it overboard instead, just like he intended to do with his shirt at first chance. But they would, as always, follow orders unerringly. And this damned corpse would stay on their ship.

Harland pressed his hands over his face in a futile effort to block out some of the lights and noise. The dead-eyed passengers were backing into each other, clustering like frightened sheep in a pen, as the scratching grew louder and louder and louder, until Harland thought he would scream.

28.

THE SECOND DIVE

Cove was weightless, but she still rested one arm against the passageway's wall, feeling, in her bones, that she needed the support.

She'd managed to keep her tone light when the audio reconnected them with Vanna and Hestie, but the reality was their escape from the hold hadn't been half as smooth as she'd made it sound.

Aidan, frightened out of his mind, had clawed past Roy and dragged himself up Cove's body in an effort to escape whatever was around his ankle. Even through layers of wool and dry suit, she was fairly sure she'd have bruises from it.

Being fully honest with herself, she would be unerringly grateful if bruises were *all* they had to deal with. Aidan had come close to knocking her face mask off, taking the oxygen with it. For a brief moment, she'd thought something similar must have happened to Roy; he'd lost his grip on her, and although she stretched her legs out to feel for him, she couldn't find him. The idea that he might be drowning in the thick silt even while she struggled with Aidan terrified her.

But then Roy's hand had snagged on her leg, and Cove had managed to twist Aidan around enough to pin his arms at his sides.

All of that desperate fighting had happened with her fully blind and almost entirely deaf. Aidan had screamed, she thought, but the reverberations had come to her as a distant, strangely disconnected noise.

And then, as quickly as it had started, the world became calm again.

Cove was still blind, but Aidan ceased thrashing. Roy pulled himself slightly closer. They had hung there like that, a tether of three people clinging to each other in a void, and then Cove's back had hit something broad and hard. The wall. She'd carefully relaxed her hold on Aidan and stretched one arm out to see if she could feel anything to anchor herself to and had, to her quiet shock, found a handle.

The holds' doors were watertight. It had been a struggle to get it open, but Cove, pushed by desperation, had managed it. A gush of sediment flowed through the opening along with their three bodies, but Cove had slammed the door closed as fast as was possible, and visibility, while not ideal, at least *existed*. She could see the two dark forms of her companions, both still alive. She could see about ten feet down the hallway before the cloudiness made it feel like peering into a dense fog. And although her air supply had never once been interrupted, she felt like it was possible to breathe again.

She'd gone to Aidan first, clapping both of his shoulders and doing what she could to reassure him without any audio. She could feel him shivering through her gloves. He'd tried to sign back—apologies, she thought, coming thick and fast—but in the end they'd both held up the universal okay sign and that had been enough.

Roy had been restless, swimming the width of the hallway in an imitation of pacing. When he neared a wall, he put out a hand and used his momentum to bounce himself away again. Cove wished he would stop. The constant motion was too much after the claustrophobia of the hold, and she would have given the world for just a moment to sit in quiet and gather her mind. But forcing him to stop would only make his agitation worse, she knew, so she let him burn his anxious energy in whatever way he chose.

And then, the ship had shuddered as though it planned to collapse beneath them, and mercifully, the audio came back on.

Now, Cove hung in the hall with her two companions, trying as well as she could to remember how the ship's lower levels had been arranged.

The *Arcadia* used a very familiar design for steam-powered ocean liners: boilers at the back, with massive smokestacks rising through the ship to expel the smoke on the surface. At the front, ahead of the boilers, about a third of the ship's footprint was used on holds. The *Arcadia* had four, from what she could remember: all rooms just as large as the one they had come through. She had no intention of visiting any of the others.

The ship's above-water and below-water levels were kept largely separate. While large stairwells connected the higher passenger sections and made traveling easy, the *Arcadia* had been designed to keep passengers from accidentally stumbling into the lower boiler and storage areas—and to keep the grimy stokers from wandering the passenger halls. The stokers not only worked in the below-water levels of the hull but ate and slept there too. Only a few narrow stairwells connected the crew and passenger floors.

Cove checked her oxygen levels and grimaced. Technically, they should already be outside the ship and making progress on their decompression stops. They'd need to find one of the stairwells up—very soon. She figured their chances would be best if they tried around the boilers. With stewards bringing meals down three times a day, they wouldn't want their access too far from the dining area.

She pushed forward. Aidan followed, sticking so close to her that Cove was afraid she might accidentally kick him.

Through the audio, she listened to Hestie make plans with Vanna. She had to assume the dive instructor was nodding or giving other nonverbal signals, but it was disconcerting to only hear one side of the conversation. Cove kept the line clear for them. She knew where she was going; she only needed the others to follow.

Which is why she had to bite down on an exasperated "Really?" when she heard the whine of straining metal, looked back, and saw that Roy had opened one of the other hold doors.

He waved a hand to call her closer, then pointed inside the room. She couldn't be sure thanks to the mask, but she thought he must have his trademark lopsided grin in place.

Fine. Okay. We might be able to find a hull breach and, if we're lucky, get out without having to go to the higher levels at all. He shouldn't be calling the shots in this—but, sure, humor him.

Cove backtracked to the door, glad that the mask would hide her irritation. She caught herself on the doorframe's edge and pulled out her spare flashlight to help light the space.

This room was different from the hold they'd entered through. It was far less crowded, and more pathways ran through it. Room had been cleared immediately inside the door, almost as a kind of landing. She had a moment of wonder over whether the first hold had been packed so tightly when it was originally loaded but decided to save those kinds of questions for when they reviewed the footage later.

If there's a later.

It was a horrible but ludicrous thought, and Cove would have tried to laugh at it if she weren't so bone tired.

The space cleared inside the doorway hadn't been left empty. Strange, long sacks were scattered about. They had probably been placed neatly, maybe in rows, but the sinking had left them with the appearance of being tossed about the room: some hung from the remaining storage on the walls, and others clumped together at the edge of the clear space, piled on top of one another.

Roy bumped past her as he glided into the room.

"Don't touch them," she warned.

"Relax, I'm not going to."

She pressed her lips together as she leaned forward to follow him.

Pathways had been cleared through the storage to reach the far wall, and Roy aimed for one of them. Cove couldn't see what had caught his notice but followed at a distance. She kept a close eye on him. The last thing they needed was a repeat of what had happened in the first hold.

Aidan made a very small noise that might have been nerves or might have been him trying to gain their notice, but when she looked back at him, she saw he was staring at one of the bundled shapes.

"Check it out. They cut a hole in the wall." Roy's glove traced the edges of where a metal sheet had been torn free from the hull. Behind were narrow compartments to create pockets of air space between the two shells.

"They must have been doing repairs." Cove frowned, even as her mouth formed an acceptable explanation. The hull piece was discarded nearby, and while it was badly dented from its removal, she couldn't see any reason to pull it out midtransit. All ocean liners from that time period had engineers, woodworkers, and electricians in case of faults while at sea. In early maritime history, stocks of spare cloth for sails and wood for structural repairs had been carried on ships, since long-distance voyages could last between months and years.

By the time of the *Arcadia*, though, advancements in steamship capabilities meant voyages were generally much shorter—even the transatlantic ones—and most repairs could be carried out once the vessel was safely back at dock. Engineers were still needed to keep the boilers running and for any other technical issues, but problems with the hull were more likely to be patched, rather than…whatever had happened *here*.

"There's another one." Roy nodded to their right. About ten feet away, a second segment of the interior wall had been stripped—this one closer to the ceiling. "Huh. Wonder how hard it would be to just punch through that second layer of metal and make our own exit."

"Pretty hard." The ship's walls were made to endure hundreds of tons of pressure from the ocean. They could probably break through with a good-sized crowbar and some time, but the effort would deplete their oxygen too fast for a gamble.

What happened here? Cove leaned back and kicked away from the wall. *Was there massive structural failure? Leaks they couldn't find? I would have expected to see more damage, but, then, an expert would probably be able to—*

"Guys?" Aidan cleared his throat. "I don't want to, uh…"

"It's okay, go on," Cove said.

"Well, I don't want to freak anyone out, but these are, uh, bodies down here. Y'know?"

Roy, who had been examining the gap torn in the wall, turned. Cove leaned forward as she neared Aidan. He was still only just inside the door, examining one of the long, cloth-bound objects. Ropes had been wrapped around the shape, holding it in place, but sometime during the sinking or after the fabric had been pulled free from one end, exposing a pair of bare feet.

"Huh." She cleared her throat. "You're right."

Hestie came through the communications unit: "You found more?"

"Ah, these aren't like the body in the dining hall." It was hard to remember that Hestie was half a ship away, even with the audio crackling like it was. "It looks like these individuals passed during the voyage. They've been wrapped in shrouds to be brought back to land. There are…at least a dozen of them."

Roy muttered something. Before Cove could react, he was barreling past her, urgently trying to get back to the hallway.

To her surprise, Aidan seemed the less perturbed. Maybe he, like her, was too exhausted to exert much more effort. Or maybe he was in shock and his reactions were dulled. She would have to assess him when they got back to the ship.

If you get back to the ship.

She shoved the thought aside, more irritated at its presence than uncomfortable. If her brain wanted to cope with edgy, morbid comments, well, it could at least do it discreetly.

Cove paused to give her head-mounted camera a moment to record the scene. There was less sediment in the room, thanks to its watertight door, but a thin dusting still coated every surface. She tried to get an accurate estimate of the shrouded bodies. At least fourteen, she thought, but more could be hidden behind the stacked crates or disguised in the pile to her left.

She beckoned for Aidan to follow her. Someday the hold that she was beginning to think of as *the shroud room* would need to be more closely examined. It wasn't unheard of for people to die on a transatlantic voyage, but she'd never heard of a ship racking up a dozen corpses in the span of less than two weeks.

Was there some kind of viral outbreak? A hallway was blocked off, almost as though quarantined. But then, why sail into the Gulf of Bothnia? Was it a mutiny, instead? Maybe the more outlandish rumors had some basis and the ship was overrun.

She didn't know what to think. Thankfully, it wasn't her *job* to think. Not at that moment. Devereaux and whichever experts Vivitech wanted to bring on for the documentary could postulate for as long as they wanted. Right at that moment, there were still five living humans inside the ship who needed to find an exit before their oxygen ran out.

29.

Harland knew it was night. His watch said so; the officer who had reminded him he was due on shift said so; the slop that had been turned out for food had been labeled as dinner.

Except for those, he might not have known. The fog was so impossibly dense that he couldn't even see the distant glow of the moon that he knew must exist somewhere behind the clouds.

He'd been given a lantern again, for all the good it did him. The whistle hung about his neck. It dripped with condensation, and he could feel how cold it was, even through his layers of coats.

But for the first time since the infernal fog had begun, Harland was actually grateful to be above deck. Since they'd opened the panel in the hold, the smell had grown far, far worse. He'd always believed the stench came from the fog, but now he began to wonder whether the *fog* came from *it*. Like some kind of corporeal manifestation of the sickness and the evil that had inhabited the ship.

He felt something move behind him. Harland turned, but all he saw was the billowing white.

There was a restlessness about the crew and passengers that he neither liked nor trusted. He hadn't seen Fitz since the scene in the hold, but everywhere he turned were echoes of his friend's legacy. Whispers at the tables. Whispers between officers. Captain Virgil had reportedly locked himself in the bridge and was not to be disturbed.

A heavy boot slammed against the deck. Harland craned, straining to see anything beyond the abysmal, all-consuming white. "Hello there!" he called. Even his words were stolen from him. They faded, muffled, steadily dismantled by the walls of emptiness. A drop of condensation fell from his nose and hit the already-saturated scarf. He was cold in a way he thought he might never be rid of. The kind of cold that burrows deep and lives in a man's bones, where no number of hot baths or warm beds can ease. Not that he was to be offered much of either for as long as the ship sailed.

They should have arrived at port by now, he was certain. He'd lost count of the days sometime before, but they were passing, and alarmingly quickly. The ship's speed still had not slowed. The stokers had to be working extra shifts to keep it running at this pace.

For a second, he questioned whether he would trade places with them. The boiler room, at least, was hot. The men who worked there were kept lean, no matter how much they ate. It was the sweat, Fitz had always said. They lost their body weight in perspiration every day, and a man could not sustain much fat when it all bled out of him like that.

Harland bared his teeth in a bitter grin. Cooked in the oven or frozen in the icebox that was the surface. Despite the opposite roles, the watchmen and the furnace stokers both had short—but frequent—shifts to account for the way it broke a man down.

No. He preferred it here, Harland decided. His fingers seemed to creak whenever he tried to curl them around the lantern's handle and he could not feel much of his face, but at least he was farther away from the hellish display in the lower storeroom.

He hadn't found out where the blackened, mummified body had been moved to. But it was still down there, somewhere. Beneath their feet. In the heart of their ship. And it was a desperately bad omen that it should be so.

Frenzied whispers passed between passengers and crew. They all agreed: the body represented a rot in the ship. As long as it remained there, things could not get any better.

It should be thrown overboard, they decided. Still, no one volunteered to move it. No one dared touch the shriveled remains, for fear of incurring the brunt of its curse.

A rope groaned, fell quiet, and then groaned again. Harland barely reacted to the noise. He'd been able to see the other sailors' lanterns on the earliest watches. They'd been distant, seemingly cut off from him by an uncrossable expanse, but they had at least been there. Now, there was just the fog and the wet.

It dripped from the rigging above Harland: the foretop, a relic from a time when steam had yet to be harnessed aboard ships, now used solely for the crow's nest, a familiar position for Harland and his fellow watchmen. A spiderweb of cables spread out from it, lashing it in place despite winds and hail and whatever other battering forces the ocean chose to throw at them.

A distant bell rang. It was to signal something, but he'd been out in the cold and the wet for so long that he was no longer certain what. Shift change? Dinner? No, they had already had dinner—hours ago. Unless he had been standing on the deck through the night, mindless and unfocused, and this one was now for breakfast. Unlikely, but with how scattered his mind was, not impossible.

Another sound came from above him. The ropes again, creaking, and he had the vague idea that the crow's nest shift must be changing and men were navigating the narrow rope ladder up to it.

Only a second later, the body hit the deck.

It landed with a dense crunching sound. The splintering of bones, the bursting skin. A skull, cracked open like a coconut.

Harland swallowed a deep, aching groan. Through the fog, the shape on the deck was barely distinguishable from a sack of flour. Only one hand was clearly visible; cast out to the side, extended from the cuff of an expensive pinstripe suit, the fingers twitched once, twice, then became still again.

He didn't want to move closer, but his feet dragged him toward the fallen figure regardless. His lantern shuddered as he stretched it forward. From a distance, the body barely looked harmed: the clothes were neatly pressed, if damp. A gold watch chain lay next to the body, and for a second, Harland imagined the man might stand, brushing his pants down and murmuring polite apologies before picking up the watch and returning to his business.

But there were enough signs to tell Harland that wouldn't be happening. The bend to the legs was unnatural. The head, turned to the side, stared blindly. He still had an impeccable head of dark hair, so neatly combed that only small parts had been mussed out of place. The top half looked fine, but the lower half of the face, the cheek pressed to the deck, had been flattened.

Harland lowered the lantern. Its golden light flickered over a steadily growing pool of crimson spreading out across the wood.

He felt for the whistle. It took two tries to fit it between his numb, wet lips. And even then, he only managed half a blast before he was forced to leap out of the way.

A second body hit the deck near where he stood. Harland didn't get a closer look at that one, only enough to see it was a larger man, and he had collided with the deck headfirst.

Harland raised the lantern as high as he could and stared toward the sky. Dark shapes plunged through the gloomy mist. Their limbs were outstretched, as though reaching for the heavens. He couldn't count how many—only saw there were *too* many. A shoe tumbled off one. It bounced off the wooden deck near Harland's own feet in the same instant its accompanying body disappeared over the ship's side.

Another heavy slap behind him: a woman, crumpled, not yet dead but very close to it. Harland averted his gaze, pressed the whistle between his lips, and blew. The sharp, piercing cry nearly drowned out the sickening crackle of a spine hitting the railing. That body spiraled away, overboard, but another collided so close to Harland that he felt the reverberations shudder through his own legs. He dropped to his knees. The lantern fell from his hand. The flame was extinguished. And Harland was left alone in the dark, his hands pressed over his head, as he was forced to listen to the slap of bodies hitting the deck around him.

Over the following days, the crew would debate the event in hushed tones, looking for some answers as to what caused the men and women to jump. Many of them had berths near one another, but no closer links could be ascertained. Had the sounds in the walls driven them to it? Were they trying to climb higher than the fog? Was it a suicide pact, or had there been some misguided idea of escaping the ship?

Whatever the truth, something had compelled them to climb.

A few had tried to scale the cables anchoring the smokestacks in place. But most had chosen the foretop, seeing it as the highest place they could reach. Only a few had plunged over the ship's edge and into the ocean. Blinded by the fog, most had met a faster and harsher end on the deck instead.

As the man who had witnessed the act, Harland was pardoned from the effort to clean the bodies off the deck. He was later told that they had been wrapped in shrouds and stored in the same hold as the miserable, shriveled creature from inside the walls. He silently prayed that his duties might never ever send him to that room again.

30.

THE SECOND DIVE

The passageway leading between the holds was narrow. They moved single file, with Cove at the head and Roy bringing up the rear.

Aidan had seemed strangely okay about the bodies in the hold, but she couldn't discount a delayed reaction due to shock. By contrast, Roy had become irritable again—almost as though he viewed the existence of the shrouded figures as a personal affront. The body in the dining hall had caught him by surprise, and he'd gone to great lengths to avoid passing it a second time, and now the ship had disrespected his wishes by filling a whole room with human remains. It was deliberate, designed to needle his weaknesses.

Or some logic that amounted to that. The long and short of it was that he was simmering, and Cove didn't have any way to calm him down.

Not that there was much time for anything save for *getting out*. Ironically, despite calling an end to the dive early, this was likely to run longer than the previous day's trip.

Ahead, a heavy, bolted door led to the first of the boiler rooms. Cove pushed her back against the opposite wall to gain some leverage as she strained against the seal. The dive tanks dug into her shoulder blades. For a fearful second she thought that perhaps the door wouldn't budge at all, but then the metal screamed as it shuddered inward. Roy pushed past Aidan and joined Cove, and together they dragged the watertight door open just enough to move through.

Cove, breathing heavily, hung in the water while she waited for the shapes around her to become clear. For all the wattage their headlights boasted, they felt strangely inadequate in the *Arcadia*. It hadn't been nearly enough to properly light the hallways, and, in the boiler room, the effect was magnified so far that she began to fear that the batteries were near empty.

"Huh." Roy had emerged through the door and stopped to Cove's right.

She supposed that sentiment was as good as any, given what they were facing.

As with the storage holds, the *Arcadia* had multiple boiler rooms, each divided by a wall and a watertight door. That didn't mean the boiler rooms were small though. They were at least three floors tall and had been built with multiple levels of walkways. The space did feel cramped, but only because both walls were lined with rows of massive furnaces.

Nearly twice the height of a human, the furnaces had a circular front with multiple hatches allowing the coal—which was unceremoniously dumped on the floor—to be shoveled into the infernos inside by stokers working around the clock to keep the fires fed.

Cove couldn't imagine how intensely, unendingly hot the room must have gotten with four furnaces on each side of the ship, towering over the narrow passageway between.

Suspended walkways had been built above the furnaces to accommodate the trimmers, the men who shoveled the coal down chutes to the stokers. Those platforms had collapsed during the *Arcadia*'s sinking and were now a tangle of metal and stairs, blocking most of the floor.

Cove's first instinctual thought was: *Damn, we won't be able to climb them.* Followed by the mental slap of: *You're weightless, idiot. Float up.*

She bared her teeth in a grin as she began to rise. Here she was, the woman who would climb any mountain and raft any river, the woman who taught viewers every level of survival skills—whether they were likely to need them or not—and she'd straight-up forgotten that she was underwater.

The fallen walkways created a web she needed to navigate through, but none of it was so dense they couldn't figure out a way past. Cove picked the route, carefully twisting her way between the metal. There was a temptation to take hold of some of the bars and pull herself along to give her legs a break, but she couldn't tell how sound the formation was and didn't want to risk a repeat of the storage hold.

As they moved higher, she hazarded a glance down, toward the boilers. The massive structures created the illusion of a floor: the true path was barely visible between them, a mess of scattered coal pieces and—

And an arm.

Cove clenched her teeth. She didn't say anything; Roy's mood was sour enough as it was. But beneath where they swam, jutting out of fallen metal, was a man's arm.

She'd stayed up until the early hours of the previous night researching how and why bodies could be preserved underwater. She'd thought she needed to understand what they were facing when revisiting the *Arcadia*. Now that she was here, though, she wasn't entirely sure the extra knowledge led to an improvement of her mental state.

Hestie's summary had been pretty well correct: with no oxygen, the body's natural bacteria was only able to start the earliest stages of decomposition before suffocating. From then on, the bodies could remain in a state of stasis: never truly being able to decay and unable to return to the surface.

Just like the furniture and just like their own clothes, the bodies were held in a state remarkably close to life. But not *entirely* close. A hundred years changed a body, even one that hadn't been allowed to rot.

Adipocere was the waxy layer of fat exuded by the body after death—specifically, a body that was exposed to water and a lack of bacteria. The body's natural fats gradually seeped through the skin to form a layer on top. It was thicker in the parts of the body where fat was more plentiful. If allowed to dry, it would turn into a hard case across the body...but held underwater like in the *Arcadia*, it would stay soft and oily indefinitely.

Cove had noticed the unnaturally lumpy, white appearance of the body they'd encountered in the dining hall. Combined with the harsh lights from their helmets, it was hard to tell where the skin ended and the lumps began. She'd only had an opportunity for a closer look when the images were enlarged and paused on Devereaux's screens.

Now, she'd been given another chance for a view of adipocere in action...and she genuinely would have preferred not to.

The hands were one of the least changed parts. The fingers

were still distinct and recognizable, though the skin had shrunken around the joints.

As the arm continued, though, the bubbling pockets of corpse fat made an appearance. They started as small patches: a cluster here, a mark there, easy to mistake for a trick of the light. But it had caked around the biceps. Parts had started to fuse to the ladder that lay across the body.

A human is only human for as long as it's alive. Her father had told her that on a relief mission to Thailand after massive floods had destroyed villages. *Once we die and once the soul separates, we are no longer human but only a body to be returned to the soil.*

He'd given her those words when they'd found a half-undressed, bloated corpse among a house's wreckage. The words had been intended as a comfort. But watching the flies creep over the distended stomach, Cove had simply felt a deep, numbing horror.

It might only be a body now, but it had been a human not so long ago. A human that had woken one morning, unaware that she was gazing at the last sunrise she would ever see.

Isn't that the truth for all of us though? Isn't it, in some ways, a blessing that we don't know when our time will end? Think, Cove—how much attention did you pay to your *sunrise this morning? Did you make the most of it, as though it could be your last?*

She fixed her eyes ahead again, but the image of the arm was seared into her head, just as the body in Thailand had been. She believed she would still see those images just as clearly in another fifty years, heaven willing she lived that long.

Aidan followed close behind Cove, and his headlight glanced over her arms when she stretched them ahead of herself. Roy was focused on the ceiling though. His beam attempted to cut through the near impenetrable dark above them as they struggled across the boiler room's wreckage.

Cove's rebreather let out a rush of air. She lifted her head to visually chase the bubbles toward the ceiling, and that was when she saw it: the ragged end of the broken walkway, still attached to one of the upper walls. And connected to that, a door. Their way out.

31.

Hestie's chest was tight. The communications line had been almost completely silent since the other team's discovery of bodies in one of the storage holds. At once, she'd wanted to know more…and had dreaded to ask.

If a ship's crew had been shrouded and stored, that rarely meant good things. A sinking would happen too fast to care for the dead; the survivors would simply be focused on getting themselves to safety at all costs. Some kind of hostile takeover would usually result in the victims' bodies being thrown overboard, where there would be less evidence—and less guilt—for the remaining crew to worry about.

Shrouded bodies meant there had been deaths, and there had also been time to grieve them and tend to them and consider an eventual funeral for them.

They were being given clues about what had happened to the *Arcadia* but not enough to see how they fit together.

She and Vanna had stopped in their hallway, facing another puzzle piece. A message, written on the walls.

On their previous dive, they'd uncovered two messages. Or three, if they counted the outline in the first-class berth. At the time, there had been arguments over whether one person had penned those messages or whether they had been made by different hands. Hestie thought they might now have their answer.

KEEP THEM CONTAINED

The words had been written on wood paneling, where the disintegrating paper couldn't interrupt their message. And it had been written with a very distinctive hand. It was slanted and jarring and rough, with many letters sloppily sliding over each other as though the writer had misjudged the space they needed, but it was still legible. An arrow led from it, pointing along the hallway.

In the direction they had been traveling.

Very slowly, Hestie rotated to stare along the passageway. Some effort had been made to seal this hall as well. Chairs and tables and spare beams of wood had been stacked. But the attempt had been less thorough than on the port side. Here, on the starboard, the gushing water from the sinking ship had broken through the blockade…to some degree. It would be a squeeze, but Hestie was fairly certain they could get through a gap near the ceiling.

Vanna glanced at her, wordlessly waiting for her opinion. She'd been doing that frequently. Hestie was used to letting others call the shots, doubly so on this kind of dive, where she was one of the less experienced members. At first, there had been a small thrill that Vanna might be treating her as the default leader in Cove's absence. Following that had been a much, much stronger sense of dread: she was very much not qualified to be making these kinds of decisions, and the pressure of making the *right* choice had become paralyzing.

Now, though, she thought she might understand. It wasn't that Vanna was treating Hestie as the leader; it was more that she, with over four thousand cave dives under her belt, was comfortable with almost any challenge the *Arcadia* could provide. Those questioning looks weren't her waiting for instruction; they were checking whether *Hestie* felt like she was able to keep up.

She took a second look at the tangled furniture, measuring it up, and nodded. She was fairly sure she could fit. They would try to go through and maybe even clear a slightly larger passage for the others, in case that hallway led to a way out.

Vanna's mask dipped in a nod, then she moved forward, one hand unreeling extra dive cord as she rose. Hestie watched in awe as the agile woman curved her body and slipped through the gap without so much as brushing the furniture.

It reminded her of a seal: heavy and slow on land, but a sleek machine in the water. Hestie had never been like that. She wasn't going to claim her land coordination was anything spectacular either, but it was still better than the way she felt in the water.

She loved marine biology with all of her heart, but she hadn't been born to live in the waves like some of her colleagues. Hestie's passion lay in the statistics. Comparing data, tracking a coral's life cycle over years, studying the minute and not-so-minute changes as coastal towns began dumping more microplastics in the ocean. She was good at numbers.

Now, though, this lack of actual diving practice meant she was less of a sleek seal gliding through the gap and more of a fumbling, exhausted human clambering very slowly across the debris.

Her tanks scraped the ceiling, raining flecks of plaster over her, and Hestie flinched. Technically, the dive was to be as close to no contact as possible. They were here to document, not to alter any part. She supposed that had already gone out the window when they'd started opening doors, but well, it was a balance.

She'd had some small fear that the other side of the blockade would be an even worse jumble, but the hallway was once again clear. She let herself float back down. Vanna was waiting for her, head tilted as she examined the right-hand wall.

"Oh," Hestie murmured. A hole had been gorged through the wood paneling and plaster. The ragged edges of wood had something clinging to them. Algae, was Hestie's first thought, except the gulf didn't allow for life-forms even as simple as the single-cell goo. She felt a sad smile rise. She hadn't expected she would miss *life* quite so much that she would grow nostalgic for algae, the bane of almost every marine biologist's career…excluding, of course, the weirdos who studied it.

She dipped closer to the loose, drifting shapes. They flowed like a mirage. Almost like…

Hestie recoiled. She was looking at a clump of hair. *Woman's* hair, judging by the length. It came from inside the hole: lose gray strands, clogged with silt, floating in tiny eddies.

Hestie was already certain she didn't want to see any more of what was inside the hole. But she also knew the footage would be reviewed by the others later that night, and they would have questions. It was her job to document the wreck, even when she dearly wished she'd taken a different hallway.

She managed to repress a groan as she felt for her spare flashlight. It flickered as it switched on, and she felt a pang of anxiety that it would malfunction, just as the audio had. Then the light settled, and Hestie, breathing deeply, angled it inside the hole.

It took a second to register what she was seeing. The hole

had broken through to the room beyond, which, she was fairly certain based on the distant flashes of tile, was a bathroom.

In between was a mesh of pipes and electrical cables. And a woman's body.

The head was wedged to one side, the skin mottled and swelling with a strange white substance. The head and shoulders filled the hole. Her arms were pinned back at her sides, while the lower half of her body was still inside the bathroom.

Hestie backed away, uneasy. It looked as though the woman had been locked inside the bathroom and had chosen to escape by...breaking a hole in the wall and attempting to climb through?

It made very little sense. She doubted a bathroom would even supply enough tools to cut through the hard plaster and wood. And she couldn't guess why that had been the woman's first plan, instead of attacking the much flimsier door.

Or why she'd been locked in there in the first place.

Or why, when she'd clearly become wedged, no one had tried to help her back out.

Stop it. Stop thinking. Stop looking. We need to get out of the ship—focus on that and that alone.

She caught Vanna's attention and nodded along the hallway, indicating that she wanted to continue. Vanna needed no encouragement. She hadn't tried to get a closer look at the body in the wall and seemed perfectly content to leave it behind.

Ahead, the hallway formed a strange bend to compensate for the ship narrowing. The hallway first turned right, then a new pathway branched off to the left, continuing toward the ship's rear. Hestie paused in the intersection. Ahead, she saw the distinct sheen of a wooden bannister. They'd found a second stairwell. She pointed to it, and Vanna gave a minute nod in return.

The *Arcadia* had windows on its lower levels, but they were almost entirely cabin portholes that were too small to fit a body. The windows in the higher levels, though, farther from the ocean's spray and closer to the sun, were larger. The *Arcadia* had been fitted with lounges for each of the three passenger classes, as well as smoking lounges and a writing room. Photos of those spaces had shown large plate glass windows that, without a doubt, would have broken during the sinking. As long as they could get to one of those areas, it shouldn't be hard to find a passage out.

As Hestie passed the hallway leading left, her headlight flashed over a sign on the wall: *Hospital.* That placed them very close to the stern. They'd entered at the bow, which meant they had managed to work their way along the *Arcadia*'s full length.

The hospital sign came as a slight shock. It was the first sign Hestie had seen on the ship. The small metal placard was set onto the wall at the corner, with a discreet arrow leading the way. From what she understood, there should have been signs like that on almost every corner of the passenger decks, like in any hotel or modern cruise ship.

Maybe she'd missed them. But the glinting metal—bronze, probably, though the depths had robbed it of its distinct color— should have easily caught her eyes before.

She tried to put it out of mind as she turned toward the stairwell. Vanna had already begun ascending but had stopped partway up. The stairs were wide enough for two people, and Hestie let herself drift to her companion's side as they stared at a third jumble of furniture and wooden boards blocking their path.

I should have expected this. They blocked both hallways. If they were that desperate to contain whatever was in here, they would have blocked the stairs as well.

Hestie reached for a chair leg and gave it a cautious tug. The structure groaned. Vanna grabbed her arm and dragged her back. "Unstable" was all she said.

"Right. Sorry."

Stupid. Of course we don't want to break through. We'd end up in a silt-out as bad as they had in the cargo hold...and that's if the collapsing furniture didn't crush us in the process.

Unlike the barricade they'd come through, Hestie could see no way to squeeze around the edges of this one. Table legs and chair backs angled out at her like a row of hostile spears. It had been packed so tightly that not even the tons of water rushing through the sinking ship had budged it.

That left them with very few options. They could search for another exit on this level, not knowing what they might find, or they could follow their path back to the stairwell and use Cove's original plan, which was to ascend through the dining hall despite Roy's complaints.

It was hard to admit it even to herself, but Hestie very dearly wanted to find a way out in that section of the ship. Part of it was because she didn't want her search to be wasted. But more than that, she didn't want to have to pass the woman in the hallway again.

Her eyes turned toward the shining bronze *Hospital* sign. It was a gamble. The hospital would have larger windows than most of the berths on that floor...but she also didn't think it was a coincidence that the three pathways leading to it had been barricaded.

Perhaps there really had been some kind of viral outbreak. Maybe something that had led to paranoia or even insanity. And the crew, desperate to escape whatever was killing them, had sealed the infected in this one section.

If that was true, at least the dive crew should be safe. The full-body dry suits kept them warm in the near-freezing waters, but they had the extra side effect of protecting them from any contaminants in the water—like an underwater version of hazmat gear—and viral particles were unlikely to have survived in the water for the past hundred years.

The light on Hestie's mask faded, then regained its focus. She held still, waiting, willing it to hold, then ran her tongue across her cracked lips. None of their technology had worked quite right since they'd entered the *Arcadia*. And she didn't think she could lay that at the feet of a potential viral infection. In her heart, she believed that whatever had happened to the *Arcadia*, it had been something they hadn't even considered before.

She leaned forward and led the way toward the hospital.

32.

A drop of cold, greasy water fell from the ceiling. Harland shuddered as it pinged off the back of his neck and trickled down beneath his collar.

The sickening mist had thickened inside the ship. Visibility had been reduced to less than fifteen feet.

Very few of the *Arcadia*'s original lights remained. The crew used whatever lights they could get their hands on to find their way about the ship. Sometimes, the only warning that someone was coming toward you was a distant glow swinging through the gloom.

Harland held a candle in an open-top jar. Its flame was weak. Like him and like everyone else in the cursed ship, it was being smothered by the heaving fog. Harland's stomach refused to settle. He hadn't eaten in days and had barely drunk. The water had drawn in the rotting odor and left his tongue slimy and foul. Even the daily ration of rum tasted wrong.

"Hey, help me with my light."

Harland glanced at his companion. He'd been paired with a man about his age: Boswell. With the far-brighter lanterns all being taken by the officers and with the flashlights refusing to hold power, most of the crew were reduced to using candles. The ship's official store had run out quickly, but someone had entered the hold to retrieve boxes that were being shipped to Britain.

Boswell's face was narrow and clean-shaven, with a small chin and too-large lips. He'd struck Harland as nervous and jumpy. Though weren't they all? At least he was largely quiet. Crew members were supposed to move in pairs now, and some of the older sailors had begun muttering—a constant stream of babble that made no sense to anyone around them, falling through barely parted lips at a whisper's level. They obeyed instructions and could even answer questions but seemed unable, or unwilling, to halt the noise. Harland thanked whatever luck had held for him to be paired with a silent man.

He'd been taken off deck watch after the incident with the falling bodies. Someone probably thought they were doing him a favor, though even with the images of the victims splashed across the promenade seared into his mind, he would have greatly preferred to be above deck.

Below levels, every breath felt like a struggle. Water dripped from the ceiling and ran in trickles down the walls. Harland had to step carefully; the carpet was becoming spongy and slippery, and twice he had lost his footing—and his light.

Now, Boswell held his own jar toward Harland. His candle had gone out. Again. This was part of the reason they were being sent out in pairs: not just for safety, but also to protect them from losing their lights. If both of their candles were to fail, they would be trapped in the pitch-dark hallway, condemned to either creep along by their sense of touch alone or wait until another crew member's faint glow appeared in the distance.

Harland tilted his own jar so that Boswell could touch the candles' tips together. The dead candle hissed back to life, though the flame was even smaller than Harland's, something he hadn't thought was possible.

They had been given a list of rooms to visit: passengers who hadn't been seen at meals for several days. They were supposed to locate the travelers. Alive, if possible, though no one held out a huge amount of hope. The first room of the morning had been a lucky find—a family of four, all still present, but simply too frightened to leave their berth.

Harland and Boswell had brought them fresh water and some food from the kitchens and left them there. Harland couldn't blame them for wanting to stay hidden.

The next passenger room they were scheduled to check was in the third-class hall. An older couple, according to the hasty notes scribbled on Harland's paper. Not seen for three days.

Liquid rose from the carpet with every footfall, blooming around the edges of Harland's shoes. His candlelight barely did more than put his own tired, pale face into relief. The fog teased at the edges of his vision, painting phantoms just out of view.

"Ah." Boswell tugged on Harland's sleeve, bringing him to a halt. Something rattled through the walls to their left. The clacking, scraping fingernails, beginning somewhere near the floor and then rising as they raced along the wall. Harland saw the edges of the peeling wallpaper shiver as the unseen being rushed past them. It had moved as high as the ceiling by the time it reached the intersecting hallway, and then the scratching sounds faded as it burrowed deeper into the ship.

Boswell's light had gone out again. Possibly because the man had jumped when the noise passed close to his shoulder, but Harland thought more likely in response to the sound itself. Things in the ship changed in minuscule ways when the *others* moved through the wall. Harland didn't know how many there were or how they had spread so far through the ship, but their presence left changes. Sometimes it was only a little more moisture in the air. Sometimes more dust.

Harland held his jar still so his companion could light his candle once more, then turned back to their path. A message had been painted on the wall:

THEY CAME THROUGH HERE

Someone—passengers or crew or officers working under the captain's command, Harland wasn't sure—had started marking the unseen beings' most-used passageways. No one had yet seen them step into the hallways, though most believed they could if they wanted to. Instead, they had built their paths through the walls. They traversed the ship in those secret tunnels, built to accommodate piping and wires, and the whispers said it was a bad omen to hear them pass you. It meant misfortune was sure to come.

As though we don't already have enough misfortune.

Boswell seemed rooted to the spot, his wild eyes fixated on the place where the sounds had vanished, and Harland gave him a quick slap to the upper arm to startle him back to awareness.

They were close to their berth. It had been built to accommodate four, like most of the third-class passenger rooms, but with the low numbers of attendance on that crossing, the passengers—the Whites—had been given the space to themselves.

Harland stopped by the door and, raising the jar high enough to ensure he had the right number, knocked firmly enough that no one inside could fail to hear him.

He waited, straining to hear the squeak of a mattress or the yawn of someone waking, but the berth was silent. He tried the handle. Locked.

Boswell had been given charge of the rooms' keys. He took one out of his pocket and offered it to Harland, who fit it into the lock. The latch turned, and Harland shoved the door open.

The berth held two bunk beds, pressed against opposite walls, with a simple sink and mirror between them. Pale light came through a small porthole behind one of the bunk beds.

The Whites had left their room in disarray. Sheets had been stripped and left in the sink and the room's corners. Their luggage had been taken from the under-bed storage and strewn about, and coats and undergarments created a blockade on the door's interior side that Harland had to shove away in order to open the door fully.

A sickly smell was present. It was different from the fog. Both had an undercurrent of decay, but the fog smelled of the ocean: rotting seaweed, rotting fish, queasy, and salty. This room smelled of blood and metal and fleshy corruption. They were not going to find the Whites alive.

Boswell, at Harland's back, swung around to face the hall again. The rattles had begun afresh, starting nearer to the ship's bow and racing overhead, before dipping to the right and entering the walls again. Harland waited only until the sounds had ended before pulling his scarf up over his mouth and nose and stepping into the room.

For himself, he would have only needed to catch that smell before locking the door and declaring the Whites deceased. But the officer's orders had been clear: find and identify the bodies. They wanted an accurate count of how many were dead and how many were missing.

There were very few places in third-class berths to hide. The room had no wardrobes or chest of drawers. However, each bunk had a drawer built in beneath the mattress, designed for storing luggage. Harland crossed to the nearest one and wrenched it open. Empty. He tried the one above, also empty, but found what he was looking for in the lowest drawer against the external wall.

The drawer jammed as he tried to drag it open and Harland, gagging, had to press one boot against the wooden frame to get leverage. The drawer slid open with a heavy, slick noise. Inside was a man's body, bloated and gray and contorted. He'd managed to place himself inside the drawer and drag it closed, even though it would have been a struggle for a person half his size.

The surgeon called it the burrowing disease. When passengers or crew felt they were very close to death, they would try to find a small space and wedge themselves inside of it. Perhaps to hide. Perhaps it gave them some comfort in their last minutes.

The steward in the boiler room had been their first recorded instance, but the numbers grew each day. Kitchen staff had to check all cupboards and large drawers before beginning work in the mornings. A man had reportedly even been found in the hold, squeezed in behind the stack of shrouded bodies that had perished from throwing themselves off the foretop.

And now, this. Harland checked the final drawer, but it was empty. Mrs. White had left the room, then, and likely found a place of her own to burrow.

Harland left the berth. He was breathing in shallow gasps, spit marking the inside of his scarf. The cabin's odor faded slightly as he closed and locked the door.

Boswell was missing. Normally the man waited in the hallways while Harland checked the berths and would note down their findings in the notebook to be presented to the officers later. But now, he had vanished, leaving only the glass jar with its unlit candle sitting in the center of the damp carpet.

Harland stopped next to the jar, his own raised in a futile effort to shine light on his surroundings. His view faded quickly as the weak flame and heavy fog conspired to mask the depths of the passageways. Harland closed his eyes and listened.

In the far distance, to his left, was a very soft scratching noise. Harland snatched up the jar from the floor and moved in the sound's direction.

He'd known what he was likely to find, but that didn't stop the burning ache from forming deep in his stomach as he finally caught up with Boswell. The man was burrowing into the wall.

Since the shriveled, mummified remains had been retrieved from the hold, some of the crew had become obsessed with the thought that there were more of them. No matter how often the officers or even the captain impressed on them that the original body was the only one—a freak accident from the ship's construction, nothing more—they were not believed.

When passengers and crew began to suspect they'd identified a part of the wall that hid another mummy, they would tear through metal, drywall, and wood to prove they were right. So far, no other mummified remains had been found. But that didn't stop the ship's walls from being dotted with holes. In some areas—especially the lowest regions, around the boilers and the storage—there could be a half dozen carved openings in any one room.

Harland himself wasn't sure what to believe about the bodies. He simply wished the crew would cease digging holes…if only to stop whatever was *in* the walls from getting *out*.

Boswell had found one of those man-made gaps. The space wasn't large—less than two feet high and barely as deep—but by the time Harland caught up to him, he had crushed his entire body inside. Knees pulled to his chest, head facing down, one wide, bloodshot eye peering out at Harland as he knelt at his companion's side.

There was nothing he could do for Boswell now. The burrowing disease had him, and once it started, there was no way to make it stop. Even if Harland tried to pull Boswell out, the man would simply crawl back in the first chance he was given. That hole was his now, and he would doggedly cling to it until death.

"I am sorry," Harland said.

Boswell didn't reply, and he didn't try to stop Harland from feeling inside his pockets and retrieving the keys and notebook.

Harland lit Boswell's candle and placed the jar beside the burrowed sailor. It was a last gift to a man who would very soon become all too similar to Mr. White.

Boswell showed no reaction. His eyes were glistening and unfocused, as though in terror, but the dull slackness about his face suggested he had precious little of his mind intact. Harland rose, his chest aching, and turned down the hallway to continue his job. He tried not to notice as Boswell's candle flickered and died.

33.

THE SECOND DIVE

Hestie paused outside the hospital's doors. They had been designed to blend in with the ship's decor; made of deeply carved wood and flanked by sconces, they looked more fitting for access to a ballroom than as a space intended for medical treatment.

All ocean liners from the time had been like that. There was a lot of money to be made in the business, and the ships were all competing to be the largest and most luxurious. Anywhere the passengers stepped was supposed to reinforce that sense of top-of-the-line accommodation.

However, it was notable that the sense of all-encompassing opulence vanished once you entered the crew areas. Double-berth rooms were replaced with quarters that could sleep twenty with rows of beds stacked to the ceiling. The wood paneling and elegant lights were switched for dim, featureless metal and cramped walkways.

But the hospital had been considered a passenger-facing room, and as such, it had been given the same treatment as the lounges and the first-class berths.

Hestie shot a glance back at Vanna, silently asking if she was making the right choice. Vanna was, as always, unreadable. She simply watched Hestie, any expression disguised under the blank dive mask.

If it's bad, we can leave again. She braced her hands on the left-hand door and began to push. *We just need a large enough window. If we can't get to one quickly and easily, we'll turn around.*

The wood shuddered. A deep groan rose from it, and the sound seemed to extend beyond just the doors and encompass the entire ship. Hestie paused, biting her lower lip so hard that the split reopened. A small dusting of silt fell from the ceiling to land on her shoulders. She took one quick, sharp breath and pushed again.

The door scraped inward, fighting against its own aged hinges and the debris on the floor. As soon as the gap was wide enough, Hestie tilted her head to allow the light through.

Her first impression of the room was *chaos*. White sheets scattered over the floor. Curtains hung at angles, their fabric pooling across beds and tables. Pillows had clumped together in the corners.

Hestie held still, trying to keep her breathing slow and deep as her light shimmered across the room. The hospital had most likely been in perfect order until it had been subjected to the same deluge as everywhere else on the ship. She almost wanted to laugh at herself for expecting it to look otherwise.

She slipped through the gap in the doors. Even through the chaos, it was possible to see how the room had been intended to look. Rows of hospital beds ran along each wall, creating a broad

passageway between them. The doors had made her think of a
ballroom, and that instinct wasn't too far off, she realized. The
space was genuinely large enough to host a ball in—and included
nurses' stations and beds for at least forty passengers.

Most of the beds were still in their positions. Although they
had wheels, they had been locked into the walls to prevent them
from sliding during rough weather.

The privacy curtains had fared worse. They had toppled, creating an unnerving, heaving effect across the room: dips and gullies
and the gentle slope of broad, dusty cloth wherever she looked.

And on the room's starboard-side wall, there were windows.
They weren't huge, but they were at least larger than the
portholes. The glass had broken free during the sinking, leaving
empty frames looking into the endless water.

"I think we found a way out," Hestie said, knowing the second
half of the team would hear her. "We're in the hospital, near the
ship's rear."

"Good." Cove's voice was, as always, confident and encouraging, but Hestie thought she caught a trace of relief underneath it
too. "We're nearly at the stairs. We'll bring the dive line with us."

Hestie moved past the doorway, careful not to kick her legs
too hard as she passed over the delicate layers of sediment covering the fallen curtains.

As she moved, she darted her eyes from bed to bed, driven
by the slow, creeping fear that there might be presences in the
room. The closest bed was empty. And the one after that. The
one beyond that though...

Hestie leaned back, arms sweeping ahead of herself to halt
her momentum. The bed beneath the window she'd been aiming
for was occupied. A man, lying on his back, jaw slack, with thin
gray hair creating a halo around his head. He'd been tied down

to the bed. Three broad leather straps ran over his body, at his shoulders, his hips, and his feet, anchoring him in place.

It was both hypnotizing and horrifying that he should still be here, held down for so long. A strange impulse passed through her: the desire to untie the straps. Her hands were actually moving toward him before she caught herself and forced her head away.

He wasn't the only body, she realized. The beds closest to the door had been empty, but most others—at least twenty of them—had been filled. Each passenger wearing the same blue hospital pajamas, each held down with three thick leather straps.

She'd heard of something like that years ago. It had been a common practice in the 1800s and earlier for ship crews to tie their passengers to their beds during extremely rough seas. It had been done to ensure the guests, unused to holding their balance on heaving waters, wouldn't fall and hurt themselves. The practice had been commonplace before it was realized that, in the case of a sinking ship, passengers had no way to free themselves or reach the lifeboats. The practice had been abolished long before the *Arcadia* ever set sail.

A question flashed through Hestie, searing her. Had these men and women still been alive when the ship sank?

She imagined lying in the bed, possibly sick, possibly delirious, as the nursing staff raced from the room. Waiting for someone to come back and free her. Waiting, even as the gushing, pounding water burst underneath the doors. Feeling the mattress growing wet beneath her back. Then water lapping at her arms but still waiting, believing that someone would return for her. And then the water was up to her face, slipping over her lips—

Hestie flinched. She realized, with a vicious shock, that she'd been in the process of untying one of the leather straps.

She shoved away from the bed, her gasps turning into

low moans as queasiness swamped her. The man's shriveled, whitened body lay still, but the gently swirling hair gave the impression of movement. The head was tilted back, the jaws wide open, and Hestie wondered if that had been the position he'd died in: gasping for a final mouthful of air that would never reach him.

She turned. Vanna floated behind and above her. The dark, faceless figure seemed to loom over them in the hospital's gloom, somehow otherworldly and as though she had always belonged there. The sleek, black dive suit was superimposed against the backdrop of white. Shadows spread out from her back, and the shapes they painted across the opposite wall looked for all the world like wings.

An angel. Or an angel of death?

Hestie's breathing had become labored. She was sinking, slowly, and knew she should correct her buoyancy but couldn't remember how. Vanna was moving nearer. One of her long, powerful arms reached toward Hestie.

"What's happening?"

Cove threaded her way along the dive line, winding it into loops around her elbow as they followed the path laid out for them by Vanna and Hestie. The static persisted in their audio systems, but underneath were strange noises. A gasping, gurgling sound. The rustle of a struggle. Something that might have been a moan.

And then Hestie's voice, slurred and slow: "What are... I..."

"Hestie?" Cove was moving faster than she knew she should. Clouds of silt kicked up behind her, but Roy and Aidan were doggedly keeping pace with her as they hunted their way along the hall. "Vanna?"

A gasp. The sound of someone choking.

The dive line tilted upward, and Cove realized, a second too late, that she was powering straight into a barricade of furniture. She corrected her angle at the last second and speared over the top. The rattle of a disturbed chair told her that she'd bumped something, but the structure held together well enough for Roy and Aidan to slide through.

The other side of the audio had grown strangely quiet.

Catching up the dive line was slowing her down, so Cove dropped the coils, and instead focused on following the white cord that seemed to glow through the *Arcadia's* darkness. It followed a bend in the hall, then turned sharply to the left and disappeared through an open door.

Cove's headlight flickered, then flared twice as bright as before and vanished with a sharp pop. Perfect darkness swallowed her. She'd been aiming for the opening in the door but misjudged it with her lights gone. Her head collided with the wood first. A heavy cracking noise flooded around her. The headlight flickered on, then died again. She reflexively clamped her mouth shut and held her breath, but the most dreaded outcome—icy saltwater rushing across her face—didn't follow.

Her neck ached. A low, throbbing headache started in the back of her head. But she thought she was still all right.

"Hey, Cove, you good?"

Roy's hand lightly touched her back. His headlight was still working. It swamped the door beside her, the harsh white light refracting off the polished wood and redoubling the ache at the back of her skull.

"I'm okay. Lost my light. Vanna? Hestie?"

There was no reply, just ragged breathing, and Cove didn't know if it came from Aidan, Roy, or even herself. No lights came from behind the door.

In that second, the room terrified her. She didn't know what— or who—she might find inside, only that, without her lights, the space would be pitch-black.

Reach your hand inside. See if anything reaches back.

Cove recoiled but then, sucking in a tight breath between clenched teeth, shoved through.

She was blind. It was a different kind of blind from what she'd experienced in the hull; that had been constant swirling flecks, dizzying and endless. This…this was just *black*. A pitch-dark that her eyes would never adjust to. Crushing, limitless. She could have twenty feet of clear swimming space ahead or she could be within inches of a sharp metal spike, and she had no way of knowing.

And then Roy followed her through the door's narrow gap. The blush of light started in jittering stages, catching on the wall, some of the toppled curtains, the sleek metal edges of the beds. And then his head turned and the circle of light fixated, like a spotlight, on the two bodies floating ahead.

Hestie seemed both limp and rigid at the same moment. Her head was tilted slightly to the side. Her body seemed to heave.

No—please, no—

Vanna was at her back, arms encircling the marine biologist. She was pinning Hestie's arms down. The angle had to be difficult with the dive canisters between them, but she'd managed to wedge her shoulder in at Hestie's neck, propping her head up.

Fear pounded through Cove, pushing her forward. Hestie's arms were kept still by Vanna, but her legs were still moving— strange, twitching kicks that reminded Cove of a dying insect.

"Roy, bring your light over here." Cove moved too fast. She hit Vanna's side before she could stop her momentum. There, close enough that she was nearly pressing her mask against Hestie's, she was able to see through the glare.

No. Please. Not like this.

Hestie's face was impossibly pale, and the skin around her cheeks was slack. Her eyes had rolled back in their sockets, revealing the whites. She didn't show any response to Cove's presence.

"What happened?" Roy was at Hestie's other side, though he seemed reluctant to touch her. He glanced down and swore. Cove followed his gaze and saw they were floating nearly on top of a body strapped to a hospital bed. She looked away.

"I'm not sure." Vanna's voice seemed too cool, too calm for this situation. "A seizure perhaps."

Roy choked on his words. "You're telling me—"

Hestie's chest heaved, her head rolling back, her eyelids fluttering. Cove found her gloved hand and gripped it tightly.

"She can still breathe," Vanna said. "The mask will ensure that. But we need to keep her airways clear."

That was the purpose behind propping her head up, Cove saw. She looked toward the nearest wall. It had a window the size of a small dining table—easy access out.

"We're going to begin ascent," she said, and her always-steady voice held again, disguising the sheer panic coursing through her. "The sooner we can get to the surface, the better. Vanna, hold her head. I'll keep her body steady. The rest of you, follow closely. Let's go."

34.

That night, the *Skipjack's* kitchen was more crowded than it had any right to be. Aidan had made a beeline for it as soon as his equipment was packed away, under the excuse that it was his job to start dinner. Devereaux had gone with him, gently mentioning that Aidan shouldn't be expected to do all the work alone, and Sean had tailed him.

Then Roy, at a loose end, had followed and now stood with his back to the fridge, inconveniencing anyone who needed to collect ingredients.

The kitchen had been designed for two cooks—maybe three at a pinch—and Cove had to stop in the doorway with her arms crossed to avoid being jostled.

Sean and Devereaux were both pretending to help Aidan cook, but that was neither of their motives. Her father would have called them stickybeaks. She was simply calling them *nosy*.

To be fair, she hadn't spoken to them since she and Vanna had pulled the still-weak Hestie out of the water. With Cove helping

Hestie to bed and Vanna vanishing into the hold, where she seemed to spend most of her free time, very few avenues were left for them to get information. She wasn't sure how much Aidan or Roy had told them, but the irate turn to Sean's lips told her it was not as much as they wanted to know.

Aidan was unusually cheerful with so many people to keep him company and was trying to show them his methodology behind spaghetti Bolognese. "The recipe sites always say to put the salt in the water, but I like to salt the pasta *after* it's drained."

Sean, standing at Aidan's side, looked like he was in physical pain.

"Ah, Cove." Devereaux put down a block of parmesan as he caught sight of her in the doorway. "We were just wondering—"

"Hestie's okay." Cove allowed them a second to murmur among themselves. "We're not entirely sure what it was, but the symptoms match up with a seizure. She's never had one before— you can't dive if you suffer from seizures, for obvious reasons—but it's always possible for them to crop up later in life. She doesn't want to go back to shore, but she'll be resting for tonight."

"Did she say…" Sean was pretending to stir the meat sauce but was really only patting the surface with the spoon's edge. He worked his jaw as he picked his words. "She was with Vanna when it happened, wasn't she?"

"Yes." Cove sent him a sharp glare. "Vanna helped."

"But did she *say* that, or…"

"Yes. That's what she said."

Cove had meant to keep the warning note subtle, but Roy still picked up on it. He glanced between her and Sean, one hand lazily scratching his stubble. "What're you talking about?"

Sean breathed in. Cove raised her eyebrows pointedly, and he sighed. "Nothing. I guess."

"Nothing?" Roy's curiosity wasn't abating. "It doesn't sound like nothing to me."

Sean's eyes were sharp as they flickered across the gathered group. All eyes, even Aidan's, had turned to him. His heavy eyebrows lowered a fraction. "I saw her journal. There's some messed up stuff in there."

Cove was simmering. He'd promised her he wouldn't tell the others about it, but apparently, promises went by the wayside when he thought he had clues to piece together. "Sean brought this to my attention last night. I spoke to Vanna about it. The situation has been resolved."

"Huh." Roy continued to scratch his stubble. "What kind of messed up stuff?"

"None of your business." Cove pointed a finger at Roy to make her point, then turned it to Sean. "Don't harass Vanna about this. You shouldn't have been looking through her things to begin with."

Sean made a disgusted noise and slapped the spoon into the sauce hard enough to send flecks of beef and tomato onto the splashboard. "Vanna and Hestie split off alone. Hestie gets sick for no reason anyone can tell. Don't say that's not weird."

"Sean, I swear—"

"What excuse did she give you? How come you're so eager to believe her when one of your crew members nearly drowned?"

Furious bubbles of frustration built inside Cove. She slammed down on them before they could come out as angry words. Her breathing was too hard and her skin felt hot, but she hoped, at least, she was able to keep most of the emotion out of her face. "We will not be continuing this discussion."

"If we're, you know, on the topic of weird stuff?" Aidan cleared his throat but avoided looking any of them in the eye. "Some weird stuff's going on with the ship. You know?"

It was a diversion, and Cove seized it, softening her voice to encourage the crew's youngest member. "What kind of weird things, Aidan?"

"Well, okay, I know you guys think the thing that grabbed me in the hold was a rope. And maybe it was. But strange things have been happening since we first arrived. It started with the ROVs. Then our audio went out. And Cove's light broke—"

"She ran into a door," Roy interjected.

Aidan blinked furiously. "I thought—uh—didn't she—after?"

"She ran into a door and broke her light," Roy said. "Sorry, buddy, but I'm tagging that one as pure clumsiness."

"Okay, well." His eyebrows were deeply furrowed as he struggled to put his thoughts into words. "I think… I think the bodies down there are… I don't know. Maybe they did something to Hestie. I think maybe I saw one of them move."

Sean made another disgusted noise and hauled the meat sauce off the stove. It had started to develop a burnt scent that Cove knew didn't bode well.

"Sometimes things underwater can appear to move," she said. "But it's really only the eddies disturbing them. Normally, when we see, say, a blanket or a piece of paper move, we can accept that. But in this case, we're still perceiving these bodies as *humans* and that's adding a level of eeriness to the motion that wouldn't otherwise be there."

He frowned, not looking convinced, but mumbled, "I guess."

Cove rolled her shoulders as she regarded the room. Devereaux, as seemed his habit, was contributing very little but listened with great interest. Sean looked quietly furious. And Roy was watching her with a level of suspicion she really didn't appreciate. She would have given almost anything for Sean to have kept his mouth shut.

"Well, Hestie won't be returning for any further dives," Cove said. "Not here and maybe not anywhere else, depending. But we still need to decide what the rest of us are doing."

Sean's head jerked toward her, nostrils flaring. "You're not thinking of—"

"Right now, we don't have enough footage to meet Vivitech's contract." Cove, arms folded, lifted her shoulders in a shrug. "We can try submitting what we have. I figure our justification for not completing the work is about as solid as it could ever get. But... they may not honor the payments."

Roy choked on his laughter. "There's, like, an actual cemetery's worth of bodies down there. They wouldn't reasonably expect us to...and besides, this isn't just trashy B-roll stuff we're sending them. The things we've captured would be enough to win them awards. They're not just going to *walk away* from it."

"No. Of course they couldn't." Cove's lips twisted in disgust. "But they could do what they did with the *Endless Worlds* documentary and cut payment for, and I quote, *substandard work*."

"*Endless Worlds*..." Aidan bit his lip. "Wasn't that the thing about insect life in the Amazon?"

"That's it. The host developed an infection while trying to reach a remote location. He had to be airlifted out, and they only barely managed to save his leg. He still has a limp. But because he was eight hours short of the footage quota, he was barely paid enough for the food they ate on the trip. Never mind any of the other expenses."

A hush fell over the kitchen. It was only disturbed by Aidan, who began draining the pasta in a colander in the sink.

"You think they'd do that to us?" Roy asked.

"I don't know." She couldn't look him in the eyes. "But yeah. Probably. Vivitech is cutthroat. As long as we meet the contract's quota, we should be okay. But they'll take advantage of any missteps we present them."

Aidan began messily scooping pasta and sauce onto plates, and Cove supposed they were eating in the kitchen that night. She was glad. As tight as the space was, it felt cozier than the sparse mess hall. The stove had kept it warm, and that was a blessing when the biting winds whistled about their vessel.

"Do you want to tell them the *real* reason you're pushing so hard?" Sean asked. One of his eyebrows had risen, but his lips remained curled down. It wasn't an expression she liked.

When she didn't answer, Roy said, "What?"

Cove closed her eyes, knowing what was coming next.

"She had to file for bankruptcy last year." Sean rolled his shoulders as he leaned back against the kitchen cabinets. "I did some digging while you were on the dive. Right now, she's got *nothing*. She had to borrow money just to go on this trip. What do you think happens to her if it fails?"

Roy flicked his gaze to Cove, faintly incredulous. "Is that true?"

"It is," Sean said. "She needs this dive to be a success because she's desperate. If she weren't, maybe she'd, I don't know, value your lives a little more highly."

The familiar flush of humiliation had been a regular visitor for most of a year. Cove tamped it down just as hard as she always did. She took a second to breathe slowly, even though it hurt on the way down. "I have nothing to hide. Yes, I filed for bankruptcy. My father was sick. The doctors said he wasn't going to last six months. So I paid for an experimental treatment for him. So you're right, I need work right now. But give me some credit. I have taken none of this flippantly. At every turn, I've left the choice to continue up to each of you."

"Did it work?" Roy asked.

She hesitated. "Sorry?"

"The treatment. For your dad."

"No." The act of smiling felt like it was ripping a hole deep inside her. She and Roy had been working together on and off for years, not exactly close friends, but warmer than simple work colleagues. She realized, with a shock, she'd never told him about her father's passing. And apparently, he'd missed the articles plastered all over the news. Her father had spent his life working for humanitarian causes, but it had been Cove's own modest fame that had qualified his passing as newsworthy.

"Damn," Roy said, scowling at the floor.

Aidan approached her, holding out a plate of pasta and cutlery. "I'm sorry."

She knew what he meant, but partnered with the plate, it gave Cove the impression that he was apologizing for the food, and a wild, helpless kind of laughter tried to bubble up before she tamped it down too. "Thanks."

Roy cleared his throat. "I'm game for another dive."

"Me too," Aidan said.

Sean grimaced and slammed past Cove, leaving the kitchen with his food untouched.

Cove tried to hold her hands steady as she twirled pasta onto the fork. "Please don't make this choice based on me. This isn't some request from a friend that you can't turn down without being impolite; it's still a work contract. And if at any point you—"

"I said I'm in." Roy shoveled some of the meat sauce into his mouth and, to Cove's horror, managed to grin and chew in the same moment. "I want to get paid too."

"Okay," Cove said as her heart beat furiously against her ribs. "We'll talk about it."

35.

The captain almost never left the bridge. Rarely, he would summon one of the officers or shipmates for hushed conversations, but they never stayed long. He didn't allow any of the other crew to see the controls or catch a glimpse of where they were heading.

Fourth Officer Swain had been watching the door for days. In case he was questioned about it, he had a handful of excuses at the ready: that he was waiting to carry a message from the captain, that he had been stationed as a guard, or that there was a report to pass on once the door next opened. But so far, no one had asked him.

The crew seemed universally dead-eyed. They moved, and they did their jobs with the rigid conviction of men who have forgotten how to say no, but there seemed to be very little of them left inside.

Even the officers were behaving abnormally. They would nod as they passed him in the halls, as they always did, but they never spoke to him unless he spoke first, and none of them—not even the most hardheaded—seemed to be questioning the captain's decisions in the way Swain was.

He didn't have the long naval career of the others, to be fair. This was his first stationing, while many of the others had worked under Captain Virgil for upward of a decade. Being the newest, there was heavy pressure to conform. To not ask too many questions, to simply follow orders.

And yet...

It had been days since the captain had left the bridge for any significant length of time. When was he sleeping? Was he even eating? Trays of food were delivered three times a day, but when they were next carried out, they seemed as full as they had when they went in.

A ship was not meant to be sailed by its captain alone. It should have been buzzing with quartermasters, officers, and stewards. The captain's role should be to give orders and see that they were carried out, rarely more.

Which left Swain with a cold fear in the pit of his stomach: What if they were not being led to land?

No one had seen the charts or the coordinates. No one, except for the captain, knew exactly where they were or where they were going. At one point, a rumor had passed through the mess hall that land had to be close. It couldn't be seen, not with the unnatural mist that clouded their every waking moment, but it could be heard: other boats and far distant mechanical noises. But that had been a full day ago, and the ship continued to power on under full steam, and no word had been given that they were anywhere close to making land.

It was as though they were destined to sail forever.

The thought was like ice in Swain's chest. Stories of ghost ships, once ubiquitous in the navy, had petered out as the world entered a more modern age. They were past the era of superstition, seances and rappings and apparitions in the back of drawing rooms. Very few crew members still entertained the idea of ghost ships, and while Swain would have considered himself the least likely out of anyone, wasn't that akin to what they had become?

A wraithlike ship, gliding through a mist it never quite managed to escape. Sailing on forever, under the command of a captain who might have been sent mad by the ocean. The crew, tirelessly working their stations, following orders without question, as the days dragged into weeks and the weeks to months and the months, eventually, to years.

Swain suspected it was paranoia whispering those thoughts into his mind, yet they should have docked by now. Days passed and still no one saw their coordinates. If they had been able to escape the fog for just an hour, Swain could have made some rough estimates on their heading based on either the sun or star positions—but the mist refused to give them any respite.

And so he stood outside the bridge, waiting for his chance.

This chance.

The door groaned as it opened. Very rarely, perhaps once a day, the captain would leave the bridge, usually in response to some urgent situation elsewhere in the vessel. He always locked the door behind himself, and he was rarely gone for more than half an hour.

Swain hoped that today's crisis might delay him slightly longer. Crew members had begun coughing up blood. It had happened once before, when a stoker was found delirious in a bathroom. He hadn't survived a full day. These new cases presented very

similarly. There was a lack of coordination, a fever, and a delirious state. Almost a mercy, Swain thought; he wouldn't want to
be conscious in that condition, slowly bleeding out from his nose
and eyes and ears.

The four new cases had been brought to the hospital. The
officers in charge of the efforts had been given instructions not to
share anything with the crew or the passengers, but the whispers
had started to swell regardless.

Swain hated that. No one seemed to speak any longer. They just
passed things on in *whispers*. Everywhere he walked was the soft
murmur of hushed voices that grew ever quieter as he neared them.
As though he couldn't be allowed to hear their secrets. As though
even the ship's most vital updates were to be kept from him.

The captain stepped through the open door. Swain stood
to attention, eyes fixed on the wall, but not even the captain
acknowledged him as he locked the door with a heavy metal key.

Captain Virgil had always struck Swain as an imposing man,
the way a captain ought to be. He inspired awe. He could bring
a room to silence with a single word. And with a career of thirty
years backing him, he'd earned that respect.

Now, as Swain caught glances of him from the corner of his
eye, he found himself questioning whether the captain's shoulders
had always been this bowed or his face this gaunt. His eyelids
hung heavy, while bags filled below. Once, nothing had escaped
his notice. Now, he walked past Swain as though the officer were
no more than a decoration.

The changes in the captain frightened Swain and strengthened
his resolve. He could be put in the brig for disobeying orders—
possibly even charged once they reached land—but at that
moment, a court hearing would almost be a blessing; it would
mean the SS *Arcadia* had made it back to land.

Swain waited until the captain's footsteps had nearly faded and then knelt in front of the door. Generally, the bridge was not ever supposed to be locked. Officers and stewards needed to move in and out freely, and the constant motion had meant that limiting their access to the room would have only been a hindrance. Even in the dead of night, someone had to be steering and manning the communications.

But not under Captain Virgil's watch apparently.

Swain fit his small metal bobby pin into the keyhole, then gently inserted a second metal hook. One of the crew—a Fitzwilliam, the man who had uncovered the desiccated remains in the hull—had taught Swain how to pick locks when they were stuck on a dull shift together. At the time, Swain had been vaguely aghast at the older stock master's willingness to admit to the activity, even if, as he swore, he never used it for anything illegal.

Now, Swain had never been more grateful. He'd fashioned the hook himself, and the bobby pin had been taken from one of the abandoned passenger berths. He'd practiced on his own cabin's door to ensure it would work, but now, as he crouched outside the bridge, his hands shook too much to get a solid grip on the slim implements.

Every few seconds he stopped, listening for the heavy thud of boots on the stairs, the only warning he would have if the captain was returning.

A click, and the lock finally gave way. Swain was breathing far too loudly as he slipped inside the bridge and gently closed the door behind himself.

There was a problem though. The bridge's lights were out. Swain could barely make out the curved tops of the steering and navigational gear ahead of the windows.

The captain hadn't carried anything when he left, which meant there had to be a lantern or, at the very least, a candle somewhere close by. Swain reached blind hands out toward the desks he knew were beside the door. His fingertips touched a stack of books, then felt the metal shell of a compass, then knocked over a full glass of water.

He swore under his breath as he fumbled to catch the glass before it could topple over the desk's edge. He couldn't afford to disturb anything. The captain's eyes were sharp, and if a single item were left out of place…

Swain used his uniform sleeve to swipe the water off the table. He couldn't see to tell whether he'd gotten it all or if he was putting the glass back in the right place. As his fingers brushed the wooden tabletop, they came away tacky and slimy, as though the water hadn't been fresh after all, as though it had, perhaps, been sitting there for weeks.

Still no source of light, and his time was ticking away. Was it possible the captain had actually been steering the ship in the dark? He should leave and try again later, making sure to bring a candle of his own.

But how long would it take for the captain to step out of the bridge again? A full day? How many more deaths could occur in those hours? How far would they sail?

Bent double in case he might be seen through the windows, Swain jogged to the tools at the ship's front. The steering wheel was positioned at the center, before the compass's binnacle and a row of tools to measure speed. He tried to read their coordinates, but despite having time for his eyes to adjust to the dark, he still could not make out any of the numbers.

Something heavy knocked on the wood behind him, and Swain's heart nearly died. He swung around, still crouched, his weight pressing on his toes. He was still alone in the bridge.

The knocking sound repeated, traveling along the wall, circling him.

The *things in the walls*. That was what the crew called them. The sounds that could never fully be traced. They seemed to hunt through the walls, following paths of their own design, rising between levels and slinking along every passageway.

Swain was not the kind of man to believe in such fictions, but then, he himself had begun to think of the *Arcadia* as a ghost ship.

There was precious little he could do in the bridge with no light, but he couldn't just *leave* when the ship was in this state. There was one avenue he could yet try. The radio. He hadn't been trained in it, but he'd stood beside the communications officer for enough months to pick up some ideas of what his station entailed. Even blind, he thought he might be able to achieve something with it.

Swain narrowed his eyes as he urged the barely there traces of light to help guide his hand. He could see the faintest sheen of the edges of the knobs, and his roving fingers found the plush headset. He put on only one of the earmuffs, leaving the other hanging behind his left ear so he might still hear the warning footsteps in time. Then he began fiddling with the settings.

Did this warrant the emergency mayday code? People were dead, and more were in the sickbay. But the ship was not, technically, sinking. As much as it *felt* like a mayday to Swain, he knew there were repercussions for using the code erroneously, so instead, he whispered the lesser alternative into the receiver. "Pan-pan."

Silence. His fingers roved over the settings, trying to find what he had done wrong. There were dedicated frequencies that ships listened for, but with no light, he couldn't pick them; instead, he spoke to whatever frequency he had managed to find, silently praying it would be near enough for a ship to hear. "Pan-pan."

Again, silence. He had already pushed his luck to breaking. The captain rarely spent this long away from the bridge.

A different setting, then, again, "Pan-pan."

Shivers ran through him as a voice answered. It was warm, fully vibrant, and loud. It was the first time Swain had heard someone speak at a normal volume in days.

"This is the SS *Rambolt*, Communications Officer Lee. I hear you. What's your situation?"

Swain was grinning, half-wild with relief and hope, his eyes wet in spite of himself. "Thank heaven. I'm calling from the SS *Arcadia*. We need urgent help."

"Received. What are your coordinates?"

"I...I don't know." Swain's smile fell. He had done it; he had made contact with another ship, a ship that could help them, maybe even save them. But how could they find him when he didn't know where they were supposed to be?

The man on the line was speaking again, but Swain's ears were pulled in another direction: toward the stairs. They groaned as heavy shoes pressed on the metal.

He threw down the headset and slammed the switch to turn off the radio system. There was no time to be stealthy and no time to do anything about the empty glass of water. He raced for the door, his heart in his throat, and hit it with a heady reverberation that was far louder than he'd intended.

Then he was out, the door closed behind him. There was no chance to hide. The only possible locations for concealment were down the same hallway that Captain Virgil was tracing. Instead, Swain pressed his back to the wall, in the same position he had been in when the captain had left, and prayed.

Captain Virgil turned the corner, his gaunt features visible in the single bulb that still operated in that stretch of hall. He showed no acknowledgment of Swain, which was a mercy, since Swain himself was sweating and shivering despite his best efforts to keep still.

The captain's key came from his pocket and was pressed into the keyhole. Captain Virgil's shoulders tensed, and Swain felt his heart miss a beat. He had not locked the door on the way out.

This was it; in a second, the captain would turn and fix him with those steely, shrewd eyes, and he would have no way of hiding the fear or the color on his face and—

The captain simply shoved the door open and stepped inside. The door closed, then the lock clicked as it was, once again, sealed.

Swain held his rigid position for a full minute before allowing the tension to bleed from his limbs. His shoulders slumped, his hair falling forward as he let his head droop forward. He couldn't stop gasping thin, ragged breaths.

Only then did he see the color on his sleeve. He'd noticed that the water from the glass had been tacky and sour when he used his coat to mop up the spilled residue. Now, he saw it had also contained streaks of red.

As Swain silently crept away from the bridge, questions clung in his mind like frantic moths: Had the *Rambolt* raised an alarm? Would a search begin? Could the *Arcadia*, ghost ship that it was, even be found?

And above all, how long had the captain been coughing up blood?

36.

THE EVENING OF THE SECOND DIVE

Aidan wore his furry slippers. They'd been a gift from his mother years before, and they represented comfort. Not only because they were the coziest item of clothing he'd ever owned but because of who they had come from. It had been his first year living away from home, and his mother had bought the largest, puffiest pair of slippers she could find and express posted them to him because she'd heard that there was unseasonally cold weather coming to his area.

They'd arrived when he'd been at a low point: missing home, struggling to find friends, and fearful that he was wasting his life. The slippers, showing up at his door unexpectedly, had gotten him through that first autumn.

He'd brought them on this trip half as a reminder of home and half because he'd suspected he might need to be comforted. Turns out, that premonition had been very correct.

It was half past eleven and he was wandering the ship, searching for someone who might still be awake. A pale light came from under the lounge doors. Aidan knocked lightly. There wasn't a response, so he gingerly nudged a door open to peek inside.

Cove sat on one of the lounges, one leg pulled up and the other curled under herself. A single lamp lit the room. Her computer sat on the table in front of her, and although Cove stared at it, the screen had gone black.

Aidan tentatively knocked on the door again, and Cove startled. The familiar warm smile rose as she saw him, and she beckoned him. "Hey, Aidan. Come on in. Couldn't sleep?"

"No." He shuffled into the room, pulling his tattered jacket higher around his neck to protect against the chill. "You too?"

"Hmm." She nodded toward the laptop. "Trying to do some more last-minute research. This…" She flicked a hand vaguely, then cleared her throat. "*None* of this should have been so complicated. It was meant to be four days of filming with the ROVs, then a dive to fill out the footage. It should have been so much simpler."

He found a chair near her and shuffled into it. "Not your fault. Y'know? You didn't plan for this to happen."

"No." She was still smiling, but there was a wry twist to it. "But I'm the leader. I'm supposed to be looking after my crew. And I can't stop thinking about what Sean said. Is he right?"

"About…" Aidan frowned, fidgeting at the edges of his jacket. "About my spaghetti being garbage?"

"What? Did he say that? No. Your spaghetti's great." She found his forearm and gave it a squeeze. "Seriously. Best Bolognese I've had in years."

He squinted one eye at her. "Is it…the only Bolognese you've had in years?"

"Damn, you got me."

They both broke out into soft laughter. Aidan kicked back in the chair, rubbing his slippers together. It was a habit he'd developed shortly after getting them, and it was turning them threadbare, but he liked the sensation too much to stop.

"Something's on your mind," Cove said. She closed the laptop and the soft whirr of its fans faded instantly.

"No. Well, yeah, I guess. Roy hasn't gone to bed yet, and I kept worrying about that, and it made it hard to sleep."

"Huh. Have you found him?"

"No. But I haven't really looked far."

"You would've found him in the kitchen." The lounge room's door creaked open. Roy, haggard and wearing a rumpled T-shirt and grease-splattered shorts, leaned in the doorway, a crooked smile in place. "He was looking for beer. Or, you know, any other kind of alcohol the owners of the ship might have had the foresight to stock."

"Ah. I don't think Devereaux drinks much." Cove pushed out of her chair and stretched. "But I did bring something. Give me a minute."

She stepped through the door Roy was leaning against, and they gave each other a lazy high five on the way past. From what Aidan could tell, that was a habit that had sprung up between them years ago. He smiled but also ached inside. He so readily found himself thinking of Roy as his best friend that it was easy to forget that Roy probably didn't think the same in return.

"Hey," Roy said, dropping into the couch on Aidan's other side and kicking his feet over the armrest. "Getting cold feet about the dive tomorrow?"

How can I answer that? Tell Roy that, for the second dive in a row, I came within half an hour of running out of oxygen? That

I only started to calm down when I was too exhausted to feel any more fear?

Or do I tell him about the arm in the boiler room?

Cove had noticed it first, but she'd looked away quickly so she wouldn't draw Roy's attention to it. He hadn't been very chill about the bodies up until then. But Aidan, last in the procession, had looked. His mask had released a burst of bubbles that had clouded his vision, and when it cleared, he could have sworn the hand had been in a different position.

All of those thoughts jumbled through his head, tumbling over each other, and in the end, all he said was, "I'm fine."

The door swung open again. Cove had returned, this time carrying three mugs and a bottle of champagne.

"I brought a few of these to share after the final dive." She set the mugs onto the coffee table beside the laptop and began working the cork out of the bottle. "Figure that's no longer the mood, so we may as well have it now."

"I'm not sure it's the mood for tonight either," Roy said, "but I'm not going to turn it down."

The cork popped free, and Aidan jolted. Roy laughed, using his elbow to bump Aidan's knee. "Bit jittery, huh?"

"I mean, I don't blame him. Today was...how do I say this? Not great." Cove poured the first mug and passed it to Roy, then narrowed her eyes at Aidan. "Are you old enough?"

"I'm twenty-two." He managed some indignation, but Roy only laughed louder.

"Right, of course. Pretty sure I checked that before letting you join the crew." She poured his serving and passed it over.

He wrapped his hands around the cup and gazed down at the tiny spitting bubbles forming on the champagne's surface. There was something surreal about the setting: late at night, wearing comfortable clothing, and holding mugs. By all rights the drink should have been hot chocolate or coffee, something rich and warming to match the atmosphere. Instead, the sparkling alcohol made everything feel just a little off.

It was like a metaphor for the *Arcadia*, he thought. A ship but just a little off. So much of it matching his idea of what a shipwreck might look like…but with a whole band of emotions that shouldn't have been there.

"I'm glad you're both here actually." Cove reclined in her chair, gazing at her own drink with the look of someone who wasn't sure they actually wanted it.

Roy drank deeply and sighed as he came up for air. "This is about tomorrow's dive, huh?"

"Yeah."

"So you…" Aidan ran his thumb over the edge of the mug as he hunted for words. "You don't want to go down again tomorrow?"

"If it were just me? No, I'd go on the final dive. But I'm used to that. It's always been a bit of a game: How far can I go? What can I get away with? But it's different with a team. I have to make a judgment call on what's best for you guys and your safety. I checked in with Vanna. She's willing to go again. But…she does this professionally. And this is a lot more than either of you signed up for. I was thinking that maybe just Vanna and I should go down tomorrow."

"You need us though," Aidan said. The thoughts had clicked into place in the back of his head without him even noticing. "You need enough divers to split into two teams. That's the only way you'd get enough footage in just three dives."

She grimaced, confirming his theory.

"At what point, in our sordid history together, have I ever shown myself to be a quitter?" Roy asked.

Cove snorted, a smile forming. "I don't know. You quit that game of chess pretty fast."

"You took my queen on the third turn! I don't think that's legal. Chess is a stupid game anyway."

Cove extended her mug toward him, and he tapped it with his own.

"Nah," Roy said. "My point is, I signed my own contract, and I'm seeing this through to the end."

"Me too," Aidan said, with a level of conviction he wasn't entirely sure he felt. "This is my, my one chance to do something big, and—"

"Hey." Cove's voice took on a soft note. "Don't believe that. Life is full of opportunities. Sometimes you need to go out looking for them, but if you want them, you'll find them."

He chewed his lip. "Still. I…I don't want to quit when we're so close to finishing it."

Cove continued to watch him, her striking green eyes taking his measure. Aidan knew what she was thinking. He cleared his throat. "I'm really sorry about the thing in the hold. I won't do that again."

"I don't blame you for that." She shrugged. "It's not a measure of your character in any way. You just…you have less experience. Most of us have a decade more of diving practice. We shouldn't have expected you to be at our level—"

"Let me do this." He couldn't meet her eyes, but the sudden desperate need to be deemed *enough*, to be seen as acceptable, was overwhelming. "I can—I'm getting better. The thing in the hold was a mistake, but I know where I went wrong and I can do better next time."

There was something pained in Cove's expression. She opened her mouth, then closed it again, then took a slow breath and said, "Okay."

"Okay." His smile was shaky. "Great. Okay. Yeah."

"I want to keep tomorrow's dive simple." Cove sipped from the edge of her mug. "We've gotten footage in the holds and the boiler room. I figure it will be enough to give the experts *something* to ponder over. Tomorrow, we'll spend our time somewhere easier to access. Maybe around the decks or in the higher passenger areas. No more gymnastics in crowded rooms."

"Sounds like a plan to me," Roy said. He downed the last of his mug and reached for the bottle, but Cove grabbed it first. She rose and carried it to the door.

"Nope. You're not getting drunk the night before the dive. Technically, you shouldn't have had any alcohol at all, but…"

"C'mon," Roy called, but Cove was already gone. He sighed dramatically. "Well, if even the world's saddest substitute for beer has been taken from me, I guess I'm going to bed."

"Yeah, I'll be down in a moment too."

Roy gave him a firm clap on the back, then rose with a groan and loped toward the door. Aidan looked down at his own mug. He'd only drunk half, but he didn't hold alcohol well and was already feeling on the edge of tipsy. He put it aside, then sat back as he rubbed his slippers together. The fluffy edges were just high enough to hide the bruising around his ankle.

Warm metal grazed his chest every time he moved. He carefully drew out the ring he kept there and turned it over in his hands. The small diamond shone beautifully in the lamplight. It didn't look even a fraction as old as it was.

"Excuse me." The door creaked as Devereaux's head appeared around the edge. "I'm looking for Cove."

"Ah. Just missed her. She might be in the kitchen."

"Excellent." He hesitated. "You'll have to forgive my curious streak, but that's an engagement ring, isn't it?"

Aidan dropped it, feeling color flame over his face, but Devereaux stepped into the room, letting the door drop closed behind him. "You're not planning to propose to someone on the trip, I hope. They all strike me as being a little too old for you."

"N-no. When I get back home. Penny. It's, uh…" He picked the ring back up. "I let it slip to her parents last month. And they offered me this."

"Ah." Devereaux, beaming, took a seat. "A family heirloom?"

"Yeah, exactly. It's been passed down for, like, three hundred years or something." Aidan couldn't stop the deeply nervous smile. "So, like, I really hope she says yes, or else it's going to be pretty awkward giving it back to them."

"Mm. Sounds like they like you. Which probably bodes well for the lady's reply." Devereaux removed his glasses and began polishing them on his cardigan's corner. "I wish you the best of luck with it. Are you going back down to the ship tomorrow?"

"Yeah. We just finished talking about that. One last dive."

"Then I'll wish you the best of luck with that as well." He replaced his glasses and gave Aidan a shrewd glance. "You know, I was going to ask Cove about this, but you might be interested as well. I've been reviewing the footage and noticed something peculiar in the hold…"

37.

They'd started to leave the walls.

The tormentors were only seen in distant glimpses, far away in the dark hallways, shrouded by the fog. The few among the crew who were bold enough to approach them claimed they vanished when you grew near.

For most, though, the sight of one of the wall-dwellers was enough to drive them into retreat or to freeze them in place in terror.

Harland had only seen one: right at the edges of his vision, barely touched by his candle's flickering light. Strange and pale, seeming to be made of the very fog that flooded the *Arcadia*, it had fixed him with a single piercing gaze and then turned and vanished into the wall. Harland had needed nearly half an hour to gain enough courage to approach that section. The wall was smooth and untouched: no holes and no secret doors.

A band of passengers had gone into a frenzy, rushing the decks, attempting to launch the lifeboats themselves, demanding that they be allowed at least an attempt at escape. The captain's orders had been swift. The lifeboats were to be hurled into the ocean…empty. Oars were thrown overboard and left to drift away on the ocean.

It had taken the entire crew twenty minutes to achieve. While many of the crew worked to unceremoniously drop the lifeboats over the *Arcadia*'s edge, others had forced the passengers back belowdecks.

It was for their own safety, the captain said. That was what he considered above all else.

Following that, orders had been given for the crew to begin work on boarding over the higher levels' windows. He believed that the fog must be leaking in through them and that the fog was the source of all of their sickness. If they wanted to survive, they needed to block any holes it might be entering through.

No one was allowed outside any longer, not even watchmen. The doors to the deck had been sealed and made airtight.

There were too many windows in the passenger holds to seal, so they locked the doors instead, usually with the passengers inside. Not a perfect defense, but the best they could manage under the circumstances.

Supposedly, once the work was done, the only remaining windows on the upper deck would be in the bridge, to allow for navigation. The captain was exposing himself to enormous risk by being in their proximity, and he refused to share that risk with any of his officers.

The crew had tried to maintain a docket of deaths, but more and more individuals had vanished, presumably claimed by the burrowing disease, and their hiding places had yet to be found. The officers had given up on trying to track missing passengers.

They were running out of storage space in the hull and had begun hanging sack-wrapped corpses from its ceiling, like cuts of meat in a butcher's store.

They had opened another crate of candles, but there was only one more after this. They needed to conserve the lights. If they weren't careful, they would very soon be living in the dark. Lost, never to be found again.

THE THIRD DIVE

Cove's body was angled for the dive: head down, feet toward the surface, as she followed the snaking white dive line laid out two days before.

She'd had some faint idea that the journey would grow easier each time, but the anxiety had been worse than ever that morning, the impulse to hold her breath harder to override, the plunge toward the ocean's floor faster, her nerves tighter.

As had become their pattern, Vanna led the team, with Roy and Aidan in her wake and Cove bringing up the rear to watch her crew. She studied their body language now, in the same way she had studied their expressions as they suited up. Roy was dogged and rigid. Aidan, breathing a little too fast but seemingly still in control of himself. Vanna, as expressionless as a stone.

She was feeling the loss of Hestie. The slim marine biologist had seen them off on deck but then quietly returned to her room. The experience on the last dive had shaken her. And it was no wonder; a seizure underwater would have been almost certain death if she'd been using a traditional scuba mouthpiece. They could thank their luck that the full-face mask hadn't accidentally been knocked free.

Their dive weights ensured the descent happened at a near-uncomfortable speed. Cove tracked their depth on her dive computer, checking off each of their milestones. Past the point where nitrogen turned toxic. Past the point where the equivalent of eight atmospheres was pressing on them. Past the point where natural sunlight was all but blotted out.

And then, all too soon, the *Arcadia* loomed into view. That ship had once filled Cove with immeasurable excitement. Now, staring at its bow, she only felt the slick dread of obligation.

She had to make this final dive count. The previous day's had been cut short, even though, in their panic, they had all burned through their measure of oxygen and then some.

"Let's start by going across the deck," Cove said. "The first-class lounges all had major windows. It shouldn't be too hard to find a way in."

"Gotcha," Roy said. Cove noticed a slight crackle to his voice.

Sean had examined their audio equipment the previous night. He'd come back to Cove over breakfast with the light on her dive mask replaced and the news that nothing else seemed amiss. At surface level, at least, everything worked exactly as intended.

They rose along the ship's bow and gently dipped over the railing. It was Cove's first time getting a clear look at the ship's decks. They were almost entirely bare, washed clean during the descent.

"Looks like they tried the lifeboats after all," Roy noted.

He was right. The locations where the boats were traditionally anchored were empty. Now, all that remained of them were tangled, silt-covered rigging.

The ship's main promenade deck extended as far as they could see. Rising out of its center was the complex of lounge rooms, smoking rooms, and writing rooms. Two massive smokestacks cut between them. One had partially collapsed, its upper half tumbling down to crush a section of the promenade, but the fore smokestack stood like a man-made mountain ahead of them.

"Here's the plan." Cove's smooth, calming voice didn't betray her. No matter how much trepidation she felt at this last trip, she still sounded fully in control. "We'll pick an entrance and mark it as our meeting point. Then we split into two teams and each pick a direction. Everyone check your watches. It's one fifteen. If we lose communications with each other, we'll meet back at this point in exactly one hour, at two fifteen."

"Gotcha," Roy said. "I was thinking for the team split—"

Vanna cut across him. "I'd like Aidan."

That was followed by a heavy second of silence, then Roy's disgusted snort. "Nope. He's my friend, yeah? I think I'd like to keep him with me."

This was going to be a repeat of the previous dive. Cove fixed her face into a smile as she prepared for a battle. "I like Vanna's suggestion. We've always worked well as a team, Roy."

"That we have. But I promised Aidan I'd stick with him."

They were approaching the first block of rooms: the smoking rooms, if Cove wasn't mistaken. Something seemed off about the windows, but Cove could only afford to give it half her attention when Roy was being so stubborn.

"I might want to explore some tight spaces," Vanna said. "Cove wouldn't fit. But Aidan would."

"Oh, sweet," Aidan said, and he sounded like he meant it.

"Really?" Roy asked. "You're going to push the issue, Vanna? Fine. I don't want Aidan with you after what Sean said last night."

Vanna's reaction was so minuscule that Cove wouldn't have noticed it if she hadn't been looking for it. But there it was: the stiffening of her shoulders, the new rigidity in her neck.

Cove grit her teeth. "Sean has a big mouth and gossips about things he shouldn't. All you know, Roy, is that Vanna keeps a journal. That's hardly shocking."

"He said there was *weird* stuff in it. And he was pretty damn concerned about what company Hestie was keeping when she collapsed—"

"Roy, enough." For the first time in years, Cove's composure cracked, just a fraction. She took a slow breath, reeling herself back in, then focused on maintaining the calm levelness to her voice. "I'm crew leader and as such I expect you to follow instructions. Aidan will be paired with Vanna. You will be paired with me. I don't want any further arguments about it."

"But—"

"Roy, seriously."

The silence that followed was the kind that stretched and stretched until it ached in their bones. But then Aidan piped up: "I don't mind. Vanna's cool."

"Fine," Roy muttered. "But you damn well better look after him, or I swear I'll break your bones once we get back to the surface."

"You could *try*." Vanna's words held just a hint of humor, and Cove managed to smile.

"Ah…" Aidan cleared his throat. "I don't want to be, like, a wet blanket on this experience or anything, but I'm not sure the windows will be as easy as we were hoping."

Cove finally brought her full attention back to the broad walls in front of them. At the time the *Arcadia* was built, windows couldn't be especially large. It had been constructed a decade before tempered and laminated glass became viable options, and subjected to gale-force winds, rapid temperature changes, and even occasionally unfortunate marine bird impacts, larger windows presented a significant risk to crew and passengers.

But like with many parts of the *Arcadia*, safety was often compromised for aesthetics. The windows had been built as large as possible. They were still tiny by modern standards, where floor-to-ceiling views and even entire walls made of glass could be found in luxury architecture. But by the *Arcadia*'s time, their modest size was considered impressive, especially since they didn't use crossbars.

The windows should have been large enough for the dive team to fit through comfortably, albeit single file and while being careful not to bump the frame. But as Cove faced the row of shattered glass rectangles, she could only frown. They'd all been boarded up from the inside.

"What in the world?" Roy, identifiable by his broad shoulders, kicked closer to the smoking room windows. He stretched a hand out to pry around the window frame. "It's just wood. I bet we could knock it in if we gave it a good kick or something."

"Better not. Too much silt." Already small clouds were rising from where Roy's questioning fingers probed the ship. The promenades—exposed to the slow-moving gulf currents—created a perfect net for the underwater equivalent of dust. It had been bad inside the ship, but on the surface, every small detail was utterly drowning in the silt. It muffled the metal and ropes and wood as thoroughly as a snowfall.

"We'll try farther along," Cove said. "I can't imagine any reason for them to board over *every* window, but even if they did, there should still be some that were knocked free during the sinking."

Vanna fell back, allowing Cove to move first as she swam alongside what she believed were the smoking rooms. She couldn't be sure though, because every single window was blocked.

This was more than a single broken plate of glass being boarded over until it could be repaired. This was systematic and thorough. The barricades had all been treated seriously enough that none of them had broken free during the sinking—not an easy feat, when the moment a ship plunged under often caused enough stress to fracture the metal hull.

Trying to keep something out? Cove's mind flashed to the barricade of furniture in the hallway leading to the hospital. *Or... trying to keep them in?*

She had the sudden, irrational idea that there was something following them on the other side of the walls. She could almost hear it, creeping along inside the rooms, matching their pace, waiting for a gap that might allow it access to the divers. Bulbous, white eyes staring into the dark and long, emaciated fingers scraping over the wooden barricades.

Stop it. Find a way in. One hour. Then you're done.

They passed the first block of rooms. Cove tilted her head back to admire the smokestack. Barely any light reached those depths, but what did was easily blotted out by the structure. Being mostly vertical, it hadn't collected as much silt as the horizontal sections, and the white paint was still clearly visible. It was more than simply formidable; it would have been enough to take Cove's breath away if she'd had much left.

She forced herself to breathe again, belatedly realizing that her lungs were near empty. It was the stress. She'd been in unpleasant situations before: peeling leeches off her legs, the first time she'd fallen off a white-water raft, trying what felt like a thirtieth take on freezing tundra because she couldn't get the audio right. But this, she thought, was perhaps the first time she truly, genuinely did not want to be in the situation.

The times before might have been filled with frustrations and exhaustion, but when she got back to base and collapsed in the evening, she had always felt deeply gratified. As though the hard work was worth something. Cove suspected, when she returned to the ship that evening, it would not be with high spirits, but rather a deep, sinking relief that it was finally over.

They had reached the second block of buildings, what should make up the writing room and the lounge area. The sinking confusion intensified as she saw that these windows, just like the first, had been boarded up.

"We might be able to get in through there." The crackle in Roy's audio had become more noticeable. Cove silently prayed it would resist whatever influence that part of the gulf was exerting on it...at least for the next hour.

She lifted her head. The smokestack behind the second set of rooms had partially collapsed. Massive shards of concrete had crushed the rear of the lounge area and, if her eyes weren't deceiving her, there was enough of a gap remaining to fit through.

"Okay." *This is okay. We can make this work. One final trip inside.* "Let's go."

38.

"Hey."

Devereaux startled as the bridge door slammed. He'd been dozing off again. The previous night had been spent pouring through fresh hours of footage, and he'd fallen asleep slumped across the desk somewhere around three in the morning, earning himself a glasses-shaped imprint across the side of his face and a crick in his neck.

He blinked at the tall, thin man stalking through the bridge and smiled. "Oh, hello, Sean. Did you want to review some footage with me? There's a lot I still haven't—"

"No." Sean, breathing hard, shoved a small leather bag onto an empty space on the console. "Your comms system is still broken, right? I want to try to fix it."

"Ah." Devereaux's eyebrows rose. He swiveled his seat so he could face Sean directly. "You want to listen to the dive while it's still happening. They should have reached the gulf's floor by now; by the time you fix it, I can't imagine there will be much left to listen to."

"Doesn't matter. This is it, right?" Sean was already unscrewing the metal casing on the communications system. "I should have done this sooner. But I actually believed Cove would call it off—"

"I suppose this relates to Vanna."

Sean didn't answer, but the harsh angle of his shoulders told Devereaux all he needed to know.

"You fear...she might try to hurt one of the other divers." Devereaux's eyes were still sore. He removed his glasses, massaged the stinging lids, then replaced his eyewear to get a better look at Sean. "You want to be connected to the audio so you can hear if she does."

Sean flicked the communication console's power off then on again, testing to see if he could get a response. "Cove's either too trusting or Vanna has some kind of sway over her. After what happened to Hestie, they never should have gone back in the water."

"You really think she might sabotage the dive after being a caving instructor for so many years?"

"A lion might let a dozen gazelles run past it while it waits for the right target. Doesn't mean it never intends to strike." Sean shot him a cold glance. "She either threw her journal overboard or hid it somewhere that I can't find it; otherwise, I'd show you. But there's something seriously wrong with that woman."

"Vanna's okay."

Hestie had entered the room so quietly that neither man had heard her. She leaned against the doorframe, a dressing gown loosely tied over her clothes, her wildly curly hair struggling to break free of the scrunchies she'd applied to it. She gave Devereaux a wan smile, but it was impossible not to notice how drained she appeared. Her skin had taken on an ashen shade of gray, and dark patches had formed around her eyes.

"Oh, my dear." Devereaux rose and extended a hand to her.

"You don't look well. Perhaps we should have begun the return to shore last night."

"I'm fine, don't worry." She found his hand and pressed it. Her fingers seemed chilled. "Just tired. Cove made the same offer yesterday, but I didn't feel like dealing with an emergency room, especially when they were probably just going to tell me to sleep it off."

"Still." He sighed. "Would you take a seat? I'll get you something warm to drink."

"I'd like that." She slid into the port-side spare seat, pulling the gown more tightly around herself to block out the icy air. As Devereaux crossed to the door, he glanced back at his two companions.

Sean still knelt over the console, watching Hestie out of the corner of his eye. He seemed to be trying to judge whether it was appropriate to question her about what had happened during the last dive.

Hestie caught his look and gave him a thin smile. "Vanna isn't the problem." Her voice was soft and barely carried through the bridge. "But you should get that working if you can. There's something very, very wrong with the ship."

Aidan watched as Vanna slid through the gap in the walls. She made it look so easy, like a smooth, sleek fish gently curling between ridges of coral. Roy followed, and the illusion was shattered. He struggled to wedge himself between the slabs of cracked concrete, his fins kicking and a soft but constant flow of profanity issuing from the communications units.

"Take it easy," Cove said, a hint of humor in her voice. "Don't force it."

"The damn hole just needs to be a few inches wider." He tried a different angle, his shoulders twisted down, and finally managed to creep through. "Someone needs to add some warning signs to this damn wreck."

"Ha." Aidan glanced at Cove, but she nodded for him to go first. He licked his lips and approached the gap.

The smokestack had crushed part of the room, tearing chunks out of the concrete, but the rubble only allowed for a narrow chasm into the darkness beyond. Aidan began to twist his body into the same shape Roy had but then stopped, picked a different angle, and slid inside.

The back of his canisters and one knee bumped the walls, but then he was through, breathing fast and grinning to himself.

"It's like I said." Vanna, suspended in the water ahead, held her lights trained on the opening to help them see their way. "You'd be good at cave diving."

Aidan moved aside to let Cove through, then turned to examine the room.

It must have been absolutely decadent. Intricately carved wooden pillars were spaced along the room's edge, and what remained of the furniture must have been in deep mahogany shades and plush, royal-colored fabrics.

Many of the chairs were missing though—either used to block off the halls leading to the hospital or dismantled to board over the windows. Now that he was inside, he could see just what lengths the crew had gone to in order to construct their barricades. The boards were reinforced and hammered into place with massive nails and rivets. It hadn't been a quick patch job; each barricade had layers applied to it, as though one level had been deemed not enough. Aidan was grateful Roy hadn't tried to kick his way through. He'd have better odds of breaking his foot.

"Good," Cove murmured, slowly rotating as she examined the space. "The writing room is to the left. We should still be about to reach the smoking rooms through that corridor to the right. Who wants to call dibs?"

"Ah, could I have the smoking room?" Aidan said. "I've never seen one before."

"Neither have I," Roy said, indignant. "How old do you think I am?"

"Smoking room's yours, Aidan." Cove nodded to the passageway. "You might find a stairwell down, and if it's clear, feel free to have a quick look into the lower level. But we're not going to push this one, yeah? Any sort of barricade or tight space or cloudy water is a no-go. Just stick to the easy areas, don't stray too far, and stay safe."

Aidan fired off a clumsy salute, then turned to follow Vanna, who was already moving through the open door in the room's far-right corner.

The smokestacks, which contained a single long tunnel running down to the boiler rooms below, were broad enough to take up most of the deck. The first-class leisure rooms had been built in the gaps between them, accessed by the stairwells that ran down through the passenger levels.

Although the smokestack prevented them being built next to each other, a long passageway had been constructed to run alongside the concrete structure. Aidan gazed up as they followed the dim, carpeted hall. Cracks had formed in its ceiling, spreading along the molded plaster like spiderwebs.

The wallpaper had probably been elegant and warming when it was installed, but three hundred feet underwater and with large shreds of it torn free from the walls, it only made the passageway feel darker and narrower. Aidan dipped his head to avoid touching the strands that danced in Vanna's gentle wake.

Then, ahead, their lights caught across the dark edges of a new doorway. Aidan sped up a fraction, eager to get out from under the oppressive walls, and they emerged into the smoking room.

Like the lounge area, much of its furniture had been scavenged, but enough remained to give Aidan a sense of the space. It must have been grand—even grander than the lounge area—and decked out in dark wood colors that would have disguised the steadily building layers of tar across the walls.

This room had paintings too: elegant landscapes and images of ships that were at least a hundred years older than the *Arcadia*. He swam past them slowly, letting his camera linger over each image for a few seconds before moving on. It wasn't likely that any of the paintings were very valuable—they wouldn't have been put in a room that was constantly saturated with smoke otherwise—but they definitely weren't prints either. It made him question how much the *Arcadia*'s contents had been worth when it went down.

At the room's back, closest to the smokestack, were the doors to the stairwell down. Aidan glanced around for Vanna. She floated just a few feet away, passively watching him, like a tour guide waiting for her guest to have their fill.

Aidan licked his lips, then pointed to the stairwell. Vanna nodded, and Aidan approached the doors. They groaned as they shifted inward but were, miraculously, less jammed than the doors he'd encountered on the earlier dives.

Below, the stairwell led down to a landing before turning, hiding the lower level. Aidan took a slow breath and flexed his hands. He'd been happy to be paired with Vanna. He needed to return to the lower storerooms, something Cove would never in a million years agree to.

Roy was usually on board for most kinds of rule bending, but his reactions to the bodies in the hold made it hard for Aidan to think he'd be chill about revisiting them. Out of the crew, only Vanna was likely to let Aidan lead her into the lowest levels... and, more importantly, allow it quietly.

I'm sorry, Cove. She'd been so adamant that this was going to be a chill, safe dive and that they weren't to stray too far from the lounge area, but Devereaux had asked Aidan a favor and he was pretty sure that, as long as Vanna didn't stop him, he could complete it quickly and quietly without anyone getting mad at him.

He tilted so his head was below his feet to navigate the stairs down, turning gently at the landing. He was going to be careful with his oxygen this time. He was going to keep his too-fast heart calm. And if all went to plan, he was going to be able to contribute to this dive, instead of simply holding the others back.

The landing led down into the first-class hallway, but Aidan turned again, taking the next level of stairs down. He glanced back. Vanna still followed him, sleek and dark in the harsh glare of his lights. As he'd hoped, she hadn't said a word about their detour. They were going to visit the hold.

39.

Cove kept one eye on her watch as she recorded the lounge area. Fifty minutes to go. If she could burn fifteen minutes in the lounge and another fifteen in the writing room, then she would only need to make a brief trip to the floor below; a few meters each way along the hall and a glance inside a couple of rooms and she'd be done.

That kind of behavior went against her nature. She was used to going above and beyond for her jobs: pushing for the perfect smile when every muscle in her body screamed, keeping her enunciation clean when suspended over a gorge.

And if it had just been her, she might have pushed her limits a bit harder.

But this wasn't just about her. In every sense, her team had gone above and beyond for Vivitech. They would have enough material to pad their documentary to twenty episodes if they so choose. If she'd had any greater faith in their sponsor, she would have delivered the material under the good faith that they would be thrilled.

But Vivitech's reputation meant Cove couldn't rely on that. It was a bad-faith agreement, and so she was, in essence, letting her team wait out the clock.

Only, she hadn't fully factored Roy into that plan. He was already growing tired of the lounge room. She'd never imagined someone could become bored in a ship of bodies three hundred feet from air, but Roy continued to find ways to surprise her.

He slouched past a row of abandoned chairs, his shoulders hunched, one finger casually prodding the dust-soaked fabric. Then, when he saw Cove was watching, he pointed toward the double doors that would lead into the writing room.

All right. We'll just take our time on the way out instead.

She let Roy lead through the doors. They passed the stairwell to lower levels, and Cove felt a wash of anxiety flow over her. She'd have to face it eventually. She just hoped the writing room would have more to interest Roy so she could prolong their visit there.

The collapsed smokestack had left cracks in the writing room's ceiling, so the room contained a higher level of sediment—not just on the surfaces but suspended in the water as well. A thousand tiny particles flashed in Cove's light. Unlike the lounge area, most of this room's furniture seemed to be in place, albeit somewhat shifted after the sinking. Rounded seats butted against bookcases, and desks still showed imprints where the fallen lamps had stood. The space was used not just for reading but to write letters for friends and family at home and was perhaps the only room on the *Arcadia* where silence was enforced.

A gush of air escaped Cove's rebreather. She imagined a dozen sullen faces turning toward her, glaring with irritation at the interruption.

Roy had stopped by one of the tables. He raised a hand to call Cove over. Countless books had fallen from their shelves and now lay scattered over the floor like autumn leaves, but one in particular seemed to have caught his attention.

Cove eased herself over to his side and peered down at the book. It was small—only a little larger than her hand—and bound in leather. Unlike the novels and reference books scattered about, this contained handwriting.

The ocean had gradually leached the ink out of the pages, but they had left enough of a stain that very faint words teased Cove's vision. She drew herself closer, until she was hovering just a few inches over the delicate, waterlogged pages.

Strange that this doesn't have sediment covering it. That was what must have drawn Roy to it at first glance, she realized. Everything else in the room was covered with the fine, sandy material, but this book held nothing more than a light sprinkle. It must have been propped up on a higher surface and fallen recently—possibly by the groaning, shuddering movements they'd felt on previous dives.

Her lips twitched as she tried to make out the words. A heading at the page's top said something about records. She skipped down the neat lines below:

> Mr. and Mrs. Van de Berg, alive.
> Mr. White, deceased. Burrowing disease.
> Mrs. White, missing.
> James Boswell, removed from roster. Burrowing disease.
> Mr. and Mrs. Muller, missing.
> Miss Brooks, deceased. Burrowing disease.

Cove swallowed around a lump in her throat. The words, though badly faded, were penned in a stiff, legible hand. Like a storekeeper noting down the quality of his wares. At first she'd imagined she'd misread the phrase "burrowing disease," but it repeated often enough that there was no mistaking it.

Roy hung by her shoulder, also attempting to read the writings. She could imagine the disgusted tilt to his lips. He'd had enough of death in this ship. He extended one finger. The glove's tip grazed a smear on the page's upper-right corner. Cove squinted and realized the shape was actually a date: 16 April, two days before the *Arcadia*'s final distress call.

Roy jerked his head aside as he floated away from the journal. He refused to even glance back in its direction, and Cove realized this was more than just frustration at being reminded of the ship's body count; it had actually seriously unnerved him. He pretended to examine some of the bookcases, but it was clear his heart wasn't in it.

Cove checked her dive computer. Forty minutes to go. Her oxygen was still at a good level, but apparently, she was not as skilled at wasting time as she'd anticipated. She grit her teeth. *We'll go into the lower level now and get it over with. It should, at least, bother Roy less than this space does.*

He followed her motion toward the stairwell, his posture instantly picking up. An okay sign confirmed he was ready to go, and Cove reluctantly headed back through the open double doors.

A plume of air rose from Roy's rebreather. Almost as though in response, the ship's heavy hull shuddered. A sound accompanied it: groaning metal, deep and pained. Cove reached out, preparing to steady herself on the door's edge, as the water reverberated. It passed within seconds, leaving only an eerie silence in its place.

Cove looked back through the entrance to the writing room. Fresh flecks of sediment fell through the cracks in the ceiling, confirming to her that the murky water was a result of the ship settling.

Though it shouldn't be moving, especially not this much, after a hundred years on the ocean floor.

Cove had done what she could to make sure their impact on the wreck was minimal. Even the rebreathers had been purchased specifically because they released less air than traditional scuba gear and would therefore introduce fewer contaminants in to the wreck.

Though when she thought about it, this wasn't the first time the ship had shifted following one of their rebreathers releasing air.

She blinked, trying to bring her focus back to the task at hand as she tilted into the dark, curving stairwell. It had to be a coincidence. She couldn't imagine any way that the introduction of a breath or two of air could impact the ship to that degree.

Hestie said the wreck is utterly devoid of oxygen. That's why it's been able to survive in this stasis for so long. The rebreathers aren't releasing much, *but it's probable this is the only oxygen the wreck has had since it sank.*

Against her will, her mind was brought to the idea of hibernation. Not just mammals like bears, which could go months with no food, but the creatures that could survive without air as well. She'd read a paper about nematodes found frozen in the Arctic ice. Scientists estimated they had been there for thousands of years, but when thawed, they had begun wriggling again.

And the *Arcadia's* environment mimicked those conditions surprisingly closely. It wasn't frozen, but it was as close as an ocean could get.

Hibernation. The ship, waiting to come alive again. Waiting... for air?

She suddenly felt immensely tired. Energy was normally never an issue for her, but at that moment, she wished she could just lean her head against the wall and let the tension fall away as she closed her eyes.

A heavy hand touched her shoulder. Roy's helmet loomed through the darkness. It took her a moment to realize why he was staring at her: she'd come to a halt halfway down the stairs.

This is what you get for burning the midnight oil too many nights in a row. Keep it together. Thirty-five minutes, then you're out for good.

She pushed onward, following the stairs' curve. The wallpaper, borrowing from art nouveau inspirations, messed with her eyes, making it hard to judge her distance from the walls. She held one arm ahead of herself as a defense.

As she rounded the stair's corner, some slight movement behind Roy caught her eye. She pulled herself back with some effort, hands pushing against the water to reverse her direction. Her headlight glanced over the aged, carpeted stairs leading up, each shelf a hard line of glare against the dark. She could have sworn she'd seen something pale drift past the doorway above, but now the space was empty.

Roy was watching her again. Breathing took more effort than her pressurized tanks of air should have required, but Cove managed it and then turned back to their path down.

Thirty-five minutes. You just need to get through another thirty-five minutes.

40.

Aidan descended through levels with a near wild sense of desperation. He didn't have a path in mind, he simply knew he needed to get *down*. The question of retracing their way back up would fall to Vanna, whose sleek, white dive line painted a history of their path through the ship like a trail of bread crumbs.

Though in the original bread crumb story, don't Hansel and Gretel become lost because the forest's birds eat the bread away?

He'd have to let Vanna worry about that. His jaw hurt from how tightly he was clenching it. Nervous adrenaline throbbed through his veins. There was elation—the thrill of having a purpose, of a secret task only he could complete—but that spark was being overshadowed by the crushing anxiety of just how far off the set path he was traveling.

Vanna still hadn't spoken up. He was grateful. The communications units meant that if she questioned where they were going, Cove would know that he'd deviated from the plan, and he would be in more trouble than he wanted to think about.

One of Roy's favorite sayings was *it's easier to ask forgiveness than permission.* Aidan hoped he was right.

He'd lost track of how many levels they'd descended, but they'd left the first-class passenger stairwell and seemed to be passing through the third-class regions of the ship. The halls were still decorated, but they seemed a few inches narrower and the trimmings were more modest.

A door caught Aidan's eye. It was slimmer than the cabin doors and didn't match the bathrooms'. He tried to avoid looking at Vanna's faceless mask as he wrenched on the handle. It squeaked, painfully, and refused to budge.

Vanna's glove lightly tapped his shoulder. She didn't speak but pointed upward. Aidan, knowing the expression wouldn't be visible through his gear, grimaced. He held up a finger: *One minute?*

She didn't respond, but she lightly drifted back from him, giving him free access to the door again. He applied more weight to the handle. This time, the jammed metal began to grind inward. Through the narrow gap, he saw thin metal stairs leading down.

Come on! His legs floated up above his head as he shoved on the door. It gave way in a sudden jolt, almost dragging him through in its wake.

He was smiling and panting and too nervous to check his oxygen levels, but the elation lent his shaking muscles extra strength as he descended the stairs.

This region was very clearly crew only. The metal slats descended steeply, then abruptly turned at an angle before connecting with a hallway that split into two directions. Aidan chose blindly, turning right, and within twenty paces, they were facing another set of stairs down.

The crew hallways were narrow. It was easy to imagine them being claustrophobically dark during operation. Now, though, the metal reflected their flashlight beams back at them in painful angles. It was almost blinding at moments, and Aidan held his fingers in front of his head-mounted light to dull its effect.

A final set of stairs down let out into a slightly wider hallway. To their left was a familiar sight: the first boiler room door, still open from their trip through it the previous day. That meant, to their right, were the storerooms.

Aidan twisted in the water and raised a thumbs-up to Vanna, then quickly corrected it to the okay sign. After a second's hesitation, Vanna raised a confused okay back at him.

He swung around toward the holds. The room farthest to their left led to what had once been their entrance to the *Arcadia*. He wondered whether the silt might have started to settle or if it was still blinding. The watertight door gave no hints, not even a creep of sediment around the edges.

Aidan turned to the right instead. The door to the other hold, first opened by Roy, was still ajar. His light grazed over items inside, and he thought he saw the edge of one of the shrouds.

He wanted to tell Vanna that she could wait outside if she wanted, but Cove was still connected to their audio.

Give me one more minute, Vanna. One more minute and then we can go back up.

Keeping his movements light, he turned sideways to fit through the doorway and then drew in a deep breath to gain height. His fins floated above the shrouded bodies. Feet, strangely shaped and mottled white, protruded from one of the blankets. He tried not to look at it or any of the other uncomfortably human-shaped bundles slung about the room.

When Devereaux had spoken with him the previous night, he'd politely inquired if there was any way to revisit one of the lower storerooms and, if possible, collect something he'd spotted on the cameras. Aidan tried to follow the directions he'd been given: near the room's back-left corner, suspended from the ceiling in one of the bundle-filled nets. Devereaux had described the package as having a red logo, but with red filtered out of the light spectrum, they all looked gray to Aidan.

He crept closer to the back corner. Four nets were suspended there. The one to the far left had a shrouded body propped against the wall right beside it. Aidan's jaw hurt from how tightly he clenched his teeth as he approached the far-right net first.

A square logo with the letters PT inside. The first bundle was full of boxes, splitting from the dampness and the pressure of their goods, and their stamps were nearly unreadable. The second bundle had small wooden boxes with only an address printed on them.

Aidan couldn't prevent himself from glancing at the body as he sidled ever closer to it. From that angle, he could see that the shroud had come partially away from the head. A gap existed, just wide enough to see an eye, swollen shut, and bared teeth behind retracted lips.

His stomach became sour. He turned away, breathing slowly, trying to stop his pounding heart. According to Cove, he could technically survive even if he was sick into his gear. It would just make an extremely unpleasant two-hour ascension.

Devereaux hadn't warned him that the corpse was exposed. Maybe he hadn't been able to see. He'd only been able to use the footage gained from their own cameras, and no one had gotten this close to the back corner during the previous dive.

Aidan painstakingly fixed his eyes ahead and fought the instinct to look back at the body, even as he drifted closer to it. The fourth bundle, the one closest to the shroud, held large sacks of cloth. On their front of each sack was a square shape and inside were two letters: *PT*.

How did Devereaux recognize this from so far away? I guess the cameras are HD, but still. He must have been zooming into the footage to pick out tiny details.

Aidan's tongue tasted sour as he ran it across the back of his teeth. He felt across his belt and cautiously drew out two items. The first, a knife, was a universal tool in a diver's belt. He'd only needed to use his once before, on a reef dive with Roy, where fishing line had become tangled around one of his fins. The ocean was littered with line and abandoned nets, and the knife was a necessity to get out of trouble quickly.

The second item was very much unique to Aidan: a small glass jar taken from the *Skipjack's* kitchen, gifted to him by Devereaux. He struggled to get the lid open. It had one of the metal spring latches and a rubber ring to form an airtight seal, and when it popped open, two large blobs of air shot out and scattered into smaller bubbles above his head.

Something seemed to shift in Aidan's periphery. He nearly turned toward it before catching himself and fixing his gaze back on the sacks of cloth. If he turned, he would have to look at the cold, dead eye of the shrouded body again, and he didn't think he could endure even one more minute in the hold if he did that.

Aidan held the jar in the crook of his arm, pressed against his chest, as he used one hand to grip the rope net and the other to slip the curved blade into the fabric and jerk it repeatedly toward himself, gradually working a tear in the cotton.

Even though he was holding the net as still as possible with his other hand, puffs of sediment rolled free with every jolt. Memories of the previous dive rose: trapped in the endless, bleak clouds of silt, his hands and legs knocking against objects he couldn't identify, the sharp spike of panic that followed the realization that he was no longer sure which way was up.

The silt he sent into the water wasn't yet at those levels, but it was beginning to cloud the edges of his vision and give the water a thickened appearance. He kept focus on his breathing: a slow inhale, hold for five, and a slow exhale. The count to five during the hold grew faster as his knife tore free from the sack and sent a thick plume of dust coursing around him. Aidan swallowed, trying to regain control over his pounding pulse and panicked mind, then slipped the knife inside the fresh tear in the sack.

Fabric spilled free. The fabric's base was probably a deep gold, he thought, but the only color still visible came from blue detailing.

He released his hold on the net and instead pinched the edge of the cloth and began sawing at it. The knife was sharp and the fabric tore beautifully, giving him a scrap slightly smaller than his hand, which he stuffed into the glass jar.

Okay. His hands shook as he worked on closing the spring lid. *We did it. Cove never knew. We still have time to get back to the smoking room. This…this actually went as well as it could have.*

He fit the knife back into his belt. There was another shimmer of motion in his periphery. This time, he was too slow to stop himself from looking.

The shrouded body leaned on the wall close to his side. Aidan had half a second to register that it was no longer in the position he'd first seen it. The head, barely visible through the narrow gap in the cloth, had turned toward him. Its eye had opened. The space behind the lid was milky white but fixed on his face.

There were voices in his comms unit, but he barely heard them. He'd frozen in mindless horror. The body shifted again. A long, bone-thin arm snaked out from between the folds of cloth. The skin was mottled with white and shrunken, the joint around the wrist uncomfortably prominent.

The corpse's clawlike fingers spread open as they reached for him.

41.

The wall-mounted lights—uncomfortably large shapes, considering the hall's size—cast strange shadows in Cove's beam. To both the left and right were closed doors, slightly indented from the path, each bearing a small bronze number. First-class passenger berths.

Cove's communications unit had been silent since the teams split up, but subtle ambient noises reassured her that it was still working: her companion's breathing, the infrequent rattle as their rebreathers purged air, and the soft crunching of their dive suits being flexed. She suppressed the urge to ask the other team for a report. They'd speak up if they were in any kind of trouble. Not that she expected them to meet any. Vanna was both solid and reliable, and she couldn't imagine a scenario where Aidan would deviate from the path she'd laid out. He had a better eye for detail than Roy, and Cove suspected it would take a lot longer for him to grow bored with the smoking room's furnishings.

They were following the hallway toward the ship's stern. That level was largely first-class accommodation, with occasional bathrooms and steward berths. Cove was hoping for an open door that would give them a fresh room to record. After that, she could justifiably say it was time to head back up.

Though, strangely, since they'd entered the hallway, a soft ticking noise had begun to tease at the edge of Cove's hearing. Masked by the other ambient noises through the audio, it was so faint that it felt like it was creeping out of the back of her imagination alone.

Cove lifted her wrist to glance at the dive computer just in case. Although the computer displayed the time, it was all digital and made no noise. The sounds echoing in the back of her ears weren't quite like the ticking of a clock anyway. They were too irregular.

Someone clicking their tongue? Cove frowned. It was too quiet for that. Maybe someone was working a stiff jaw or cracking their knuckles…though she couldn't imagine why they were doing it without a break for so many minutes.

It was probably another malfunction from the audio. The cousin of static or some kind of feedback error.

Whatever the cause, it shouldn't matter. The documentary would only use the audio if they spoke, and a sound engineer should be able to edit out such a faint noise, if it even was recorded in the first place.

Ahead and to her left, a dark line appeared on the wall: the open door Cove had been hoping for. She checked behind herself. Roy's head was up, warily shifting from side to side as though looking for something on the walls, but he was following closely enough. Cove pointed to the door. He nodded.

The gap wasn't quite wide enough to fit through, but the wood shifted easily enough under a light touch. As the door moved inward, Cove's light picked over the heavily shredded wallpaper and dark-wood furniture adorning the berth.

She drifted into the room in increments. It was far more spacious than the third-class cabin she'd seen on her first drive. A large wardrobe occupied one wall, opposite the four-poster bed. The bed's canopy was drawn back, revealing blankets that had been tucked so tightly that they'd barely shifted in the water. She wouldn't know without opening the wardrobe, but the lack of personal effects or suitcases suggested the room had been unoccupied.

Good. An easy room. Fill up a few minutes of footage, then you can start heading back.

Her dive computer said she only had twenty minutes until their film quota was filled. She moved toward the porthole on the outside wall and angled her head so the camera could get a clear view out. There wouldn't be much to see beyond—just endless, dark water, maybe a few floating specks to be highlighted by her light—but it would still make for a good shot.

As she backed away from the window, she caught Roy in her periphery. He was opening the bedside table's drawers.

Looting on shipwrecks was a hotly contested issue in the diving community. One party said that it was a finders keepers principle: the wreck and its contents had been abandoned, which meant it was fair game for anyone with a dive tank and an adventurous spirit. Another group said that it still counted as theft, even if the ship's owners had relinquished rights to it and the ship's occupants were deceased. Either way, it would look bad if anyone on Cove's team were found to have taken passenger goods.

She was fairly certain Roy wouldn't find anything, and even if he did, she wanted to believe that he wouldn't pocket it, but she still kept an eye on him as she moved to film the four-poster bed.

The strange clicking noise had stopped at least. Maybe there was some quirk of the hallway that messed with the audio. She wasn't sad to be free of it. There had been something oddly melancholy about the ticks that didn't sit right in her ears.

Cove panned her gaze across the bed, moving slowly so the camera could get good footage. From that new angle, she was able to see that one of the wardrobe's doors was open a crack. Something pale had slipped out of it, near the base.

Maybe the room had an occupant after all. Cove shifted nearer, focusing her light on the shape as she tried to identify it. Pale and small, it emerged from the narrow gap and bent slightly across the wood.

Fingers. Her heart skipped a beat as her tongue turned dry. She was looking at long, slim fingers, curled around the wardrobe door as though holding it closed.

She felt the shocking impulse to wrench the doors open and reveal the person inside. Her mind's eye painted a picture: a skeletal figure huddling on the floor, wrapped in gently drifting fabric, a skull face peering up at her.

No. Definitely no. Time to leave.

Roy had finished exploring the bedside table and drifted toward Cove. It took a lot of effort to turn her back to the wardrobe, but she managed it, blocking his view with her body. She couldn't trust her voice not to betray her stress, so she wordlessly pointed to the door.

He shrugged and moved to the opening. The wood's faint creak reached Cove's ears, even with the layers of dry suit. Roy swam into the hallway and turned left, continuing their exploration along the hall.

Damn it. Cove checked her clock. Eighteen minutes until they were due back at the lounge area. "Hey, Roy, it's about time to head back."

"Really? I was just starting to get into it." He rotated languidly, then, as his light flashed over Cove, his form turned rigid. The smooth sweeps of his arms and lightly kicking feet fell still as he stared, blankly, toward her.

"Roy?" She strained to see through the cool, blank curve of his mask. His light was glaring in her eyes, half blinding her, and she raised a hand to block it. "What's up?"

"Ah—ah—"

It sounded like he was trying to speak, but his mouth wouldn't form the words. The light was still in her eyes, but it wasn't pointing directly at her, Cove realized. It was angled at something over her shoulder. Her lungs ached, and she realized she'd stopped breathing as she slowly, carefully turned.

The hallway stretched ahead of them. Patchy, weblike wallpaper floated across the edges of her vision. Every ten feet or so, the walls dipped inward to accommodate another door. The water held fragments of silt that had been accidentally kicked up during their trip, but Cove still had a near uninterrupted view of at least twenty feet.

Right at the edge of her light, almost invisible in the shadows, multiple dark shapes floated in the hallway. They were too large to be scraps of wallpaper and too solid to be sediment. Cove's mind scrambled to remember what they'd swum through, but it came up empty. The hallway had been clear as recently as five minutes ago when they'd passed along it.

She blinked, and the shapes came into focus. Bodies. Four of them. Suspended upright, their arms coiled around themselves as though wrapped there by currents. The heads tilted up, toward the ceiling. The feet hung limp, toes pointed down, nearly a foot off the floor.

The nearest body shifted. Its head turned, lowering to face Cove, and her ears were filled with the distant clicking noise of old joints being flexed: the sound that had dogged her ever since she'd left the stairs.

42.

A sound rang through the *Arcadia*'s lower levels. Deep, pained, metallic. Harland, barely conscious of his feet moving, followed the sound.

His candle had nearly burned out. Its flame flickered low, near drowning in the melted wax pool. He lifted the jar high, as though its weak light could do much more than tease the closest walls.

Figures moved through the hallway ahead. *Those from within the walls?* No. They were too solid, too staggering and bone weary to be the spirits of the damned that tormented the ship. These were his fellow humans, crew and passengers blending together as they trailed down the narrowest, darkest passages to reach the hold.

The sound was ceaseless. It rang like a chiming bell—on repeat, unavoidable. It reverberated through the walls. It fell in a horrible discordant rhythm with Harland's own heart rate, the beats threatening to align but never quite managing it.

He didn't know if he wanted to stamp the sound out of existence or if he wanted to be closer to it.

The things moved through the walls. One rattled past Harland's left side, causing the old paneling to shiver.

Down the stairs, following behind a faceless, nameless passenger. The rhythmic ring of metal against metal grew harsher the deeper they descended. More people came behind Harland, stumbling like he was. An *other* ran through the walls again. They shied away from it, some of them closing their eyes, but made no noise of protest.

Into the passageway leading to the hold, then. Doors had been left open. Harland glimpsed the cloth-wrapped bodies to his right. They had amassed so many of them, but that wasn't even half the total the ship had exacted. Too many had been lost over the railings. Some of the burrowers had dug themselves so deeply into the holes in the walls that they could not be removed even in death.

He'd avoided this level since the shriveled, black remains had been removed from the hull, but he now knew that was foolishness. The corpse—and the corpse's curse—could not be avoided. It had claimed the ship and every soul inside. They were trapped within its snow globe now, clinging to whatever gave them comfort as their world was shaken. They could not be saved through hiding.

The sounds came from the last hold to the right, just as Harland had suspected. That was where it had started. It felt right to be returning to that space again.

As he stepped through the open door, his boots hit water. That was not unusual, with the eternal, inescapable mist dripping from every surface and soaking the carpet. What was unusual was how deep it was here. Every step caused it to splash up.

The procession did not pause, and so neither did Harland. He set his burning eyes ahead, his feeble light joining the dozens of other glass jars raised around him, as they rounded the storage hold's barriers to see the wall where it had begun.

Fitz worked at it. His clothes were in tatters. He'd neither changed nor washed them since leaving port. Tears ran down the sleeves where he'd scavenged fabric to patch his cracked hands. The threads at the seams were frayed, much like Fitz himself.

He used his makeshift crowbar to work at the hole he'd already created. The sharpened tip stabbed repeatedly at a seam on the external wall, where a black stain still showed where the corpse had once been pressed. Salt water gushed through the hole he'd formed.

The procession had come to a halt in a ring around him. Everywhere Harland looked were gray faces and dark, unfocused eyes. He felt as though he were in some type of slow, disquieting dream, the kind that wasn't quite a nightmare, but regardless left him waking in damp sheets and with fear in his blood.

Metal shrieked as the seam was pried open. More water gushed onto the floor. The pools shifted with each swell they passed over, sometimes leaving the floor at Harland's feet merely damp, sometimes splashing frothy water across his ankles.

Fitz staggered back from the wall, gasping. His body was drenched from the spray. Strands of hair hung glued to his face. Feral eyes glanced out from behind them, seeming neither conscious nor quite human; their cores appeared to Harland to be a sick tar black, with tiny pinpricks of light at their center. They flashed as they fixed on him.

"Harland…my lad." Fitz stretched a hand toward him. The bandages around his fingers were bled through and hung in scraps. "I found the answer. There are others. So many others. But they hide *deeper*. We peeled back one layer of skin and found the first infection. But to purge the others, we must go farther. Peel back layer on layer, until the flesh is bare and the parasites are exposed to our lights. I will get them, my lad. Like *this*."

He swung back to the wall, hurling his strength into the bar as he stabbed through the metal.

Harland felt strangely detached as he watched. Fitz's mantra felt *wrong* to him. The water gushing through the widening hole was, in increments, rising across the floor. He couldn't believe that there could be any more layers beyond that, despite what Fitz said.

But Fitz had been right before, hadn't he? He'd found the blackened mummy. Maybe he knew something no one else did. Dark secrets, whispered into his ears during those hours he'd spent alone in the hold.

A dark shape shifted near the opposite wall. Captain Virgil's imposing outline was hidden under the layers of shadows. He was flanked by four of his officers, their hands clasped behind their backs. They were his attack dogs. Focused, unthinking, scarcely breathing. They were contained but braced to lunge forward at a flick of their master's wrist.

The captain regarded Fitz with something that bordered on curiosity. The past days had been harsh on him, as it had on all of them. His broad shoulders were still set, but he'd lost both color and fullness to his face. Dark patches marked around the edges of his eyes. As Harland watched, a trickle of shockingly vivid blood seeped from the corner of his nose. He swiped the back of his hand over it with the passionless irritation of a man brushing a fly away.

Fitz released a cry. The metal plate broke free on one side, lurching inward. The subtle flow of water turned into a deluge. It spread outward, coursing over Harland's feet in frothy ripples.

"They're here," Fitz muttered, but his raspy voice was nearly impossible to hear beneath the thick rush of the ocean. "They're here…they must be here…"

He tried to jab his metal bar through the gap, but the water pressure sent him staggering back. Fitz stopped in their loosely formed circle, doubled over, his face going slack as he drew gasping breaths.

Captain Virgil tilted his head a fraction. The officers at his side tensed, prepared for movement.

"It seems to me that the body in the walls served a vital purpose." The captain's skin might have turned papery and pale, but his voice still held the rigid quality that made the dull-eyed onlookers turn toward him. "It was required there to block the flow of water. In removing it, we created a weakness in our ship."

Every face in the room focused on the captain, save for Fitz's. Salt water dripped from his whiskers as he stared into the hole he'd formed, manic, utterly possessed. He showed no reaction to the words as the captain continued speaking.

"The body shall be replaced," Virgil said. "Stock master Fitzwilliam has offered himself."

The captain's hand flicked up, and the four officers moved. Fitz barely had the breath to make a sound as they grasped his arms and dragged him forward, toward the chasm gushing water.

Harland's body turned numb. Blood rushed through his ears as loud as the foaming waves. The jar slipped from his sweaty grip, and the swelling water at his feet flooded it and extinguished the flame. No one else seemed to notice.

He tried to move, even to raise his hands, but it was as though his free will had been stolen. He could do nothing except stand there, his jaw slack and his eyes staring, as his friend was forced into the jagged hole he'd carved.

43.

THE THIRD DIVE

Aidan's mouth gaped open, but no sounds came out. His throat had closed over so tightly that he couldn't form even a whisper, let alone draw air.

The mottled, shriveled hand fastened around his wrist. The shroud slipped farther from around the corpse. A larger slice of its corrupted face became visible. The lips had pulled back from yellowed teeth, creating the impression that it was grinning at Aidan. Milky eyes were fixed on his face with more intensity than their blindness should have allowed.

He tried to squirm his hand free, but the grip was like a vise. The corpse tugged on him, dragging itself closer, the shroud slipping further.

Aidan's mouth stretched wider, fighting to release the scream that echoed through his head, but he was choking on his own saliva.

Large arms gripped him from behind. Aidan shuddered, shocked into paralysis, before he glimpsed the form in his periphery. Sleek, dark dry suit material cloaked the arms. Gloved hands dug around his waist as Vanna found a grip.

She dragged him backward, away from the shrouded body. He was barely aware of her shallow, ragged breathing through the communication unit.

The corpse didn't release its grip. As Aidan lurched backward, it was pulled in his wake, dragging the cloth in heavy billows behind it. The leering, skull-like grin fixated on him as its gray hair swirled. He choked on the lump in his throat as he fought to breathe.

Vanna released him. One hand planted on his shoulder to pull him backward in the same motion as she pushed herself forward. Then both of her gloved hands fastened on the corpse's fingers, fighting for any give they might have, trying to dig the clutching hand free.

The pressure on Aidan's forearm increased. A stuttering gasp filled his lungs as sparks flashed over his vision. He felt his very bones groan from the pressure as they were crushed to the edge of fracturing.

Vanna reached into her belt. Aidan was barely able to focus on a flash of metal as her dive knife rose and then plunged into the corpse's forearm.

The blade embedded itself, slicing through skin and muscle. The grinning corpse showed no reaction. It was drawing itself closer to Aidan in increments, pulling his wrist toward its chest, its face angled up to meet his.

A second arm extended from the coils of off-white cloth. It was bony and seemed frozen into a fist, but it stretched forward regardless, moving to Aidan's throat.

Vanna rolled away. Her fin came up and she kicked it into

the reaching hand. The corpse rocked. A horrible crackling noise rose from the neck as its head snapped backward, then slowly drifted forward again, the blank white eyes unerringly coming down to fasten on Aidan's own.

Another aching breath whistled through his constricted throat. Vanna still held the blade embedded in the corpse's arm. She twisted it, wrenching it from side to side, and Aidan only realized what she was trying to do when splinters of cracked bones began floating from the wrist.

He closed his eyes and turned his head aside. Even through the muffling suit, he heard the crack as the hand was severed. The pressure on his arm instantly relaxed. Aidan grit his teeth as the severed hand slid off him. It floated on the edges of his peripheral vision, spiraling loosely, slowly descending to the floor.

The corpse didn't stop. The shroud tangled around the lower half of its body as its staring, emaciated face drew closer to Aidan.

Vanna's foot came up again. Her fin hit the corpse's face, and for the second time, Aidan's stomach turned at the sound of the crackling joints being moved in unnatural ways.

Slowed by the water's resistance, Vanna's kick hadn't had as much power as she'd clearly wanted to give. It was enough to direct the corpse away from them though. The gray body bumped against the suspended nets, sending additional sediment flooding into the already clouded water.

"Cove. Roy." Vanna shoved her knife back into her belt and then fixed her grip on Aidan's arm as she pulled him away from the shrouded figure. "End the dive. Do you hear me? Leave the ship immediately by the nearest exit you can find."

She'd been unnervingly silent when focused on the shrouded body. Now though, Aidan could hear the heavy undercurrent of fear in the sharply enunciated words.

His own panic rose as the other side of the communications units stayed silent. He might have expected objections from Roy and questions from Cove, but not this: the endless, faintly staticky quiet.

"I repeat, exit the dive immediately." Vanna moved ahead of Aidan, her hand on his bruised and aching wrist as she pulled him toward the hold's door. Her head moved on a swivel, and the harsh white beam from her headgear lit up the stacks of crates and seemingly endless amounts of white fabric bundled in every corner. "Cove. Roy. Please acknowledge."

Still silence. Vanna's movements drew to a sharp halt, and Aidan tilted his body back to keep from colliding with her.

The door existed as a dark arch ahead, its metal frame glaring in the lights and the space beyond forming a shadowy block. That darkness had been interrupted though. A long, shriveled arm reached across the opening, its pale-gray skin in sharp contrast to the darkness.

Vanna's rebreather purged a rush of air as she began backing up. Movement came from their sides. Bundles of white writhed as disfigured limbs crept out of the shrouds.

The bodies around them were rising.

"Cove. Roy. Please acknowledge."

Vanna's words hung over Cove, echoing through the headset long after the static-filled voices had faded. She couldn't reply.

Four bodies were suspended in the water ahead. Their clothes hung loosely, twisting into strange shapes in the eddies. Their arms were curled about their bodies. Their heads turned upward, directed toward the ceiling, while their feet hung nearly a foot above the floor.

They were in a room we passed. We created currents that pulled them out into the hallway. That must *be what happened.*

Even as she made that promise to herself, Cove wasn't able to believe it. They hadn't passed any other open doors. There was nowhere in the hallway that could have conceivably concealed one corpse, let alone four. It seemed impossible that the forms were now blocking their path back.

Nitrogen narcosis. Oxygen poisoning. Your dive computer's clock malfunctioned and you've been at depths longer than you should have. You're hallucinating.

The four forms were nearly twenty feet away, right on the edge of her light's reach. At that distance, they appeared more shadow than human. And the darkness could very easily force a mind to concoct shapes to fill the void. It was plausible.

Except Cove knew she wasn't alone in seeing them. Roy had turned rigid at her side.

If it hadn't been for Roy, Cove might have actually approached the figures, intent on proving her theory. But she could feel the tension rolling off of her companion as his fight-or-flight instincts kicked in, and it sent her own pulse into a raging tempo that she couldn't stop.

There must be an explanation. This must be some kind of mistake, or—

The first figure, the one closest to them, moved. Horrible clicking, cracking noises echoed along the hallway as the body rotated to face them, its head slowly lowering to fix them with heavy-lidded, sightless eyes.

Cove found Roy's arm and shoved. His head jerked, as though he was coming back to life again.

They were all moving now. Bone-thin arms twitched in sharp, insect-like jolts as they unraveled from around the bodies. A mess of hair washed over the closest one's face, obscuring its eyes, as its jaws creaked open.

The clicking sounds were growing louder, and Cove realized, with a tinge of disbelief, that the corpses were gaining on them. Their forms, which she had only glanced at the edges of her light even half a minute ago, were becoming clearer as they twitched through the murky water.

A noise came from the communications unit. A gasp. A hiss of pain from Vanna. Cove's heart froze.

"Vanna. Aidan." She kept her voice to a whisper, hoping that the sound wouldn't reach the distant forms. "Are you safe?"

"Trying—" Another sharp noise from Vanna, the static rising to swell over her words. "Get out of the ship. *Get out now.* I can't help you. Do you understand? You need to get out."

"Yeah." That was Roy, his voice hollow with shock, the words almost drowned out under the static. "I'm pretty sure we understand."

The nearest body reached an arm toward them, fingers raking the water, and Cove knew it wasn't just searching the water blindly: it could sense their presence.

The door beside them was the only one open that they'd found along that hallway. Without moving her eyes from the approaching figures, Cove felt for Roy's shoulder and shoved him toward the dark opening. He shuddered at her touch, then pushed through the gap, leaving room for Cove to follow. The moment she passed through, Roy forced the door closed.

Its hinges set up a shrieking, scraping sound as they moved. *Gently*, Cove thought, but it was already too late; sediment rose from the motion, hanging heavy in the water.

"What is *that*?" Roy asked. "What kind of—"

Nitrogen narcosis. Shared delusions. Hallucinations.

None of them felt fully true to Cove. But what other explanation was there?

"Doesn't matter. Whatever's happening, we can figure that out later. Right now, we just need to *get out.*" She was already moving to the window, her steady voice belied the way her heart pounded out of control. "Vanna, Aidan, we're a fair way from the door. Can you find the exit without assistance?"

"Working on it" was Vanna's short reply. Static hissed at the edges of her audio.

Cove felt around the porthole's seal. It was fused in place...not that it would have been much help either way. If she'd removed her tanks, Cove might have been just able to squirm through the opening, but it would be too narrow for Roy's shoulders.

Think. If our intended path back is blocked by... Her mind shorted out as she tried to fit any kind of word into that space. *If our path back is* blocked, *we'll need an alternative.*

The ship had dual hallways running its length, occasionally connected by intersecting halls. Cove and Roy were on the starboard side of the ship. If they kept following their path, they could eventually cross over to the port and use it to get back around to the set of stairs they'd been trying to reach. It was a circuitous route, but it at least meant they wouldn't have to get any closer to the shapes blocking the hallway.

"Roy, we're going around." Cove pushed away from the window. Roy stood frozen, his fingers spread at his sides. He stared toward the wardrobe. The door was creeping open.

Don't. Don't think about it. Don't dwell, or you'll lose whatever's left of your mind.

She shoved Roy's shoulder, pushing him toward the door.

Outside, coming from the hallway, she could faintly make out the clicking sound of long-dead corpses.

44.

Aidan's eyes burned. He didn't have the courage to blink. A trickle of sweat ran down his back, making him itch for a second before it was absorbed into the layers of wool.

Vanna was at his side. They'd wedged themselves in behind a row of crates. Through a gap in the stack, Aidan thought he could glimpse the path to the hold door. It seemed impossibly far away. He fixed his eyes on it, unwilling to look away for even a glance in case it somehow vanished in the gloom.

Something heavy and dark shifted past, blocking his view. He tried to squirm backward, but there was nowhere to go.

Vanna's head moved in sharp jerks as she assessed their options. Her headlight glanced over sacks, ropes, and wood before coming to rest on the crate less than six inches ahead of her. The backwash was strong enough to illuminate her features, even through the smooth mask. So far underwater, her skin looked a sickly gray. Spots of perspiration dotted her cheeks.

The lights. They're like a beacon, calling everything toward us.

Aidan's hand twitched, but he repressed the movement. Switching the lights off wasn't going to be any kind of solution. It would be as bad as being trapped in the silt-out again. They'd be blind.

Even as he thought that, the bulb in Vanna's light dimmed a fraction before coming back to full strength.

The batteries should have all been fresh. Part of Vanna's work was to check and recheck the equipment after every dive and he doubted someone with as much caving experience as her would leave the lights to chance. The bulb dimmed again, then came back once more. His stomach turned to knots.

Vanna tapped his wrist, then, barely moving her hand, indicated to her left. She'd decided on a route. Aidan, scarcely breathing, nodded once. Going left put them farther from the door. But he also couldn't *see* the door any longer, since the dark silhouette had drifted across his view.

The space between the crates could barely be considered a walkway. The sailors navigating the space must have rubbed shoulders with the walls of cargo. Now, burdened by the dive tanks and with gravity no longer rooting Aidan to the floor, he glanced off the walls with every small movement.

Ahead, Vanna moved like a wraith through the water. Her light shimmered over stacks of cargo that stretched to the ceiling. It seemed endless. Aidan's ears hummed with the labored breathing of his three companion divers and the growing hiss of static.

Something moved between the walls of crates, squirming near Aidan's feet. His throat closed over and he drew his legs up, a pantomime of leaping over the creature even though he only managed to pull his center of gravity lower. His flashlight picked out something that looked like long, mottled fingers, but then he was past it, the fear ringing in his ears and the adrenaline pushing him until he was close to bumping Vanna's back.

The wall to their right opened up, giving them a path through. Vanna paused at the corner, one hand held toward Aidan to halt his progress as she searched the dark waters ahead with her flashlight. The light didn't seem as strong as it had been a moment ago. Neither was Aidan's.

More than a dozen narrow sacks hung from the ceiling, blocking their path, but past them appeared clear. Vanna glanced back to Aidan. He managed a shaky okay, and she turned and pushed into the sacks, carefully weaving between them in an effort to not disturb them too much.

Aidan followed. He hadn't seen bags like this in the holds before; they widened at their lowest points, around near Aidan's knees, and tapered in a teardrop shape above his head. Hooks, large enough to be meat hooks, had been fastened into the wooden ceiling and used to stab through the bags, just below where they were tied.

He put his hand out to push the nearest sack aside. A gush of air flowed from his rebreather, a hundred tiny bubbles merging and breaking apart again as they battered against the cloth and disappeared between the hooks.

The bag had an unpleasant weight to it as Aidan shoved through. At his first touch it seemed as soft as the suspended sacks of fabric, but when he pushed, it had a firmness hidden beneath. It barely moved, and Aidan was forced to turn his body at an angle to squeeze between it and its neighbor.

Vanna's fins teased at the edges of his vision ahead. The sacks swayed slightly as she pushed through.

Aidan used his hands as much as his legs to keep moving. He reached forward, splayed fingers attempting to stretch through the gaps and forge a path. The bags bumped his body as he passed, heavier and harder than he'd imagined they could be.

Unlike most of the other storage in the hull, these bags had no clear logos or labeling on them. They almost looked as though they had been sewn out of sailcloth. The seams were irregular, the threads coming loose in places and tattered edges peeking open.

One of the sacks squirmed.

Aidan's tongue stuck to the roof of his mouth. He couldn't have made a noise even if he'd wanted to. The bag pressed against his left-hand side seemed to have come alive. It writhed languidly, like a snake waking on a cold day, then fell still again.

One of the cloth seams next to his right had come nearly undone, exposing part of the dark insides. He knew he didn't want to look. He knew what the sacks contained. As tall as a human, hung like cuts of meat from the ceiling, heads and arms tangling at the lowest point while the feet were strung up above. It couldn't be anything else.

Vanna had pulled ahead of him. Aidan wanted to call to her to come back, to not leave him in this sea of bags, but his throat was closed over. He couldn't back out. The only available path was to move forward.

Something shifted inside the bag to his right as he dragged himself past it. He glimpsed the outline of a thin arm pressing across the fabric.

His headlight dimmed, returned, then dimmed again. The sharp, stabbing panic rising through his chest redoubled as the light failed entirely. He was alone in the dark, blind and surrounded by the moving, writhing bags. Then his headlight glowed to life again, spearing a circle of harsh white into the web of fabric.

A sack behind him shuddered as the *something* inside began to move. The heavy sacks bumped him, again and again, as he forced his way between them. One grazed along his thigh and he swore he felt teeth, even through the layers of cloth.

There were too many. More than he'd thought when they'd first entered the maze. He could no longer see Vanna. Just the off-white cocoons, layers of them, twitching in strange motions as their contents awoke.

No. No more—no more—

His lungs screamed from lack of air, but his throat was too tight to get more than a whistle of oxygen through. Something pushed out of a frayed seam ahead. An elbow, cold blue veins mapping underneath layers of white growth. It bumped Aidan's shoulder as he tried to pull away from it.

They kept knocking into him, slowing him and robbing him of his sense of direction. Fingertips peeked through a seam to his left. The bag ahead rocked as the body inside twisted itself around.

And then, abruptly, an arm thrust toward him through the mess of cloth. Aidan tried to recoil. But the arm wasn't the horrible, pallid white of death and oily growth. It was covered in a black dry suit and glove. Vanna. Aidan reached for it, grasping the hand, and almost cried out as she dragged him forward, pulling him from the last layers of twisting, writhing sacks.

Their momentum shoved them into the metal hull. They clung together, both breathing in harsh, ragged gasps. The cocoons twisted at the edges of their sight, their movements turning sluggish again.

Aidan's light could no longer cut through the expanse of dark storage around them. He wasn't sure which way would lead to the exit. Everywhere he looked, he imagined he saw movement. Sometimes it was just a flash of old rope floating in the currents or a speck of sediment. But sometimes he couldn't find words for what teased at the edges of his sight.

Vanna's faceless mask turned toward him, and he imagined she was about to speak. Instead, she shook her head.

What exactly could either of them say?

I'm sorry I brought you down here. I'm sorry I don't know how to get us out.

45.

Fourth Officer Swain stood outside the bridge. He shook. The jar held in his right hand rattled, its base full of wax, its stub of a candle unlit.

He'd dressed for the occasion, as though that might actually do anything to help. His officers' uniform was many days from being pressed, but he'd brushed it down for lint and applied some polish to his shoes. He held his cap in his left elbow, his dark hair combed.

Even as he stood outside the captain's den, he knew his appearance was laughable. There had been some idea of pretending he was still normal, still healthy and sound of mind.

He knew he wasn't. He was trying, fighting every moment of every hour to cling to clear thought and to line up his behaviors in a way that could make rational sense, but things were slipping.

The rattling in the walls was growing louder, faster, more persistent. And for all the times he told himself it was *impossible*, that this was some kind of delusion encouraged by his fellow crew's paranoia, he still flinched every time it passed.

He'd had a second opportunity to enter the bridge the previous night. The store master, known to his fellow crew as Fitz, had been causing havoc in one of the holds. Captain Virgil had gone down, taking four other officers with him.

Swain had rushed to unlock the door, knowing every minute was precious. He'd been prepared. He'd brought light. But as he connected to the wireless system, he found the *Arcadia* would not let him escape so easily.

Whether by a trick of the pale, flickering light or by the drenching mist that enveloped the room or from his own beleaguering exhaustion, the coordinates did not make sense. He'd tried to stammer them to a crisp voice on the other end of the radio, but they'd danced before his very eyes, the digits swirling and shifting in place until he had no concept of what he was looking at.

He'd hoped his confused, near-delirious message had at least reached someone, but no ships had arrived. It was as though they had been forgotten, left adrift on the empty ocean.

Now, he had a final chance to reach the outside world before it was all too late. Things were devolving at a dangerous speed. The store master—thanks to his distraction the previous night—was dead at the captain's hands. Yet no one seemed to care.

Swain himself had to repeatedly jolt his mind back to cognizance about the enormity of the crime. The *Arcadia* had seen many deaths, but this was its first murder.

His head swam at the thought. It should be shocking...but he did not feel shocked.

Very little perturbed him any longer.

One of the older officers had said that the captain was making a visit to the hospital. Swain hadn't been sure whether to trust the officer's slack-jawed words, but opportunities came so infrequently that he couldn't afford to ignore any.

Swain's fist made a sharp rapping noise on the bridge's door. He didn't know who he was trying to deceive with this formal act. The brushed-down uniform, the combed hair, the official-sounding knocks. All he was achieving was to set himself apart. No one bothered with presentation any longer. Even the captain's beard had grown unkempt.

There was no response to his knock. A good sign. Swain licked condensation off of his lips as he felt for the lockpicking tools. His vision was blurred at the edges, his head aching from the effort of holding his mind together. It took him more than one try to get the pin and hook lined up.

The latch clicked as it opened. Swain glanced down the hallway a final time before slipping inside the bridge.

He was not under any delusions about what would happen to him if he were caught. The stock master's fate had cut through any remaining ideas that law and order mattered on the *Arcadia*. Now, the only question was of survival.

The bridge was pitch-black, just as it had been when he'd visited before. Swain closed the door behind himself and paused for a second to bring a box of matches out of his pocket. He was close to running out of them and had to fight his shaking hands as he struck one and lit his candle.

The sickly glow spread across the carpeted floor and the nearest wooden desks. Swain put the matches away before approaching the controls. They looked horribly neglected, their colors washed-out and their forms indistinct.

His candle shivered as it fought for life. Swain gently placed the jar beside the wireless station as he pulled the headset on and brought the radio online. Despite the urgency, he still didn't dare raise his words past a whisper.

"Pan-pan. I'm on board the SS *Arcadia*. We require assistance urgently. Pan-pan."

He listened to the hissing, cracking emptiness on the wireless's other side. The dial made no noise as he turned it, adjusting the frequency. The light was so dim that he could barely read the numbers through the coiling mist. He would have to bring more lights—stronger lights—next time.

There won't be a next time.

The sticky fear on his tongue tasted like oil and blood. He swallowed it the best he could before speaking into the microphone again. "Pan-pan. This is the SS *Arcadia*. So many of us are dead. If anyone out there can hear me, I beg you, help us before it's too late."

Deep groaning sounds rose from the ship's hull. The candle light spluttered. Swain watched in growing horror as it grew smaller, dropping into just a pinprick of light, and then, unable to sustain itself, died.

He pulled the crackling headset off and dropped it on the table, then felt inside his pockets for the matches. He couldn't find them. Couldn't even remember where he'd placed them. His grasping became more frantic. Without a light, he wasn't even sure if he could find the door again, and he'd already spent a dangerous amount of time inside the bridge. Too much time. The captain never left his nest for long, and if he caught Swain inside—

A lighter clicked. Its flame flickered to life, bathing Swain in a small, shivering circle of light.

He turned, dread rising like a tidal wave in his chest.

The captain sat in his chair. Always had, even before Swain

entered the room. The jar's light had been too weak to reveal more than a crescent around his body, and Swain's mind had been so wholly focused on the wireless system that he hadn't even thought to search the room.

The captain held the lighter in his scabbed, cracked hands. It bathed his face in a sickly yellow glow. His eyes, heavy lidded, bore into Swain with a chilling fury.

The ship shuddered beneath them, great groaning noises rising to drown out any excuse Swain might have fumbled for. Not that there were any. Not that it would have been accepted, even if he'd had one.

Sweat stuck between his hairline and the carefully brushed officer's cap. He still had his hands wrapped about the jar with its lightless candle. It was the only thing nearby that could even be remotely considered a weapon. He raised it in the same instant that the captain lurched out of his chair, charging Swain in a blur of hands and bared, bloody teeth.

Swain didn't emerge from the bridge for nearly twenty minutes. When he did, he was pale and shaking. The cap was gone, and the hair he'd so carefully combed was hanging in damp strands about his face.

Blood dripped from his hand, where the shards from the glass jar had bitten him. He couldn't remember what had happened. Couldn't even remember why he'd entered the bridge in the first place. But he understood one thing: the captain was dead.

Holding the bleeding hand against his chest, Swain staggered the length of the hall to reach the stairs. The sticking mist had grown heavy in his gasping lungs. And he had grown tired.

He would find his berth, Swain decided. Find his berth, seal the door, and not come out again for a very long time. Perhaps not ever.

46.

THE THIRD DIVE

The wardrobe door teased itself open in increments. Something white crept around the edge. Fingers, old and spongy and swollen. The nails were missing, leaving pale white semicircles where they belonged.

Cove's mind was trying to cope with what she saw, to give it a label, an identity, some way to describe it that would allow it to make at least partial sense. She had nothing.

Roy grabbed her elbow and pulled her toward the cabin's door. Cove, shaken free from the impossible image, wrenched her head aside and fixed it on their only way out. *Left, down the hall. Find an intersection. Follow the port-side hallway back to the stairs. Get out. Get to the surface. And this ship can rot on the ocean floor for the remainder of its years.*

They were at the door. Roy shoved on it, the handle rattling in his gloves. It wasn't opening. Cove hung as close as she could.

She was acutely aware that *one* door was moving on its hinges. A faint whine rose behind them as the wardrobe quivered open.

She refused to let herself look, but her mind supplied the images regardless. It would be a giant black maw, endlessly deep, the layers of shadow going farther and farther and pressing all light out of existence. Those long, pale fingers would extend from long, pale hands. Spreading, reaching out, welcoming Cove in.

Roy shoved his shoulder into the door. It cracked, then crashed open, the wood shivering as it forced its path through the water. Clouds of silt spiraled in its wake, temporarily blotting the hall from view.

Those figures—are they still out there? How close did they come?

The wardrobe doors stopped creaking. They were fully open. Still, Cove refused to let herself glance back. Roy found her arm. He squeezed: a quick, reassuring pressure. At least, no matter what, she wasn't alone. She caught his hand and squeezed back.

Then, together, they crept through the open door.

Cove knew there was no way she could actually feel it—not through the layers of dry suit and fleece—but it felt as though the water's temperature dropped outside the room. Silt continued to circle around them. The shreds of wallpaper reached out like dust-clogged cobwebs caught in a breeze.

She looked right, around the open door. Her light trailed across the walls and the indents marking closed doors. She couldn't see the floating figures.

Somehow, that felt worse. She wanted to believe that they'd been some creation from her mind—nitrogen narcosis materializing as a nightmare before her eyes—and that it had now vanished as easily as it had appeared. But the thought rang so false that she couldn't even get away with lying to herself.

She leaned forward to look past Roy, toward their left. There seemed to be more shadows in that direction. She couldn't see the hall's end, but at least there was no glimpse of the gaunt, floating shapes either.

Is it safe to go right, then? If we try to go directly to the stairs— bypass the loop—will that be a mistake?

Roy's own misgivings were palpable as he repeatedly glanced in each direction. His gloves clenched and relaxed. Then, cautiously, he started to the right, toward the stairs.

Cove was closest to the door, and she saw it first. The wash of gossamer-thin hair teasing around the wood's edge. She threw herself back, hitting Roy and forcing both of them away from the door.

A pale, malformed body had hidden behind the door. It reached out from the shadowed cave. Glints of light shone from under heavy eyelids. The jaw seemed to widen. The creased edges of where lips belonged gaped, and the space behind seemed endlessly, impossibly dark.

Cove's shoulder hit the doorframe. She made to scramble back into the room. Roy's arms wrapped over hers, tangling them, as he dragged her back into the hallway.

She looked over her shoulder and saw why. The *thing* in the wardrobe had emerged. Its body contorted in strange ways, its skin cracking as it dragged itself toward them. It was nearly at the door.

Cove's fingers dug a clump of wallpaper free as she fought to put space between herself and the unnatural forms. Plaster and silt spilled out, creating a temporary barrier as it swallowed the white figures.

She didn't stop but paddled backward. Roy's arm was around her shoulders, as well as he could manage with the canisters between them.

They would be faster if they faced the direction they were swimming, but instinctually, she knew turning away from the misshapen forms would be a dangerous game. The gray dust swirled through the water, teasing her eyes. Something dark moved through it.

Roy gasped. Cove swung, hands rising, but he'd only backed into a wall. The passageway turned inward, then split: they could choose to go left, following the ship's length toward the stern, or cross the liner's width to reach the identical halls on its other side. Those other halls would eventually circle them back to the stairwell they'd entered through, provided it wasn't blocked.

And that was the main risk: any of the passageways could be dead ends, either stacked with furniture or with…

The shapes had emerged from the clouded sediment. Cove stared at the suspended forms. They twitched closer, gaining ground at an alarming speed.

How many are there? As many as drowned in the Arcadia? We passed dozens in the hold alone; how many more might there be?

She couldn't let herself think about it; she simply had to act. Cove shoved Roy's shoulder, pointing along the passageway that crossed the *Arcadia's* width. He shook his head once but still followed her instruction, sweeping his arms in wide arcs to pick up speed.

She followed. Moving around the corner was worse than she'd anticipated. It blocked the suspended forms from sight, which should have been a blessing, except now she had no way of knowing how close they were—or if they were even following.

Cove flipped around so she faced the hall they were traveling along. She hated not being able to watch her back, but it at least gave her a speed advantage. The faster they could navigate the pathways that ringed that central part of the ship, the better their odds of beating anything else back to the stairs.

Someone had damaged the hall. Holes had been carved into the plaster and wood, leaving dark crevices dotting their path. The sour taste of fear coated Cove's tongue. She pulled ahead of Roy and aligned herself to the runner's center, as far from each wall as she could possibly manage. It was nowhere near as far as she would have liked. Even though this was a first-class passenger hall, Cove could have put out both arms and just about bumped each set of paneling.

She kept her head moving as she swam forward, directing her light into each of the gorged holes as she passed them. Her instincts begged for her to slow down and be more cautious, but time was a luxury she didn't have. It was impossible to guess how close the suspended figures might have gotten to the corner, except underneath her ragged breathing and the heavy static, she could still hear the faint clicking of damaged joints.

Movement flashed to her left, and Cove jolted away from it, swinging her light about. Something soft drifted inside a narrow, horizontal gash. Like fine seagrass or like algae strings in a pond. Cove blinked. She was looking at a gently swaying curtain of hair. The gap seemed impossibly narrow, but somehow, a body had been wedged inside. As the hair shifted, it revealed something beady and white behind—an eye, swiveling to fix on Cove.

She licked dry lips. "Roy, careful to your left."

"I hear you."

The static was bad. Cove prayed the audio would hold at least enough that she could still communicate with the second half of her team. The silence from their radios was alarming.

She drifted right to put more space between herself and the figure wedged into the wall. A dark smear stood out on the paneling to her side. As she neared it, the words became clearer, painted in the same deep shade of paint that had been used elsewhere.

THEY CRAWL ABOUT IN THE DARK

Cove put her head back down, her skin itching. More holes appeared through the gloom ahead. They'd been cut with wild abandon. Scraps of rubble were still strewn across the floor. The holes' edges were frayed with sharp, jutting shards of wood, and it made it nearly impossible in the dim light to tell if she was looking at a piece of debris or at a protruding hand.

She felt more than heard a disturbance behind her. The static redoubled as she turned. Roy struggled. A cloud of silt billowed around him. He yelled something into the radio, but the static swallowed the words.

Cove grabbed for the second light on her belt. Its beam flashed, harsh, as she turned it toward Roy.

The figure inside the hole had moved. Long arms reached from its dark home, the bony fingers digging into Roy's legs like claws.

47.

Harland had come to visit Fitz.

It was probably his last chance, he knew. He had the stub of a candle in a glass jar, one he'd managed to squirrel away and keep hidden from the others. They were out of lights. Sometimes officers would tie an old shirt around a metal bar and set it alight to see. Sometimes they found fat in the stores or in the kitchen and gave it a wick to help it burn. But mostly, they just felt their way along the *Arcadia* blindly.

The *others* liked the dark. They showed themselves more boldly in it. He'd sensed their presences, creeping along behind him or standing in his way and waiting to see if he walked into them or pressed against the walls and watching him with their monstrous eyes as he passed. Every time he felt they were close by, he was tempted to light the last of the candle, to ward them back. But he didn't. Because once this final light was gone, he would have nothing left.

The *others* had congregated around the hospital. The men and women there wailed through the night, begging to be let free, to be allowed to crawl into holes. Their noise attracted the creatures from the walls, and the patients' pleas had turned to shrieks of terror. And so, in an attempt to keep them contained, the crew had built barriers around the hospital's halls. Furniture scavenged from wherever they could find it, stacked high, crammed into the stairwell and the passageways until the *others* might never get back out.

It hadn't stopped them, of course. The halls were only a shortcut for them; their true homes were inside the walls, and through the walls, they accessed any part of the ship they liked.

They were watching him now. He sat in the cargo hold, the jar clenched between numb fingers. The mist was making his body swell, as though he'd spent too long in a bath. His fingers had become wrinkly, his skin pallid. He dreaded what it must be doing to him inside. He imbibed it with every breath, drawing it deep into his lungs, into his core, and there it was setting root and slowly consuming him from the inside out.

The captain was to make an address that night, it was said. No one had seen the captain since that day in the hold. A few of the others still whispered of hope: the captain was bringing them news. Perhaps they were close to land. Perhaps help would be arriving soon.

Harland had no such hopes. He knew in his bones what this address would be: a farewell. An instruction for each man to make peace with himself in the minutes he had left. To pass them over into the hands of the things in the walls, the only individuals on the ship who still walked freely among them, who still thrived.

The boilers had been shut down, the flames extinguished, the stokers attempting to cool the cavities by any means necessary. Too many passengers had crawled inside, seeking a hole to hide in, the flesh cooking off their bodies before they could pull their feet in behind. They were out of coal regardless. The *Arcadia's* furious pace had finally quieted, and she was now all but adrift in whatever mercy-forsaken ocean they had found themselves in.

Harland leaned forward slightly, extending his flickering light for Fitz's benefit. He'd saved his candle for this very occasion: a final goodbye to his friend, the man who had tried to warn them. Had Fitz known this was how it would end? Harland had tried to ask him, but Fitz had not answered.

Water wallowed across his thighs. It continued to seep through the hole in the hull and slowly flood the lower levels, despite the captain's effort to fill the leak. The ship sat low in the water from the additional weight. It was close to its tipping point.

Harland tried to imagine what might be below them, waiting for them. An endless ocean of nothing? A seafloor full of the strangest and most nightmarish creatures that the earth had to offer?

Or would it be more of *them*? The ones that moved through the walls. The ones that slowly consumed all that was good aboard the ship. Somehow, he didn't think the ocean would stop them from moving. They would continue tapping and scraping and skittering through the dark, even when the ship lay fathoms down, in the deepest parts of the world. It was where they belonged.

Fitz's eyes regarded Harland coldly, as though he was waiting for an apology. And he *was* due one, Harland reasoned. There was no way to get him free any longer.

The water swirled around them, achingly cold. The liquid was dark, even under Harland's weak candle. It was absorbing all that was inside the ship: the tar, the smoke, the poison that seeped from the walls. And it turned the lapping, swelling waves into inky madness. As deep as a night sky, but with no hope of dawn ever coming.

The candle fluttered, weak as a dying heartbeat.

Fitz was pinned into the hole he'd carved. He was in the earliest stages of decomposition. His eyes, normally so blue, had clouded over as they stared into the empty space between them.

The jagged metal edges held him in place like a vise. The ocean, so desperate to get through the hole, could neither suck him out nor expel him back into the ship. Instead, it spilled around his swelling form, pouring over his clothes and his limp, cracked fingers.

He would sit with Fitz until the candle was out, Harland decided, but then he would have to leave. Because left to the dark, he was certain Fitz's stiff lips would begin twitching and his raw, raspy voice would start whispering dark, dangerous secrets.

THE THIRD DIVE

Devereaux's fingernail lightly fidgeted over the rim of his mug, searching for imperfections or chips. There were none. He'd bought the mugs himself from a vendor in India, and they'd served him as well as he could hope for the last fifteen years. Well enough that he'd stocked the *Skipjack* with them, eager to do his part—no matter how small—to make sure the trip was perfect.

He'd chosen those mugs when making drinks for Hestie and Sean. Hestie, in the chair by his side, nursed hers, though she'd barely drunk any. Sean let his sit neglected on the floor beside him. He crouched, muttering under his breath, occasionally swearing, as he worked on the communications unit.

Hestie watched the work with dull eyes. She shuffled her feet, but the way her back slumped into the chair betrayed how utterly exhausted she was.

"There's something wrong with that ship." She'd barely spoken after uttering those words, and Devereaux hadn't been able to pry much more out of her.

If there was ever going to be a wreck that held true mystery and horror, he supposed it made sense for it to be the *Arcadia*.

He'd first heard about the ship in a history book at age twelve. The untethered questions had lodged themselves inside of him and refused to let go. In a world where advances in technology were solving problems Devereaux hadn't even known existed, it felt unfathomable to have such a mystery exist with no visible answers.

Of course, it wasn't the only naval mystery to captivate him. But over the decades, the others fell like dominoes, sometimes all at once, like when the *Titanic's* wreck was found. Sometimes in gradual steps, like his growing awareness that the Bermuda Triangle was not some godforsaken portal to the underworld, but simply a rough patch of ocean with an uncommonly high amount of traffic and a corresponding ratio of wrecks. Or sometimes the mysteries were not entirely, conclusively solved, like the *Mary Celeste*, but the experts were able to present such plausible theories that it felt foolish to believe in magic any longer.

But the *Arcadia* had defied all of that. As Devereaux passed his sixtieth birthday, he'd begun to imagine that this would be the only one of the big wrecks that might not have any resolution before his death.

And then, the miracle he'd been waiting for. Ocean surveys had discovered a ship's silhouette matching the *Arcadia*. It correlated with the heavily debated oar discovered on the Polish coast.

Answers were within his grasp. Devereaux had known that someone would leap on the chance to document the wreck sooner or later and had been waiting in the wings, ready to volunteer himself and his beloved *Skipjack*. He'd had custom modifications made to it, including a fill station installed so that the dive team could recharge their tanks between trips. He'd made his offer as attractive as possible and had positively danced across his study when he received the acceptance call.

He was far, far too old to dive to the *Arcadia*'s depths. If he was being honest with himself, even recreational scuba would have been outside of his comfort level. He would not himself be allowed to lay hands on the mythical ship. But he could be close to it, floating just above the wreck. And he could be the first to review the footage that came back to him. That in itself was more than he'd dreamed he might achieve in a lifetime.

Now, though, things were crumbling in ways he wasn't sure he understood. Sean's breathing ran rough as he stabbed a screwdriver into something under the console. Hestie watched him with the dogged urgency of someone who not only wanted but *needed* him to succeed.

Devereaux gently cleared his throat. "Hestie, perhaps—"

"I'm fine." It was a rote answer. She shot him a glance. Her eyes were bloodshot around their edges. "No, maybe I'm not. I can't stand that they got to return to the *Arcadia*, and I didn't. Is that crazy?"

Devereaux tilted his head. "The *Arcadia* is a remarkable ship, not only for its history but for its construction as well. Though I was under the impression that perhaps it held less allure for you after the first dive."

"I should have told them to cancel the whole thing. There were plenty of opportunities. I could have begged Cove to cut it all short, take me back to shore, get us all as far from the wreck as possible. Do you know what I did instead? I begged her to let me go down for the final dive."

Sean lifted his head from the console, eyebrows heavy as he scrutinized her. She didn't seem to notice, her eyes glassy as she stared into her mug.

"Perhaps…" Devereaux tried running the words through his mind before he committed to them. "You felt as though your work were incomplete. I've known some professionals who would put themselves into harm's way in order to fulfill a commitment, no matter how inadvisable—"

"No. It's the ship. It wants me back. Because it didn't want *any* of us to leave."

Sean muttered something as he ducked back under the dashboard.

Devereaux put his mug aside. He knew Hestie was trying to communicate something to him—something more than the sum of her words. He tried a slightly different tack. "You speak about the ship as though it's sentient."

Her mouth worked, lips twisting down at their edges. "I don't know if I'd say that."

Devereaux didn't try to fill the silence but let it hold, showing her that there was room to speak if she so desired. After a beat, she did.

"The *ship* isn't aware. It's just the shell. But…the things *inside* the ship…"

A sudden jolt of static blared from the speakers. Sean scuttled out from under the console, his face lit up, a triumphant hiss escaping through clenched teeth. He reached for the settings and flicked several switches.

The static continued—an awful, unending blur of white noise—but then a new sound joined in. Noise from the dive team's communications units. Distorted and muffled but still present.

Roy was screaming.

48.

It was all happening too fast. Cove swiveled, feeling the dense water drag against her as she attempted to turn back to Roy. He struggled, his headlight flashing in jagged lines across the walls, ceiling, and floor. Air burst from his rebreather. It mingled with the silt that was gradually turning the hallway into a haze of maddening dust particles.

One long arm stretched out of the hole in the wall. Its fingers, thin and bony, looked impossibly fragile but had latched on to Roy's leg, digging into the layers of fabric.

He kicked at it. The arm retracted and then extended again but did not let go. It was like a vise around his ankle, and as Cove pulled herself closer, she thought she could hear the creature inside the wall releasing slow, raspy hissing noises.

"Cove! Cove, I—"

She could barely hear him through the deafening static, but she knew what was causing his distress. The arm was beginning to pull. It dragged him closer to its hole, as though determined to crush Roy inside with her, to somehow get them both into a space that scarcely allowed room for one.

Cove aimed a fist at the wrist. It looked too thin, like a bird's leg or a rotted, knotted stick. One good impact should have been enough to break it. Her blow landed squarely below the woman's wrist, and she was rewarded with a distinct crunching sensation beneath her hand. The arm bent as it broke, creating the impression of an additional nightmarish joint between the wrist and the elbow.

But still, it did not let Roy go.

Through the static, Cove was faintly aware that the clicking noises were growing nearer. Past Roy's thrashing form, figures had emerged around the hallway's corner. She could see four but didn't know if more would be coming. The contorted limbs twitched. Their heads seemed frozen on stiff necks, but the eyes tracked Cove. The nearest one extended its jaw into a ghoulish oval, a voiceless scream.

Cove pulled her dive knife out of her belt. The woman's fingers dug deeply into Roy's leg. She pried the knife in around the index finger's first knuckle and began sawing. The blade cut through the skin easily enough. There was no blood, just a clean line through gray flesh. The blade became caught on the bone. Cove knew she had to be careful; she couldn't risk slicing his dry suit.

"Cove—Cove—behind—"

She almost missed the words through the static. By the time she lifted her head, the creature was nearly on her.

It had crept out of one of the other holes. A trail of sediment hung in the water like a plume of smoke, marking its path. It wore a sailor's uniform, and a beard still clung to its gaunt cheeks, which were coated in the milky-white adipocere.

Cove snatched the knife away from the gripping hand and swung it toward the sailor just as he reached for her.

The curved knife embedded in the side of his hand, sinking through the mottled white and gray skin like cutting into a dense cake. The sailor swept his arm outward. It broke Cove's grip on the handle, and she gasped as the blade was wrenched away from her.

His other hand came out and reached for her face. She hauled herself back, trying to put herself out of reach, but her tanks hit Roy, who was blocking the passageway. The clicking was growing closer. Cove fumbled across her belt, her mind running through every item she stored there but unable to think of any that could possibly work as a weapon against the gaunt-faced *being*.

Its hand pressed over her mask. Splayed fingers covered the screen, blocking her view, filling her vision with nothing but the gray, cracking skin and the white corpse fat. It began to pull. Cove sucked in a desperate breath as she realized what was happening. The straps holding the full-face mask in place were stretching. A gap appeared around her chin. At three hundred-odd feet, the ocean water took less than a second to flood the space, forcing the oxygen out as it surged over her mouth, her nose, her eyes.

Cove thrashed. The mask slipped further. She dragged her hands over it, desperately attempting to hold it in place. The dead-eyed sailor was stronger. Its other hand rose to grip her around her neck. The fingers, which appeared so bony and fragile, held a ferocious, unnatural strength. Her windpipe closed over. Cove gaped her mouth open, futilely trying to draw in air that didn't exist. Bubbles flowed from her rebreather in a constant stream, failing to do more than graze across her face, as ocean water filled her mouth.

A painfully sharp light speared past her. It turned the sailor's face into a shocking palette of white, highlighting the creases across its cheeks and the gray of its eyes.

The face mask snapped back against Cove's head as the dead

creature released it. The pressure on her throat released. It rocked away from them, clawlike hands slowly rising to cover its face.

They don't like light.

Cove's lungs were aching for air. She dragged the mask back over her head, her hands shaking as protocol ran through her head. *Make sure the seal is firm. And then purge—*

She pressed the button. Air flooded through the mask, expelling the water. She spat ocean from her mouth and began gulping down air, coughing and shaking.

Roy had his hand extended over her shoulder, she realized. He held his light—not the headlight, but the flashlight they all carried in their belts—and shoved it as close to the sailor's face as he could reach.

The clicking sounds were almost upon them, and Cove didn't need to look to know how bad it would be. Drops of the near-icy water continued to run from her face as she took Roy's hand and brought it around, toward the creature in the wall.

It had been pulling on him while Cove was distracted by the sailor. His foot had disappeared through the gap in the plaster and wood. Her lungs still ached and her tongue tasted like death, but Cove took the light from Roy's hand and bent closer, searching for the creature inside. She found it. Coiled more tightly than she thought it was possible for a human body to achieve, the entity's bobbed hair floated about its face like a cloud. A glint of light flashed through: the eye.

Cove shoved the flashlight against it. The hissing noise, which had all but blended into the static, suddenly redoubled. The woman writhed, her arms coiling back into her body. Roy's leg scraped her arm as he pulled it free. Cove grabbed his shoulder and hauled him forward, away from the clicking entities, just as their bleached fingers scraped her back.

The sailor still blocked their path. One of its arms snaked out toward them, but Cove brought the light up, and it convulsed as it rolled back.

The flashlight flickered. Its beam dimmed to almost nothing, then when it came back, it was less than half its strength. Cove grit her teeth but kept them moving. Roy needed no encouragement. They passed the sailor, squeezing close to the opposite wall in an effort to avoid touching the body. Its hands stayed up around its face, but it rotated warily, watching them from between clawed fingers, and Cove had no doubt it would be following them as soon as the light grew distant enough.

Roy patted her shoulder, and that was when she realized he was trying to speak to her. His words were distorted and disjointed, and not just from the audio, she thought, but from the panic. "Okay—? You all right?"

Her throat ached; it would be ringed by bruises come morning. Her lungs still gulped down the air faster than she really needed it as the fear of drowning three hundred feet underwater took hold. Her tongue continued to taste foul, no matter how many times she swallowed. And a smear of the corpse wax, the adipocere, ran across her mask. She raised one sleeve to feverishly wipe at it without slowing. "I'm fine. You?"

She couldn't see his expression, but she could imagine it as he tilted his head at her. *Nothing* about this situation was okay with him.

The handheld flashlight was dimming with each second. She passed it back to Roy. She still had her own strapped to her belt and could only pray it would work if she needed it. Her knife was gone though, snatched away by the *thing* dressed like a sailor.

They were at the corner. Cove reached around first, tilting the top half of her body so that she could withdraw in a rush if necessary. It was hard to be sure with the flowing wallpaper and the dark doorway indents, but she thought the path was empty. She beckoned for Roy to follow. "Vanna, Aidan, can you hear me?"

The static was horrendous. She strained to hear voices beneath, but if they were still there, they were drowned out. She licked her lips and tasted the drops of water that still clung there. "If you can hear me, use your lights. They don't like brightness. Okay? Use your lights."

She let the quiet stretch, praying for some kind of answer. Something bubbled up underneath the hissing white noise. A man's voice.

"—Cove—happening—?"

She frowned. "Sean?"

"I'm here. You—" Sharp bursts of dead sound cut across his words.

"I can't hear you, Sean." She threw a glance over her shoulder. The hallway's corner cut a sharp line through the gloom. Pale fingers reached around the edge.

"What's happening?" The static dropped, and Sean's voice rose as it made it through. "Vanna's done something, hasn't she?"

Abrupt frustration bubbled up through Cove. "Vanna has done *nothing*. We're dealing with a situation here. We're just trying to get out."

"But if she's done something you need to tell—"

Roy cut across, panicked laughter filling his words. "It's the ship. The bodies. They're all coming back to life."

A beat of silence followed, filled only with static. Then Sean, disgusted, "I'm not in the mood for jokes."

It's the truth though, isn't it? Cove had steadfastly refused to put any kind of name to the figures. It seemed insane to even

49.

"They don't like brightness. Okay? Use your lights."

Cove's voice faded from the communications unit. Aidan didn't have enough moisture left in his mouth to answer.

Vanna was frozen at his side. Her hand gripped his forearm, almost painfully tight.

They had their backs to a stack of crates. Aidan was shivering, his whole upper body locked as he fought to avoid knocking the canisters against the wood.

Ahead, one of the dead lurked.

It moved from between the narrow passageway to their right and passed ahead of them. Aidan didn't think it knew they were there, even though their headlights were trained on its form. It passed them unflinchingly, aiming toward a gap in the crates ahead.

Despite being blind, it seemed to know the pathway perfectly; the gaps were narrow, but it still didn't so much as graze the walls.

And it *had* to be blind, didn't it?

Half of its head was missing.

The entity passed directly ahead of them, close enough that Aidan could have stretched a hand forward and grazed its white-mottled cheeks. Vanna's hold on him increased, and beneath the pressure he felt her hand shake.

The entity wore a dinner jacket. The pants were gone, fallen away and lost somewhere deeper in the hold. Aidan thought the body must have been large in life, but the belly had sagged and deformed during its years in purgatory. Clumps of waxy fat extruded between buttons in the dinner jacket, matting the fabric to the body until it appeared like an additional layer of skin.

The top part of the entity's head was gone. Everything from the bridge of the nose above was crushed away. The jaw was slack, its irregular, brittle teeth visible inside.

Use your lights, Cove had said. That would have given Aidan some measure of hope, except that their lights were failing fast. Vanna's headlamp was almost gone; it flickered in sickly patterns, threatening collapse. His own was scarcely better. Vanna had brought out her backup flashlight, but its bulb seemed weaker than it should have been, and he didn't have the courage to question how much longer it might last.

He'd been about to take out his own spare light when Vanna had shoved him back against the crates. That had been when the eyeless figure had glided into view. They'd held still. It had continued moving.

As they stood frozen against the cargo, Cove and Roy had continued speaking. Only the faintest outline of words had been audible. The static had swallowed everything else.

The headless figure passed by them, slipping like a phantom into another of the narrow passageways. Aidan couldn't see the door, only an endless maze of crates and hanging sacks, but he knew their way out had to be *somewhere* ahead.

Vanna lifted two fingers and used them to tap on Aidan's wrist. *We'll go now.* He nodded once, grateful that she couldn't see how uncertain he truly felt.

They leaned forward. Motion came from their left. Aidan yanked on Vanna, pulling them both back, their canisters hitting the crates behind them and sending billows of silt around them.

The half-headed figure had returned. The face turned toward them, and Aidan had a glimpse of the pulpy insides of its head through his failing light. He squeezed his eyes closed.

It can't see us. It can't see…

Vanna pulled his arm closer. He cracked his eyes open to see she was pressing buttons on his dive computer. Settings flashed up, then flicked away as she scrolled through them.

The figure with the crushed head drifted toward them. Its feet curled under itself. Its jaw gaped open. The fat extruding through its dinner jacket glowed a hollow white in his headlamp.

Its eyes were gone, but its ears were still attached. One of the figure's hands rose, stretching toward Aidan's helmet.

It can't see us. But it can still hear us.

Vanna pressed a final button, and his audio cut out. Aidan silently forced his breath out as he and Vanna sank down, bending at their knees to drop into a crouch. The headless figure's outstretched hand bumped into the crate directly behind where his mask had been. The thick-knuckled fingers were contorted into a claw but grazed across the surface as it searched for them.

At that angle, the deflated, fat-covered stomach was immediately in front of Aidan's face. He turned his head slightly, his breathing shallow as he relied on his lungs' buoyancy to keep him at the lower level, beneath the grasping hand.

A low, ragged gurgle rang from its throat. Now that the static was no longer filling Aidan's ears, he could hear it clearly. Vanna must have turned her radio off as well, he realized; her helmet was tilted slightly toward him, one eye watching the presence, the other keeping track of Aidan.

The figure turned. Although blind, it seemed to know exactly where to go as it resumed its path back toward the narrow passageways.

Aidan finally let himself breathe deeply enough to rise back up. Vanna matched his movement, but as she floated away from the floor, her headlight finally faded into nothing.

He bit the inside of his cheek. His own headlight was flickering too, weak bursts of light cutting through the gloom before fading again.

Vanna took his hand and forced her handheld flashlight into it. The beam was steady, at least, though not as strong as it should have been. Aidan tried to pass it back to her. He still had his own backup flashlight on his belt; he didn't need to take hers. It took him a second to realize she wasn't trying to give him the flashlight but merely asking him to hold it. She uncoiled a length of dive line from her belt, then cut it free and tied the two remaining pieces back together. The spare length—barely more than a meter—was shaken out. She fastened one end to Aidan's wrist, then the other to her own.

So that we won't be separated if…or when…our lights go out.

He swallowed through a painful thickness in his throat. Vanna checked the knots twice, tugging on them to make sure they wouldn't come loose, then tapped the back of Aidan's hand and pointed toward where he knew the opposite wall must be.

He looked in that direction. Stacks of crates and hanging nets cluttered the area. In between them though, he caught hints of movement. White shroud, shivering. Strange figures, floating. One turned toward him, and his headlight reflected off the glazed eyes, causing them to glint like an animal's. He turned away.

Vanna tapped his wrist again, then pointed to his light. She raised her other hand over her mask, pantomiming blocking her eyes.

The meaning caught up to Aidan. They'd been able to hide from the half-headed figure because it couldn't see them. The others would have no such problem. If they wanted to get to the door, they would have to pass over the bodies waiting in their path…and that would mean swimming with their lights off, moving blind.

Cove said the light would keep them away. But Aidan had already realized the truth. Their lights were dying. Each minute spent in the hold robbed their brightness and sapped their power. They couldn't rely on the lights to force a path.

He hated the thought so intensely that bile rose in the back of his throat. But he still nodded. Vanna reached around his headlight and found the switch to turn it off. Then she took the backup light back from him and switched it off as well.

Perfect darkness rushed in to surround them. It felt like a physical weight pressing on Aidan's chest, crushing the air out of him. The moment he stopped being able to see, he lost context for where his body belonged in the void. Were his feet still pointing down, or had they started to drift up? He tried to correct them, but for all he knew he'd moved them in the wrong direction and was now beginning to tip over.

The rebreather released air with a muffled rushing noise. He reached out a hand, hoping he might be able to tell which way was up by finding the bubbles, but he couldn't even feel them through his gloves.

He felt something though. The soft tug on the cord tied to his wrist. They were moving.

Aidan leaned forward and relied on gentle nudges of his fins to push away from the crates. They had to move softly to avoid detection—no noise, minimal currents. His right foot grazed something, and he couldn't tell whether he'd bumped a crate or whether the half-faced figure had returned for another loop.

Moving into the darkness was terrifying. He kept expecting to hit a wall of boxes or one of the suspended nets. He held his right forearm ahead of himself to shield his head from the inevitable impact. It was impossible to know how far they had traveled.

Then, from his left, a soft clicking noise. A wedge of light appeared from Vanna's flashlight. She swept it across the scene ahead of them, then turned it off again.

In that second-long glimpse of the world ahead, he'd seen that they were trending toward the ceiling, and a stack of crates was blocking them to the front and right. Vanna tugged on the cord, pulling them left. Aidan overcorrected and hit her shoulder. They straightened then, their arms grazing as they moved toward the narrow gap they'd seen during their second of light.

The tethered boxes grazed Aidan's side as they moved between them. He had no idea what was ahead. They hadn't been able to see into this area as they were huddled and waiting for the half-faced creature to pass. They could be moving into a dead end. Or into the claws of countless shrouded bodies.

Again, Vanna flashed her light on. Again, she switched it off after less than a second, giving them the slimmest chance to glimpse the path ahead.

The crates created a natural tunnel pushing them right, away from where the door should be. But Aidan didn't like the idea of retracing their steps. If the dead were following them by their lights, they would be clustering in their wake.

Their formation had to switch to single file to accommodate the narrow passage. Vanna moved first, and Aidan stretched his tethered hand ahead to give her slack. Every few seconds, the cord gave a light tug. At first it felt like a comforting signal; she was still there and still pulling him forward. But gradually, that emotion morphed to one of dread.

Would he know if something had happened to her? The tugs were sharp. Would he be able to tell if it were truly Vanna pulling him forward or simply her severed arm being dragged along like a lure by one of the dead?

Aidan clenched his jaw until his teeth ached. He waited for her light. She'd have to turn it on again soon to correct their course. Soon…soon…

Something soft and malleable ran along Aidan's thigh. He pictured one of the dead bodies raking its limp hands across his side, or perhaps one of the swaddled, shrouded figures struggling toward him.

Aidan took a deep breath. It was a long time since he'd checked his dive computer for his oxygen level. He was frightened to look at it. A small part of him registered that, even at that moment, it might be too late to escape. Even if they got past the grasping hands and out of the cursed ship, they might not have enough air to reach the surface.

And then, ahead, Vanna's light flicked on.

Rows of glinting eyes filled their path. The light turned off immediately. The cord, which had been tugging him, became slack.

Turn back and risk being cornered? Or push forward and risk being caught?

Two short, sharp tugs on the cord answered Aidan's question. They were going forward. And they were going to do it fast.

Vanna lunged forward. Aidan moved with her, kicking his feet furiously, no longer cautious about the silt or creating currents.

Hands raked across his chest. Something hit his mask, shifting it a fraction of an inch, and Aidan grappled with it to push it back into place.

Light flashed again as Vanna turned her flashlight on. It glared across the closest faces, and the gaping jaws stretched wider as the figures coiled back.

Aidan grappled for his own spare flashlight. His left hand was still tied to Vanna's right, but he held his light in his spare and directed it toward anything that came close to them.

It helped. A bit. The bodies didn't fully retreat, but the grasping, clawlike hands rose to block their eyes. It struck Aidan that, after living in the dark and the cold for more than ninety years, the sudden illumination must hurt their eyes.

His flashlight was weakening rapidly though. The bulb grew dim, as though each grimacing face it pointed toward was stealing some of its power. Vanna's was fading just as fast.

But he could see the door ahead. No more than fifteen paces away, it still had the white dive line floating through the opening like a marker.

His light blinked, then stuttered as it fought for life. Aidan kicked forward again, the edges of his fins scraping over reaching, shriveled arms. Vanna moved at his side, both of them propelled by pure adrenaline. Her flashlight failed first. Aidan pointed his ahead, no longer bothering to shine it on the shrouded figures clustering toward them but using it to guide their path.

A broad, dim silhouette moved in front of the doorway. Aidan's flashlight flickered across the sagging stomach and the faded dinner jacket, then up, toward the slack jaw and the blunt end of its head where the bridge of its nose began.

And then his flashlight died.

Aidan dropped it and instead reached his hands forward to claw through the water. They were moving too fast to stop... not that stopping was an option either way. Movement swelled behind them, eddies dragging on their fins as the figures tried to claw them back.

Aidan's outstretched hand dug into something bony. He didn't think but simply pulled on it, using it to aid his speed as he clambered toward freedom. It was only when bony plates shifted and his fingertips sank into something soft that he realized what he was touching: the insides of the half-headed man's skull.

A scream boiled in his chest but choked on the lump in his throat. He couldn't breathe as he snatched his hand free. The doorframe scraped his shoulder, and fingertips ran down his calf, searching for purchase, but were shaken free when he kicked his feet.

They were through the hold's door and out into the hallway.

50.

The captain called a meeting just before midnight. One of the officers, Pulley, had sent word that they were to be summoned to the bridge. That came as a surprise to many: the bridge had been off-limits to all—even the officers—for days.

Harland felt numb as he traced the passageways. He could no longer feel his feet or his hands through the cold. It was almost possible to imagine that he had slipped over the veil between life and death without even noticing it, except that he still tasted *it*. The rotting, sticking fog, drenching his clothes, filling his lungs, like glue on the inside of his nostrils. If he were dead, he should have at least been set free from *that*.

Though he could be mistaken, he reasoned. Perhaps this *was* hell.

The ship certainly felt like it. Voices mumbled from the hospital on the floor below. No one had visited them since the hallways were barricaded, but their raving and shrieking ensured they were not forgotten.

As Harland trailed after his companions on the route to the captain's bridge, arms reached from holes in the walls, languidly plucking at his pant legs as though trying to draw him into their hiding places. They were all familiar faces, some of them even friends. Now, he barely spared them a glance.

The bridge door was open. The captain occupied his chair, facing away from them. He stared toward the controls and the broad windows overlooking a wall of white.

The fog was thicker on the bridge, and Harland raised his sleeve over his mouth in a vain effort to block it out.

There was no rhyme or reason to the people who had been summoned. Harland half believed that Officer Pulley had simply grabbed the sleeves of whoever he passed in the halls. For all he knew, that could be the truth. They had stopped keeping records of which staff were still alive and still willing to work. Indeed, work had almost entirely ground to a halt. The engines were rapidly growing cold as the surviving stokers congregated in one of the staff mess halls, staring into empty mugs with empty eyes and never seeming to leave their seats.

Nearly thirty individuals lined up inside the bridge. That was about as many as the space could take, but although it was cramped, they all avoided moving too close to the captain's chair. Only Pulley, his favored officer, stood at his side, one hand on the chair's leather back.

Still, the captain remained facing away from them. The top of his cap was visible above the seat. His elbows lay on the armrests, unnervingly still. The dim light of burning fat in a jar did a pitiful job of lighting the space, and Harland squinted. Were those flecks of dried blood on the captain's sleeves?

He, along with several colleagues, shuffled backward, trying to pull deeper into the crowd that was already packed shoulder to shoulder.

"The captain thanks you for joining him this evening," Pulley said. He was a small man with sloped shoulders but a few years older than Harland. He'd had keen eyes before the journey set out, and they seemed to have only sharpened since then. Harland had a flash of memory: Pulley's lips pulled tight with a harsh kind of glee as he and his fellow officers rushed Fitz in the hold. He turned aside so he wouldn't have to see that same maniacal glint again.

"The captain has special instructions for you tonight," Pulley continued. "I suggest you listen closely."

He pushed on the edge of the captain's chair. Slowly, creaking, it rotated to face them. Harland squinted as the dull light burned his eyes. It was impossible to read any detail clearly. He had the strange impression of a crooked smile on the captain's lips as the chair came to a halt, then abruptly took another step back.

Quiet murmurs rose from those around him. The captain faced him, a jar of burning fat held between his hands. He'd been tied to the chair with coarse rope. Even his hands had been lashed together, to prevent the jar from falling and spilling. If not for the ropes, Harland was certain Captain Virgil would have been entirely limp.

There was no crooked smile on his lips. His cheeks and jaw were slack. His eyes were cast downward and fogged. His head rocked with every small movement, giving him the illusion of motion. A harsh, jagged line cut across his throat. Blood ran down from it like a cravat, to paint his shirt in dark crimson.

The whispers were growing into a crescendo. Pulley's eyes drew tight. "Silence," he barked, and the crew fell quiet.

The captain is dead, Harland thought, and although he knew he should feel some kind of emotion at that revelation, all he experienced was a dull sort of surprise.

It was because it had been inevitable, he realized. He'd been too slow to read the signs, but they were all there: painted across the walls as messages, carved into the plaster and metal, present in the inhuman creatures that stalked through their secret passages. This was as inevitable as winter following autumn, as inevitable as the passing of an elderly relative. It was always going to happen... and he was the fool who hadn't felt the need to prepare.

"The captain has orders," Pulley said, still standing uncomfortably close to the captain's chair, still resting his pale fingers on its back. "Listen."

Against his better judgment, Harland edged closer. The captain was dead. And yet...was he really? The harder Harland listened, the more he became convinced that he could hear whispers. Not from his fellow crew; they, along with him, were holding their breath. But as he leaned in, he swore he saw the captain's lips twitching. Secret, rasping phrases dropped from between bloodied teeth and bruised lips.

The captain was dead. And yet...he was not.

"You hear that?" The sharp glint in Pulley's eyes had grown dangerous. "You understand it, don't you? The captain wants the holes widened. We must root out these intruders. Go to work; begin digging. Peel away the layers. Don't stop until you find them."

Yes, Harland thought. *That's what the whispers say. We're supposed to dig.*

The captain's bloodshot, faded eyes fixed on nothing, but the lips continued to twitch, those dark phrases he couldn't fully understand falling from them as smoothly as snakes.

Yes, they were supposed to dig, and dig deeper and not stop until the *others* were uncovered—and maybe not even then.

51.

THE THIRD DIVE

Just get to the stairs. That's all that matters. Get to the stairs.

Cove had their path mapped out in her mind. Ahead, the hall turned to the right. There would be the stairwell, one-half leading down, but the other half taking them up, back into the writing room, and then out into the ocean.

And the misshapen, once-human figures creeping in their wake wouldn't follow them into the ocean, Cove was certain. Somehow, they felt as much a part of the ship as the plate metal walls and wood panels: fixtures that could not be removed without carving something vital out of the ship.

Loose wallpaper coiled over her face mask as her too-rapid pace sent eddies rolling through the hall. Roy was close behind her, his dark form visible in brief flashes at her side. She hadn't heard from Vanna or Aidan. She only hoped they'd already found their own way out. They couldn't have been far from the smoking room when Vanna's first warning came through.

She didn't know what she'd do if she and Roy arrived outside the *Arcadia* and found they were alone. The thought tied her stomach into knots. With her lights threatening to fail and the audio so broken it was close to useless, she had no plan for how she would even go about locating her missing crew...let alone retrieve them.

Don't think about it. They'll be there. You just need to focus on getting yourself out; that's all you can afford right now.

Quiet clicking sounds echoed from around Cove. She could no longer identify them as coming from *behind* her. They seemed to surround her—inside the rooms they passed, from the floor above, from the floor below. She refused to twist her head in search of the sounds but instead fixated ahead, eyes glued on the hall's end. Every fiber of her body was wound tight at the idea of *something* shifting in to block her path. She thanked whatever luck they held on to for each passing moment that the hall remained clear.

Up the stairs. Through the writing room and into the lounge. Out through the hole. Then you'll be safe.

A heavy, sonorous noise rose from the ship. Beginning at the stern and rushing along the ocean liner like shivers along a spine, the reverberations vibrated the water around Cove and shook sparkling lines of sediment loose from the ceiling. She swallowed around the lump in her throat and coaxed herself to breathe. There was no luxury to stop and wait the noise out; they simply had to keep moving as the shudders passed around them and faded at the stern.

The ship's waking up. She'd had that thought once before, but it seemed so much more possible at that moment. They'd brought the oxygen back into the *Arcadia*. They'd fed the bodies that had been dormant for so many decades. They hadn't risen from their resting places at once; the first dive, they'd been in hibernation, still and silent and reluctant to be roused.

But Cove and her team had been given warnings during the second dive. The safety line being severed. Doors closing. Signs that something did not want them to leave. And Hestie—reliable, logical Hestie—collapsing in the hospital.

It had taken those first two dives to fully rouse the sleeping dead. But now they were awake, and Cove didn't like to think how little time they had to escape the *Arcadia*'s jaws before they were closed forever.

They were at the hall's end. Cove knew they couldn't afford to stop, but she still slowed her pace to lean around the corner, sending her fading headlight cutting into the gloom beyond.

The stairs were to her left. The sharp edges of the railing caught the light, casting hard shadows on the opposite walls. Specks of waterborne sediment floated across the stairs, marking the path Cove and Roy—and presumably, the stiffly suspended figures—had followed.

Cove beckoned to her companion as she leaned forward. The clicking noises had grown louder and more consuming and bled into the static in a way that put Cove's teeth on edge.

Roy pushed forward to come up beside her, just as eager to leave the vessel. Cove pointed herself at the stairs leading up and began to rise.

Almost…

A gray figure turned toward her. Cove pulled up, her hands cutting through the water as she tried to halt her momentum.

One of the unnaturally stiff creatures blocked the stairs. Its shoes were missing, and its toes curled under themselves, grazing the steps as it moved toward them. Its back was bowed and its hands wrapped around its torso, but as it moved nearer, they uncoiled, slowly spreading out from its body.

Cove froze as she stared up at it. She couldn't afford to turn away from the stairs, but the figure blocked the path, and it was growing nearer.

The lights worked before—

Just as that thought registered, the bulb on her head flickered, its strength fading dangerously. Cove clenched her teeth, willing it to hold.

The figure's arms spread, reaching out toward them. Two more shapes filled the shadowed recesses behind it, and Cove's heart missed a beat.

Roy backed away from the stairwell, his motions sharp. He was moving toward the other passageway, the path they'd originally taken when entering that level.

Cove felt ice flood her veins. The creature from the wardrobe twisted through the water at his back. Cove reached toward him, desperate, and managed to snag his gloved hand. She pulled on him. The wardrobe-creature's too-long fingers reached forward, snagging Roy's canister. Cove heard him yell, not through the static-flooded communications units, but through the water. He writhed, frantic. The creature's grip slipped, and Cove pulled her friend to her.

The figure on the stairs was nearly at the landing, its bony, wax-crusted arms twitching through the water as it reached for her. Cove backed away from it, moving toward the passageway they had just come from. Slick fear flowed across her tongue. The four figures, the ones that had followed them around the loop, were nearly on top of them.

Can't go up. Can't go forward. Can't go backward.

Cove turned, her hands sweeping the water to back her away from the threats drawing closer on all three sides.

There was one path that still remained empty, but terror gripped Cove at the thought of it. The stairwell down was an ink-black tunnel of shadows under her failing light, but nothing blocked the stairs. Yet.

Roy grasped her shoulder and hauled her toward it. They were out of choices. Reluctantly, she let herself tip into the hole leading to the lower level, knowing it likely wasn't a coincidence that the only path left open to them was the one that carried them deeper into the ship.

The hallway between the holds was so perfectly silent that Aidan could hear his heart beating. He tried to drift forward, toward where the doors to the upper levels could be found, but the cord still tied to his wrist pulled taut.

Vanna. Is she stuck? Is she okay?

He felt for the controls next to his headlight, desperately hoping it had survived the struggle through the hold. The sound of metal shrieking put his teeth on edge. He found a switch and pressed it, and sharp white light flickered across the scene.

Vanna was at the hold door, forcing it closed. Scabbed, cracked hands reached past the door's edge, trying to curl around far enough to snag her. Aidan pressed his lips together, hoping it might somehow be enough to keep him from being sick, and raised himself in the water. He kicked at the hands in quick, sharp jabs, never leaving his foot there long enough to be snagged in return. The door shuddered as it ground home, and Vanna leaned her shoulder against it, her chest heaving from the exertion.

The dark mask covering her face tilted toward him, and Aidan tentatively raised an okay sign. The head dipped, then Vanna gave him an okay in return.

Aidan reached for the knot holding the cord around his wrist, but Vanna placed her hand over it, refusing to let him untie it. They were going to stay tethered until they left the ship. That made sense, Aidan realized; they only had one light left—his— and no radios. If the headlight went out unexpectedly, they might never find each other again.

Vanna bent to pick the white dive line off the floor. She tugged on it, and all of Aidan's thoughts of following a simple pathway to the outside faded. The cord snaked toward them, loose in the water, and Vanna caught its end.

They don't want us finding our way out. We should have expected that.

Vanna dropped the severed line and pointed ahead, toward where the hallway met the boiler rooms. Aidan nodded. Vanna had spent the previous journey in the higher levels, but Aidan had been with Cove when they went past the furnaces. There were pathways that would take them back to the passenger halls. As long as the majority of the dead had been restricted to the hold—and he dearly hoped they were—they should be able to get out of the ship in less than ten minutes.

He just hoped his light would last that long.

The watertight door was still left ajar from the previous day. It was a narrow fit, and Vanna passed through first, her arm extended behind herself to give the tether slack for Aidan. He squeezed through after her, the canisters scraping the metal walls, and turned his light across the room.

The beam reached far less than it had on his first visit. Back then, the team's lights had given him a sense of the scale of the cathedral-like room. Now, it could barely pick out the edges of the tangled metal walkways that created a weblike maze across the floor.

Aidan tapped Vanna's shoulder and pointed forward and slightly up, to where he remembered the door Cove had found the previous day. They'd had to cross almost all of the boiler room to reach it, but it had brought them out near the main dining hall.

Vanna nodded and let Aidan lead. He ran his tongue over dry lips as he rose, putting space between himself and the tangled metal and wires.

He wasn't used to being the lead on *anything*. But Vanna didn't know where the door was, and with the weakened light, Aidan wasn't sure if even he could find it on the first try. The thought of low oxygen dug at the back of his head, but he still refused to let himself look at the dive computer's metrics. They were getting out as quickly as they possibly could; it would either be good enough or not.

Everywhere he turned, metal glinted out from beneath layers of sediment. The massive boilers rose on either side of the room, their dark holes impenetrable to his light. Above, scraps of the fallen walkways and piping created threateningly jagged edges across the ceiling.

A shadow shifted below. Aidan's pulse quickened. Part of him didn't want to look at it. Part of him didn't have a choice. His headlight flickered as it turned downward.

Small, silvery disks of light shone from between the metal. Aidan's pace slowed and his eyes narrowed as he tried to understand what he was looking at. Some of them winked in and out of view, like stars or dull fireflies. They were hypnotic. Strange, otherworldly. Beautiful. He couldn't stop watching as they flickered, dozens of them creating a tapestry of dull lights across the disorienting wreckage of the floor.

His mind felt empty. He was drifting down toward them, he realized…and he couldn't stop. Vanna gave a light tug to the cord connecting them. Aidan barely felt it. His legs no longer wanted to swim. Those winking, blinking disks of light below seemed to drain his buoyancy. They were drawing him down, sucking him toward them, and he no longer had the presence of mind to fight them.

A quiet thought floated through his head. *Nitrogen narcosis.* These were the symptoms the dive instructors had warned about. The looseness to his limbs. The quiet calm. The haziness, as though he'd been disturbed from deep slumber and was on the verge of falling back under again.

The lights continued to blink up at him. A night sky on the ocean floor, quietly calling him toward them.

Vanna tugged on the cord again, harder this time, and Aidan realized he was pulling her down with him. Something at the back of his mind told him that was wrong, that he shouldn't do that, but the closer he got to the lights, the harder it became to think of anything else.

The nearest two disks of illumination winked out of view and back, and Aidan's heart slipped. They weren't stars. They were eyes. Horribly shiny, white-glazed eyes.

Strength returned to his legs in a rush. He kicked and thrashed to pull away from the countless bodies buried inside the silt and metal.

They were faster. The nearest figure reached its arms up, its spreading hands and too-long nails grasping for his legs. Aidan flipped, dropping his torso in order to gain height for his feet to put them out of reach.

Another body, one he hadn't seen before, rose out of the

darkness, hands extended like claws, and dug into Aidan's neck on either side of his mask. Aidan felt the pinch through the dive suit and gasped, his airway squeezed until he struggled to draw oxygen.

The creature gripping him sank back into the silt and metal like a worm, dragging Aidan with it. More bodies rose around them, enormous plumes of sediment dragging over their twisted forms, as they latched on to him. Fingers dug into his legs, his stomach, his back. His mouth gasped wide as they pulled him into the thickly stacked layers of silt.

Only one part of him remained free: the arm with the cord attached. Vanna, tied to him, hauled on it as she urgently tried to pull him out.

Fingers worked their way around his dive mask, picking at the connections as they looked for a way inside. Something tore. Aidan gasped as achingly cold water poured over his chest, soaking through the fleece to press against his skin.

Fingers squirmed through the tear in his dive suit, their long nails picking through the material to reach his skin. He beat at them, but they wouldn't let go.

Vanna still pulled on him. She wasn't going to get him out though. Even Aidan knew it was a lost battle. Arms folded over his torso, his legs, his throat. The silt had become an impenetrable layer over his mask, blinding him.

The grips were like a vise, unyielding, as they sucked him deeper and deeper into their tangled nest of metal. They weren't going to let him go. But at least *she* could still get away. As the ice water flowed into his suit, Aidan pulled his hands together and began digging at the knot. At the very least, he could set her free.

Vanna's hands pressed over his, trying to stop him. He closed his eyes. Tears, both from the ache of the freezing water and the sheer terror of what he was doing, stung his cheeks. He pushed

Vanna's hands aside. The knot was stubborn. He shouldn't have expected anything less; she was a cave diver after all.

Her hands left. Aidan, working blind, managed to find one loose end and began working it free. If Vanna was smart, she would have already begun on the knot around her own wrist. The hideous, silt-covered bodies had to be clutching at her too. She would have a limited window to escape.

Then, abruptly, the cord went taut. It jerked Aidan's arm up, pulling it out from the sediment. Vanna had already tried to drag him free, but she hadn't been able to get enough momentum. This was something more, something almost unstoppable, heaving them toward the ceiling.

The corpses clung to him. Hissing, gasping noises rose from them as they sensed their prey attempting to pull away. The arms tightened around his limbs, hard enough to make his bones ache.

But whatever Vanna had done, it was working. Aidan's head pulled free from the bed of sediment and twisted metal. Specks of sand clung to his mask, but through it, he glimpsed Vanna suspended above him. Her legs bowed up, pointed toward the ceiling, while her head remained facing him, her arm pulled taut against the tether.

He couldn't see her expression, but her helmet was fixated on him. She reached her spare hand back and tapped something on her belt.

The buoyancy compensator.

Aidan forced his untethered hand back into the squirming mass of bodies. He felt around for his own compensator, then flooded it with as much air as it would hold.

Hideous hands raked the length of his body as the sudden lift dragged him free. He exploded from the mounds of silt and writhing bodies, rushing alongside Vanna toward the ceiling.

Their tether snapped tight, and Vanna pulled on it, dragging him closer. Bubbles spiraled around them as their ascent ran unchecked.

Aidan glanced above. The ceiling was nesting endless lengths of twisted metal and broken pipes. There was no time to stop their rise and no time to aim. He simply coiled over, back exposed and hands held up to shield his face.

The impact forced air from his lungs. He grunted, flinching, as his back slammed into the concrete ceiling. A pipe dragged across his sleeve, tearing through the dry suit. Not that there wasn't enough of that happening to begin with. Fresh water flowed through the gaps as he stabilized, his back pinned to the boiler room's ceiling.

Through the flickering flashlight, he caught sight of Vanna. She pulled herself closer to him. One hand snatched up his wrist, examining the cut. Then the other hand felt around the hood flap that had been torn. She took Aidan's free hand and used it to form a grip across the tear, clamping it closed. It was enough to stop more water from entering, but Aidan wasn't sure how much that might help. The cold water had flowed over his torso and was spreading into his legs and across his back. Already, he was shivering as his core's warmth was sapped away.

Vanna moved in frantic, stiff motions as she adjusted the buoyancy compensators so they were no longer pressed so fiercely against the ceiling. Then she gripped him on either side of his head, her gloves squeezing his helmet, and touched her own screen against his. As she drew away, she raised one hand and pointed to her side. Twenty feet away was a door marking where one of the walkways had ended. It wasn't the exit Cove had taken them through the day before, Aidan was sure, but it was still a way out—wherever *out* led to.

Aidan gave a shaky, breathless nod.

Trapped with the squirming corpses on the boiler room floor, he'd been ready to give up. A few more seconds would have been enough for him to undo the knot and allow himself to be pulled ever deeper into the endless silty floor. He would have breathed his last there, clasped in a deathly embrace that would never ever let him go.

He'd believed he was finished. But apparently, Vanna wasn't ready to give up on him yet.

52.

Cove didn't know how far they plunged down. The stairs disappeared beneath her as she sank, seemingly endless. The enduring sound of clicking, cracking joints flowed from above. They never seemed to escape it. Worse, shapes moved at every landing they rushed past—creaking arms stretching toward them, glinting eyes leaving streaks of light across her vision.

One dark thought stuck in her mind. *They're funneling us. To where?* There was no chance to break through though, no time to pause and assess. She could only try to match Roy's pace. He was rushing down furiously, his ragged breathing blending into the static as he fought to put distance between them and the figures.

The stairs flattened out. Roy swung around, preparing for another bannister and another set of steps to carry them down, but there were none. They were at the lowest passenger level, which meant they were only barely above the *Arcadia*'s waterline.

Cove reached for her headlight and jostled it. The fluttering light refused to stabilize. It flashed across white-painted walls and heavy gray carpet. After the stairs, the hall seemed almost unnaturally quiet.

"Roy?" she tried, but if he heard her, he didn't react.

The hall was stark compared to the higher levels. The paint cracked and peeled, leaving shards of itself across the floor, and the ornate sconces felt eerily out of place.

Cove dug through her mind as she tried to guess what part of the ship they might have found themselves in. Exercise rooms? Staff lodgings? It couldn't be the hospital; they'd already found that on a higher floor. It didn't help that their lights had grown so weak; she had to fight to pick out even the nearby cracks in the walls.

The stairs were at their backs. To their left was a narrow doorway with a tarnished lock below the handle. Some kind of staff room, Cove suspected. The path to their right continued on for a stretch. It was partially blocked; three chairs, either washed down during the sinking or carried there, tangled together. Cove couldn't fully see its end, but it appeared to turn to the left.

Straight ahead were double doors. Square windows had been set at eye level, but they were too blurred by age to see through.

Take the hall, or try the room? Cove looked to Roy, wishing she could see him beneath the glaring mask. The creaking, clicking sounds had never quite disappeared beneath the static; their pursuers were still following.

The hall must wrap around the room. Whatever this place is, it probably has a door on its other side. They'll both take us in the same direction. The question is—are we safer in a hall that might be blocked or a room that could hold additional surprises?

A crackling noise warned Cove that one of the creatures in the stairwell was flexing its neck. She made a snap decision and shoved on the doors. Technically, this level was still above the waterline. She held some small hope that it might have windows.

A fine curtain of silt grazed over them as the aged hinges responded. They were smoother than most of the doors Cove had struggled through before. She hoped that was because the wood had swollen less; she dreaded the alternative, that things had been moving through the door before them.

Her headlight struggled across foreign shapes. Railings to Cove's left and right. Tiles beneath her. And some kind of depression ahead, vanishing into what felt like an ocean of darkness.

The pool.

The *Arcadia*, like most of the ocean liners from its time, had attempted to offer cutting-edge luxury. Including a miniature ocean in a ship surrounded by the ocean.

Roy tried to say something, but his words were lost in the static. Cove thought she could guess though. *Do you think it still has water?* Only Roy would use humor as a defense against pure fear.

Cove passed the threshold as the door closed behind them. The swimming pool had no windows. Opposite, across the pool, were the changing rooms and a doorway back into the ship's higher levels. That would be their best chance.

Cove raised a hand, indicating to Roy that they were going to swim over the pool. He gave a short, terse nod.

Railings ran on either side of the pool, but the front and rear had been left clear for stairs. Cove inhaled to rise as her tiring leg muscles pushed her forward. Her light, faint as it was, glinted off a thousand tiles. The water inside the pool rippled in a way that bordered on hypnotic. She fixed her eyes on the faint outlines of the opposite wall and door.

Her mind snagged a second too late. *The water in the pool... is rippling?*

Cove looked down. Beneath her, cracked tile edges surrounded a deep rectangular depression. And inside *that*...

Cove choked on her own breath. The pool was full of bodies. Her headlight grazed across silk dresses and dinner jackets, crew uniforms and steward outfits. The bodies almost appeared to have melted into one solid form. As though they had tried to dig between one another and became trapped like that.

Some forms squirmed, long limbs adjusting as they tried to sink into the mass. Most of them were still though. *Dormant,* Cove thought, and clenched her hands as she prayed they would stay that way.

Roy reached out and gripped her forearm. He'd noticed too. The hold was tight to the point of being painful, but Cove didn't try to push him away. They began moving more carefully, keeping their kicks soft enough that they barely disturbed the water. One of the bodies below them rolled over. Cove held her breath.

It wasn't enough. A rush of air escaped her rebreather. It arced toward the room's corner as Cove swallowed a moan.

The pool of bodies below shifted. Heads rolled over; lamp-like eyes turned toward them.

"Fast!" Cove yelled. She didn't even know if Roy could hear her, but he certainly understood the message. He released his grip on her as they both pushed forward, legs moving as sharply as their drained muscles could stand and then some more.

Cove's lungs ached. Her eyes burned. She fought against her instinct to look down. She was afraid that if she did, she might never be able to stop seeing them: the turning, grasping creatures with their howling jaws.

She could feel them though. They were surging upward, leaving their cloistered home. Cove tilted up, angling her trajectory so she rose as well as moved forward. Roy gasped. She shot him a fearful glance, but he was still moving at her side, one of the stiff limbs grasping in his wake.

The swimming pool's edge was close. And beyond that was the silvery outline of the door Cove had been relying on. It was already open. Both Cove and Roy were moving fast, and the denizens of the pool were slow to stir. They were going to make it. Hope burned in Cove's chest like a flare, pushing her forward, lending energy to her drained muscles.

A dark figure shifted into view beyond the door. Long strands of hair washed past flickering eyes as it turned to face them.

No…

More eyes blinked to life behind it. Their forms weren't even visible in Cove's light, but they hung in the water, unmoving, constantly watching.

No.

She and Roy had been funneled to this level for a reason. It was a dead end, and no matter which path they had chosen—hall or pool—they were not coming back out.

Cove felt paralyzed. Her legs, which had been propelling her forward, fell still. The writhing mass beneath them continued to rise, but her mind had dipped into emptiness. There was no way forward. No way back. The ceiling pressed close above them. Cove drew a stuttering breath and she was hit with the stark understanding that it might be one of her last.

Her headlight was nearly gone. She pulled her backup flashlight from her belt but knew it very likely wouldn't make it much further. Both of Roy's lights were out. And even if her flashlight was enough to break through the first wall of creatures blocking their path, she had little hope that it would carry them very far beyond. They were in one of the ship's deepest realms, and soon they would be blind.

Think. There must be something. There must be.

Roy caught her arm and pulled. Cove kicked into motion, following him. He dragged her down, toward the doorway.

Does he think we'll be able to break through? He knows we can't get far—

He abruptly pulled her to the left. The walls had been built in on that side of the room, and a row of narrow doors created bands of shadow across the smooth wall.

The changing rooms.

Cove pushed forward. Her lungs ached and her legs shook. The figures ahead were edging inward, long limbs and billowing scraps of clothing spreading through the doorway.

Something snagged at her foot. Cove clicked on the handheld flashlight and shone it back at the creature. The hand twitched, loosening just enough for Cove to pull free.

And then they were at the changing rooms, and Roy was barreling into the nearest heavy wood door, forcing it open in a cacophony of screaming metal hinges and swollen wood. Cove fastened a hand on the door's frame and dragged herself inside.

The dead crowded against the open door. Stiff hands and bared, blunted teeth fought at the gap. Cove slapped her open palm against her handheld light. The beam, which had been waning, flashed bright. After struggling to see with the dimming bulbs for so long, the full strength was shockingly harsh; it flashed the changing room's wall and door in polarizing white, bleeding the details out of them. The mass of dead outside recoiled in a horribly slow shock wave, fingers creeping up to block their eyes, jaws gaping wider. The bulb burst in a hiss of dying electricity.

Roy shoved against the door, taking advantage of their second of surprise. Hard bodies hit its other side just as the latch found home. He shoved the lock into place and slumped away, gasping.

Cove squeezed her eyes closed as blunt fingertips and cracked nails scraped over the wood. They were searching for a way in. Clawing, tapping, exploring.

And she and Roy were back to just one light: Cove's flickering, fading headlamp. She let herself sink, her body sliding down the wall in graceful slow motion as she drew sharp, pained breaths.

They were alive. Surrounded in the worst way in a tiny, claustrophobic room but, for the moment, alive.

Roy coiled over, his arms wrapping around his knees. He hung suspended for a second before very slowly beginning to drift to the floor, like Cove. She reached out her hands. He took them, their gloves snagging together as they held on to each other.

The static wasn't so bad in that part of the ship, she realized. It remained a constant, like rain on a tin roof, but it was no longer deafening. She ran her dry tongue across her lips. "Roy?"

"Yeah."

He was still smothered, still distant, but audible. She smiled. "For what it's worth, I'm glad it's you I'm stuck with."

He patted the top of her hands, and Cove suspected it was partially an effort to hide how badly he was shaking. "Same, girl."

They huddled together. The creatures outside the door clawed around its seams. The handle rattled, but with the lock engaged, it didn't open.

Maybe if we stay silent for long enough, they'll leave.

She knew it was a fool's hope as soon as she thought it. These weren't mindless monsters, blindly roaming the halls. She couldn't guess how intelligent they might actually be, but they were conscious enough to plan. They'd ambushed her and Roy, diverting them away from the exits and down into one of the deepest levels of the ship. After a hundred years of dormancy, Cove somehow doubted they would lose interest in the locked door anytime soon.

The dead would keep clawing at the flimsy, waterlogged barrier for as long as it took. Until… *What? They break in and eat us? Is that their only goal?*

The answer came unnervingly easily, as though the thought had long ago squirmed into and embedded itself in her mind without her noticing. *They don't want to eat us. They don't even want to hurt us. They just want us to stay here, with them, inside the ship forever.*

She pictured her drowned body, still weighed down by the empty canisters and heavy dive suit, suspended in the *Arcadia's* cold halls. Aware but unmoving. Eternally frozen inside the ship that had become home to the dead.

Cove closed her eyes as the terror swamped her with nausea. Roy continued to pat her hand, and beneath the static, she heard him wet his lips several times, as though preparing to speak. He never actually did though. He wanted to give her some kind of comfort, but there was none to find.

The headlight flickered again, losing another iota of strength. Its batteries were almost gone. Against her better judgment, Cove lifted her wrist to read her dive computer. Oxygen: 12 percent. She grit her teeth into a smile as she squeezed Roy's hand. That was it, then. Even if they had a way out right that moment, there wouldn't be enough air to reach the surface.

She didn't ask Roy for his number. She didn't want to know. Traditionally, on the underwater shoots they'd completed together before, his air ran out slightly before hers. That was just a side effect of his larger body mass. Now though? When both of them had lost so much of their oxygen fighting and panicked? She had no idea.

If they were lucky, his would run out first. At least that way he would have someone to hold him and comfort him through the suffocation. Cove pictured herself spending the last moments of her life locked in a tiny cubicle with her friend's body and was nearly sick again.

The static spiked, and with it, her light blinked, threatening to fade completely. Cove pressed her tongue between her teeth, begging it to hold. It did.

The static jogged something in her memories though. She took a deep breath. "Sean? Are you still there?"

"Yes. I've been trying to reach you for the last half hour." His voice was distant and distorted, but Cove could still hear traces of irritability around the edge. Irritability, she suspected, that came from pressing anxiety. "Are you close to getting back?"

Cove closed her eyes. It was a small balm, being able to talk to another person, but it was enough to make her heart ache. "Not really. I don't think we're coming back up, Sean."

The silence hung for so long that she worried the static might have separated them again. But then Sean asked, "What happened?"

A lot. Too much. The fingers scraped and tapped and clawed at the door behind her. Cove thought she could hear parts of the wood splintering off. Instead of answering Sean's question, she asked, "Have you heard from the others? Roy's with me, but we've lost contact with Aidan and Vanna."

"Nothing. I've only spoken to you two."

She'd feared as much, but the news still pressed on her. She'd hoped, if nothing else, their cave diver might have been able to navigate herself and Aidan out.

"Talk to me," Sean said. "Tell me what I can do to help. Are you trapped?"

Yes. Cove's shoulder pressed against the door and she felt every time it shuddered. Roy still held her hands, and she squeezed them. "This is important, Sean. No one else can come into the *Arcadia.* Not anyone trying to recover our bodies and not future dive teams. Okay? I need you to make sure the wreck stays off-limits. Permanently."

Again, empty static flooded the radio. This time, it was Hestie who broke the stillness. Her voice was so quiet that Cove had to strain to hear the words. "It's the crew, isn't it?"

"Yeah," Roy answered her. "And the passengers. I guess you know, huh?"

She laughed, a weak, miserable noise. "Yeah. I guess so."

Then Sean again, sharp annoyance in his voice, as though he'd started to think he was the butt of some joke he didn't yet understand. "I'll ask again. What can I do to help?"

Cove opened her mouth, but the words died in her throat. The clicking, scraping noise echoed endlessly from her back, maddening. She'd put such effort into ignoring its presence that it had taken her too long to realize fresh clicking noises had begun…ahead of them.

She leaned forward, craning her neck to shine the pale light as far into the room as possible. It wasn't a large space, but it had become clogged with disturbed silt, and trying to read the details was like fighting to see faraway shapes through a foggy twilight.

A bench ran along one side of the room, still coated with an undisturbed layer of sediment. The rear wall had some kind of mottled stain on it. A chair was propped opposite the bench, its delicate wooden legs making it look like a malformed insect. It, too, was choked with dust, its wooden bars dulled around the edges.

Wait…the sediment. There wasn't this much in the swimming room. Or in the hallways. You only get this much silt…when there's a window to outside.

Cove's heart spiked. At the same time, the dark blot at the opposite side of the room shifted. She'd mistaken it for a stain; instead, she realized, tiles had been torn aside. A layer of plaster created ragged edges, and then, beneath that, torn metal.

Inside that nest was one of the crew. It had coiled around, elbows bent against its ears and its arms pressed into gaps in the torn hull. But it was emerging. Bony fingers crept over the tiles' edges as the jaw worked, clicking as it opened and closed.

"Damn it," Roy muttered.

The hole goes all the way to the external hull layer. How wide is it? Cove, against her better judgment, crept forward. Her light flickered across dull gray flesh speckled with white. The figure's body was blocking the gap, making it impossible to see past. But maybe—just maybe—

The creature lunged.

53.

This was their final hour.

Harland climbed the stairs. His clothes were wet up to his shoulders, leaving a trail of drips to mark his path.

The crew had dug, as they had been instructed. Holes were carved, peeling away layers of metal in search of the things that walked between walls. Sometimes, the holes opened into the drowning white mist, allowing it to seep into the ship. Sometimes, they opened into biting water, and it flooded about their legs and sucked their breath away.

The water inside the ship had risen. Fitz was gone beneath it. So were the boilers. The furnaces had been cool enough to avoid exploding. Harland doubted that could be called a blessing; there was no such thing in the monstrous, cursed vessel.

A tipping point had been reached, and the ship no longer

cared to coast above the waves but wanted to merge with them. The enormous metal construction groaned and rattled as water entered through a dozen breaches, rising and rising with gushing bubbles and clattering furniture.

Soon, the ship would be given to those in the walls. As they had always intended. Harland had put down his tools and now simply sought a nest of his own.

The first-class dining hall, he decided. He'd always admired it, wondered what it would be like to afford to sit at the dark-wood tables with their delicate wineglasses and soft cloth napkins.

The ground floor had already been submerged, so he kept climbing. He passed crew mates and friends coiled into holes in the walls. Their wide, unblinking eyes watched him pass as the rushing water rose across their bodies. Harland kept climbing until he reached an elegant set of doors. He pressed through them.

The balcony formed a ring surrounding the dining room. Thick curtains created nooks, each with its own table settings.

He would have preferred a smaller nest: something narrow, something tight, that he could wedge himself inside and be sure he might never come out. But all of those smaller spaces had already been claimed. He'd left it too long, and now he had to make do with what remained.

Still, Harland thought as he passed through a layer of curtains, this wasn't too bad. The space was larger than he needed, but it was dark, and he could be sure he would be alone there. He lowered to his knees and crept between the chairs to nestle himself beneath the table.

As he pressed his cheek to the carpeted floor, he felt the first rush of icy ocean brush across his skin.

Soon, he promised himself. *No more mist. No more sounds. Just quiet and peace and safety. Soon.*

THE THIRD DIVE

The emaciated form lurched out form its hole in the wall in erratic jolts. The arms were crooked from being wedged at odd angles for too long and unfurled in strange increments.

Roy made a sharp, horrified sound. He kicked at the nearest item—the chair—to force it as a barrier between them and the twisted figure.

The space was too small. Designed only for a single person to change for the pool, it gave them almost no room to avoid the dead crew member. Its arms passed through the chair's slats, fingers spreading wide like a waiting vise.

Roy kicked the chair again. It fractured, its delicate wood splintering. The grasping hands snapped around Roy's ankle. He cried out in mingled horror and pain.

Cove shoved forward. Her open palm slammed into the dead creature's face, snapping its head back. The vertebrae made awful clicking noises as they rotated. The half-lidded eyes shimmered as they rolled toward her.

Roy twisted, turning onto his stomach. The momentum dragged the creature around, pulling it off balance. The fractured chair jammed against the bench. Cove slammed her hand into the creature's face again, silently begging it to let go, begging it to just *die* and *stay dead*, but the jaw only continued flexing with increasing eagerness.

The sounds beyond the door redoubled as the dead sensed activity. Wood creaked as shards were broken off.

Cove grabbed for the chair. Roy rolled again, and the additional pressure broke the chair's leg. Its lower half came free, the point of fracture a vicious, jagged edge.

Cove raised the wood and plunged it down, aiming for the center of the dead crew member's head.

Bones fractured. Wood fractured. The silt made the scene unreadable. But Cove felt the skull give way under her makeshift spear. It jerked, pulled free from her hands, and Cove, nearly blind, rocked to keep herself from tumbling backward.

"Roy?" She felt for him, her heart pumping out of control. Through the endless blur of sediment, his hand found hers.

A heavy creaking sound echoed from behind them. Cove couldn't see it, but she could picture the door breaking apart.

"Get your tanks off," she said, holding on to him as tightly as she could manage as she dragged him to the rear of the room, where the crew member had made its nest. "You'll go first."

"I might block it. You first; you have a better chance of fitting."

Cove was struggling with her own straps. It was a nightmare when the silt-out reduced her sensory input to touch alone. "You'll follow my instructions. Go first."

"You always were bossy," he mumbled, deep fondness in his voice. The hand squeezed hers, then let go. Her headlight blinked one final time, then died. Not that it was much help any longer. The cracking wooden door groaned, and Cove knew it wouldn't survive more than a minute.

Roy grunted. Faint metallic sounds rose through the static. Cove kept one hand pressed to the wall to maintain her sense of direction as the other hand slung the tanks down at her side. She could still breathe through them, but they couldn't stay on her back. Not if she hoped to fit through the hole in the wall.

"Cove," Roy said, and she moved. She extended her arms ahead of herself as she pushed the tanks into the hole first, then began squirming into the space behind them. A vicious cracking noise marked the end of the door. Cove lunged forward, moving faster than was safe and felt ragged metal dig into her shoulder.

The hands clamped over her fins. She kicked, trying to bat them free, but she'd been too slow. They'd found their grip on her and began dragging her back.

A choked noise died in Cove's throat. She knew the connection to the tanks was still intact, but it seemed impossible to breathe.

Roy's gloves fixed over her hands. He pulled, and Cove cried out as the rough metal dragged a line down her back, bruising her through the dry suit. She broke free from the hands. And suddenly, she was past the hull's second layer, and back into the endless expanse of the ocean.

Cove kicked, fear urging her to put space between herself and the ship's wall. It took her a moment to realize Roy was patting her shoulder, encouraging her to calm.

She turned. Barely any sunlight reached those depths, but after spending so long in the increasingly dim halls, her eyes had adjusted. The *Arcadia*'s hull hung like a colossal wall ahead of them. A dark circle marked the hole they'd crawled through. Cascading silt spilled from it, a cloud that slowly extended into the water.

Gray hands reached through the hole. Their clawlike fingers extended, grasping, as they blindly searched for their lost quarry.

"Back to the dive line," Cove mumbled. Her mind was numb, fragmented from stress, but it still ticked over, searching for the next step, the next thing she would need to do to stay alive. "Look for Vanna. Look for Aidan."

And what next? Her mind went empty. She had no answers for what came after. She could only move forward in tight increments and focus on whatever came immediately next. And that meant finding the dive line.

She and Roy slung their canisters onto their backs again. They held close together as they moved along the *Arcadia's* side, toward the bow, avoiding drifting any nearer to the ship than was necessary. When the rock walls squeezed them inward, they ran so close to the stone that they could have brushed their hands across the jagged, silt-clogged edges.

At last, the bow ended, and they entered into the clear water beyond. Cove's instincts wanted her to swim to the rocky outcrop where they'd begun their dive as quickly as possible, but she moderated herself. Slower movements would consume less oxygen. That was one of the paradoxes of diving, and something that took a lot of practice to grow used to.

Roy didn't try to speak. Vaguely, she was aware that he might be sinking into the numbing effects of shock. The bodies had always unnerved him worse than anyone else on the team. There wasn't much she could do to help him...not until they reached the surface.

If we reach the surface.

They could race up, following the line that brought them to the buoy near the *Skipjack*, and surface as quickly as possible. But then carbon dioxide bubbles would shred their insides. On the other hand, following the prescribed decompression stops would leave them dead before they were halfway up. They could try to compromise—rising fast enough that their air would last until the surface and crossing their fingers the bends wouldn't be too bad—

"Hey," Sean barked, distant but unmistakable. "Are you still there?"

"Yes. Quiet. I'm trying to think." The endless depths pressed on her. The exhaustion left her mind fogged and sparse. They were so close to getting out; she just needed to push a little further, find some way to get them more air...

Everything has a price. You either pay by being prepared or you pay with your life.

"Spare canisters are at the rock," Cove said, the memory rushing back to her. Vanna had laid three of them on their first dive. That had only been two days prior, but it felt like a lifetime ago. Cove had vaguely noted the existence of backup canisters on the safety log prepared prior to the dive, but she'd been so focused on the ship that they had blurred into the background of her mind, all but forgotten.

Vanna knew how dangerous a dive could be. She knew how vital it was to prepare for every contingency.

And Vanna's forethought was going to save their lives.

The gray stone outcropping still had the vertical dive line connected, leading up to the buoy. Cove snagged on to the cord. The three silver containers were neatly tied in place beside it.

Despite everything, she'd hoped she would find their two missing crew members already at the rock. Or if not that, clinging to the line as they ascended. The ocean was empty in every direction.

She swallowed, hoping her always-steady voice would hold once more without cracking. "Roy, switch over your air and head for the surface. I'll meet you there."

"What do you mean?" He sounded faint and unnaturally flat. Shock was setting in. "We're going up together, right?"

Cove turned back to stare along the *Arcadia*'s immense bow as her fingers traced over the edge of her fresh canister, her throat burning. The air would be enough for a journey back to the ship. It was an idiot's hope, she knew, a decision that was tantamount to suicide and with very little optimism to motivate it. But she was missing two members from her crew. And if there was even a tiny chance they were still alive…

Something shifted above the ship. She squinted. The light was so poor that at first she thought she was looking at a mirage. But second by second, a distant shape crept closer. Something emerging from the *Arcadia*'s deck, traveling directly toward them.

Not the drowned crew. Not now—

Her breath caught in her chest. The shapes had fins. Two bodies moved abreast of each other, one hunched and clutching its chest, the other with an arm holding on to its companion. Based on their direction, Cove could only imagine that they'd risen through the dining hall's ceiling.

The larger body reached for its dive computer. A second later, a fresh burst of static poured into the comms unit.

"Start your ascent," Vanna said, her voice clipped. "Take one canister each and follow the decompression schedule. I'll share the third tank with Aidan. His suit's torn and he's going hypothermic. He'll need to go up fast."

54.

The *Skipjack* was on the edge of chaos. Hestie kept her back pressed to the lounge area's wall, listening as the voices rose and dipped in waves.

Vanna and Aidan had arrived back first. Aidan had been so severely chilled that he'd needed Sean's help to even get out of the water. Hestie couldn't blame him; his suit had been torn and nearly all of his underlayers were soaked. Vanna explained that she'd brought him up fast and that they would need to watch him for signs of decompression sickness. He'd been helped to the showers, where, teeth chattering, he asked for some privacy while he got his body temperature back up.

He still hadn't returned. Twice, Hestie had suggested someone should check on him, but no one had listened. Instead, Sean had dogged Vanna around the ship, spitting questions at her. Hestie hadn't fully caught what was going on between them, but the same phrase kept recurring: *What did you do?* Only once had Vanna snapped back, telling him to leave her alone. It hadn't worked. Since then, she'd refused to speak but simply went through her routine of checking and logging her equipment.

Cove and Roy surfaced forty minutes later. Hestie had hoped their presence would cool the atmosphere, but it did very little to help. Roy seemed quietly stunned. He'd accepted the blanket Cove put around his shoulders and the drink and crackers she forced into his hands but didn't meet any of their eyes.

Sean, his patience thin, hovered close by them, quietly simmering. Devereaux tried to make himself useful by politely offering anything on his ship that might help. Cove had told him to unmoor and get them the hell out of there.

"My dear, we can't. There's a storm—"

"Doesn't matter." Cove's words had been flat. "However dangerous the storm is, it can't be worse than this. Get us moving."

Devereaux, conflicted, had glanced toward the dark windows. "I understand you're eager to leave, but perhaps we could wait until dawn?"

For a second, Cove had looked as though she was going to argue. Then she sighed, a heavy, resigned noise. "Fine. At dawn."

Hestie herself stayed quiet and waited. She didn't know exactly what her fellow crew members had encountered three hundred feet below, but she could guess.

The dressing gown bunched around her throat. She hadn't felt properly warm since her encounter in the hospital the previous day. The weather didn't help. A storm was rolling in, and the water had grown choppy. The sun no longer made it through the clouds. Even though the *Skipjack*'s heaters were running, they did very little to keep the chill at bay.

Vanna had stayed to ensure Cove and Roy were both taken care of, then discretely turned toward the door to disappear back into the hold. Sean's sharp eyes noticed. He snapped his fingers at her. "Not so fast."

She looked utterly drained; the dark rings around her eyes were more pronounced than ever, and her dark hair was slick with drying sweat. Still, she only blinked at Sean, seemingly impassive. "I don't believe I'll be any further help here."

Laughter caught in his throat. He glanced at Cove for backup, but she was still preoccupied with making Roy drink the heated milk. "I don't think it's wise to let you wander the ship alone," Sean said. "Not after today."

Finally, Cove lifted her head. Exhaustion was etched around her expression. Her voice, usually so upbeat and positive, sounded hollow. "Sean, give it a break. If Vanna wants space, I think she's allowed it."

His cheeks had been pale, but at that, color flushed through them. The glare he fixed on Cove was achingly harsh. "I don't get it. Why do you keep protecting her? You almost *died* down there—"

"Ha." Roy stirred, a grim smile breaking through the stunned shell. He finally seemed to be coming back to himself. "I dunno, man, if you want to blame someone, maybe get mad at the zombies instead."

Sean glanced back and forth between them, waiting for some sort of clarification, and when none came, he began pacing. He ran his fingers through his short hair before turning back to them, flames of frustration burning bright on his cheeks. "Please. *Please.* Someone explain to me what's going on. I feel like I'm trapped in some prank sketch, except there's never any actual punch line."

Cove's chest rose as she took a deep breath, then let it out in increments. At last she said, "We brought the cameras back. Watch the footage. I can't promise you'll get any answers because

I really don't think there *are* any, but at least you'll have all the same info we do."

"Okay." Sean swallowed. "The footage. Okay. Good."

Their dive helmets were haphazardly scattered on one of the desks. Sean pried the chips free while Devereaux retrieved the laptop from the bridge. Hestie, all but forgotten in the room's back corner, drew further into herself.

She knew she shouldn't want to see what the cameras had captured, but somehow the idea of returning to her berth and hiding there alone was far, far worse. She remained as the files downloaded, the little green bars spearing across the screen to track their progress.

"Hey."

Hestie jolted and turned. Aidan had approached the room silently. His clothes were a riot of color: reds and blues across his T-shirt, yellow and black on his sweatpants. It only helped emphasize how pale his skin had become and how deeply shadowed his eyes were. His hair was still wet from the shower, and he clutched something in both hands.

Some of the tension dropped from Cove's shoulders. She reached toward the younger crew member, beckoning him into the room. "How are you doing? I made you some cocoa. Come and have a seat with us for a minute."

Aidan took a step into the room but didn't approach the chair Cove had offered to him. His eyes seemed slightly glazed as he glanced between them, his fingers fidgeting over what Hestie now saw was a small glass jar. "Did, uh…did anyone *take* anything off me when we got out of the water? Like a piece of jewelry or…?"

Sean, barely paying any attention, began opening the loaded files and scrolling through the footage.

Roy leaned forward in his seat though, a weary smile forming creases around his mouth as he braced his forearms on his knees. "Sorry, no one touched your equipment. What are you missing, bud?"

"It…" He fidgeted, one shoe scraping across the carpet, his eyes struggling to meet any of the gazes directed at him. "Never mind. I just had something when I went down, but it's gone now, and I was hoping someone might have… It doesn't matter. Devereaux, I got this, like you asked."

He stretched the small glass jar forward, and Devereaux gasped as he took it. "That is excellent. I truly hope it didn't put you into any danger—"

Aidan pushed his hands into his pockets, shrugging. "I mean, I'm pretty sure we weren't going to have a super fun dive no matter what."

Cove, moving discreetly, had retrieved a spare blanket and now draped it around Aidan's shoulders. One hand guided him toward the seats. "What is it?"

"A pet theory." Devereaux cradled the vial reverently in both hands. He leaned close over it, squinting through his glasses. Even Hestie couldn't help herself and shifted forward. What looked like a scrap of cloth floated in the water. "You all know the *Arcadia* has been my passion project for almost my whole life. Many of the laymen theories never held much water under scrutiny: pirates, spontaneous whirlpools, aliens, and the like. But rubbing shoulders with other enthusiasts, there were a small number of alternate theories that many believed may have some merit…only there simply wasn't enough evidence to give them widespread support."

"Did you believe them?" Cove asked.

"In the same way you believe a restaurant owner when they claim their burgers are the best in town." Devereaux shrugged.

"Perhaps. But who can prove it? I always kept them at the back of my mind, occasionally dabbling in whatever modest research I could achieve but never truly putting weight in them." He drew a deep breath. "Until the footage came back."

Behind Devereaux, Sean's shoulders were tightly hunched as he faced away from them. The laptop's screen illuminated his silhouette. One elbow rested on the desk, the hand propping up his chin; the other clicked keys, jumping through scenes on the recordings. His hand was the only part of him that moved. Hestie didn't think he was even breathing.

"Cove, you inadvertently stumbled on what I hope is the missing puzzle piece," Devereaux continued. "When you, Roy, and Aidan passed through the holds, your camera caught the corner of several sacks with a distinctive logo."

Sean flinched but still made no noise. His finger tapped aggressively to rewind one of the recordings.

"Around the time the *Arcadia* sank, the American textile business was booming. New dyes were being introduced, new fabrics, new styles. It was a race to innovate. And not all innovation was a step forward. In 1927, Prescott Textiles suffered a major scandal after nearly thirty of their workers committed suicide by leaping from the roof of their factory. It was revealed that a process they had developed to make their cotton thinner and softer had created a dangerous neurotoxin."

Devereaux gave the vial a slight shake, prompting the scrap of cloth inside to spin. "One of my colleagues proposed the theory that some of that fabric could have been stored on board the *Arcadia*. It wasn't the most ludicrous idea—the two disasters happened scarcely eight months apart, and Prescott Textiles operated near the port where the *Arcadia* picked up its fares. But his idea was easily dismissed. The *Arcadia*'s manifest listed all cargo: while some cloth was among it, none matched the company or the description."

"People went over that manifest countless times," Cove murmured. "But they were mostly looking for anything that could have exploded or caught fire."

"Exactly. And there was nothing concrete connecting Prescott to the *Arcadia*…until your footage from the hold gave validity to the theory." Devereaux was growing animated, shuffling forward in his seat, eyes shining behind his glasses. "You inadvertently recorded some bags in the hold that bore a logo with remarkable similarities to Prescott Textiles' logo. My colleague who supports the fabric theory suggested that the cloth could have been stored on the ship under a fake company name and description. After all, no one would have wanted to purchase the tainted material after so many news stories ran about it. But Prescott Textiles, on the brink of bankruptcy, might have been unscrupulous enough to unload the material on overseas stores, where it could less easily be connected to them."

"I'm losing you." Roy, slumped in his chair, ran a hand across his face. He looked exhausted. They all did, Hestie thought. As though that final journey into the *Arcadia* had drained something more than mere stamina from them.

"It's still very speculative—we might not ever get complete answers—but I'd hazard to suggest that several hundred pounds of the material was stored inside the *Arcadia*'s hold. Yards and yards of cotton that contained neurotoxins, slowly degassing into a ship that did not have much air circulation on a good day. The material would have caused paranoia at first and then hallucinations that grew increasingly intense the longer the exposure lasted. Those closest to the material—those who worked in the holds or nearby—would have felt the effects soonest, but it's possible it would have reached everywhere inside the ship, given enough time."

"You think…" Roy's hand was still pressed across his face. He didn't look annoyed though, just lost. "Some fabric made them crazy?"

"Or tipped them into a state of shared hallucination. Or a level of paranoia that drove them to self-destruction."

"The upper floor's windows were boarded over," Cove murmured. "Almost like they wanted the ship airtight."

"It's more than just toxins." Hestie's voice sounded dry and faded to her own ears.

Devereaux tilted forward to see her better. "How do you mean?"

She thought again of the images from the hold: bodies stacked high, wound in cloth, heaped into piles. And the thing in the hospital. Strapped to the bed but straining, its whited-out eyes boring into hers. "Maybe the Arcadia truly was cursed."

"Ah, the cursed ship theory." Devereaux dipped his head in acknowledgment. "Not one of the most mainstream hypotheses and not a personal favorite of mine, if I'm being honest, but several notable people through history have put stock in it."

Cove closed her eyes, one hand softly massaging the back of her neck. "Hestie's right though. Toxins might explain why the ship sank. But what we saw down there…it's not a delusion. It's something real."

"Maybe it's both," Hestie murmured.

The others all looked at her.

"Come again?" Roy asked.

Hestie's tongue was tacky as she ran it over her teeth. Her dreams from the night before had been thin and scattered, disturbed frequently as she jolted awake, but one image had repeatedly resurfaced. A shriveled, black body, captured in the footage from the hold for barely a second.

The body had been unlike any of the others on the ship. Those were all pallid, their hair and beards intact. This body had been far, far older.

"Something was wrong with the ship to begin with. Something *bad* was inside it. But that badness wasn't enough to hurt them on its own."

"The ship had been crossing the Atlantic safely for years," Cove noted.

"Exactly." Her voice still felt thin, but her conviction was growing with each word. "They were fine until that final voyage, when they had the fabric inside the hold. If it did what you said, Devereaux—if it made them paranoid and caused delusions—then maybe their fear was enough to tip the balance. They opened themselves to whatever badness was inside the ship. Started to obsess over it. It's like…they invited it to haunt them."

Again, she pictured the bodies stacked in the hold. Each death would have brought more fear, and the fear made the danger worse, and the danger claimed more lives. It was like a whirlpool; the ship had been safe for as long as it skirted around the edges, but once it tipped over, it was funneled down unrelentingly, plunged ever deeper with no hope of escape.

Cove nodded, but Roy's mouth held a doubtful twist. "We don't know any of that for sure. We don't even know if the cloth actually *was* toxic."

"Of course. It's only a theory at this point." Devereaux shrugged, gently turning the bottle in his hands. "But it's perhaps the most promising one we have had in a very long time. Thanks to Aidan, we'll be able to send this sample in for testing to determine if it truly was tainted."

"Hold up." Cove blinked, then turned toward Aidan. "Where exactly did you get this?"

Devereaux cleared his throat. "I must apologize to the both of you. As dearly as I wanted to obtain a sample, I never would have asked him to revisit the holds had I known it would become such a perilous situation."

"The *holds*?" Her eyes blazed as she fixed Aidan with a scorching glare. "Tell me you didn't go into *the holds*."

His jaw was set, but he still squirmed in his seat, gaze resolutely fixed on his shoes.

"Vanna." Cove swung.

The older woman remained close to the exit, back leaned against the white-painted wall, hands loose at her sides, her heavy eyes watching the room's occupants. She didn't answer Cove but tilted her head slightly to one side, waiting.

"You were paired with him." Hestie had never seen Cove this angry before. "Did you actually let him go down to the holds? What were you *thinking*?"

"I was hired to be safety officer." Vanna's voice held no inflection, and she showed no signs of defensiveness. "I step in if I recognize a situation to pose an unnecessary danger to the team. Otherwise, I follow instructions."

"Follow…" Cove grit her teeth. "Sure. But not from *him*."

"Wow," Aidan managed, still not lifting his eyes from the floor. "Ouch."

"Hey, let's cool it a bit," Roy said. He tried for a lopsided grin, one hand held toward Cove. "It was dumb, sure. But he didn't mean any harm."

"And he could have jeopardized the remainder of the team

regardless." Cove pushed out of her chair. She paced toward the wall near Hestie, then abruptly turned again. "We had a plan, Aidan. You absolutely had no right to disregard orders."

"Yeah, well, we didn't exactly know there were...were... whatever's in the *Arcadia*." His voice sank to a miserable mutter. "Even though I tried to warn you something grabbed my leg in the first hold. You all said I was making it up."

Cove pressed a hand across her eyes. The thumb and fingers massaged her lids as she breathed in slow, deep lungfuls. When she spoke again, her voice was both cooler and calmer. "It doesn't matter now either way. I'd say you were banned from any future dives to the *Arcadia*, but we're done with the ship. We'll unmoor and begin the journey back to port as soon as the sun rises."

Aidan rose from his chair, the blanket sliding from his shoulders. He continued to scowl at the floor, but it was only as he passed Hestie that she saw the red tinge around his eyes. "Maybe you can ground me while you're at it."

Roy muttered something unhappy as Aidan left the lounge, but no one tried to stop him. Cove folded her arms, eyes squeezed closed, lips pale. Devereaux continued to hold the bottle with enormous care, looking both contrite and grieved. Vanna waited for only a moment, then, when no one spoke to her, slipped out of the room as well.

Cove's words reverberated in Hestie's mind. *As soon as the sun rises.*

She should have pressed Devereaux to leave at once, storm or not. The *Arcadia*, the most dangerous thing any of them had ever encountered, was barely three hundred feet below. Even if the figures they'd encountered were trapped within the ship's walls, Cove should still have wanted to put as much distance between them and it as possible.

Hestie wondered if Cove, like her, was feeling the draw of the ship. It was like a riptide that refused to lift its grip on her. She knew they should leave. But she didn't want to go. Not really.

Even Roy, the most volatile when it came to the ship, made no demands to unmoor sooner. After what they'd seen, none of them would ever suggest returning to the wreck. But they still lingered, as though it was painful to let go, as though they were reluctant to lose even this proximity.

The silence was only broken by Sean, whose chair creaked as he slowly turned it around. All of the heated color he'd gained had faded into a mottled gray. Deep creases ran around his mouth. "Is someone going to tell me this is a joke now?"

There wasn't any accusation left in his words. Just a dull kind of uncertainty, as though he'd lost his footing and had no idea how to regain it again.

Hestie tilted to one side. Behind Sean, illuminated clearly on the screen, was something that must have once been human. Faded clothes clung to its shrunken body. One stiff, coiling arm reached toward the camera, while the blind eyes and yellowed teeth caught refractions on the flickering light.

Cove didn't unfold her arms but merely shrugged. "If it's a joke, I don't think any of us get it."

"Did you actually…" He waved one hand toward the computer, then let it drop back into his lap. "I mean…"

No one answered. Hestie couldn't drag her eyes away from the image. She still felt cold in a way that no amount of warming food or tightly tied dressing gowns could fix. The sensation was crawling deeper into her: ice shards in her veins, frost spreading through her heart.

As cold as the Arcadia.

Her eyes burned, fixated on the grimacing, poorly lit creature on Sean's screen. It had been reaching for the camera, but with the hand distorted by the lens, it almost appeared as though the arm were stretching through the screen, straining toward Hestie.

"I need some space. I'll fix something for dinner in a couple of hours," Cove said. She was trying to force some energy back into her voice, but it was like it had all drained out of her when she'd confronted Aidan, and now all she could manage was slow resignation. "Sean, Devereaux, the footage is yours. Please don't ask me any questions though. I just can't take it right now."

55.

Cove's stomach ached. She pushed her fork through her meal: tuna casserole, her father's favorite dish, something she'd made for him every week for the last few months of his life. She'd had enough practice that the process was muscle memory, which was why she'd chosen it that day: no recipe, no unfamiliar processes, no fuss.

Now, though, picking through the pasta and tuna chunks, she wasn't sure it had been the best choice. It was reminding her of her father too much. And not of his life...but of his death.

Death. A person can only have a soul for as long as their body stays alive. Once the soul leaves, they're gone.

That was what her father had taught her. And now the *Arcadia* seemed bent on teaching her lessons of its own. Dark lessons. Unnatural lessons. The gaping jaws of the sailors lost so many decades before shook as they howled at her through her mind.

Dead. But not gone.

"So, uh..." Roy, sitting near the table's opposite side, stared at his own untouched plate. "Should I set up the camera or...?"

She forced a chuckle. "I'd be surprised if there were much exciting discussion for it to capture."

Devereaux sat in his usual place to her right, enjoying the meal that was causing her own stomach to squirm. Hestie was to her left, wearing her dressing gown over a thick jacket, with Sean opposite. Only Vanna and Aidan were missing. Vanna wasn't a surprise; she'd likely appear toward the end of dinner to take her own plate back to the hold, but the table felt like a colder, less familiar place with Aidan missing.

Why did I have to yell at him?

She could blame the stress. The shock. The way she'd felt scraped thinner than any of the previous documentaries had ever pulled her. But blaming some external force wasn't going to unwind her words. Just like becoming angry wasn't going to wind back time and change the dive.

Cove surreptitiously checked her watch. It had been nearly four hours since they'd surfaced. Night had set in. The rain, which had been steadily growing through the afternoon, battered the ship's walls, and the swell lifted them ten feet each time. Cove had spent enough weeks on ships that she wasn't at risk of seasickness, though Hestie looked pale.

She'd stop by Aidan's room after dinner, she decided. They could talk it out and hopefully clear the air. She wasn't about to apologize for what she'd said—he should have in no way deviated from their plan, doubly so without telling her—but she *would* apologize for the way she'd said it. He deserved at least that much respect.

Opposite her, Sean lifted his head. He'd only spent half an hour watching the footage before switching the computer off. Although he hadn't said anything, Cove understood; it was overwhelming. The things caught on the static-smattered cameras defied words. Whatever a person believed about death—whether they had faith in a higher being and a soul or whether they held fast that death was simply an end of consciousness—the moving bodies below tore those preconceived notions into shreds. No matter how well Cove tried to patch it into some acceptable understanding, it only fell apart again.

The images were like a punch to the face with no apology. You were simply left nursing your bruise and questioning where you'd gone wrong.

"So." Sean lifted a forkful of dinner, then let it drop back onto his plate. "What...do we *do*?"

"About the ship?" Roy asked. He'd been unusually quiet through that afternoon. Now, he scowled at even the reminder of what lurked three hundred feet beneath them. "We sail the hell away from it as soon as possible and let it rot on the ocean floor."

Sean made a slight disgruntled noise. "Sure, obvious answer. That's not what I was talking about though."

Cove thought she understood. She'd been asking herself the same question. "What do we do with the footage? With everything we've seen?"

His sharp eyes met hers, and he gave a very small nod.

She gave herself a moment to simply breathe. Contractually, they were obligated to pass the footage over to Vivitech. Her skin squirmed at the very idea.

What would happen if the film made it out to the general public? Some people might believe the footage, but she knew most would default to thinking it was an enormous hoax, like Sean had initially wanted to believe—CGI and special effects; a static filter at the edges of the footage to ramp up the eeriness, someone's attempt at making a budget horror film go viral.

If a stranger had tried to show her the footage, Cove suspected she herself wouldn't have put any faith in it either.

"I don't know," she said at last. "Do we burn the footage? Do we edit it? Do we tell Vivitech the system was corrupted and hold on to a copy ourselves? Should we pass it on to someone…and if so, who? The government?"

"What's the government going to do about a ship full of not-dead sailors?" Roy asked. "Except send more people down there, that is?"

Cove, despite herself, shuddered. "Yeah."

"And what about the public?" Sean asked. "Aren't they, I don't know, *entitled* to know about this?"

Devereaux, the only one out of them to finish his meal, carefully placed his knife and fork on his plate. "Would you welcome some well-meaning advice, considering it's coming from a person with remarkably little skin in the game?"

Cove's smile came out crooked. "Right now? I'll take any sort of advice I can get."

He gently dipped his head as he removed his glasses. "Philosophers have been torn on this subject for almost their entire existence. Are individuals entitled to the truth as a basic human right? Or is it acceptable to disguise facts if they ultimately do more harm than good? In the modern day, where we're exposed to government cover-ups and ingenuous PR campaigns from mega corporations, most people believe the truth to be an ultimate good. How can a lie be wholesome? How can deceit be kind? But I would posit this is one of the few instances where deception would have no victims. Perhaps you would not be in the wrong to protect others from this."

"If I was given the option to go back a month and stop myself from ever seeing the *Arcadia*, I would." Dark shadows lurked around Hestie's eyes. "I can't stop thinking about it. Every time I close my eyes and try to sleep, I see it again."

Cove drew a slow breath. "In the hospital, before you had the seizure—"

"I was trying to untie one of the bodies on the beds." Her mouth twisted at the words. "I don't know why. I just stopped thinking… and *did.* I got one hand free before I realized. That night, while I was trying to fall asleep, I told myself it was just eddies in the water moving the corpse. But it wasn't. It was raising its hand toward me."

Cove put her arm around Hestie's shoulder and squeezed. It was very poor comfort, but it was all she knew how to do at that moment. What was there to say to a woman who had seen the dead rise?

"We'll have a two-day journey to return to port," she said at last. "That's not a massive amount of time, but it's *some.* Hopefully enough for us to come to a consensus on what to do with the footage."

After dinner, Devereaux and Roy helped Cove clear the table and wash the dishes. Sean, normally keen to return to his computer, instead spent the time wiping down the table. They were all trying to focus on simple, easy tasks to get the ship of the dead out of their minds—to feel safe again.

Aidan still hadn't emerged, so Cove took a plate of dinner and carried it down to his cabin. She paused outside his door. The squirming discomfort ate at her insides. She allowed herself just a second to collect her thoughts, then knocked. There was no answer. She knocked again, then, calling out, "Aidan, it's just me," shoved on the door.

The berth was empty. Roy's duffel bag lay on the floor beneath the window and one of his spare jackets had been cast aside on the carpet, but there was surprisingly little trace of Aidan there: just a messily made bed on the top bunk and whatever he'd put inside his locker.

The door opposite creaked open, and Vanna appeared in the entrance, one shoulder leaned against the frame as she blinked tired eyes at Cove.

"Sorry," Cove said, noting how rumpled Vanna's dark hair had become. She'd obviously been trying to sleep off the dive-induced exhaustion. "Didn't mean to disturb you. I'm just looking for Aidan."

Vanna moved into the hallway, squinting into Aidan's room to be sure he wasn't there. "Could be in the hold," she murmured. "He sometimes spends time down there."

That made sense to Cove. It was a dark, quiet part of the ship. The storage held on the walls muffled sounds from the higher levels, and the gentle rocking of the ship could be calming. It was where she would go too if she desperately wanted to be alone.

Cove nodded in thanks and turned. Vanna stepped back into her room but emerged again a second later, dragging a jacket over her arms as she followed Cove to the stairs.

The lowest storage area bore the brunt of the cold weather. Cove hunched her shoulders as she switched on one of the overhead lights and stepped into the narrow mazes of shelves.

"Aidan?" Her own voice echoed back to her. She rounded a corner, searching along the shadowed walls. "I'm here to apologize. And I brought you some dinner."

No voice answered her, and a shiver of unease prickled its way along Cove's skin. Aidan hadn't struck her as the kind of person to harbor grudges or to stay quiet when he was called.

Where is he? None of the showers are running. I didn't see him in the lounge when I passed it. I can't imagine him staying on the bridge...

Cove had reached the rear wall. Vanna emerged from the shadows behind, her cool eyes scanning the racks of equipment.

"Aidan?" Cove raised her voice, letting it carry through the *Skipjack's* levels. It bounced back toward her from every wall.

He can't be far. It's not like he could vanish.

The *Arcadia* had left her unnerved, Cove reasoned as she shifted the plate of tuna casserole to her other hand. That was the only reason she was reacting with such gripping fear. Aidan wouldn't be far. Maybe on the bridge. Maybe in one of the other berths. Maybe he'd already emerged to meet up with Roy, and Cove had merely missed him on the way. She shouldn't be feeling this level of queasiness, and her skin shouldn't be rising into goose bumps, and her heart shouldn't be quickening like this. An overreaction prompted by that day's dive, that was all.

Then Vanna turned, her eyes flashing with fear, and her words were almost enough to stop Cove's heart entirely. "We're missing a dry suit."

56.

Cove took the stairs two at a time. The plate of food threatened to spill, but she barely registered she was still holding it. Her voice had turned hoarse as she called into the ship, *"Aidan!"*

Roy appeared in the kitchen doorway, eyes squinted in irritation. "What's going on? Why are you—"

She pushed past him, almost throwing the plate onto the kitchen counter as she scanned the room. "When was the last time you saw him?"

"What? Aidan? In the lounge when you were—"

Cove flew back out of the room. Roy ran after her, his irritated tone taking on an edge of fear. "Hey, slow down!"

She pushed into the lounge. Seats circled the windows, which looked out into a heavy deluge of gray rain. The laptop still stood open on the table from when Sean had scrolled through the footage. The room was empty. Cove left the door swinging as she dashed up to the bridge. "Aidan, *answer me.*"

More voices rose through the ship: Devereaux asking what

was wrong, Sean speaking to Hestie in quick tones. None of them Aidan.

The bridge was bare and dark. Cove felt as though her insides were turning to ice as she staggered back down the stairs. She met Vanna in the hall by the lounge. "Not in the bathrooms," Vanna simply said.

"What the *hell* is happening?" Roy had caught up to them, his barrel chest rolling with every breath, fear and frustration prickling through his words.

Cove's mouth opened, but no kind of answer came. She had no idea what to say. The fear was turning to a battering storm inside her head, and she could not make it quiet.

"Aidan's missing," Vanna said. "Hestie's dry suit has been taken from the hold."

Roy's uneasy laughter only lasted for a second. "What? It's not like—He's not going to—"

"One of the helmets is also gone." Vanna, cool as always, swallowed. "And a set of canisters."

Devereaux, Hestie, and Sean crammed into the hallway around Cove, making her feel claustrophobic. She stepped into the lounge, her fingers dragging over her face as she tried to simply *think*.

"You're not saying he went back to the *Arcadia*." Sean followed her into the room, his wiry form seeming to tower over her.

Roy tried, once again, to laugh. "He wouldn't. Obviously. That would be—He's not—"

When Cove dropped her hands, they came away damp. She clenched them at her sides. "When was the last time anyone saw him?"

A second of silence followed the question. Hestie broke it. "During the meeting in the lounge."

"Same," said Roy, followed by murmurs from the others. "I thought he was in his room."

Think, Cove. Think. "Vanna, did you go into the hold at all?"

"Only briefly." Her cool eyes flickered as she thought back. "After the meeting. To stow the equipment. It was all accounted for at that time. I went to bed. That was…nearly four hours ago."

"Have you searched the ship?" Devereaux asked.

"Everywhere," Cove confirmed.

"It doesn't make any sense," Roy said, this time real panic bleeding into his voice. "Why would he go back? Why would *anyone?*"

Hestie's breathing was audible "Because the ship wants him."

"Cove belittled him," Sean interjected. "You all treat him like a child. Maybe he's trying to prove himself. Reclaim some pride."

"He was upset, sure, but he wouldn't go back down just because of *that*." Roy swung around, jaw working. "He's young but he's not *stupid*."

Then Devereaux simply said, "Oh," and the others turned to stare at him.

He raised his hand. A shaking finger pointed toward the laptop. Its screen had been frozen on an image taken inside the *Arcadia*. Thick sediment blotted almost all details out, except for a bar of twisted metal and several long, grasping hands reaching toward the camera.

"That's not where I left the footage," Sean said.

Cove stepped closer, frowning. "Where is that? I don't think it's from my camera."

"From Aidan's," Vanna said. "In the boiler room. That's where his dive suit was torn."

"But why—"

"Look," Devereaux interjected. He stumbled toward the laptop, one finger tracing across a shape that Cove had first mistaken for a streak of sediment. She bent toward the screen, fighting to see the shapes through the disorienting silt and thought she could make out the line of a broken necklace. It looped across one of the grasping hands, suspended on the highest finger. Something shiny hung from it.

"That's his ring." Devereaux removed his glasses, one hand dragging up part of his cardigan to polish them. A nervous habit, Cove thought. His face was shining with perspiration. "He wanted it to propose to his girlfriend when he got home."

"What? No." Roy's teeth were bared in something that tried to be a smile but came out as a grimace. "Where'd you hear that? He wasn't planning to *get engaged*."

"He was," Devereaux said, and Cove remembered when Aidan had first returned from the showers. He'd asked if any of them had taken something from him when bringing him up from the *Arcadia*. "And I believe that ring meant a great deal to him."

She swore, then plunged back into the hallway. Stairs rang under her feet as she flew down them to reach the hold. Racks held their still-damp dry suits, one of the complement missing. Cove dragged hers off its hanger and began pulling it on.

How long ago? She could barely think, but that simple question spun in endless circles through her mind. *How long has he been underwater? How long would his air last?*

Something moved at her side. Cove, dazed, lifted her head. Vanna had taken her own suit from the rack and was pulling it on with sharp jerks.

"You don't have to," Cove said.

She didn't so much as look up from her work. "I do."

Roy staggered off the stairs and rounded the shelves. He was dragging in deep, gasping breaths. "Sean and Hestie are refilling the dive tanks for us," he said. His hands shook as he grappled for his suit. "They'll meet us on deck."

Cove swallowed thickly as she zipped her suit into place. "It might be best if you—"

"He's *my* friend." Roy fought the clinging material as he tried to fit his foot into the boot. "I'm not leaving him in that damn ship, you understand?"

She did. All too well. The calculations her mind was running through didn't look good. No one had seen Aidan since their confrontation on the bridge, which meant he must have descended more than two hours before. If it was *just* two hours, they might still have a chance. But it could have been as long as four. And the tanks were unlikely to last that long.

Cove grabbed her helmet. The storage hold held an assortment of spare equipment, some belonging to Devereaux, some brought by Cove herself. She paced along a shelf, grabbing for items that might be useful. Spare flashlights to replace the ones that had already burned out, underwater flares—they would only last for a moment, but they were bright. Vanna took one. Cove gave another two to Roy and kept the final two for herself as she jogged toward the stairs.

Rain thundered across the deck. The ship heaved, rising across white peaks before plunging back down. The part of the deck closest to the door was covered, and as Cove paused there, she tasted salt as the wind drove ocean spray across her face.

Devereaux appeared behind her. He clutched his cardigan across his chest. His eyes flickered, anxious as he searched her face. "Are you certain you want to do this?"

She hadn't thought to ask herself that question, but now she answered without hesitation. "Yes."

"Be careful. Please." He let go of the cardigan and reached

out, pulling her into a tight hug. Cove felt something rise in her throat. As she leaned her head on his shoulder, she realized, with a pang, this was the first time she'd been held since before her father's passing. Devereaux murmured, "Be safe, my girl," and Cove had to pull away before he could feel her shake.

Sean staggered onto the deck, Hestie close behind. They each carried two sets of canisters. Cove took one from Sean and slung it over her back. Normally, she would have taken the time to check the equipment herself. But every second that ticked by felt like a hammer driving a nail of fear deeper into Cove's chest. She rushed to connect the lines to her mask.

"I'll be on the audio," Sean said. "Anything you need, just ask."

"Thank you." She pulled the mask over her head. Her wet hair snagged, and she tugged the strands free with a hiss, then switched on her air supply.

"You said they don't like light." Hestie pulled small cylindrical shapes out of her pocket. "I found some glowsticks. They're not bright, but they might help."

Cove didn't think she could speak without her voice cracking. Vanna accepted the glowsticks, tucking them into a pouch on her belt.

The *Skipjack* dropped into a deep trough. The slanting rain came through the overhead cover, and Sean held a hand up to block his face. "Be careful," he yelled, his voice nearly drowned out by the storm.

Vanna stepped up to the drop-off point, her back toward the ocean, fingers gripping the ship's edge. Cove moved to her side, with Roy taking his place next to her. Rain lashed across them, blinding. Cove drew a breath and pressed her eyes closed and then tipped backward, throwing herself once more into the ocean's embrace.

57.

THE FINAL DIVE

The moment Cove entered the water, the storm's lashing rain vanished as though someone had put it on mute. Bubbles raced past her as they fought to escape the folds of her suit and return to the surface. Her throat closed over, unwilling to let her breathe when the ocean flooded over her face, and her first breath of oxygen whistled as she forced it down.

"Audio check." Cove didn't wait for replies but had already flipped, her head directed toward the ocean's floor as she raced down. Vanna led the descent. She carried the spare set of air tanks on her side, and its white paint flashed bright in Cove's headlight. Roy was close on her heels, powerful legs kicking to increase his pace.

"Here," Roy said.

"Present," from Vanna.

Cove hesitated, her mouth dry, her head buzzing, then asked, "Aidan, can you hear me?"

She waited. Seconds ticked by, utterly empty except for the distant hiss of static that seemed to have permanently embedded itself into their system. She felt as though she might be sick.

"I switched his audio off during the last dive," Vanna said, cutting through the silence. "It's possible he didn't turn it back on again."

Maybe. Possibly. Those words keep coming up. We're hanging everything on a sliver of a chance that we can make this right.

It's the only choice we have.

Her headset crackled, then Sean's voice reached her, sounding as intimate as though he were pressed to her side. "Hey, can you hear me?"

"I can."

"Good. Devereaux's bringing up the *Arcadia*'s floor plan. The thing looks miserable—all hand illustrated and badly scanned decades ago. We're going to do our best to give you directions though."

"Roger that. Thank you."

Silence fell over them again. Except for her fellow divers, the only visible object was the eerily still dive line. It shone like a white paint stroke cutting through the black, leading them down and down and farther down, until it vanished into the gloom.

A part of Cove prayed that they might meet Aidan on the way back up. If he'd only been gone for two hours, it was still possible he was returning to the surface but delayed by the decompression stops. But he would need to be following the dive line, meaning they couldn't miss him. Meters raced by. The white cord remained painfully vacant.

"Hey," Sean said. He cleared his throat. "I figure I should say this now. I'm sorry, Vanna. I was…maybe not fair to you."

"Mm." Her voice remained free from any kind of inflection, giving no indication of how she felt about the apology.

"Well. You keep a weird diary, but…I guess I can't blame you for what happened in the *Arcadia*. The whole thing with my ROVs made me irritable and paranoid, and I took it out on you. Sorry."

"Buy me a beer when we get back to shore," Vanna said. "I'll call that equal."

He chuckled. "Okay. You got it."

Roy's breathing came through as a faint wheeze. He was on the edge of panicking. Cove felt a spark of misgiving for letting him come.

Then Roy spoke, the words rushing out of him. "I killed the ROVs."

"You…" A pause from Sean, then bubbling fury entered his voice. "It *was* you?"

"I know. I know. It was so dumb. I just wanted to dive. I didn't want to have to watch it on the screen; I wanted to be down there. I took chips out of your ROVs. They're in my duffel bag. I was going to give them back to you once the trip was over."

A clattering sound rang through the audio, and Cove could imagine Sean shoving away from the desk. Expletives ran like water from his mouth, growing increasingly faint, until a distant door slammed and they faded entirely.

After a beat, Hestie's voice registered. "I think he left."

"Honestly?" Roy sounded miserable. "I don't blame him."

Any anger Cove might have felt was dampened by the sight of the dive line curving. They were close to the wreck.

I guess that explains why he was so irritable on the first dive. The unnerving messages, the blocked hallways—I bet at that moment he was wishing he'd let the ROVs take the first trip down, but it was too late to say anything.

The *Arcadia*'s silhouetted bow cut through the darkness ahead, and all other thoughts vanished. Her body reacted viscerally; her stomach twisted into knots, her heart's pace redoubled, and fine beading sweat spread over her body, making the layered clothes cling to her skin.

Her first sighting of the *Arcadia* had been one of pure elation. Now, it was of terror. The one place she never wanted to enter again. The one place that held someone she couldn't bring herself to give up on.

How many hours since he entered the ship? How many hours on such little air?

"He would have been trying to get to the boiler room," Cove said. "Can anyone guess which path he'd be likely to take?"

"Perhaps the route we used to leave during the last dive," Vanna said. "Through the dining room. I'll lead."

The static was starting to set in in earnest. Cove kept her eyes fixed on Vanna's fins as they left the dive line and approached the *Arcadia*'s deck.

"Keep us updated on the path you're taking," Devereaux said. Closer to the surface, the *Skipjack*'s crew had sounded intimately close. Now, the voices were fading and distorting. "That will help us give directions if it becomes necessary."

Cove knew their best chance—really, their only chance—was to pass through the *Arcadia* as quickly as they could. The ship messed with their equipment, draining their lights and distorting their audio. The longer they spent inside, the worse the effect became.

And the longer we spend down there, the more oxygen our rebreathers will be putting back into the water.

It had struck Cove that the ship's passengers had only begun to truly wake up on their last dive. They had been dormant for so long that it had been a slow process...but also inevitable.

They grazed over the *Arcadia*'s bow. Roy's fins brushed the crusted railing, sending flecks of sediment and rust flowing into the water. Ahead, built slightly above the deck, was the domed skylight that looked down into the dining hall. Vanna reached the edge first and turned her body at a sharp angle to descend through one of the broken windows.

Roy followed. Cove reached the pane less than a second after his legs had disappeared through. Beneath seemed like an endless tunnel, plunging down into the ship's stomach, lit only by her companions' headlights. She didn't let her momentum slow but rushed through, allowing the ship to draw her inside.

The three divers coursed down the multistory dining hall, aiming for the distant, silty floor beneath. Nothing tried to interrupt their descent. That made sense to Cove. The ship's dead didn't want to frighten them away. They would only begin to close in once the divers were far enough into the mazelike ship that they couldn't escape.

One step at a time. Cove kept her hands clenched at her sides, her body shimmying with each kick of her feet. Tired muscles ached from being pushed a second time in one day, but she ignored them. *Find Aidan first. Then worry about everything else.*

Vanna changed her angle as she neared the floor, swooping toward the open door. Cove thought she caught something shifting in her peripheral vision. She glanced toward it, but it was already gone.

One step at a time.

Vanna pressed through the door. The water was already cloudier than Cove would have liked, so she tried to watch her movements and not kick up additional material. It was easier said than done. The *Arcadia's* environment was precariously delicate. She'd barely made it through the door when her rebreather purged, and she flinched as jostling bubbles of air raced for the ceiling.

The deep, grinding shudders ran through the ship. She pictured it as a sleeping monster, shifting through the heavy silt and water, its bones aching. The water almost buzzed.

Vanna had swerved to one side, into a hallway, and paused only long enough to ensure Cove and Roy were following before pressing deeper into the path. Her headlight began to flicker. Sharp fear sliced through Cove's heart. She used the tightened nerves to make herself faster, pushing her muscles and burning through her own oxygen at a reckless rate. Minutes counted. *Seconds* counted. Even with the best time estimates and even believing Aidan had managed to conserve his air inside the hellish ship, it was going to be a knife's edge gamble.

A narrow metal door hung open, and Vanna aimed for it. Cove narrated their path to the *Skipjack* team as accurately as she could manage. Buried beneath the static, she could hear Hestie and Devereaux debating in hushed voices.

She was familiar with ship maps. They were not easy to read. The ship itself was a 3D shape, with rooms stacked above, below, and beside each other, but it had only ever been mapped in 2D, which meant every time they changed floors, the *Skipjack* team would have to jump between images and try to find the connecting passageway. It would have been easier if they'd taken one of the main stairwells, but they were trying to retrace Aidan's path, which meant using the narrow staff passageways that would barely be visible on the tightly illustrated pages.

The stairwell led down steeply. Its walls squeezed on either side, and Cove held her hands out to prevent herself from bumping against the painfully reflective surfaces.

Slats created disorienting patterns of shadow beneath her body. They were nearing what Cove assumed to be its end when she heard the distant cry of pained steel. She twisted to look over her shoulders. Where the hallway above had been visible through the door was now only grim metal. Something had closed the door.

One step at a time.

The stairwell hit a landing. The lower door was shut, though Cove couldn't imagine Vanna would have left it that way on the previous dive. The passage was too narrow for them to move abreast of each other, so Vanna alone worked at the door, jamming her shoulder into it as she attempted to shift the stiff metal.

For a second, Cove was forced to question what would happen if the door didn't open. If *neither* door opened. They would be trapped in the narrow stairwell, three humans in a tube that offered no escape. Fighting the locked metal on either side, waiting for the air in their own canisters to run empty.

Then the lower door groaned, bending outward, and abruptly snapped open. The static redoubled, and Cove flinched against the noise.

But they were out. Clear water stretched ahead. Cove pushed through the doorway and found the metal path vanished. It had crumpled, falling apart, like the rest of the walkways in the boiler room.

They had made it. Cove lifted her head, and her light flickered as it caught over an impossible tangle in the hall's center.

She'd been in the boiler room once two days before. She remembered twisted metal and heavy silt filling the space between the four furnaces. At first glance, it looked as though that ground had grown a misshapen kind of fungus. The coiling form rose upward, approaching the ceiling. It moved very gently in the water. The form twisted around itself, whorls and lumps and protrusions marking where branches might be expected.

Roy made a sound somewhere between a groan and a cry.

Cove let herself drift away from the open door, frowning as she tried to understand what she was looking at.

The form was made of bodies. The realization hit her like a slap, and she bit her tongue to prevent herself from making any additional noise. Layer upon layer of the stiff, discolored corpses had clumped together to form the mockery of a tree. Their limbs wove between each other, clinging, to create the effect of rippling whorls of wood. There had to be more than a hundred of them.

And there, in the formation's center, was Aidan.

58.

The growth of interwoven bodies swayed. They were a map of washed-out colors, streaks of gray fabrics and gray patterns and gray skin. They clung to each other so tightly that it was impossible to see where one ended and another began.

And trapped in the shape's center was a shimmering flash of black.

Gray skin spread over it. Gray arms coiling over the dive suit's shoulder. Gray legs cinched across the waist. The suit's lower half was no longer visible, embedded thoroughly inside the mass. Fingers pressed into the helmet's reflective sheen, blotting out whatever was beneath.

"Aidan!" Roy lunged forward, then immediately pulled back again. The tower of merging forms began twisting at his voice. They squirmed, the limbs pulling tight, burrowing further into each other. The dark dive suit sank inches deeper into the mass. It threatened to vanish from sight altogether.

"Don't move," Vanna snapped. She reached one hand toward her companions, holding them in place.

Cove's ears rang as her fear grew to overwhelming levels. Aidan hung limp. Part of his arms were still visible, but they weren't moving.

Too late…you were too late…if only you'd noticed he was missing sooner…if only you'd gone to apologize an hour earlier…

She was going to scream.

The mass writhed in languid, sluggish rhythms. Cove's light began to flicker as it traced over the pillar of coiling flesh. Like a hallucination. Like a monster from a fevered dream. No longer individuals but a tumorous growth taking root in the ship's deepest level.

Aidan's head twitched. The movement was subtle but sharp. The fingers holding his face in place tightened, drawing him an inch deeper.

"He's still there," Cove managed, but she could barely hear her own voice.

Roy took a sharp breath. Cove gripped his forearm to hold him still. She didn't know if Aidan had seen them. One of his hands rose, the glove breaking out from the pillar that was slowly absorbing him. It spasmed.

A sickly moan escaped Vanna. The sound sent chills flooding down Cove's spine. She was used to Vanna being calm, firm, unemotional. The pure dread flooding that sound sent her heart into palpitations.

Vanna launched away from them, swimming furiously toward the mass. Cove made to follow her before Vanna's gasping, barking words cut her movements short. "Don't follow! Stay where you are!"

"What—"

"He's suffocating."

One of Aidan's hands twitched again. A reflexive action, not conscious. No other part of him could move.

The howling screams were building in Cove's chest. She kicked closer, one hand still holding Roy's forearm to prevent him from doing anything rash. "What are you—"

"Getting him air." Vanna was already pulling the spare canister around from her side. Her voice was cracking. "It's going to absorb me too. I'll let it. But you have to find a way to get us out."

Aidan's hand spasmed once more. The movement was weaker. His mask had almost entirely disappeared under layers of sprawling fingers.

Vanna hit the mass. It responded instantly; the nearest bodies writhed inward, pulling away from her. Vanna didn't give it any ground though; one hand dug between the whorls of flesh, searching for the edges to Aidan's mask.

The growth swelled then. Hands broke away from the form. They wrapped across Vanna's shoulders. More spread around her legs. She didn't fight them. They began to suck her in, the sharp black dive suit vanishing in painful increments. Vanna's gasp was audible through the communications unit. Cove could only imagine how viciously they must have been squeezing her.

Please. Aidan was almost gone. Only the edges of his glove and a sliver of the mask were visible. The static in her communications unit was growing worse. In her peripheral vision, Cove was aware of dark shapes gradually moving into the room. They floated, their arms wrapped across torsos, legs hanging limp beneath them, and their heads tilted up, facing the mass. They drew in from every shadowed corner of the boiler room, emerging through the open doorways and from between and inside the massive furnaces. One of the dark forms grazed Cove's shoulder as it moved past. The bones in its neck cracked as its head slowly rotated to fix milky eyes on her. Cove held still, her teeth clenched, her heart ready to explode as it continued on, toward the conglomerate.

And at last, Vanna spoke.

"He's got air." And then softer, tinged with dread, "Don't leave us."

Cove let her eyes close for a second, the relief burning the inside of her chest. "We won't." *Not in a thousand years.*

Neither Vanna nor Aidan were visible any longer. More bodies merged with the slowly writhing growth. They were pressed thick, backs to the room, resolute as they struggled to burrow deeper into their own formation.

She needed to get her divers out. And soon.

They don't like light.

Her headlight was already fading. At her side, Roy leaned forward, straining to see into the mass, as his own lamp blinked.

Cove pulled her two waterproof flares out of her belt and used one to tap Roy's side to get his attention.

"We'll swim above and drop them," she said.

He nodded, retrieving his own flares. The lights were bright, but they didn't last long. They would have a very limited window to work through.

"Vanna, one minute. Don't let Aidan fall." Cove pushed forward, adjusting her buoyancy to carry her closer to the ceiling. There was a gap of about twelve feet between the mass and the twisting metal pipes above. It should be enough, Cove hoped. If they miscalculated—if she and Roy were drawn into the coiling flesh—she didn't think they would ever come out again.

The gray pillar writhed as she moved nearer, as though it

wanted to retreat from her. Cove took advantage of that, kicking her feet to carry her up. She waited until she and Roy were nearly on top of it before preparing the flares.

They were rated to burn for fifteen minutes near the surface, but the increased pressure would force them to consume themselves much, much faster. They couldn't afford to mess up their timing.

"Drop them on three." Cove pulled on a tab, lighting the first of her flares. Vivid hissing red lights burst out of its end, the sparks spiraling away into the clouded water.

Movement came from below her. The mass shifted down, sinking toward the floor.

Good. They don't like it. This might just be enough—

The gray form abruptly twisted and then surged upward again. Fast. Faster than Cove had anticipated the interlocked bodies could move. The space between her and the squirming mass halved in just a second, and she had a sharp moment of clarity: they were aiming to crush her and Roy into the metal-studded ceiling. She choked on her own voice. "*Three!*"

Roy made a faint gasping noise as he threw his two flares downward at the same moment Cove dropped one of hers. The heavy water slowed their momentum to a crawl. Instead of dropping into the twisting mass, they simply drifted, slowly rotating in the water.

The bodies were still rising though, rushing upward to meet them. The flare glanced off one of the bodies, and Cove felt a surge of panic.

They're all facing inward, protecting their faces. The light can't hurt them if they can't see it.

Then, like ripples passing through unsteady water, a disturbance raced outward from the mass. The clinging, clutching limbs began to break apart: a hideous three-dimensional jigsaw puzzle collapsing on itself.

The closest bodies were almost upon Cove. She reached her hands down in defense, and a mottled back hit her gloves. They didn't keep rising though. They spread apart, like a bubble bursting, their limbs separating from each other as the bodies writhed.

In their center was a blazing red flame. Vanna, crushed on all sides, had managed to light her own flare. She hunched around Aidan, one arm pinning him to her side, the flare held above their face masks.

The swelling mass was still fighting to keep itself whole. The twisting, gray figures reached back to one another, clutching and pulling as they tried to clump together again. The three flares Cove and Roy had dropped tumbled between the newly created gaps in the form, bouncing off twitching arms and illuminating a hundred slack-jawed faces.

Already the flares were starting to die. The depths were unforgiving to them; Vanna's had burned half through. In another half minute, it would be gone entirely.

"*Fast*," Cove yelled, and struck her final flare as she dove.

Bodies pulled away from her as she cut through the formation like a knife. She kept the flame ahead of herself, lighting her way, its tip pointed toward any and every distorted face that tried to block her path.

Vanna's flare spluttered as it neared the end of its life. She dropped it and instead stretched her hand up.

Cove caught her around the wrist and hauled. Roy followed at her back, using his headlight and his spare flashlight like dual swords to cut through the mass. The final clinging bodies released Vanna's and Aidan's legs as the flares spiraled past them.

Go, go, go. Her legs kicked furiously. She forced herself to breathe, even when her throat threatened to close over. The swelling mass of bodies was trying to reform…and reform *over* them. A net of the bodies spread above, slowly knitting together, limbs locking around each other as they pulled tight.

There was a small gap. Cove aimed for it. Her final flare was almost gone, but she reached it forward, piercing through the clumping, writhing bodies.

Her torso made it through, but then Vanna pulled on her hand. The bodies were sealing around them, tightening impossibly to hold them inside.

Roy snarled as he jammed his hands into two of the closest faces. He pushed, shoving them back, like tearing a hole through the fleshy net even as it tried to constrict around them. Crackling bones rang through the cold water, and then the hole was open again, and Roy was hauling them out.

Cove didn't let herself so much as slow but continued pulling upward, toward the narrow metal doors that marked where the walkways had once existed.

Not the door we came through. They've sealed the other exit. We need another way—

Shapes continued moving across her periphery. More of the figures drifting in from every corner, converging on them. The silt made it nearly impossible to see, but Cove thought she glimpsed the outline of a door on the opposite wall from where they'd entered. She aimed for it.

Behind her, Roy discarded the flashlight he'd been using, dead already. He came up alongside Vanna, with Aidan positioned between them, and hooked his arms around the boy. Aidan still hadn't moved. His legs trailed limply behind him, and his head bumped against his chest with every movement. Between them, Vanna and Roy held him upright and pulled him forward, leaving Cove to lead.

She hit the door and fought to get it open. It shuddered as it groaned inward. Cove moved to force it wider but then saw how close the dead had come to catching up to them.

The bodies climbed over each other. Their stiff, creaking fingers blindly dug into their companions as they crawled up, closer and closer to the door. Cove made a sharp noise and pulled away, her back pressed to the hallway's metal wall as she tried to make room for the other divers. Roy shifted through the narrow door first, grunting as the metal scraped his shoulder. He pulled Aidan in after him, and Vanna, silent as a wraith, slipped through.

Cove shoved on the door. Slowed by the water, it wouldn't close as quickly as she wanted. Hands hit against its other side. She pressed one foot into the wall to gain leverage and pushed. The door grated home.

There are no locks. It won't take them long to get through.

The drowned figures were slow. Stiffened by age and the cold, they were sluggish to react, and that was Cove's only real advantage. She couldn't hide from them and she couldn't fight them. Her sole hope was to move and move fast—and keep moving until they were outside the ship and beyond reach.

Vanna and Roy had paused, waiting for her, and she hissed, "*Go.*"

She wasn't certain they heard through the drowning static, but at least they understood her gesture. Moving in an awkward single file with Aidan held between them, they navigated the tight crew hallway.

Stairs will be a good sign. Doors into the passenger quarters even better. The only thing we want to avoid is becoming backed into a room with no other exit.

It was a real risk in the crew-manned levels. Cove's light was growing weak. Vanna used her handheld flashlight to substitute for her own headlight. The static became heavier with every passing second, and when a voice bubbled up from beneath, Cove had to strain to hear it.

"Do you have a location?" Hestie called. Her voice shook as she raised it to be heard over the static. "Do you know where you are?"

"Near the boiler room," Cove replied. "We have Aidan. We're trying to get out. As soon as I can identify an area, I'll—"

Her voice cut off. The hallway ended ahead. A dark doorway gaped, seeming to swallow their lights even as they strained to look inside.

They had very little choice. Already, clicking, cracking sounds behind them told Cove that the figures had found their way through the door. There were no other exits. They had to go through, whether they wanted to or not.

59.

Roy passed Aidan back to Vanna and approached first. He moved cautiously, his broad shoulders hunched as he slipped through the unfamiliar opening. His headlight flickered, dimming alarmingly. Vanna cast one look back at Cove, then, with a brief nod, followed Roy.

We can't afford a dead end. Cove's heart thundered in her throat as she followed her team through the open doorway.

Her eyes took a second to adjust. The room was littered with long wood dining tables. They had been thrown loose by the sinking and now piled up like driftwood around the walls. Chairs toppled over and through them, the legs forming an unsettling patchwork of shadows in their conflicting lights. The furniture's design was utilitarian, broad and solid, with very little effort put into make it appealing.

"We're in the crew mess hall," Cove said for Hestie's benefit. "There should be at least one other way out. We just need to—"

Roy raised a hand, pointing at the opposite wall. There was

the exit Cove needed. It was barely visible beneath the furniture that had piled in front of it.

She grit her teeth. *We can't go back. No other choice.*

Vanna had read her thoughts. She gently released Aidan, letting him drift to the floor, before pushing forward and reaching into the barricade. They were going to have to dig their way out.

Cove tried not to look too closely at Aidan as she passed him. Vanna said she'd gotten the boy air in time, but he still hadn't moved, and that terrified her. There was nothing she could do for him inside the *Arcadia* though; she could only fight to get him to the surface as quickly as possible and hope it would be enough.

She struggled to drag one of the chairs free. The room had relatively little sediment. That was a blessing for their visibility, but also a bad sign: sediment came from openings to the ocean. They had to be some distance from the exits if the mess hall was this clear.

Roy wrenched a table back, his gasps cutting through the static as he fought to unjam it. Cove put her shoulder into it, scraping it free. It rang out against the floor as it rolled aside.

They had managed to form a gap near the ceiling. Cove rose, clambering across the furniture as she tried to widen it. She caught a glimpse through the door. The other side seemed clear. She pulled at a chair, rattling it to unlock it from the jam, then tossed it back to where Vanna caught it.

Her fading light caught something dark on the opposite wall. Words, scrawled messily, almost frantically:

THEY HEAR YOUR WHISPERS

Cove set her jaw. "This should be enough," she said. "Lift Aidan."
As she reached down to take Aidan's shoulders and draw him

through the gap, something sleek grazed across the leg she'd braced against a table. Cove's breath stuttered. Fingers curled from between the wood piles. Buried far down, pinned beneath the furniture, a cool, off-white eye regarded her.

Cove leaned back, pulling herself and Aidan through the narrow opening. As she drifted back toward the clear ground on the other side, she said, "Come through quickly. There's something under the furniture."

Roy muttered a swear word and barreled after her so quickly that he sent a loose chair skittering into the hall. He caught up with Cove and took Aidan's other side, and she pretended she couldn't feel him shivering through his suit.

They waited just long enough to ensure Vanna was through safely, then Cove pushed onward. An open door to her right revealed one of the crew's rooms: bunks stacked against every wall, fitting as many of the sailors into the space as possible.

Then, to the left, another entrance opened into the kitchens.

Good. The kitchens would be close to the passenger areas. Cove's heart was starting to ache from the strain. Her light flickered out entirely for a second before returning weaker than it had been before.

She pushed into the kitchens. Unlike other areas in the ship, most of the fixings had been bolted into the walls and ceiling. A chaos of pans and shattered plates lined the floor. The passageways between the benches were narrow, but at their other side, an open door teased the edges of a set of metal stairs leading up.

Cove adjusted her grip on Aidan. Out of the corner of her eye, she saw cupboards creaking open. Shadowed eyes flickered in her light. One hand flopped free.

Move fast. They're still waking. Don't give them a chance to leave their holes.

She barely paused to check through the open doorway. It seemed clear, but with how low her lights had fallen, it was far from a certainty. They were out of time to hesitate. She moved through.

The stairs carried them up and ended on a short landing with a narrow door. Cove had to pass Aidan back to Roy as she worked on the handle, jostling it open.

They spilled into one of the passenger hallways. It was either third- or second-class. The familiar half-wall paneling was present, but the wallpaper above had a pattern she didn't recognize. They hadn't been in that part of the ship before.

Cove's light struggled to see any distance, but she couldn't hear the clicking noise behind them any longer. She felt a small spark of hope that the plan to move fast might actually be working.

"We'll look for the stairs and aim to find the dining room," Cove said. "It had a body inside of it, but only one. I think that gives us better odds than the hospital. Hestie, we just took the stairs leading up from the kitchens."

"Oh!" She sounded miles away, and Cove strained to hear her. "Okay, try turning right and take two flights up. You're close. Really close."

Please. Behind her, Roy's light died. Cove tried to keep one eye on him while also watching the hall ahead. *Let us just get to the dining hall. Please.*

The ship shuddered deeply beneath them. Cove pressed her tongue between her teeth, but focused on the pathway ahead even as cracks spread across the peeling plaster ceiling.

Just a little farther. Please.

The hallway had an intersecting hall to the left. As she moved around the corner, Cove's light hit the aged wood bannisters marking the stairwell.

She moved toward it before a distant shimmer of movement froze her. Opposite was the port-side hallway. A tall figure floated there like a lone sentinel, barely touching the farthest reaches of her light, its arms wrapped around a shredded officer uniform, its face unreadable except for two sharp, flashing eyes.

Don't hesitate. Don't give them even a second. Cove reached behind herself and grabbed Vanna's shoulder. "Fast," she hissed, and moved forward, toward the stairs.

The distant click of flexing neck bones warned Cove that they'd been seen. She pushed her way through the water, clawing for ground as fast as she could. The figure tilted its head with a hideous crackling noise. Cove hit the stairwell's bannister and put her body between the stairs and the approaching form, using herself as a barrier as Vanna and Roy moved Aidan up.

Her headlight's beam flickered, then vanished entirely. Cove pulled out her handheld spare, but it wouldn't even turn on. They were reduced to just Vanna's light.

Move fast. Don't stop. That's the only way this will work.

She held her position until Vanna and Roy had reached the higher level, then turned after them. The sediment was growing thicker. Their furious pace kicked it up and worsened visibility, but at that moment, Cove was only grateful. Extra sediment meant they were approaching their exit.

They pulled around the final turn in the stairs and emerged into the hall. There, ahead, were the open dining room doors.

Vanna, the only one of them that still had a light, moved first. She reached one arm behind herself to keep a hold on Aidan as she extended her head through the narrow opening. Her light was entirely swallowed by the room beyond, leaving Cove and Roy close to blind in the hallway.

The clicking was growing closer, rising along the stairwell. It wasn't rushing but moved with the slow confidence of something that knew this encounter could only culminate in one kind of conclusion. Cove clenched her teeth until her jaw ached.

Vanna turned back to them, gave a sharp nod, and shifted inside the dining hall. Cove followed last, her eyes still fixed on the dark pit of stairs below them.

They had barely made it past the threshold when the static worsened. It grew thicker and louder until it was impossible to hear anything except the pure rush of white noise that bordered on deafening. Vanna's headlight began to stutter. Cove, guessing what was about to happen, reached out and grasped both Roy's and Vanna's arms. The light vanished.

Cove strained to hear through the static. Without the headlights, they were blind. She was free floating. She tightened her grip, afraid of losing Roy and Vanna in the world of nothingness.

And then, abruptly, the static vanished. It was like turning a light switch—one second Cove could barely think through the onslaught; the next, the hollow silence pressed so intensely that she felt as though she couldn't breathe through it.

She wet her lips. "Roy? Vanna?"

"I can hear you." That came from Roy. He was whispering, as though the sudden quiet had pushed him to reverence. His arm shifted minutely under her hand. "I've still got Aidan."

Vanna said, "I'm here."

"Okay." Cove found herself matching their whispers as she tilted her head up. The ceiling had to be above her somewhere. "We're going to begin rising. No decompression stops until we're outside the ship."

She didn't love the idea of feeling her way through the old metal and remaining shards of glass to find one of the open skylights, but every second she spent inside the *Arcadia* made her heart feel closer to collapsing from the strain. Cove, still not letting go of the others, began to rise.

The clicking noise sounded from behind her, warning her that the stairwell figure had caught up to the door. She fought the impulse to turn toward it. She wouldn't have been able to see it either way.

Keep moving. They're slow; if you keep the pace fast, they won't be able to catch up.

Another click rang through the dead air. This time, it came from the opposite side of the room.

Cove's mouth was achingly dry. She kept her head tilted up, blind eyes searching the empty dark ahead for any sign of the ceiling. With no visual cues, it was impossible to tell how far they had risen.

Another cracking sound and then a series of soft clicks, this time closer, coming from what felt like right behind Cove's ear.

"Hold still a second," Vanna said. The arm Cove was holding moved as she felt for something in her belt. Another muffled rattle sounded, this time on Cove's other side.

And then, abruptly, a dim blue glow formed. Vanna raised one of the glowsticks Hestie had gifted them. It was pale, its light better suited to being seen in the dark instead of *seeing*, its glow diffusing quickly. It washed about them, coloring Vanna's face and suit in an eerie tinge of blue.

She raised the stick as it brightened in fractions. The wan light spread outward, across their surroundings, highlighting the rows of gaunt, expressionless faces poised just over her shoulder.

60.

The lights were dimmed. Vanna kept her eyes cast down, toward her own loosely folded hands.

"You understand why I have to ask," Cove said. Normally, she had a habit of making herself cozy in chairs: legs folded up, arms wrapped around herself, reclined as deeply as she could. Now, though, she sat with both feet planted on the floor, forearms braced on her knees as she leaned forward. Her vivid green eyes shone in the muffled lamplight. The posture wasn't hostile, but it *was* formal.

Vanna's throat ached. The room was too loud. Cove's laptop hummed at her side. The lamp's electric hiss seemed louder than normal. And the stabbing, whistling wind, normally a calming presence, cut across her nerves. "I would rather not talk about it."

Cove drew a slow breath, her hands flexing. She appeared to

be taking pains to choose her words carefully. "Sean was adamant. And from this outside perspective, what he claims he saw is a very concerning accusation. But he doesn't know your motivations. None of us do. That's why I want to hear your perspective. Help me understand."

For a beat, they were lost in a world of hissing lamps and humming laptop fans. Vanna said, "Please don't tell the others."

Cove didn't respond. She simply kept staring at Vanna, her cutting eyes impossible to escape.

Impossible to escape. This was always going to come back to you eventually.

The shame, the fear, and the pain were rising in tandem through her, like knives slicing through muscle and fat until there was nothing but a sick pulp inside of her. Vanna knew her face wouldn't betray it. A small mercy. "You would have looked me up online before hiring me."

"Of course," Cove said. "That's why I want to hear your perspective. Because every newspaper article and association profile talked about your professionalism and conscientiousness."

"Then you didn't try searching within the last three weeks."

Cove's eyes narrowed a fraction. "Should I?"

"Yes. Look up the name Abby Freeman."

The winds intensified, battering against the ship's side. Cove's eyes continued to flick over her, scrutinizing, before she dragged her laptop up to her side. Fingers clicked across keys. The pale artificial light washed across Cove's face as a page opened.

Vanna waited. Cove lifted one hand to press across her mouth, her eyes hard as she scrolled. Vanna couldn't see the screen, but she could almost see the words reflected in Cove's eyes.

Diver perishes in cave.

Cove leaned back from the screen a fraction, her tongue

running across her teeth. She was forming questions. Vanna cut over her before she could speak them.

"Abby was my dive partner. And my life partner. My... everything."

The words almost choked her. She pushed through before Cove could hear the catch in her voice.

"Eighteen days ago, we scheduled a dive to explore Arch Creek's cave system. A recreational dive, no students."

Eighteen days. She counted each new dawn and each new nightfall. The clock on the wall told her it was around one in the morning, which meant a new day, which meant she was at nineteen. Nineteen days without her other half.

Cove didn't press. She just waited, her hand still held over her mouth as the questioning eyes bore into her.

"We were navigating a narrow section that opened back into the main system. I went first. Abby's oxygen tube became caught on a rock. When she tried to pull through the opening, it tore. I tried to get back to her. Get her some of my air. I couldn't reach far enough."

Only enough to hold her hand. Vanna continued to stare at her long, pale fingers. She'd felt the spasms. It had happened so, so quickly, but in the moment, it also felt as though it had lasted a lifetime.

Her throat was sore. She pushed through, back to more neutral grounds, back to the topic that would hurt less. "I've been seeing a professional. They suggested I write down my nightmares in a journal. A way to address them in a safe environment. It helps—a little."

The silence, filled with the cutting wind and hissing lamp, seemed impossibly loud.

"Why did you still come on this trip?" Cove asked.

Vanna didn't know how she was expected to answer. "I signed a contract."

"Yes, but…" Cove's voice caught. "No one would have expected you to—"

"You needed an experienced diver," Vanna said, her eyes fixed on the floor. "I needed to be somewhere other than my home. And I had made a commitment."

Cove finally shifted, her legs turning at a more comfortable angle as she rubbed her hands over her knees. "I'm sorry."

Vanna shrugged. "My skills aren't compromised. I can still perform my duties as safety officer."

"You're sure you really want to go back down tomorrow?"

"Yes." What else was there to do? Living above the water hurt. Living below the water hurt as well, but slightly less. Under the water, she was compartmentalized. The phone calls, the bills, the mundanity of life couldn't reach her when she was under the waves. For the few hours she was below, she had clarity again.

"Okay." Cove rose slowly. One hand moved out, as though wanting to touch Vanna. She pulled away from it. Since Abby, everyone had wanted to touch her: hugs, pats, squeezes. They felt like sandpaper across her skin. Cove withdrew her hand, then cleared her throat. "If you need anything…"

"Don't tell the others." Vanna's thumb dug at a sliver of scraped skin on her palm. "I would prefer if they didn't know."

"Sure. Yeah. That's the least I can do." Cove hesitated again, then cleared her throat. One hand rose to point to her eyes. "They're implants, you know."

Vanna frowned slightly. "I'm sorry?"

"The eyes. My natural ones are brown. But my agent thought I needed something memorable, and…I got green implants. No one else knows." She rubbed the back of her neck, seeming uncomfortable. "I'm sorry, that sounds completely frivolous compared to what you just told me, but…I know one of your secrets. And I thought it might help if you knew one of mine."

In a strange way, it did. Vanna didn't respond, but when Cove left the room, she found it just slightly easier to get air into her lungs.

61.

The glowstick shimmered in the cold water. Vanna was frozen, trapped staring at the blue-washed shapes behind their team leader.

"Vanna." Cove's voice was lower than a whisper: no more than a breath. "Behind you—"

"Behind you as well." Her stomach coiled on itself as raw panic burned in her veins. They were surrounded. The forms created a ring. Not just one layer deep either; the glowstick's light barely reached the closest sets of pale, flashing eyes and gaunt, mottled cheeks, but a shimmer of moving hair and the quiet click of flexing bones warned her that there were more. How many, she couldn't say, and she didn't want to know the answer.

They were out of lights, and the glowsticks weren't strong enough to force back the pressing walls of bodies. Vanna's elbow moved as she adjusted her position and it bumped something firm.

The ceiling and its promised escape were so close. The bodies clustered uncomfortably near, but nothing blocked the water above. And the bodies weren't acting. It was almost as though they were waiting for some signal…from the dive team?

Vanna's mind flashed to earlier encounters. The mass of twining bodies in the boiler room must have had Aidan in their grasp for upward of an hour, but they only buried him inside their form when the dive team tried to remove him.

They didn't want to attack the divers. They simply wanted them to *stay*. Inside the *Arcadia*. Forever. And as long as the crew didn't appear to be struggling, the drowned figures around them would remain placid.

"Rise," she whispered, and gave her feet a very soft, experimental kick. "No sudden movements. No struggling. Move slowly. Carefully."

Her fins pushed against the water in minute increments. Neither Cove nor Roy made any sound, but by the slight shimmer to their bodies she knew they were swimming too. Their faces were invisible behind the masks, but she could hear their breathing: tight, tense, painfully measured.

The ring of the dead pulled fractionally closer. One bumped Vanna's back, and it took all of her self-control not to shove it away.

No resistance. No fighting. We just need to gain whatever ground we can.

They were moving higher, she knew—but it was impossible to tell by how much. The grim, shadowed faces around them dogged them with perfect synchronization: their heads all level with Vanna's own, their heavy-lidded eyes staring blindly at the divers. It gave the unnerving illusion that, no matter how many times she pushed the fins through the cold water, she never gained ground.

Vanna tilted her head up, trying to read the inky depths above. She very slowly raised the arm holding the glowstick. As it lifted above the clustering passengers of the *Arcadia*, she saw their mass went far farther than she had first hoped. Shimmers of blue light caught across endless fields of gently drifting hair and unblinking, staring eyes. She looked away, refusing to let them fill her vision for a second longer, as she searched the dark above.

At the farthest edges of her light, she thought she saw something. She tried to swallow through the tight ache in her throat. At that distance, it could have just been her eyes playing tricks: forcing images into the darkness to give her something to process. She didn't think so though. She was almost certain she was looking at the metal frame holding the skylights, no more than fifteen feet above.

If we can reach it…if we can make it that far, then surely…

Then surely they could find *some* way to break free. Aidan, still limp, was in the center of their formation. It would make it harder to fight past the circling monsters without letting go of him, but they had to find a way. Surely, after making it so far, after getting so close to the end, she couldn't fall short.

Not like I failed Abby.

They were gaining on the ceiling an inch at a time. Vanna's eyes hadn't deceived her. Blue-tinted glints of light marked the remaining shards of glass. She kicked slightly harder, pushing her luck, as she raised the glowstick higher.

The clicking noises increased in frequency and intensity. Vanna's skin prickled as every hair on her arms rose. She couldn't so much as blink as she stared up.

The ceiling was covered with the dead. They tangled across each other, a thick matt of twining flesh and blue-tinted clothes. They were packed so densely that there was no sign of the skylights behind them. The glints of light she'd seen were reflected off countless eyes.

She was still rising, and as she grew closer, the bodies reached their hands toward her. Like limp stalactites hanging from a cave's roof, the arms stretched down, crooked fingers quivering at the expectation of impact.

No. Vanna's heart missed a beat. Roy made a soft moaning noise, and it crackled as it passed through the communications unit.

They were not getting through this. Not even if the dead could feel the bite of their knives. Not even if their headlights had been working. Ringed on all sides and now with the wall of dead canvassing the ceiling, Vanna felt as though she was being pressed into an impossibly tight vise.

There was no static in their headsets, but there may as well have been. The clicking noises were rising in volume, growing deafening, to the point that Vanna couldn't even hear her own thoughts except for one:

This is how I die.

Static hissed. Out of nowhere, Sean's voice cut through the noise. "Found you."

A piercingly bright light flooded up from the dining room's floor. Vanna flinched as the beam cut around her legs and poured across her face. It was like a floodlight in the dark, more powerful than their headlights had ever managed to be. She moved her hand to shield her eyes.

The clicking noises redoubled. The bodies circling them began to twist, their jaws widening as light pierced across their forms.

Vanna squinted through her fingers to look down. A spherical shape slightly larger than her torso rose toward them. It seemed so foreign, so alien in that underwater world, that it took Vanna a second to recognize it. One of the ROVs.

"You got it working," Cove said, her voice filled with shock.

"Yep. Thank your lucky stars Roy didn't throw the chips

overboard." The ROV moved in a slow arc as it circled them. "Judes finally gets her hour inside the *Arcadia*. Her floodlights are really something spectacular, huh?"

Vanna was not about to argue. The dead writhed in the water as they flinched back from the machine. They released their hold on the ceiling in clumps, slowly drifting downward, their pallid bodies grazing Vanna's sides and back as they coiled around themselves to protect their delicate eyes.

Gaps were appearing across the skylight. The ROV's beam highlighted an opening: one of the broken windows, clear of glass, ready for an exit.

"Get yourselves out," Sean said. "Judes can't fit through those holes. We had to guide her in by the hospital window to even get her inside the ship. She'll keep your path lit though."

Cove's ferocious grin was audible through her voice. "Roy, you go first. We'll pass Aidan out to you."

"Got it." He pushed away from their formation. The remaining corpses stretched long arms toward him as he approached the ceiling, but the ROV chugged closer, warding them off. Roy reached his arms through the gap first, then slid out, vanishing into the darkness above. "Ready," he called.

Cove took Aidan from Vanna and lifted him. The ROV must have been blinding at that close distance. Vanna hung below, half-submerged in the darkness, as she watched their team leader pass Aidan outside.

Something snagged her leg. Vanna's throat closed over entirely.

While the light was focused on the ceiling, the dead were rising like a sick mass from the dining hall's floor. A second hand closed over her other foot. She kicked, squirming, but their fingers were like nails driving into her suit. One of them latched on to her side, covering her belt and her buoyancy compensator. They had learned.

More grabbed at her arms, her thighs, her shoulders. They were weighing her down: a hundred bodies, all linked together, all creeping over her like ink creeps across paper. Each additional set of hands added weight pulling her down. Vanna kicked, fighting for the surface

like she fought for air

but there wasn't so much of an inch to gain.

The others were focused on getting through the windows. The ROV moved in slow increments, holding its camera and its beam steady on Cove as she made sure Aidan was helped outside.

Vanna was sinking, and she couldn't even call to them. Didn't know how.

A hand pressed over her mask, blocking out her view. She closed her eyes. The rebreather let out a rush of bubbles

her bubbles, rushing through your fingertips as you tried to stop the leak

but they were gone before she could even think about them, vanishing toward the same skylight the others were leaving through.

The bodies had managed to cover her, and Vanna was out of energy to fight. She let them pile on, bury her beneath a mound of darkness and quiet clicking.

The others were going to be okay. They were out of the ship and already beginning their ascent to the surface.

She could be at peace with that. She'd done her job. She'd kept them safe.

The mass around her began to squirm. Vanna grimaced as the

prodding, stabbing fingers dug through the dry suit. Something harsh raked across her back. And then, abruptly, the bodies split apart as the painfully intense light cut through them.

"There you are," Sean said.

Vanna didn't think. She only reached out a hand.

The ROV swam forward. It hit her side, hard enough to make her gasp, and she latched her grip onto its metal surface.

And then they were rushing upward: the ROV carrying her fast, faster than was comfortable, toward the skylights.

The dark crevices around the room's edges still held the clumping, staring bodies, withered forms gathered near the curtains or coiled up at the highest corners, away from the beam. The openings in the roof were almost entirely clear.

"Go on," Sean said to Vanna. "I still owe you a beer when we get back to land, remember?"

"Huh. I almost forgot." She released the ROV and reached up. Her fingertips hooked around the metal frame where a skylight had once existed. The ROV hovered below her, its spotlight blinding as she rose through the *Arcadia*'s ceiling and into clear water.

Cove and Roy waited barely fifteen feet away, supporting Aidan between them. Cove reached a hand toward her. As the spotlight faded below, Vanna swam toward her friends.

Sean leaned back from the laptop as the four divers vanished from Judes's camera. Her battery level had dropped almost 20 percent the moment she entered the *Arcadia* and had continued to weaken dangerously with every extra second she spent inside. Now, the diagnostics bar blinked a warning at him: 2 percent power remaining.

He powered down her motors and turned off the floodlight, leaving her with just the softer beams to illuminate her surroundings. She began to drift back down, away from the ceiling and deeper into the dining hall. Within seconds, gray arms reached into frame. As they wrapped around his ROV, static blurred around the camera's edges, erasing his view until nothing but the staring, unblinking eyes remained.

"Good night, Judes," he whispered as a crack appeared across her screen and the battery dropped to zero. "You did good."

Cove knelt on the *Skipjack's* deck. She took her helmet off and closed her eyes as she let the rain wash over her face.

The storm was beginning to break, its downpour fading as the dark world pressed toward midnight.

Vanna sat close to her, equally impervious to the rain. She had her knees drawn up, her forearms resting on their tops, her dark, calm eyes gazing serenely at the sky. The rain painted her short hair across her forehead and cheeks. She looked utterly dead on her feet...but a very small smile curled the edges of her mouth.

Not far behind them, Aidan retched. He was on all fours, with Roy crouched at his side, half patting his back, half hugging him. Both Devereaux and Hestie hovered over him, waiting for the sickness to fade enough to help lift him. Sean, pragmatic as always, waited inside.

Inside. Cove knew she should make moves to get them all out of the rain. Get some food. Some warm clothes. She wasn't sure her feet would work well enough to carry her weight. For that moment, she was content to just sit, the cooling rain pouring across her face and sinking in around her collar to dampen her clothes.

"I expected to die down there," Vanna said. There wasn't any fear or alarm to her words; it was just a matter-of-fact statement. She tilted her head to gaze at Cove. "It felt inevitable. As though everything in my life had been working toward it. And in a way, it almost felt poetic."

"Yeah?"

"The water is linked. Through oceans. Through rivers. Through groundwater. I was half a world away from Abby, but I kept thinking about how we still shared the same water. We would still be connected."

Cove shuffled around to put her shoulder next to Vanna's. They watched as Devereaux and Hestie helped raise a shaking Aidan from the deck. "Do you mean…"

"The cave gap was too tight to get her out," Vanna said, and tilted her head back to gaze up at the sky. "The recovery divers tried. And they say they'll try again. I wanted to go back down for her, but the site owners wouldn't let me, so I came here instead."

She expected to die in the Arcadia. Cove continued to watch Vanna's face, but there was no trace of sadness there, just a soft kind of acceptance…and relief.

"I'm glad I didn't," she said. "It took finding Aidan in the hold to realize the *Arcadia* isn't poetry. I don't think it's even evil. It's just pure cold indifference. If I want to be close to Abby—and I *do*—it will need to be through life, not death."

Cove realized, with a quiet chill, that the sight of Aidan trapped in the twisting mass of bodies must have been a harsh parallel to the moment Vanna lost her partner.

"You got Aidan the air," Cove said. "I don't think any of the rest of us would have realized he was running empty at that moment. I don't think Roy or I would have gotten the spare tank to him in time."

"I couldn't save Abby," Vanna said. "But if I'd died down there, I wouldn't have been able to help Aidan either. But I did. And I think she'd be glad I could."

"I'm pretty sure she would."

Together, they sat in the rain, watching the waves swell around the *Skipjack*'s hull and the distant spears of lightning. They would go inside eventually, Cove knew. They would go in and run assessments for the rest of the team and make sure Aidan was safe, and then Cove would tell Devereaux that they were not going to be moored above the *Arcadia* for even one more minute and to set the ship toward port. Soon. But not yet. Right then, she simply wanted to sit and share gratitude with the universe that she was still alive.

62.

"Do you think you'll ever return to the SS *Arcadia*?"

Cove's eyes glittered in the studio lights. She reclined on a leather sofa, her posture easy, her smile warm. "Not in a million years."

Jenna Bight, host of the late-night show *Take a Bight*, leaned forward in her own identical leather chair. "That's interesting, coming from the woman who doesn't appear to fear anything."

It was a talking point that Cove was well rehearsed in. Her smile stayed calm, her cascading black hair elegantly flipped over one shoulder, her tailored linen outfit perfectly designed to appear both feminine and adventurous as she laughed. "I'll stand by that reputation, you know. But the *Arcadia* is a special case. It's not so much a dangerous location as an ethical and legal problem. As you know, many of the crew and passengers' bodies are still contained inside the ship. Out of respect to them and their families, the *Arcadia* deserves to remain undisturbed."

Jenna nodded encouragingly, her sandy hair framing her face, cue cards held tidily between her hands. "This is something that not only you but the rest of your crew have been adamant about."

"That's right. We're putting some pressure on the governing body to declare the *Arcadia*'s wreck a grave site and off-limits to divers. And it looks as though they intend to do just that."

Jenna turned over one of the cue cards and glanced at it before fixing Cove with another smile. "We're told that your expedition inside the ship captured unexpected footage of the bodies. Will any of those be visible in your documentary?"

Cove turned to the camera and winked. "You'll have to watch it to find out."

Cove strode through the studio's back passageways close to an hour later. *Arcadia*, the documentary produced through Vivitech, would be releasing in just a week. Prepublicity was in full swing, and Cove, both as host and as the most natural in front of cameras, was fielding the bulk of the interview requests.

The documentary did in fact include footage of the bodies inside the ship. Specifically, a carefully edited version of when they had first found the crew member's body behind the dining hall curtain and the hand captured underneath a bed on Hestie's video. Nothing else.

Devereaux and Sean had spent the two days' trip back to base editing the footage. They had gone through it painstakingly, cutting every frame that contained images of the bodies after they began moving.

The crew had unanimously agreed that was the best course of action. They had a pact: don't breathe a whisper about what actually happened on the ship…and do whatever necessary to prevent anyone else from diving down to it.

Already, the pressure they were applying to governing bodies was getting results. Cove hoped that, by that time the following month, the *Arcadia*'s wreck and significant ground around it would be protected from any further tampering.

Despite having to cut a massive amount of footage, the final, unscheduled journey into the *Arcadia*—including what the ROV Judes had recorded—had scraped over the threshold for their contract. After everything that had happened beneath the water, being paid had been the least of Cove's concerns, but it had been a pleasant surprise.

She pulled an elastic band out of her pocket and tied her hair back into a bun as she retraced the path to the studio's exit. She'd kept her phone on silent but unmuted it then. A text flashed up on screen. Cove opened it.

The message included a photo attachment. In it, Aidan grinned. He'd gained plenty of extra freckles on the *Skipjack*, and although he still seemed paler than he had before the trip started, he looked both healthy and happy.

A girl with strawberry-colored hair leaned against him, her head tucked in just below his chin. She was flushed and beaming as she held up a hand. A delicate diamond ring sparkled on her finger.

Aidan's message followed: She said yes!!

Cove chuckled. The message had been sent as a group chat to the crew. Roy had already replied: Say goodbye to bachelor life!

Vanna's response was more to the point. Congratulations.

I knew she would! So happy for you two! That came from Hestie.

And from Devereaux, Wishing the pair of you a long and happy life together!

Cove quickly tapped out her own message. **Good one, Aidan! I have a few hours free tonight. How about we all get together to celebrate? Seven, at the hotel bar? Sean, I know you're not doing anything, so don't try to make excuses.**

She sent the message, tucked her phone back into her bag, and slipped into the passageways leading to the studio's exit.

The night after the third dive, before realizing Aidan had gone missing, Cove had felt as though the ship was dismantling her identity. She'd felt helpless in the face of how to reconcile a wreck filled with the damned with the world she thought she knew. Or even how to reconcile it with her father.

While she still didn't have any kind of complete answer—and suspected she likely never would—it had, in a strange way, pushed her closer to peace.

Regeneration followed after death. Growth required change. Life was a constant battle of give-and-take, a bittersweet tango that demanded full participation.

The *Arcadia* had exacted an enormous cost from all of them, and it would live on as something more akin to a scar than a memory. But the experience was not utterly devoid of good. She could let it burn her, or as her friends had, she could use it to grow.

Cove pushed through the studio's doors and stepped out onto the street. She stood for a moment, drinking in the fading light and the city noises, before breathing deeply and beginning her walk back to the hotel.

She'd face the future the way she'd faced the *Arcadia*: one step at a time.

ABOUT THE AUTHOR

Darcy Coates is the *USA Today* bestselling author of *Hunted*, *The Haunting of Ashburn House*, *Craven Manor*, and more than a dozen other horror and suspense titles. She lives on the Central Coast of Australia with her family, cats, and a garden full of herbs and vegetables. Darcy loves forests, especially old-growth forests where the trees dwarf anyone who steps between them. Wherever she lives, she tries to have a mountain range close by.

THEY DROWN
OUR DAUGHTERS

IF YOU CAN HEAR THE CALL OF THE WATER, IT'S ALREADY FAR TOO LATE.

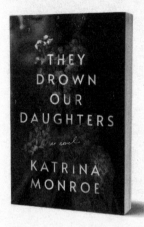

They say Cape Disappointment is haunted. That's why tourists used to flock there in droves. They'd visit the rocky shoreline under the old lighthouse's watchful eye and fish shells from the water as they pretended to spot dark shapes in the surf. Now the tourists are long gone, and when Meredith Strand and her young daughter return to Meredith's childhood home after an acrimonious split from her wife, the Cape seems more haunted by regret than any malevolent force.

But her mother, suffering from early stages of Alzheimer's, is convinced the ghost stories are real. Not only is there something in the water, but it's watching them. Waiting for them. Reaching out to Meredith's daughter the way it has to every woman in their line for generations—and if Meredith isn't careful, all three women, bound by blood and heartbreak, will be lost one by one to the ocean's mournful call.

GALLOWS HILL

IT'S TIME TO COME HOME.

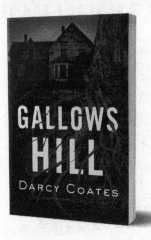

The Hull family has owned the Gallows Hill Winery for generations. Their wine wins awards. Their business prospers. Their family thrives: until Hugh and Maria Hull enter the dark halls of Gallows Hill one last time...and are found dead the next morning.

It's been more than a decade since Margot Hull last saw her childhood home. She was young enough when she was sent away that she barely remembers its dark passageways and secret corners. But now she's returned to bury her parents and reconnect with the winery that is her family's legacy—and the bloody truth of exactly what lies buried beneath the crumbling estate. Alone in the sprawling, dilapidated building, Margot is forced to come face to face with the horrors of the past—and realize that she may be the next victim of a house that never rests...

For more info about Sourcebooks's books and authors, visit:
sourcebooks.com

QUARTER TO MIDNIGHT

FIFTEEN CHILLING TALES OF GOTHIC HORROR AND SUSPENSE.

Step into a world where anything is possible—where your darkest nightmares shift and change before your eyes, taking the shape of unnameable horrors. This is a place where:

You discover a door hidden behind your bedroom's wallpaper. It's probably just a small crawl space. There's nothing unusual about it… except for the quiet tapping you hear late at night, and the growing sense of some unspeakable horror hidden just beyond sight.

A young child went missing while exploring a disused cemetery in 1965. More than fifty years later, you face the gate to the abandoned graveyard, armed with a clue that could lead to answers about the boy's fate…or your own death.

A mannequin is stored in the back of your rented basement room. Sometimes its dust cloth falls off. Sometimes you feel it watching you. And sometimes it moves while you're asleep…

For more info about Sourcebooks's books and authors, visit:
sourcebooks.com

THE RAVENOUS DEAD

HE'LL NEVER LET HER GO...

Keira, hired as Blighty Graveyard's new groundskeeper, lives surrounded by the dead. They watch her through the fog. They wordlessly cry out. They've been desperately waiting for help moving on—and only Keira can hear them. But not every restless spirit wants to be saved. Sometimes the dead hate the living too much to find peace.

As Keira struggles to uncover the tangled histories of some of the graveyard's oldest denizens, danger seeps from the darkest edges of the forest. A vicious serial killer was interred among the trees decades before, his spirit twisted by his violent nature. He's furious. Ravenous. And when Keira unwittingly answers his call, she may just seal her fate as his final intended victim.

THE HAUNTING OF
LEIGH HARKER

SOMETIMES THE DEAD REACH BACK.

Leigh Harker's quiet suburban home was her sanctuary for more than a decade, until things abruptly changed. Curtains open by themselves. Radios turn off and on. And a dark figure looms in the shadows of her bedroom door at night, watching her, waiting for her to finally let down her guard enough to fall asleep. Pushed to her limits but unwilling to abandon her home, Leigh struggles to find answers. But each step forces her toward something more terrifying than she ever imagined.

A poisonous shadow seeps from the locked door beneath the stairs. The handle rattles through the night and fingernails scratch at the wood. Her home harbors dangerous secrets, and now that Leigh is trapped within its walls, she fears she may never escape.

THE HAUNTING OF
ASHBURN HOUSE

THERE'S SOMETHING WRONG
WITH ASHBURN HOUSE...

Everyone knows about Ashburn House. They whisper that its old owner went mad and restless ghosts still walk the halls. But when Adrienne, desperate and in need of a place to stay, inherits the crumbling old mansion, she only sees it as a lifeline…until darkness falls.

Strange messages are etched into the walls. Furniture moves when she leaves the room. And a grave hidden in the depths of the forest hints at a terrible, unforgivable secret. Something twisted lives in her house, its hungry eyes ever watchful. Chasing the threads of a decades-old mystery, it isn't long before she realizes she's become prey to something deeply unnatural and intensely resentful.

She has no idea how to escape. She has no idea how to survive. Only one thing is certain: Ashburn's dead are not at rest.